THE COSSACKS
and Other Early Stories

Juliette —

One day when you're studying in Moscow and I'm drifting in Paris, let's meet up and talk about this book. And let's get lunch the next day. Also let's get dinner the day after.

I love you,
Sophie
12/27/'17

THE
COSSACKS
and Other Early Stories

—— ◆ ——

Leo Tolstoy

Translated
LOUISE AND AYLMER MAUDE

with an Introduction by
ANTHONY BRIGGS

WORDSWORTH CLASSICS

For my husband
ANTHONY JOHN RANSON
with love from your wife, the publisher.
Eternally grateful for your unconditional love.

Readers who are interested in other titles from
Wordsworth Editions are invited to visit our website at
www.wordsworth-editions.com

For our latest list and a full mail-order service, contact
Bibliophile Books, 5 Datapoint, South Crescent, London E16 4TL
TEL: +44 (0)20 7474 2474 fax: +44 (0)20 7474 8589
ORDERS: orders@bibliophilebooks.com
WEBSITE: www.bibliophilebooks.com

This edition published by Wordsworth Editions Limited
8B East Street, Ware, Hertfordshire SG12 9HJ

ISBN 978 1 84022 691 1

Text © Wordsworth Editions Limited 2012
Introduction © Anthony Briggs 2012

Wordsworth ® is a registered trademark of
Wordsworth Editions Limited

Wordsworth Editions
is the company founded in 1987 by
MICHAEL TRAYLER

Typeset in Great Britain by Roperford Editorial
Printed and bound by Clays Ltd, St Ives plc

CONTENTS

CONTENTS

INTRODUCTION

The Life of a Literary Genius

Leo Tolstoy is an emblematic figure in the history of a nation celebrated for its cultural achievement; his only rivals for the title of Russia's greatest writer are Fyodor Dostoevsky and Alexander Pushkin. He is famous for having written two of the world's biggest and best novels, and no fewer than fifty of his other prose works are still available in English translations. But he became known also as a religious thinker, a moral crusader, and an inspirational predecessor of pacifist protestors like Mahatma Gandhi. He has been the subject of thousands of biographical, literary, religious and ethical studies, books and articles in every language you can think of. And yet, he is still incompletely understood.

The first, widespread, misunderstanding concerns his two novels, *War and Peace* (1864–69) and *Anna Karenina* (1873–76). The problem with them is summarised in an event during an American 'Get Smart' movie, when Agent 86 (Maxwell Smart) is stabbed and left for dead. Somehow he survives the attack and explains how he did it by opening his coat to display a thick book into which a murderous knife has been plunged without doing any harm. His comment is, 'I figured nobody ever makes it all the way through *War and Peace*.' This is a good joke, and it says much for the author that his work is a household name.

Unfortunately, the thickness of the book seems to confirm the one thing everybody knows about *War and Peace*: it is impenetrably long and hard to read. For good measure, many people also believe that it is stuffed full of French and bogged down by the author's comments on warfare, history and the human condition. It seems to satisfy the cynical definition of a classic work as something everyone wants to have read but no one wants to read.

But the truth is different in several ways. First, although Tolstoy's early versions of the novel did contain long passages in French, including the opening lines, these were excluded from his edition of 1873, and good translations now reflect this decision.

Second, the novel is certainly a long one, running out at something like 1400 pages, but it is conveniently broken down into four unformidable volumes, each of which runs along in small sections based on individual chapters that average out at no longer than *four-and-a-half pages* in length. There is no danger of getting lost or feeling overwhelmed. Third, to make things easier still, the author has kindly relocated his various reflections in a couple of epilogues, so that they do not clog the narrative itself. No one should be discouraged from reading this splendid and easily readable work (one third war and two thirds peace) because of the myths with which it is encrusted.

Even the life of the great man has been somewhat misrepresented. Biographers, in the grip of admiration for a distinguished writer and his noble intentions, have been rather too lenient with him as a man. (One writer, Edward Crankshaw, can be exempted from this charge – see Further Reading). It is clear that this apostle of peace and brotherly love was never able to treat those around him with any degree of sympathy or charity. At every stage of his life he was a hostile and aggressive personality. Everyone spoke of his burning, malevolent glare and attitude of vindictive severity. When the novelist Ivan Turgenev called him 'a troglodyte' in 1855 he used the term at first in a spirit of light humour, only to discover that it was taxonomically exact; anyone might have employed it, at any time. In his day-to-day dealings Leo Tolstoy had the manners of a cave-man.

His life divides into four or five distinct stages. Born in 1828, he had a warmly protected childhood despite the death of his mother when he was two and his father when he was nine. In late adolescence he moved to Kazan, where he spent the time in youthful debauchery and so little study that he left the university without graduating. Rather more productively he then followed his older brother, a soldier, down to the Caucasus, where he was launched into a military career, fighting first against the local militants before transferring to other theatres and eventually ending up as a combatant in the Crimean War. In all of these places he distinguished himself as a courageous officer, and learned at first hand all there was to know about the atrocities of war. Many passages in *War and Peace* could never have been written without this direct experience of survival in close combat. When, in the novel (to take a single example), Anatole Kuragin's leg is amputated in a field hospital, and he sees it tossed across the tent still encased in its boot, this is based on a recollection of events at Sevastopol.

But this frenzy of activity was not to last. For the next half-dozen years he retired to a relaxed and still debauched life in St Petersburg, travelled abroad in leisurely style and finally, in 1862, he got married and settled down. His long-suffering wife, Sofya, was to bear him thirteen children, six of whom died before adulthood. Despite a short period of married bliss in the 1860s, and the delight of working together on what would turn out to be the world's greatest novel, the pair soon declined into a state of bickering animosity, and their long marriage ended in a terrible story of mistrust and alienation bordering on outright hatred even though shot through by inextinguishable admiration of the wife for her husband's genius. We shall return to this subject.

After the sixties (*War and Peace*) and the seventies (*Anna Karenina*) Tolstoy spent his last three eventless decades at home on his estate, sometimes writing, sometimes not. He gradually became obsessed with a search for religious truth and moral purity, setting unattainable goals of righteousness for himself and the rest of us. The remarkable thing about this period is that it produced not only a string of instructional works about how we should live our lives – according to the precepts of Jesus Christ unencumbered by the hypocritical complications created by his church – but also a string of literary masterpieces that broke their own author's self-imposed rules by avoiding out-and-out religious teaching and following the paths of good, entertaining and challenging literature. He died in 1910 at the age of 82, world-famous as an anarchist and pacifist, though as the years went by this aspect of his writing has steadily fallen away, leaving a residue of remarkable fiction by which his name is now unforgettably honoured.

There is a painful paradox right at the heart of Leo Tolstoy and his legacy. His literary achievement is at variance with his proclaimed ideas. From an early age he was obsessed with his own weakness of character. He knew the path towards goodness, self-control, but could not follow it. As a young man he gave in to every available temptation, not least the sexual ones, becoming ever more disgusted with himself and his animal appetites. It came as a relief to discover from the writings of Rousseau (see below) that all young men were as bad as he was, but this had a devastating consequence. Suddenly he knew the full extent of human weakness and degradation, and he would devote the rest of his life, not merely to self-improvement, because whenever he tried this he never succeeded, but to exposing the obvious iniquity of humankind in general. Most of his works were originally intended as didactic illustrations of human misbehaviour, intended to awaken our conscience and improve our conduct. (Many of them, including all his greatest works, escape these limitations by taking on a life of their own based on reality rather than any well-intentioned programme of improving ideas). The fact that he could never bring himself to love anyone did not prevent Leo Tolstoy from insisting that the rest of us should build our lives on love, aiming at a kind of Christ-like selflessness. As we shall see, his actual formula for human improvement would be tested in real life only to collapse repeatedly under its burden of otherworldliness.

Family Unhappiness

For the purposes of this collection of stories a little more needs to be said about love and marriage in this man's life. In September 1862 Leo Tolstoy, landowner, retired soldier and already a celebrated writer at the age of thirty-four, married Sofya Behrs, a girl not much more than half his age. His treatment of her at this time was indelicate enough to be described as brutal. A few days before the wedding he thrust into her hands a complete diary kept since his student days in Kazan; far from suppressing the sordid details of a thoroughly debauched young man's career, this document gave a full account of every imaginable lapse of character and erotic encounter, not excluding sexual diseases or even an ongoing affair with a woman on his estate which had produced a bastard child now three years old. For some obscure purpose he insisted that she, an *ingénue* barely familiar with the facts of life, had to read all of this before they were married.

Then, he showed no consideration for the emotional state of his new wife as they drove away on honeymoon, and that night, according to one biographer, 'he virtually raped her.'

Somehow she survived these shocks, and before long the two of them were like turtle doves. Visitors 'were arrested by the palpable happiness of the pair.' Their 'glowing delight' was described by friends and remembered by themselves long afterwards. Sofya's parents said they couldn't have wished for anything better for their daughter, and her husband recorded in his continuing diary a feeling of 'unbelievable happiness.' But it also includes another, rather ominous, entry. The man who had proposed to Sofya on September 16 and married her within seven days, wrote the following words only another week later: 'I love her just the same, if not more [but] today there was *a scene*. I was sad that we behave just the same way as other people.' This early misgiving was a reliable portent of bad things to come. The two lovers, whose marriage had begun in bliss, were to descend from that sublime height to depths of unhappiness known to few other people. A. N. Wilson puts this succinctly, referring to the disappointment felt by many people when they learn that, in later years, 'the great prophet of peace lived in an atmosphere of domestic hatred perhaps unrivalled in the history of matrimony.' The distance traversed in this relationship between delight and despond is outside normal experience and almost beyond understanding.

The reasons behind this catastrophic breakdown in human relations, and the results that flowed from it, lie outside our present scope, but the subject has a bearing on this volume because of Tolstoy's early story *Family Happiness* (1859), a fictional study of early romance leading to marriage but then rapidly descending into something much less rewarding and inspiring than the two lovers had hoped for. Without knowing the details of Tolstoy's biography you might imagine that real-life experience of romantic decline preceded the story, but it is not so. What did precede the story in real life was a strenuous, if ludicrous, attempt by Leo Tolstoy to make himself fall in love so that he could get married and improve his state of mind through family happiness. In 1859, for six months or more, he wooed a neighbour's daughter, twenty-year-old Valerya Arseneva, steadily arousing her expectations of a proposal, only to walk away and go abroad at the last moment, letting her down so disgracefully that he earned the reproaches of his close relatives and everyone in the locality.

Valerya didn't stay on the shelf much longer; she made a more suitable match by marrying a young man who would soon become a local magistrate, and going off into a smoother life than Leo Tolstoy could ever have given her. There was a good deal that Tolstoy disliked about this pleasant young woman – what he saw as her lack of education and a horrible taste in clothes – and even her physical charms attracted him one day and repelled him the next. It is significant that on the day of their first meeting he recorded the event in his diary followed by an entry that ended with the words, 'Sent for the soldier's wife.' Throughout his lukewarm courtship any physical stirrings on his part were easily satisfied by sending for a peasant girl.

To begin with, *Family Happiness* follows the real-life episode closely. Seventeen-year-old Masha, in mourning for her mother, is visited by Sergey Mikhaylovich, a man of thirty-six who used to be a close friend of her late father. She is attracted to him, but he seems reluctant to respond. Genuine love does arise, however, in both of them, and eventually they come together.

The situation may seem a little odd at first: he is slow to sell himself to her, and the young woman shows no interest in getting together with young men of her own tender years. This may be one reason to explain the relatively poor press that this story has received, having been considered too autobiographical, moralistic and uncertain of its purpose. The best thing to do is to forget the biographical origins of the narrative along with the author's subsequent literary achievement, and simply consider it in its own right. This will reveal greater quality and interest than has usually been acknowledged.

First, it contains two very convincing portraits. Sergey Mikhaylovich takes a long time to begin his courtship simply because his ward is so young and vulnerable. Only when she has added another year to her age and made her own attraction to him unmistakeable is he prepared to press his claim to her affection. Her lack of interest in boys and young men is only too credible, given the absence of anyone presentable in this age-group and the pressing need to find a husband to provide for her, orphaned as she now is. In the context of its day and the narrow circumstances of the two main characters, the attitudes and events of the narrative are perfectly credible. Masha's girlish passion and anxious nature, along with the gradual erosion of Sergey's reluctance, all of which is generously described, are the strength of the story.

There is a rather weak spot in mid-narrative when a couple of years speed by without enough description of events, and what happens at the end will not please everybody, even though it has been steadily gathering inevitability. Without giving too much away we can indicate that, apart from one quick flurry of distraction in mid-story, nothing sensational occurs – in healthy contrast to Tolstoy's late story The *Kreutzer Sonata* (1889), an appallingly bad work in which a not dissimilar relationship ends in bloody murder. The result here is a successful one, the tranquil consideration of a theme that fascinated Tolstoy to distraction in his own life, in many of his stories and in all three long novels (the third one being *Resurrection* (1899)). This is the transformation of young passion into mature love, which will lead inexorably to the frustration of hopes and ideals, but can end with reconcilement to a new form of contentment within marriage, far cooler in temperature but much easier to live with. Tolstoy's treatment of that idea, which seems like a cliché though it has not been exhaustively worked through in literature because of its unglamorous appeal and apparent negativity, is the signal achievement of *Family Happiness*. Young people may read this story with some impatience. They should pause and reflect, since it dramatises a dull but vital truth about human experience of which they are never advised, and which they wouldn't believe if they were – the fact that all feelings cool, but you still live on. The good thing about this story is that although it demonstrates a gradual curdling of dream into disillusionment, no one is to blame for the downturn. Instead of a bloody resolution, as in *The Kreutzer Sonata*, or blame and recrimination, as in the real lives of the author and his wife, Sergey and Masha are left with many consolations, something which usually comes about in the real life of more ordinary people than the Tolstoys.

The Cossacks

This story, also autobiographical, began life as early as 1852, suffered a good deal of rewriting and was eventually finished and published in 1863 immediately before the author settled down to write *War and Peace*. He was never satisfied with this work, and he could have left it behind in bits and pieces, had it not been for the need to raise money and pay off some gambling debts before getting married. For all that, it is taken by many people to be his finest piece before the great novels. The narrative, which begins in Moscow, concerns a young man-about-town, Dmitri Olenin, who tires of his hedonistic life in civilized society, and attempts to find happiness among the wild, free-living Cossacks down in the Caucasus. (A note on the people of the Caucasus appears below). He is, of course, a fictional version of Tolstoy himself, who was so steeped in the ideas of Jean-Jacques Rousseau that he had become convinced of man's irredeemable selfishness and depravity, which apparently get worse as people see the value of collective endeavour and specialisation, thus acquiring wealth, property and culture. This story began as an attempt to dramatise the theory that a return to primitive society might be the only way to regain the innocence and purity with which we were born, and that this would lead to permanent contentment.

If that idea sounds rather naive after the passage of six generations, it is made worse by the false comparison on which the story is based. The result is a foregone conclusion. Olenin has become so deeply immersed in his life of unthinking pleasure and immorality that he can hardly count as a decent representative of modern man against whom a primitive counterpart could be measured. Almost anybody anywhere will look morally superior to Olenin. Thus it turns out that, when the Russian encounters a true representative of the Cossack people, a huge, old Falstaffian figure called Yeroshka (based on a real person, Yepishka Sekhin, with whom the author had been billeted in 1851 during his service in the region), the simpler man triumphs in every way. He may be hard-living, cruel and quite unsophisticated, but he is a great hunter, a thoughtful person, a captivating raconteur, even a philosopher, and it is he who teaches the other man how to live.

The secret is to exist in harmony with the natural world, never losing the close contact with the earth and its goodness. All the arguments (obliquely deployed) in this story incline in the same direction. This is not good because there has been no objective or realistic comparison of life-styles. A contented man living in an apparently heroic natural state is depicted sympathetically (with his brutality as a multiple murderer conveniently played down) and set against a pathetic drop-out and failure in his own form of society. So what? (It may have been a sense of unbalanced presentation that made the author feel so dissatisfied with his endeavour for so many years after beginning it).

Do not be put off by these apparently discouraging remarks. They apply only to the ideological content of *The Cossacks*, which is not of first importance. Fortunately, there is a huge amount in this story that still makes it a rewarding read. The portraiture is splendid, among Tolstoy's best – there is certainly nothing to touch it before the big novels. This concerns not so much Olenin, who is a rather tedious character, but the natives, especially Uncle Yeroshka, Lukashka, a young Cossack warrior, and an alluring but unbiddable Cossack girl by the name of Maryanka – these are the fascinating personalities who guarantee and renew the reader's interest. Olenin cannot keep pace with any of them. Yeroshka is larger than life, but not through any exaggeration on Tolstoy's part. It is clear that such a man could exist, indeed had existed, with all his extravagance of physical stature, alluring powers of conversation, strong reputation and redoubtable character. When he is on the scene the story leaps into life. The old man uses Olenin relentlessly, beguiling him with stories, toying with him in conversation, entertaining him out in the field and forest and simulating a friendship that can hardly be genuine. In fact, at the end of the story when Olenin leaves, having failed in all his aspirations, the old man appears to be deeply moved at their separation, though moments later, when Olenin looks back, neither Yeroshka nor the girl gives even a half-hearted parting glance or wave. Only moments before, the canny native has wheedled a valuable possession out of the northern sophisticate, nothing less than his gun, which was asked for and given up during an onset of deep emotion clearly identifiable in retrospect as the Cossack hero's last act of bamboozlement and calculated acquisition. This is the last blow struck by primitivism against civilization.

In a work dedicated to an ideal of natural purity you will not be surprised to come across some glorious landscapes and rich ethnographic detail. There is time and space for this in a work of 60,000 words (sometimes categorized as a novel), and the reader will luxuriate in these passages. The best of them occur when the interest shrinks down from the towering mountains and warmly enfolds the characters, especially Olenin himself. In one passage half-way through (Chapter 20), the Russian revisits a forest glade where the previous day they had disturbed a stag, and lies down in the midst of the animal's traces. Through a mixture of skilled narrative and contemplative speculation he is miraculously depicted as blending into the natural scene until he and it are as one entity. His startling sense of the uniqueness of living; the thrill of human individuality, at first inescapable then dissolving into a shared, comfortable corner of the infinite universe; the welling up of human happiness and love – these sentiments are not merely worthy of the best moments in *War and Peace*, they actually anticipate similar occurrences in that novel, especially the famous meditation of Prince Andrey when he lies wounded after the battle of Austerlitz (Volume One, Part Three, Chapter 16). In passages of this quality the work that so dissatisfied its author attains serious stature, and at the same time looks forward to even greater things. One small detail completes our impression of consummate writing skill. The Russian word for 'stag' is 'olen', the very root of our hero's name. (We shall never know whether the author suddenly spotted this linguistic possibility, or whether, less probably, he foresaw its potential long in advance). The two syllables are deployed lovingly and repeatedly in that paragraph, merging man and beast with the natural scene, a remarkable touch of intimate lyricism hidden away in a passage of metaphysical expansiveness.

The other stories written by Leo Tolstoy in this early period, between the *Stories of Sevastopol* and *War and Peace*, may not have the same kind of quality or depth, but they are not without interest or entertainment value. *Albert* and *Lucerne* (1857) are similar in content, style and intention, each presenting the portrait of a poor amateur musician, reasonably talented but down on his luck and respected by no one. Both tales were inspired by real-life events. In January 1857 Tolstoy came across a talented musician by the name of Kiesewetter who had taken to drink. Six months later, in Switzerland, he reacted angrily when an itinerant player was rewarded with nothing by the onlookers after performing for quite a long time. The two incidents and portraits were copied into literature, and, while being rather obvious in their call for compassion towards people less fortunate than ourselves, they are interesting as small studies in individual psychology and group behaviour. What each man needs is some help and encouragement from those around him, but everyone except the narrator seems to be indifferent to their low state of morale and fortune. Once again Tolstoy is playing with the idea that sophisticated citizens in civilized surroundings lose their natural goodness and instinctive sympathy for other people.

Tolstoy wrote *Two Hussars* in 1859. Stronger in narrative interest, it describes the philandering of a father in a provincial town, followed up twenty-odd years later by his son, who returns and meets the same people, though he doesn't quite manage a similar seduction. There is a twist of irony in the narrative that seems to overturn any moral message that the tale may be thought to contain. No one was too shocked by the father's licentious behaviour because of his dashing personality and generous spirit, whereas the son, the product of a later era of scientific rationalism, is what one critic has called 'a calculating materialist prig'. He seduces no one, but leaves behind a worse impression than that left by his immoral parent. This tale is out of line with anything written by Tolstoy at this time, showing a warmer acceptance of human nature as it is rather than as it should be. It is an unusual story with a strange turn of events, and it deserves better than the relative obscurity in which it now exists.

Cossacks and Chechens

In reading *The Cossacks* you will repeatedly come across references to two different branches of humanity, the Cossacks themselves and the Chechens. But who are these peoples? The story cannot be fully appreciated without some knowledge of them and their background. The Cossacks, despite our familiarity with their famous name, are not easy to define. From hazy beginnings they became a minor nation (of two and a half million at their numerical peak in the nineteenth century), self-created, independent and not easily contained by history, geography or politics. It is uncertain when or where they arose, but they seem to have emerged as an established and identifiable group of free peasant people in the fifteenth century, by which time they were sufficiently formidable to earn respect and admiration, even fear. In order to locate them you should think of the river systems in the south west of present-day Russia and Ukraine.

The Cossacks worked along the waterways, and many of them became known by the rivers near to which they lived, including the Don, the Dnieper, the Kuban, the lower Volga and the Terek. These people were descended mainly from the Slavs, though they enjoyed a good admixture of Turkish and Tatar blood, and their language was Turkic. They remained a Christian people in regions with largely Muslim populations. They were formed from unpromising material; the earliest Cossacks were defined mainly by their inability to fit in with the societies into which they had been born. All manner of runaways, renegades, criminals, rebel serfs, freebooters, along with anyone who had resisted authority and fled from persecution – these were the people who escaped to the south and west, gathering in primitive gangs and eventually coalescing into organized societies. The standard Cossack village, known as a *stanitsa*, enjoyed a high degree of unity and good order (strictly enforced), with sound schools, elected leaders and a strong sense of shared prosperity. Eventually the loose federation of separate communities began to blend into larger units of a military character, but their fierce sense of independence precluded any possibility of the Cossacks merging into any nearby country or ethnic grouping. Cossack pride was so strong that they came to view themselves as ethnically superior to the peoples surrounding them.

Throughout their history the Cossacks behaved as they began, asserting their collective character and self-reliance through militarism. They plundered the whole region, taking anything they wanted, and woe betide anyone who objected or resisted. A Cossack boy was schooled in warfare from the cradle onwards, and when he came to maturity, already a skilled horseman, he knew he would spend at least a couple of decades away on active service, fighting for his people. It was their indomitable military prowess that made this people first of all a force to be reckoned with and then an élite martial caste valued by the various forces competing with each other for control of this volatile region. The Russians gave them generous acknowledgement in the form of large tracts of fertile land, and used them to police the area, making it safe from incursions by surrounding Muslim forces.

But, if the Cossacks could trace their occupancy of this area back through several centuries, they still look like recent interlopers compared with the indigenous population. We are speaking of the broad neck of land, only about three hundred miles across, between the Black Sea and the Caspian, known as the Caucasus. Just north of the capital of Georgia, Tbilisi, a famous mountain range rises up, the home of Europe's highest peak, Mount Elbruz (at 18,480 feet nearly 3,000 feet higher than Mont Blanc). Further still to the north, in the steep foothills of the range there is a wild region of vertiginous hills, plunging down into deep valleys and crevasses, which appears to have been inhabited sporadically by our species for at least a hundred thousand years; it has been permanently settled for the last 8,000 years. This place seems never to have known a settled existence; it is not hard to imagine an unbroken sequence, covering several hundred generations, of unresolved tribal rivalry manifesting itself in an endless series of vicious marauding, feuding and battle. And that was their own internecine strife, occurring before outsiders came in to take things over.

When the Russians felt the need to extend their empire (for *defensive* reasons) to the south, it took them about thirty years to subjugate the Caucasus (1783–1813), and at least another halfcentury to extirpate resistance from the tribesmen in the hills. You could say the job is still not done today. The town of Grozny, for instance, remains infamous in our own day as a region of unending warfare. It was so in the time of the Russian writer Mikhail Lermontov (1814–41), who wrote a wonderful narrative poem about the battle of Valerik, a small river in that very region. It is sadly significant that, before the ghastly conflict described in the poem, the name Valerik already meant 'River of Death', a testament to the uncountable run of bloody confrontations that it must have seen. This region is called Chechnya, a name that ought to be unfamiliar to us, but is not because of the brutal warfare that has been going on there even in modern times.

So now, when we learn that the enemy forces in Tolstoy's story are Chechen warriors, we know what these people must be like. They come from a line of stop-at-nothing militarism that goes back into the mists of time; they have never known anything other than the need to fight, and they are always ready to take on each other, the tribe on the next hill, or marauding foreign conquerors. Add to all of this the simple fact that they are a Muslim people on the verge of a Christian empire, and you will have a full picture of the mutual distrust, fear and hatred that have burned for so long in the hearts of every benighted inhabitant of this unhappy region. It is these two brutally aggressive oppositional forces, the Cossacks and the Chechens, who loom so large in Tolstoy's *The Cossacks*. Tolstoy will return to this subject at the end of his life; his last major work, published posthumously in 1911, was *Hadji Murad*, another short novel set in the same region and the same period. It is a curious and little-noticed fact that this great writer's first and last masterpieces were matching tales of the Caucasus, the two exotic book-ends of a magnificent career.

Jean-Jacques Rousseau

Leo Tolstoy was in his mid-teens when he came across the writings of a man who would dominate his thinking until the moment of his death: the Swiss-born French philosopher and political thinker, Jean-Jacques Rousseau (1712–78). Without some knowledge of this strange man it will be difficult to understand the life and work of the great Russian writer. Born in Geneva, Rousseau moved through Italy and Savoy before settling in France, where he made his name in 1750 with a prize essay, *A Discourse on the Arts and Sciences*, which is now described as 'feeble and almost unreadable', though in its day it was greatly praised. His instant apotheosis as a serious thinker would one day be described by a famous French critic, Jules Lemaître, as 'one of the strongest proofs ever provided of human stupidity'. Nevertheless, its main ideas became fashionable and were taken seriously by many later writers, including Leo Tolstoy. Rousseau still has a doggedly serious following today, though mainly in France and Switzerland.

Leaving aside his thoughts on other subjects (such as the education of children), which have led to excesses in our own day, particularly in connection with 'child-centred learning', now rejected by many as inefficient and impractical, Rousseau's one big idea concerned nothing less than the natural goodness of man and the reasons that lie behind his lapses into bad behaviour and consequent unhappiness. The idea is so obviously unsound (and disprovable, as history has shown) that we can only marvel at its instant popularity and stubborn endurance. The argument goes as follows. Man is originally, and by nature, virtuous, free and happy, but he has become corrupted by moving from small communities into large settlements, which have encouraged the ownership of property, the rise of inequality and immorality, as well as the imposition of despotism. There can be no happiness for mankind in this direction; the only solution would be for a fortunate few to reorganise their lives by returning to nature and living in small moral communities. It is already too late for most of humanity to adopt this strategy.

We do not have to argue this matter out in theory. In the course of history it has been tested to destruction in the most practical way, one which has involved a contribution from Leo Tolstoy, whose endorsement of Rousseau's idea carried great weight because of his reputation as a successful novelist. During the nineteenth century not a few idealists were naive enough to retreat from the distasteful world at large and form small agrarian communities based on co-operative living and self-sufficiency. Some of them, in Russia, America, England and almost every country in northern Europe, withdrew from society into 'Tolstoyan colonies'. The expectation was that under these narrowed circumstances the natural goodness of men and women would prevail over self-interest and immorality, resulting in a kind of contentment that would be the envy of the outside world and a model for all to follow. After all, these well-meaning people would, in the words of one historian, 'be leading simple, honest lives untainted by the evils of capitalism.' Every one of these communities broke down in short order. Another chronicler describes how, in the early summer of 1899, a visitor called in at the Purleigh Colony in the English county of Essex only to discover that, instead of harmony and happiness, 'argument seemed to be the farm's chief produce.' As he explains, perhaps unnecessarily, the good participants had been 'stimulated by the desire to live a perfect life in an imperfect world'.

Rousseau's obvious mistake was a wrong deduction. Driven to despair by the immorality of modern, civilised life, he assumed that this was due to the processes of modernity and civilization themselves rather than endemic in humanity's animal nature, which needed more time to evolve. Contrary to his thinking, it has been the very process of enrichment and sophistication which has led people on a huge scale out of poverty and deprivation and into multi-million communities where they rub along quite nicely. But it is a sobering thought that some of the older hymn-books in our churches still include a hymn written in 1819 by Bishop Heber, *From Greenland's icy mountains*, of which the second verse begins,

> What though the spicy breezes
> Blow soft o'er Java's isle;
> Though every prospect pleases
> And only man is vile?

This could have been the mission statement of Jean-Jacques Rousseau, and it was taken up by Leo Tolstoy, for they both believed not in the natural goodness but the natural vileness of mankind. So did the only other thinker for whom Tolstoy later developed a lifelong obsession, Arthur Schopenhauer (1788–1860), famous for his systematic philosophical pessimism. This man ('dark, distrustful, misogynistic and truculent') believed not only in the nastiness of human nature, but in the total wretchedness of the entire universe and the process of life itself. The great Russian novelist accepted the negative ideas of these two men and never repudiated them. When he transcended them in splendid literary works, he greatly regretted doing so.

The wonder is that the best of his published work travels in the opposite direction. *War and Peace* is nothing less than 'a triumphant affirmation of life', and Martin Amis captures the essence of Tolstoy in a single question: 'Who else but Tolstoy has made happiness really swing on the page?'

Despite his personal failings as a man, particularly his incapacity for love or charity, and notwithstanding his pessimistic theorising, the world's greatest novelist amazed himself by transmitting an inspiring vision of the world and its people, summarised by Russia's famous critic, Prince Dmitri Mirsky, as 'a general message of beauty, and satisfaction that the world should be so beautiful'.

The struggle between the dark moraliser and the generous lover of life raged in this writer to the end of his days; you will see it at work even in these early stories, some of them minor masterpieces that have yet to be fully appreciated.

A.D.P.BRIGGS

Visiting Research Fellow,
University of Bristol

Professor Emeritus,
University of Birmingham

SUGGESTIONS FOR FURTHER READING

John Bayley, *Tolstoy and the Novel*, London, Chatto & Windus, 1966.

Rosamund Bartlett, *Tolstoy*, London, Profile Books, 2010.

Anthony Briggs, *Leo Tolstoy*, Hesperus, Brief Lives, 2010.

T. G. S.Cain, *Tolstoy,* London and New York, Elek, 1977.

R. F. Christian, *Tolstoy: A Critical Introduction,* Cambridge University Press, 1969.

Edward Crankshaw, *The Making of a Novelist*, London, Weidenfeld & Nicolson, 1974.

Henry Gifford, *Tolstoy,* Oxford, Past Masters, 1982.

Malcolm Jones, *New Essays on Tolstoy*, Cambridge University Press, 1978.

Janko Lavrin, *Tolstoy: an Approach,* London, 1944.

Aylmer Maude, *The Life of Tolstoy*, 2 vols, London, 1908–10, reprinted, Westport, Connecticut, 1970.

Donna Tussing Orwin, *Tolstoy's Art and Thought*, Princeton, 1993.

Theodore Redpath, *Tolstoy,* London, 1960.

E. J. Simmons, *Leo Tolstoy,* Boston, 1946, reprinted New York, 1960.

Henri Troyat, *Tolstoy,* New York, W. H. Allen, 1967.

A. N. Wilson, *Tolstoy,* London 1988, Harmondsworth, 1989.

FAMILY HAPPINESS

PART I

Chapter 1

We were in mourning for my mother, who had died in the autumn, and I spent all that winter alone in the country with Katya and Sonya.

Katya was an old friend of the family, our governess who had brought us all up, and I had known and loved her since my earliest recollections. Sonya was my younger sister. It was a dark and sad winter which we spent in our old house of Pokrovskoye. The weather was cold and so windy that the snowdrifts came higher than the windows; the panes were almost always dimmed by frost, and we seldom walked or drove anywhere throughout the winter. Our visitors were few, and those who came brought no addition of cheerfulness or happiness to the household. They all wore sad faces and spoke low, as if they were afraid of waking someone; they never laughed, but sighed and often shed tears as they looked at me and especially at little Sonya in her black frock. The feeling of death clung to the house; the air was still filled with the grief and horror of death. My mother's room was kept locked; and whenever I passed it on my way to bed, I felt a strange uncomfortable impulse to look into that cold empty room.

I was then seventeen; and in the very year of her death my mother was intending to move to Petersburg, in order to take me into society. The loss of my mother was a great grief to me; but I must confess to another feeling behind that grief – a feeling that though I was young and pretty (so everybody told me), I was wasting a second winter in the solitude of the country. Before the winter ended, this sense of dejection, solitude, and simple boredom increased to such an extent that I refused to leave my room or open the piano or take up a book. When Katya urged me to find some occupation, I said that I did not feel able for it; but in my heart I said, 'What is the good of it? What is the good of doing anything, when the best part of my life is being wasted like this?' and to this question, tears were my only answer.

I was told that I was growing thin and losing my looks; but even this failed to interest me. What did it matter? For whom? I felt that my whole life was bound to go on in the same solitude and helpless dreariness, from which I had myself no strength and even no wish to escape. Towards the end of winter Katya became anxious about me and determined to make an effort to take me abroad. But money was needed for this, and we hardly knew how our affairs stood after my mother's death. Our guardian, who was to come and clear up our position, was expected every day.

In March he arrived.

'Well, thank God!' Katya said to me one day, when I was walking up and down the room like a shadow, without occupation, without a thought, and without a wish. 'Sergey Mikhaylych has arrived; he has sent to inquire about us and means to come here for dinner. You must rouse yourself, dear Mashechka,' she added, 'or what will he think of you? He was so fond of you all.'

Sergey Mikhaylych was our near neighbour, and, though a much younger man, had been a friend of my father's. His coming was likely to change our plans and to make it possible to leave the country; and also I had grown up in the habit of love and regard for him; and when Katya begged me to rouse myself, she guessed rightly that it would give me especial pain to show to disadvantage before him, more than before any other of our friends. Like everyone in the house, from Katya and his god-daughter Sonya down to the helper in the stables, I loved him from old habit; and also he had a special significance for me, owing to a remark which my mother had once made in my presence. 'I should like you to marry a man like him,' she said. At the time this seemed to me strange and even unpleasant. My ideal husband was quite different: he was to be thin, pale, and sad; and Sergey Mikhaylych was middle-aged, tall, robust, and always, as it seemed to me, in good spirits. But still my mother's words stuck in my head; and even six years before this time, when I was eleven, and he still said 'thou' to me, and played with me, and called me by the pet-name of 'violet' – even then I sometimes asked myself in a fright, 'What shall I do, if he suddenly wants to marry me?'

Before our dinner, to which Katya made an addition of sweets and a dish of spinach, Sergey Mikhaylych arrived. From the window I watched him drive up to the house in a small sleigh; but as soon as it turned the corner, I hastened to the drawing room, meaning to pretend that his visit was a complete surprise. But when I heard his tramp and loud voice and Katya's footsteps in the hall, I lost patience and went to meet him myself. He was holding Katya's hand, talking loud, and smiling. When he saw me, he stopped and looked at me for a time without bowing. I was uncomfortable and felt myself blushing.

'Can this be really you?' he said in his plain decisive way, walking towards me with his arms apart. 'Is so great a change possible? How grown-up you are! I used to call you 'violet', but now you are a rose in full bloom!'

He took my hand in his own large hand and pressed it so hard that it almost hurt. Expecting him to kiss my hand, I bent towards him, but he only pressed it again and looked straight into my eyes with the old firmness and cheerfulness in his face.

It was six years since I had seen him last. He was much changed – older and darker in complexion; and he now wore whiskers which did not become him at all; but much remained the same – his simple manner, the large features of his honest open face, his bright intelligent eyes, his friendly, almost boyish, smile.

Five minutes later he had ceased to be a visitor and had become the friend of us all, even of the servants, whose visible eagerness to wait on him proved their pleasure at his arrival. He behaved quite unlike the neighbours who had visited us after my mother's death. they had thought it necessary to be silent when they sat with us, and to shed tears. He, on the contrary, was cheerful and talkative, and said not a word about my mother, so that this indifference seemed strange to me at first and even improper on the part of so close a friend. But I understood later that what seemed indifference was sincerity, and I felt grateful for it. In the evening Katya poured out tea, sitting in her old place in the drawing room, where she used to sit in my mother's lifetime; our old butler Grigori had hunted out one of my father's pipes and brought it to him; and he began to walk up and down the room as he used to do in past days.

'How many terrible changes there are in this house, when one thinks of it all!' he said, stopping in his walk.

'Yes,' said Katya with a sigh; and then she put the lid on the samovar and looked at him, quite ready to burst out crying.

'I suppose you remember your father?' he said, turning to me.

'Not clearly,' I answered.

'How happy you would have been together now!' he added in a low voice, looking thoughtfully at my face above the eyes. 'I was very fond of him,' he added in a still lower tone, and it seemed to me that his eyes were shining more than usual.

'And now God has taken her too!' said Katya; and at once she laid her napkin on the teapot, took out her handkerchief, and began to cry.

'Yes, the changes in this house are terrible,' he repeated, turning away. 'Sonya, show me your toys,' he added after a little and went off to the parlour. When he had gone, I looked at Katya with eyes full of tears.

'What a splendid friend he is!' she said. And, though he was no relation, I did really feel a kind of warmth and comfort in the sympathy of this good man.

I could hear him moving about in the parlour with Sonya, and the sound of her high childish voice. I sent tea to him there; and I heard him sit down at the piano and strike the keys with Sonya's little hands.

Then his voice came – 'Marya Aleksandrovna, come here and play something.'

I liked his easy behavior to me and his friendly tone of command; I got up and went to him.

'Play this,' he said, opening a book of Beethoven's music at the *adagio* of the *Moonlight Sonata*. 'Let me hear how you play,' he added, and went off to a corner of the room, carrying his cup with him.

I somehow felt that with him it was impossible to refuse or to say beforehand that I played badly: I sat down obediently at the piano and began to play as well as I could; yet I was afraid of criticism, because I knew that he understood and enjoyed music. The *adagio* suited the remembrance of past days evoked by our conversation at tea, and I believe that I played it fairly well. But he would not let me play the *scherzo*. 'No,' he said, coming up to me; 'you don't play that right; don't go on; but the first move-ment was not bad; you seem to be musical.' This moderate praise pleased me so much that I even reddened. I felt it pleasant and strange that a friend of my father's, and his contemporary, should no longer treat me like a child but speak to me seriously. Katya now went upstairs to put Sonya to bed, and we were left alone in the parlour.

He talked to me about my father, and about the beginning of their friendship and the happy days they had spent together, while I was still busy with lesson-books and toys; and his talk put my father before me in quite a new light, as a man of simple and delightful character. He asked me too about my tastes, what I read and what I intended to do, and gave me advice. The man of mirth and jest who used to tease me and make me toys had disappeared; here was a serious, simple, and affectionate friend, for whom I could not help feeling respect and sympathy. It was easy and pleasant to talk to him; and yet I felt an involuntary strain also. I was anxious about each word I spoke: I wished so much to earn for my own sake the love which had been given me already merely because I was my father's daughter.

After putting Sonya to bed, Katya joined us and began to complain to him of my apathy, about which I had said nothing.

'So she never told me the most important thing of all!' he said, smiling and shaking his head reproachfully at me.

'Why tell you?' I said. 'It is very tiresome to talk about, and it will pass off.' (I really felt now, not only that my dejection would pass off, but that it had already passed off, or rather had never existed.)

'It is a bad thing,' he said, 'not to be able to stand solitude. Can it be that you are a young lady?'

'Of course, I am a young lady,' I answered laughing.

'Well, I can't praise a young lady who is alive only when people are admiring her, but as soon as she is left alone, collapses and finds nothing to her taste – one who is all for show and has no resources in herself.'

'You have a flattering opinion of me!' I said, just for the sake of saying something.

He was silent for a little. Then he said: 'Yes; your likeness to your father means something. There is something in you . . . ', and his kind attentive look again flattered me and made me feel a pleasant embarrassment.

I noticed now for the first time that his face, which gave one at first the impression of high spirits, had also an expression peculiar to himself – bright at first and then more and more attentive and rather sad.

'You ought not to be bored and you cannot be,' he said; 'you have music, which you appreciate, books, study; your whole life lies before you, and now or never is the time to prepare for it and save yourself future regrets. A year hence it will be too late.'

He spoke to me like a father or an uncle, and I felt that he kept a constant check upon himself, in order to keep on my level. Though I was hurt that he considered me as inferior to himself, I was pleased that for me alone he thought it necessary to try to be different.

For the rest of the evening he talked about business with Katya.

'Well, goodby, dear friends,' he said. Then he got up, came towards me and took my hand.

'When shall we see you again?' asked Katya.

'In spring,' he answered, still holding my hand. 'I shall go now to Danilovka,' (this was another property of ours) 'look into things there and make what arrangements I can; then I go to Moscow on business of my own; and in summer we shall meet again.'

'Must you really be away so long?' I asked, and I felt terribly grieved. I had really hoped to see him every day, and I felt a sudden shock of regret, and a fear that my depression would return. And my face and voice just have made this plain.

'You must find more to do and not get depressed,' he said; and I thought his tone too cool and unconcerned. 'I shall put you through an examination in spring,' he added, letting go my hand and not looking at me.

When we saw him off in the hall, he put on his fur coat in a hurry and still avoided looking at me. 'He is taking a deal of trouble for nothing!' I thought. 'Does he think me so anxious that he should look at me? He is a good man, a very good man; but that's all.'

That evening, however, Katya and I sat up late, talking, not about him but about our plans for the summer, and where we should spend next winter and what we should do then. I had ceased to ask that terrible question – what is the good of it all? Now it seemed quite plain and simple: the proper object of life was happiness, and I promised myself much happiness ahead. It seemed as if our gloomy old house had suddenly become full of light and life.

Chapter 2

Meanwhile spring arrived. My old dejection passed away and gave place to the unrest which spring brings with it, full of dreams and vague hopes and desires. Instead of living as I had done at the beginning of winter, I read and played the piano and gave lessons to Sonya; but also I often went into the garden and wandered for long alone through the avenues, or sat on a bench there; and Heaven knows what my thoughts and wishes and hopes were at such times. Sometimes at night, especially if there was a moon, I sat by my bedroom window till dawn; sometimes, when Katya was not watching, I stole out into the garden wearing only a wrapper and ran through the dew as far as the pond; and once I went all the way to the open fields and walked right round the garden alone at night.

I find it difficult now to recall and understand the dreams which then filled my imagination. Even when I can recall them, I find it hard to believe that my dreams were just like that: they were so strange and so remote from life. Sergey Mikhaylych kept his promise: he returned from his travels at the end of May. His first visit to us was in the evening and was quite unexpected. We were sitting in the veranda, preparing for tea. By this time the garden was all green, and the nightingales had taken up their quarters for the whole of St Peter's Fast in the leafy borders. The tops of the round lilac bushes had a sprinkling of white and purple – a sign that their flowers were ready to open. The foliage of the birch avenue was all transparent in the light of the setting sun. In the veranda there was shade and freshness. The evening dew was sure to be heavy in the grass. Out of doors beyond the garden the last sounds of day were audible, and the noise of the sheep and cattle, as they were driven home. Nikon, the half-witted boy, was driving his water-cart along the path outside the veranda, and a cold stream of water from the sprinkler made dark circles on the mould round the stems and supports of the dahlias. In our veranda the polished samovar shone and hissed on the white table-cloth; there were cracknels and biscuits and cream on the table. Katya was busy washing the cups with her plump hands. I was too hungry after bathing to wait for tea, and was eating bread with thick fresh cream. I was wearing a gingham blouse with loose sleeves, and my hair, still wet, was covered with a kerchief. Katya saw him first, even before he came in.

'You, Sergey Mikhaylych!' she cried. 'Why, we were just talking about you.'

I got up, meaning to go and change my dress, but he caught me just by the door.

'Why stand on such ceremony in the country?' he said, looking with a smile at the kerchief on my head. 'You don't mind the presence of your butler, and I am really the same to you as Grigori is.' But I felt just then that he was looking at me in a way quite unlike Grigori's way, and I was uncomfortable.

'I shall come back at once,' I said, as I left them.

'But what is wrong?' he called out after me; 'it's just the dress of a young peasant woman.'

'How strangely he looked at me!' I said to myself as I was quickly changing upstairs. 'Well, I'm glad he has come; things will be more lively.' After a look in the glass I ran gaily downstairs and into the veranda; I was out of breath and did not disguise my haste. He was sitting at the table, talking to Katya about our affairs. He glanced at me and smiled; then he went on talking. From what he said it appeared that our affairs were in capital shape: it was now possible for us, after spending the summer in the country, to go either to Petersburg for Sonya's education, or abroad.

'If only you would go abroad with us –' said Katya; 'without you we shall be quite lost there.'

'Oh, I should like to go round the world with you,' he said, half in jest and half in earnest.

'All right,' I said; let us start off and go round the world.'

He smiled and shook his head.

'What about my mother? What about my business, he said. 'But that's not the question just now: I want to know how you have been spending your time. Not depressed again, I hope?

When I told him that I had been busy and not bored during his absence, and when Katya confirmed my report, he praised me as if he had a right to do so, and his words and looks were kind, as they might have been to a child. I felt obliged to tell him, in detail and with perfect frankness, all my good actions, and to confess, as if I were in church, all that he might disapprove of. The evening was so fine that we stayed in the veranda after tea was cleared away; and the conversation interested me so much that I did not notice how we ceased by degrees to hear any sound of the servants indoors. The scent of flowers grew stronger and came from all sides; the grass was drenched with dew; a nightingale struck up in a lilac bush close by and then stopped on hearing our voices; the starry sky seemed to come down lower over our heads.

It was growing dusk, but I did not notice it till a bat suddenly and silently flew in beneath the veranda awning and began to flutter round my white shawl. I shrank back against the wall and nearly cried out; but the bat as silently and swiftly dived out from under the awning and disappeared in the half-darkness of the garden.

'How fond I am of this place of yours!' he said, changing the conversation; 'I wish I could spend all my life here, sitting in this veranda.'

'Well, do then!' said Katya.

'That's all very well,' he said, 'but life won't sit still.'

'Why don't you marry?' asked Katya; 'you would make an excellent husband.'

'Because I like sitting still?' and he laughed. 'No, Katerina Karlovna, too late for you and me to marry. People have long ceased to think of me as a marrying man, and I am even surer of it myself; and I declare I have felt quite comfortable since the matter was settled.'

It seemed to me that he said this in an unnaturally persuasive way.

'Nonsense!' said Katya; 'a man of thirty-six makes out that he is too old!'

'Too old indeed,' he went on, 'when all one wants is to sit still. For a man who is going to marry that's not enough. Just you ask her,' he added, nodding at me; 'people of her age should marry, and you and I can rejoice in their happiness.'

The sadness and constraint latent in his voice was not lost upon me. He was silent for a little, and neither Katya nor I spoke.

'Well, just fancy,' he went on, turning a little on his seat; 'suppose that by some mischance I married a girl of seventeen, Masha, if you like – I mean, Marya Aleksandrovna. The instance is good; I am glad it turned up; there could not be a better instance.'

I laughed; but I could not understand why he was glad, or what it was that had turned up.

'Just tell me honestly, with your hand on your heart,' he said, turning as if playfully to me, 'would it not be a misfortune for you to unite your life with that of an old worn-out man who only wants to sit still, whereas Heaven knows what wishes are fermenting in that heart of yours?'

I felt uncomfortable and was silent, not knowing how to answer him.

'I am not making you a proposal, you know,' he said, laughing; 'but am I really the kind of husband you dream of when walking alone in the avenue at twilight? It would be a misfortune, would it not?'

'No, not a misfortune,' I began.

'But a bad thing,' he ended my sentence.

'Perhaps; but I may be mistaken . . . ' He interrupted me again.

'There, you see! She is quite right, and I am grateful to her for her frankness, and very glad to have had this conversation. And there is something else to be said' – he added: 'for me too it would be a very great misfortune.'

'How odd you are! You have not changed in the least,' said Katya, and then left the veranda, to order supper to be served.

When she had gone, we were both silent and all was still around us, but for one exception. A nightingale, which had sung last night by fitful snatches, now flooded the garden with a steady stream of song, and was soon answered by another from the dell below, which had not sung till that evening. The nearer bird stopped and seemed to listen for a moment, and then broke out again still louder than before, pouring out his song in piercing long-drawn cadences. There was a regal calm in the birds' voices, as they floated through the realm of night which belongs to those birds and not to man. The gardener walked past to his sleeping-quarters in the greenhouse, and the noise of his heavy boots grew fainter and fainter along the path. Someone whistled twice sharply at the foot of the hill; and then all was still again. The rustling of leaves could just be heard; the veranda awning flapped; a faint perfume, floating in the air, came down on the veranda and filled it. I felt silence awkward after what had been said, but what to say I did not know. I looked at him. His eyes, bright in the half-darkness, turned towards me.

'How good life is!' he said.

I sighed, I don't know why.

'Well?' he asked.

'Life is good,' I repeated after him.

Again we were silent, and again I felt uncomfortable. I could not help fancying that I had wounded him by agreeing that he was old; and I wished to comfort him but did not know how.

'Well, I must be saying goodbye,' he said, rising; 'my mother expects me for supper; I have hardly seen her all day.'

'I meant to play you the new sonata,' I said.

'That must wait,' he replied; and I thought that he spoke coldly. 'Goodbye.'

I felt still more certain that I had wounded him, and I was sorry. Katya and I went to the steps to see him off and stood for a while in the open, looking along the road where he had disappeared from view. When we ceased to hear the sound of his horse's hoofs, I walked round the house to the veranda, and again sat looking into the garden; and all I wished to see and hear, I still saw and heard for a long time in the dewy mist filled with the sounds of night.

He came a second time, and a third; and the awkwardness arising from that strange conversation passed away entirely, never to return. During that whole summer he came two or three times a week; and I grew so accustomed to his presence, that, when he failed to come for some time, I missed him and felt angry with him, and thought he was behaving badly in deserting me. He treated me like a boy whose company he liked, asked me questions, invited the most cordial frankness on my part, gave me advice and encouragement, or sometimes scolded and checked me. But in spite of his constant effort to keep on my level, I was aware that behind the part of him which I could understand there remained an entire region of mystery, into which he did not consider it necessary to admit me; and this fact did much to preserve my respect for him and his attraction for me. I knew from

Katya and from our neighbours that he had not only to care for his old mother with whom he lived, and to manage his own estate and our affairs, but was also responsible for some public business which was the source of serious worries; but what view he took of all this, what were his convictions, plans, and hopes, I could not in the least find out from him. Whenever I turned the conversation to his affairs, he frowned in a way peculiar to himself and seemed to imply, 'Please stop! That is no business of yours;' and then he changed the subject. This hurt me at first; but I soon grew accustomed to confining our talk to my affairs, and felt this to be quite natural.

There was another thing which displeased me at first and then became pleasant to me. This was his complete indifference and even contempt for my personal appearance. Never by word or look did he imply that I was pretty; on the contrary, he frowned and laughed, whenever the word was applied to me in his presence. He even liked to find fault with my looks and tease me about them. On special days Katya liked to dress me out in fine clothes and to arrange my hair effectively; but my finery met only with mockery from him, which pained kind-hearted Katya and at first disconcerted me. She had made up her mind that he admired me; and she could not understand how a man could help wishing a woman whom he admired to appear to the utmost advantage. But I soon understood what he wanted. He wished to make sure that I had not a trace of affectation. And when I understood this I was really quite free from affectation in the clothes I wore, or the arrangement of my hair, or my movements; but a very obvious form of affectation took its place – an affectation of simplicity, at a time when I could not yet be really simple. That he loved me, I knew; but I did not yet ask myself whether he loved me as a child or as a woman. I valued his love; I felt that he thought me better than all other young women in the world, and I could not help wishing him to go on being deceived about me. Without wishing to deceive him, I did deceive him, and I became better myself while deceiving him. I felt it a better and worthier course to show him the good points of my heart and mind than of my body. My hair, hands, face, ways – all these, whether good or bad, he had appraised at once and knew so well, that I could add nothing to my external appearance except the wish to deceive him. But my mind and heart he did not know, because he loved them, and because they were in the very process of growth and development; and on this point I could and did deceive him. And how easy I felt in his company, once I understood this clearly! My causeless bashfulness and awkward movements completely disappeared. Whether he saw me from in front, or in profile, sitting or standing, with my hair up or my hair down, I felt that he knew me from head to foot, and I fancied, was satisfied with me as I was. If, contrary to his habit, he had suddenly said to me as other people did, that I had a pretty face, I believe that I should not have liked it at all. But, on the other hand, how light and happy my heart was when, after I had said something, he looked hard at me and said, hiding emotion under a mask of raillery: 'Yes, there is something in you! you are a fine girl – that I must tell you.'

And for what did I receive such rewards, which filled my heart with pride and joy? Merely for saying that I felt for old Grigori in his love for his little granddaughter; or because the reading of some poem or novel moved me to tears; or because I liked Mozart better than Schulhof. And I was surprised at my own quickness in guessing what was good and worthy of love, when I certainly did not know then what was good and worthy to be loved. Most of my former tastes and habits did not please him; and a mere look of his, or a twitch of his eyebrow was enough to show that he did not like what I was trying to say; and I felt at once that my own standard was changed. Sometimes, when he was about to give me a piece of advice, I seemed to know beforehand what he would say. When he looked in my face and asked me a question, his very look would draw out of me the answer he wanted. All my thoughts and feelings of that time were not really mine: they were his thoughts and feelings, which had suddenly become mine and passed into my life and lighted it up. Quite unconsciously I began to look at everything with different eyes – at Katya and the servants and Sonya and myself and my occupations. Books, which I used to read merely to escape boredom, now became one of the chief pleasures of my life, merely because he brought me the books and we read and discussed them together. The lessons I gave to Sonya had been a burdensome obligation which I forced myself to go through from a sense of duty; but, after he was present at a lesson, it became a joy to me to watch Sonya's progress. It used to seem to me an impossibility to learn a whole piece of music by heart; but now, when I knew that he would hear it and might praise it, I would play a single movement forty times over without stopping, till poor Katya stuffed her ears with cottonwool, while I was still not weary of it. The same old sonatas seemed quite different in the expression, and came out quite changed and much improved. Even Katya, whom I knew and loved like a second self, became different in my eyes. I now understood for the first time that she was not in the least bound to be the mother, friend, and slave that she was to us. Now I appreciated all the self-sacrifice and devotion of this affectionate creature, and all my obligations to her; and I began to love her even better. It was he too who taught me to take quite a new view of our serfs and servants and maids. It is an absurd confession to make – but I had spent seventeen years among these people and yet knew less about them than about strangers whom I had never seen; it had never once occurred to me that they had their affections and wishes and sorrows, just as I had. Our garden and woods and fields which I had known so long, became suddenly new and beautiful to me. He was right in saying that the only certain happiness in life is to live for others. At the time his words seemed to me strange, and I did not understand them; but by degrees this became a conviction with me, without thinking about it. He revealed to me a whole new world of joys in the present, without changing anything in my life, without adding anything except himself to each impression in my mind. All that had surrounded me from childhood without saying anything to me, suddenly came to life. The mere sight of him made everything begin to speak and press for admittance to my heart, filling it with happiness.

Often during that summer, when I went upstairs to my room and lay down on my bed, the old unhappiness of spring with its desires and hopes for the future gave place to a passionate happiness in the present. Unable to sleep, I often got up and sat on Katya's bed and told her how perfectly happy I was, though I now realize that this was quite unnecessary, as she could see it for herself.

But she told me that she was quite content and perfectly happy, and kissed me. I believed her – it seemed to me so necessary and just that everyone should be happy. But Katya could think of sleep too; and sometimes, pretending to be angry, she drove me from her bed and went to sleep, while I turned over and over in my mind all that made me so happy. Sometimes I got up and said my prayers over again, praying in my own words and thanking God for all the happiness he had given me.

All was quiet in the room; there was only the even breathing of Katya in her sleep, and the ticking of the clock by her bed, while I turned from side to side and whispered words of prayer, or crossed myself and kissed the cross round my neck. The door was shut and the windows shuttered; perhaps a fly or gnat hung buzzing in the air. I felt a wish never to leave that room – a wish that dawn might never come, that my present frame of mind might never change. I felt that my dreams and thoughts and prayers were live things, living there in the dark with me, hovering about my bed, and standing over me. And every thought was his thought, and every feeling his feeling. I did not know yet that this was love; I thought that things might go on so for ever, and that this feeling involved no consequences.

Chapter 3

One day when the corn was being carried, I went with Katya and Sonya to our favourite seat in the garden, in the shade of the lime trees and above the dell, beyond which the fields and woods lay open before us. It was three days since Sergey Mikhaylych had been to see us; we were expecting him, all the more because our bailiff reported that he had promised to visit the harvest field. At two o'clock we saw him ride on to the rye field. With a smile and a glance at me, Katya ordered peaches and cherries, of which he was very fond, to be brought; then she lay down on the bench and began to doze. I tore off a crooked flat lime tree branch, which made my hand wet with its juicy leaves and juicy bark. Then I fanned Katya with it and went on with my book, breaking off from time to time, to look at the field path along which he must come. Sonya was making a dolls' house at the root of an old lime tree. The day was sultry, windless, and steaming; the clouds were packing and growing blacker; all morning a thunderstorm had been gathering, and I felt restless, as I always did before thunder. But by afternoon the clouds began to part, the sun sailed out into a clear sky, and only in one quarter was there a faint rumbling. A single heavy cloud, lowering above the horizon and mingling with the dust from the fields, was rent from time to time by pale zigzags of lightning which ran down to the ground. It was clear that for today the storm would pass off, with us at all events. The road beyond the garden was visible in places, and we could see a procession of high creaking carts slowly moving along it with their load of sheaves, while the empty carts rattled at a faster pace to meet them, with swaying legs and shirts fluttering in them. The thick dust neither blew away nor settled down — it stood still beyond the fence, and we could see it through the transparent foliage of the garden trees. A little farther off, in the stackyard, the same voices and the same creaking of wheels were audible; and the same yellow sheaves that had moved slowly past the fence were now flying aloft, and I could see the oval stacks gradually rising higher, and their conspicuous pointed tops, and the labourers swarming upon them. On the dusty field in front more carts were moving and more yellow sheaves were visible; and the noise of the carts, with the sound of talking and singing, came to us from a distance. At one side the bare stubble, with strips of fallow covered with wormwood, came more and more into view. Lower down, to the right, the gay dresses of the women were visible, as they bent down and swung their arms to bind the sheaves. Here the bare stubble looked untidy; but the disorder was cleared by degrees, as the pretty sheaves were ranged at close intervals. It seemed as if summer had suddenly turned to autumn before my eyes. The dust and heat were everywhere, except in our favourite nook in the garden; and everywhere, in this heat and dust and under the burning sun, the labourers carried on their heavy task with talk and noise.

Meanwhile Katya slept so sweetly on our shady bench, beneath her white cambric handkerchief, the black juicy cherries glistened so temptingly on the plate, our dresses were so clean and fresh, the water in the jug was so bright with rainbow colours in the sun, and I felt so happy. 'How can I help it?' I thought; 'am I to blame for being happy? And how can I share my happiness? How and to whom can I surrender all myself and all my happiness?'

By this time the sun had sunk behind the tops of the birch avenue, the dust was settling on the fields, the distance became clearer and brighter in the slanting light. The clouds had dispersed altogether; I could see through the trees the thatch of three new corn stacks. The labourers came down off the stacks; the carts hurried past, evidently for the last time, with a loud noise of shouting; the women, with rakes over their shoulders and straw bands in their belts, walked home past us, singing loudly; and still there was no sign of Sergey Mikhaylych, though I had seen him ride down the hill long ago. Suddenly he appeared upon the avenue, coming from a quarter where I was not looking for him. He had walked round by the dell. He came quickly towards me, with his hat off and radiant with high spirits. Seeing that Katya was asleep, he bit his lip, closed his eyes, and advanced on tiptoe; I saw at once that he was in that peculiar mood of causeless merriment which I always delighted to see in him, and which we called 'wild ecstasy'. He was just like a schoolboy playing truant; his whole figure, from head to foot, breathed content, happiness, and boyish frolic.

'Well, young violet, how are you? All right?' he said in a whisper, coming up to me and taking my hand. Then, in answer to my question, 'Oh, I'm splendid today, I feel like a boy of thirteen – I want to play at horses and climb trees.'

'Is it wild ecstasy?' I asked, looking into his laughing eyes, and feeling that the 'wild ecstasy' was infecting me.

'Yes,' he answered, winking and checking a smile. 'But I don't see why you need hit Katerina Karlovna on the nose.'

With my eyes on him I had gone on waving the branch, without noticing that I had knocked the handkerchief off Katya's face and was now brushing her with the leaves. I laughed.

'She will say she was awake all the time,' I whispered, as if not to awake Katya; but that was not my real reason – it was only that I liked to whisper to him.

He moved his lips in imitation of me, pretending that my voice was too low for him to hear. Catching sight of the dish of cherries, he pretended to steal it, and carried it off to Sonya under the lime tree, where he sat down on her dolls. Sonya was angry at first, but he soon made his peace with her by starting a game, to see which of them could eat cherries faster.

'If you like, I will send for more cherries,' I said; 'or let us go ourselves.'

He took the dish and set the dolls on it, and we all three started for the orchard. Sonya ran behind us, laughing and pulling at his coat, to make him surrender the dolls. He gave them up and then turned to me, speaking more seriously.

'You really are a violet,' he said, still speaking low, though there was no longer any fear of waking anybody; 'when I came to you out of all that dust and heat and toil, I positively smelt violets at once. But not the sweet violet – you know, that early dark violet that smells of melting snow and spring grass.'

'Is harvest going on well?' I asked, in order to hide the happy agitation which his words produced in me.

'First rate! Our people are always splendid. The more you know them, the better you like them.'

'Yes,' I said; 'before you came I was watching them from the garden, and suddenly I felt ashamed to be so comfortable myself while they were hard at work, and so . . . .'

He interrupted me, with a kind but grave look: 'Don't talk like that, my dear; it is too sacred a matter to talk of lightly. God forbid that you should use fine phrases about that!'

'But it is only to you I say this.'

'All right, I understand. But what about those cherries?'

The orchard was locked, and no gardener to be seen: he had sent them all off to help with the harvest. Sonya ran to fetch the key. But he would not wait for her: climbing up a corner of the wall, he raised the net and jumped down on the other side.

His voice came over the wall – 'If you want some, give me the dish.'

'No,' I said; 'I want to pick for myself. I shall fetch the key; Sonya won't find it.'

But suddenly I felt that I must see what he was doing there and what he looked like – that I must watch his movements while he supposed that no one saw him. Besides I was simply unwilling just then to lose sight of him for a single minute. Running on tiptoe through the nettles to the other side of the orchard where the wall was lower, I mounted on an empty cask, till the top of the wall was on a level with my waist, and then leaned over into the orchard. I looked at the gnarled old trees, with their broad dented leaves and the ripe black cherries hanging straight and heavy among the foliage; then I pushed my head under the net, and from under the knotted bough of an old cherry tree I caught sight of Sergey Mikhaylych. He evidently thought that I had gone away and that no one was watching him. With his hat off and his eyes shut, he was sitting on the fork of an old tree and carefully rolling into a ball a lump of cherry tree gum. Suddenly he shrugged his shoulders, opened his eyes, muttered something, and smiled. Both words and smile were so unlike him that I felt ashamed of myself for eaves-dropping. It seemed to me that he had said, 'Masha!' 'Impossible,' I thought. 'Darling Masha!' he said again, in a lower and more tender tone. There was no possible doubt about the two words this time. My heart beat hard, and such a passionate joy – illicit joy, as I felt – took hold of me, that I clutched at the wall, fearing to fall and betray myself. Startled by the sound of my movement, he looked round – he dropped his eyes instantly, and his face turned red, even scarlet, like a child's. He tried to speak, but in vain; again and again his face positively flamed up. Still he smiled as he looked at me, and I smiled too. Then his whole face grew radiant with happiness. He had ceased to be the old uncle who spoiled or scolded me; he was a man on my level, who loved and feared me as I loved and feared him. We looked at one another without speaking. But suddenly he frowned; the smile and light in his eyes disappeared, and he resumed his cold paternal tone, just as if we were doing something wrong and he was repenting and calling on me to repent.

'You had better get down, or you will hurt yourself,' he said; 'and do put your hair straight; just think what you look like!'

'What makes him pretend? What makes him want to give me pain?' I thought in my vexation. And the same instant brought an irresistible desire to upset his composure again and test my power over him.

'No,' I said; 'I mean to pick for myself.' I caught hold of the nearest branch and climbed to the top of the wall; then, before he had time to catch me, I jumped down on the other side.

'What foolish things you do!' he muttered, flushing again and trying to hide his confusion under a pretence of annoyance; 'you might really have hurt yourself. But how do you mean to get out of this?'

He was even more confused than before, but this time his confusion frightened rather than pleased me. It infected me too and made me blush; avoiding his eye and not knowing what to say, I began to pick cherries though I had nothing to put them in. I reproached myself, I repented of what I had done, I was frightened; I felt that I had lost his good opinion for ever by my folly. Both of us were silent and embarrassed. From this difficult situation Sonya rescued us by running back with the key in her hand. For some time we both addressed our conversation to her and said nothing to each other. When we returned to Katya, who assured us that she had never been asleep and was listening all the time, I calmed down, and he tried to drop into his fatherly patronizing manner again, but I was not taken in by it. A discussion which we had had some days before came back clear before me.

Katya had been saying that it was easier for a man to be in love and declare his love than for a woman.

'A man may say that he is in love, and a woman can't,' she said.

'I disagree,' said he; 'a man has no business to say, and can't say that he is in love.'

'Why not?' I asked.

'Because it never can be true. What sort of a revelation is that, that a man is in love? A man seems to think that whenever he says the word, something will go pop! – that some miracle will be worked, signs and wonders, with all the big guns firing at once! In my opinion,' he went on, 'whoever solemnly brings out the words 'I love you' is either deceiving himself or, which is even worse, deceiving others.'

'Then how is a woman to know that a man is in love with her, unless he tells her?' asked Katya.

'That I don't know,' he answered; 'every man has his own way of telling things. If the feeling exists, it will out somehow. But when I read novels, I always fancy the crestfallen look of Lieut. Strelsky or Alfred, when he says, 'I love you, Eleanora', and expects something wonderful to happen at once, and no change at all takes place in either of them – their eyes and their noses and their whole selves remain exactly as they were.'

Even then I had felt that this banter covered something serious that had reference to myself. But Katya resented his disrespectful treatment of the heroes in novels.

'You are never serious,' she said; 'but tell me truthfully, have you never yourself told a woman that you loved her?'

'Never, and never gone down on one knee,' he answered, laughing; 'and never will.'

This conversation I now recalled, and I reflected that there was no need for him to tell me that he loved me. 'I know that he loves me,' I thought, 'and all his endeavours to seem indifferent will not change my opinion.'

He said little to me throughout the evening, but in every word he said to Katya and Sonya and in every look and movement of his I saw love and felt no doubt of it. I was only vexed and sorry for him, that he thought it necessary still to hide his feelings and pretend coldness, when it was all so clear, and when it would have been so simple and easy to be boundlessly happy. But my jumping down to him in the orchard weighed on me like a crime. I kept feeling that he would cease to respect me and was angry with me.

After tea I went to the piano, and he followed me.

'Play me something – it is long since I heard you,' he said, catching me up in the parlour.

'I was just going to,' I said. Then I looked straight in his face and said quickly, 'Sergey Mikhaylych, you are not angry with me, are you?'

'What for?' he asked.

'For not obeying you this afternoon,' I said, blushing.

He understood me: he shook his head and made a grimace, which implied that I deserved a scolding but that he did not feel able to give it.

'So it's all right, and we are friends again?' I said, sitting down at the piano.

'Of course!' he said.

In the drawing room, a large lofty room, there were only two lighted candles on the piano, the rest of the room remaining in half-darkness. Outside the open windows the summer night was bright. All was silent, except when the sound of Katya's footsteps in the unlighted parlour was heard occasionally, or when his horse, which was tied up under the window, snorted or stamped his hoof on the burdocks that grew there. He sat behind me, where I could not see him; but everywhere – in the half-darkness of the room, in every sound, in myself – I felt his presence. Every look, every movement of his, though I could not see them, found an echo in my heart. I played a sonata of Mozart's which he had brought me and which I had learnt in his presence and for him. I was not thinking at all of what I was playing, but I believe that I played it well, and I thought that he was pleased. I was conscious of his pleasure, and conscious too, though I never looked at him, of the gaze fixed on me from behind. Still moving my fingers mechanically, I turned round quite involuntarily and looked at him. The night had grown brighter, and his head stood out on a background of darkness. He was sitting with his head propped on his hands, and his eyes shone as they gazed at me. Catching his look, I smiled and stopped playing. He smiled too and shook his head reproachfully at the music, for me to go on. When I stopped, the moon had grown brighter and was riding high in the heavens; and the faint light of the candles was supplemented by a new silvery light which came in through the windows and fell on the floor. Katya called out that it was really too bad – that I had stopped at the best part of the piece, and that I was playing badly. But he declared that I had never played so well; and then he began to walk about the rooms – through the drawing room to the unlighted parlour and back again to the drawing room, and each time he looked at me and smiled. I smiled too; I wanted even to laugh with no reason; I was so happy at something that had happened that very day. Katya and I were standing by the piano; and each time that he vanished through the drawing room door, I started kissing her in my favourite place, the soft part of her neck under the chin; and each time he came back, I made a solemn face and refrained with difficulty from laughing.

'What is the matter with her today?' Katya asked him.

He only smiled at me without answering; he knew what was the matter with me.

'Just look what a night it is!' he called out from the parlour, where he had stopped by the open French window looking into the garden.

We joined him; and it really was such a night as I have never seen since. The full moon shone above the house and behind us, so that we could not see it, and half the shadow, thrown by the roof and pillars of the house and by the veranda awning, lay slanting and foreshortened on the gravel-path and the strip of turf beyond.

Everything else was bright and saturated with the silver of the dew and the moonlight. The broad garden path, on one side of which the shadows of the dahlias and their supports lay aslant, all bright and cold, and shining on the inequalities of the gravel, ran on till it vanished in the mist. Through the trees the roof of the greenhouse shone bright, and a growing mist rose from the dell. The lilac bushes, already partly leafless, were all bright to the centre. Each flower was distinguishable apart, and all were drenched with dew. In the avenues light and shade were so mingled that they looked, not like paths and trees but like transparent houses, swaying and moving. To our right, in the shadow of the house, everything was black, indistinguishable, and uncanny. But all the brighter for the surrounding darkness was the top of a poplar, with a fantastic crown of leaves, which for some strange reason remained there close to the house, towering into the bright light, instead of flying away into the dim distance, into the retreating dark blue of the sky.

'Let us go for a walk,' I said.

Katya agreed, but said I must put on galoshes.

'I don't want them, Katya,' I said; 'Sergey Mikhaylych will give me his arm.'

As if that would prevent me from wetting my feet! But to us three this seemed perfectly natural at the time. Though he never used to offer me his arm, I now took it of my own accord, and he saw nothing strange in it. We all went down from the veranda together. That whole world, that sky, that garden, that air, were different from those that I knew.

We were walking along an avenue, and it seemed to me, whenever I looked ahead, that we could go no farther in the same direction, that the world of the possible ended there, and that the whole scene must remain fixed for ever in its beauty. But we still moved on, and the magic wall kept parting to let us in; and still we found the familiar garden with trees and paths and withered leaves. And we were really walking along the paths, treading on patches of light and shade; and a withered leaf was really crackling under my foot, and a live twig brushing my face. And that was really he, walking steadily and slowly at my side, and carefully supporting my arm; and that was really Katya walking beside us with her creaking shoes. And that must be the moon in the sky, shining down on us through the motionless branches.

But at each step the magic wall closed up again behind us and in front, and I ceased to believe in the possibility of advancing farther – I ceased to believe in the reality of it all.

'Oh, there's a frog!' cried Katya.

'Who said that? and why?' I thought. But then I realized it was Katya, and that she was afraid of frogs. Then I looked at the ground and saw a little frog which gave a jump and then stood still in front of me, while its tiny shadow was reflected on the shining clay of the path.

'You're not afraid of frogs, are you?' he asked.

I turned and looked at him. Just where we were there was a gap of one tree in the lime avenue, and I could see his face clearly – it was so handsome and so happy!

Though he had spoken of my fear of frogs, I knew that he meant to say, 'I love you, my dear one!' 'I love you, I love you' was repeated by his look, by his arm; the light, the shadow, and the air all repeated the same words.

We had gone all round the garden. Katya's short steps had kept up with us, but now she was tired and out of breath. She said it was time to go in; and I felt very sorry for her. 'Poor thing!' I thought; 'why does not she feel as we do? Why are we not all young and happy, like this night and like him and me?'

We went in, but it was a long time before he went away, though the cocks had crowed, and everyone in the house was asleep, and his horse, tethered under the window, snorted continually and stamped his hoof on the burdocks. Katya never reminded us of the hour, and we sat on talking of the merest trifles and not thinking of the time, till it was past two. The cocks were crowing for the third time and the dawn was breaking when he rode away. He said goodbye as usual and made no special allusion; but I knew that from that day he was mine, and that I should never lose him now. As soon as I had confessed to myself that I loved him, I took Katya into my confidence. She rejoiced in the news and was touched by my telling her; but she was actually able – poor thing! – to go to bed and sleep! For me, I walked for a long, long time about the veranda; then I went down to the garden where, recalling each word, each movement, I walked along the same avenues through which I had walked with him. I did not sleep at all that night, and saw sunrise and early dawn for the first time in my life. And never again did I see such a night and such a morning. 'Only why does he not tell me plainly that he loves me?' I thought; 'what makes him invent obstacles and call himself old, when all is so simple and so splendid? What makes him waste this golden time which may never return? Let him say "I love you" – say it in plain words; let him take my hand in his and bend over it and say "I love you". Let him blush and look down before me; and then I will tell him all. No! not tell him, but throw my arms round him and press close to him and weep.' But then a thought came to me – 'What if I am mistaken and he does not love me?'

I was startled by this fear – God knows where it might have led me. I recalled his embarrassment and mine, when I jumped down to him in the orchard; and my heart grew very heavy. Tears gushed from my eyes, and I began to pray. A strange thought occurred too me, calming me and bringing hope with it. I resolved to begin fasting on that day, to take the Communion on my birthday, and on that same day to be betrothed to him.

How this result would come to pass I had no idea; but from that moment I believed and felt sure it would be so. The dawn had fully come and the labourers were getting up when I went back to my room.

Chapter 4

The Fast of the Assumption falling in August, no one in the house was surprised by my intention of fasting.

During the whole of the week he never once came to see us; but, far from being surprised or vexed or made uneasy by his absence, I was glad of it – I did not expect him until my birthday. Each day during the week I got up early. While the horses were being harnessed, I walked in the garden alone, turning over in my mind the sins of the day before, and considering what I must do today, so as to be satisfied with my day and not spoil it by a single sin. It seemed so easy to me then to abstain from sin altogether; only a trifling effort seemed necessary. When the horses came round, I got into the carriage with Katya or one of the maids, and we drove to the church two miles away. While entering the church, I always recalled the prayer for those who 'come unto the Temple in the fear of God', and tried to get just that frame of mind when mounting the two grass-grown steps up to the building. At that hour there were not more than a dozen worshippers — household servants or peasant women keeping the Fast. They bowed to me, and I returned their bows with studied humility. Then, with what seemed to me a great effort of courage, I went myself and got candles from the man who kept them, an old soldier and an Elder; and I placed the candles before the icons. Through the central door of the altar-screen I could see the altar cloth which my mother had worked; on the screen were the two angels which had seemed so big to me when I was little, and the dove with a golden halo which had fascinated me long ago. Behind the choir stood the old battered font, where I had been christened myself and stood godmother to so many of the servants' children. The old priest came out, wearing a cope made of the pall that had covered my father's coffin, and began to read in the same voice that I had heard all my life — at services held in our house, at Sonya's christening, at memorial services for my father, and at my mother's funeral. The same old quavering voice of the deacon rose in the choir; and the same old woman, whom I could remember at every service in that church, crouched by the wall, fixing her streaming eyes on an icon in the choir, pressing her folded fingers against her faded kerchief, and muttering with her toothless gums. And these objects were no longer merely curious to me, merely interesting from old recollections — each had become important and sacred in my eyes and seemed charged with profound meaning. I listened to each word of the prayers and tried to suit my feeling to it; and if I failed to understand, I prayed silently that God would enlighten me, or made up a prayer of my own in place of what I had failed to catch. When the penitential prayers were repeated, I recalled my past life, and that innocent childish past seemed to me so black when compared to the present brightness of my soul, that I wept and was horrified at myself; but I felt too that all those sins would be forgiven, and that if my sins had been even greater, my repentance would be all the sweeter. At the end of the service when the priest said, 'The blessing of the Lord be upon you!' I semed to feel an immediate sensation of physical well-being, of a mysterious light and warmth that instantly filled my heart. The service over, the priest came and asked me whether he should come to our house to say Mass, and what hour would suit me; and I thanked him for the suggestion, intended, as I thought, to please me, but said that I would come to church instead, walking or driving.

'Is that not too much trouble?' he asked. And I was at a loss for an answer, fearing to commit a sin of pride.

After the Mass, if Katya was not with me, I always sent the carriage home and walked back alone, bowing humbly to all who passed, and trying to find an opportunity of giving help or advice. I was eager to sacrifice myself for someone, to help in lifting a fallen cart, to rock a child's cradle, to give up the path to others by stepping into the mud. One evening I heard the bailiff report to Katya that Simon, one of our serfs, had come to beg some boards to make a coffin for his daughter, and a ruble to pay the priest for the funeral; the bailiff had given what he asked. 'Are they as poor as that?' I asked. 'Very poor, Miss,' the bailiff answered; 'they have no salt to their food.' My heart ached to hear this, and yet I felt a kind of pleasure too. Pretending to Katya that I was merely going for a walk, I ran upstairs, got out all my money (it was very little but it was all I had), crossed myself, and started off alone, through the veranda and the garden, on my way to Simon's hut. It stood at the end of the village, and no one saw me as I went up to the window, placed the money on the sill, and tapped on the pane. Someone came out, making the door creak, and hailed me; but I hurried home, cold and chaking with fear like a criminal. Katya asked where I had been and what was the matter with me; but I did not answer, and did not even understand what she was saying. Everything suddenly seemed to me so pety and insignificant. I locked myself up in my own room, and walked up and down alone for a long time, unable to do anything, unable to think, unable to understand my own feelings. I thought of the joy of the whole family, and of what they would say of their benefactor; and I felt sorry that I had not given them the money myself. I thought too of what Sergey Mikhaylych would say, if he knew what I had done; and I was glad to think that no one would ever find out. I was so happy, and I felt myself and everyone else so bad, and yet was so kindly disposed to myself and to all the world, that the thought of death came to me as a dream of happiness. I smiled and prayed and wept, and felt at that moment a burning passion of love for all the world, myself included. Between services I used to read the Gospel; and the book became more and more intelligible to me, and the story of that divine life simpler and more touching; and the depths of thought and feeling I found in studying it became more awful and impenetrable. On the other hand, how clear and simple everything seemed to me when I rose from the study of this book and looked again on life around me and reflected on it! It was so difficult, I felt, to lead a bad life, and so simple to love everyone and be loved. All were so kind and gentle to me; even Sonya, whose lessons I had not broken off, was quite different – trying to understand and please me and not to vex me. Everyone treated me as I treated them. Thinking over my enemies, of whom I must ask pardon before confession, I could only remember one – one of our neighbours, a girl whom I had made fun of in company a year ago, and who had ceased to visit us. I wrote to her, confessing my fault and asking her forgiveness. She replied that she forgave me and wished me to forgive her. I cried for joy over her simple words, and saw in them, at the time, a deep and touching feeling. My old nurse cried, when I asked her to forgive me. 'What makes them all so kind to me? What have I done to deserve their love?' I asked myself. Sergey Mikhaylych would come into my mind, and I thought for long about him. I could not help it, and I did not consider these thoughts sinful. But my thoughts of him were quite different from what they had been on the night when I first realized that I loved him: he seemed to me now like a second self, and became a part of every plan for the future. The inferiority which I had always felt in his presence had vanished entirely: I felt myself his equal and could understand him thoroughly from the moral elevation I had reached. What had seemed strange in him was now quite clear to me. Now I could see what he meant by saying to live for others was the only true happiness, and I agreed with him perfectly. I believed that our life together would be endlessly happy and untroubled. I looked forward, not to foreign tours or fashionable society or display, but to a quite different scene – a quiet family life in the country, with constant self-sacrifice, constant mutual love, and constant recognition in all things of the kind hand of Providence.

I carried out my plan of taking the Communion on my birthday. When I came back from church that day, my heart was so swelling with happiness that I was afraid of life, afraid of any feeling that might break in on that happiness. We had hardly left the carriage for the steps in front of the house, when there was a sound of wheels on the bridge, and I saw Sergey Mikhaylych drive up in his well-known trap. He congratulated me, and we went together to the parlour. Never since I had known him had I been so much at my ease with him and so self-possessed as on that morning. I felt in myself a whole new world out of his reach and beyond his comprehension. I was not conscious of the slightest embarrassment in speaking to him. He must have understood the cause of this feeling; for he was tender and gentle beyond his wont and showed a kind of reverent consideration for me. When I made for the piano, he locked it and put the key in his pocket.

'Don't spoil your present mood,' he said, 'you have the sweetest of all music in your soul just now.'

I was grateful for his words, and yet I was not quite pleased at his understanding too easily and clearly what ought to have been an exclusive secret in my heart. At dinner he said that he had come to congratulate me and also to say goodby; for he must go to Moscow tomorrow. He looked at Katya as he spoke; but then he stole a glance at me, and I saw that he was afraid he might detect signs of emotion on my face. But I was neither surprised nor agitated; I did not even ask whether he would be long away. I knew he would say this, and I knew that he would not go. How did I know? I cannot explain that to myself now; but on that memorable day it seemed that I knew everything that had been and that would be. It was like a delightful dream, when all that happens seems to have happened already and to be quite familiar, and it will all happen over again, and one knows that it will happen.

He meant to go away immediately after dinner; but, as Katya was tired after church and went to lie down for a little, he had to wait until she woke up in order to say goodby to her. The sun shone into the drawing room, and we went out to the veranda. When we were seated, I began at once, quite calmly, the conversation that was bound to fix the fate of my heart. I began to speak, no sooner and no later, but at the very moment when we sat down, before our talk had taken any turn or colour that might have hindered me from saying what I meant to say. I cannot tell myself where it came from – my coolness and determination and preciseness of expression. It was if something independent of my will was speaking through my lips. He sat opposite me with his elbows resting on the rails of the veranda; he pulled a lilac-branch towards him and stripped the leaves off it. When I began to speak, he let go the branch and leaned his head on one hand. His attitude might have shown either perfect calmness or strong emotion.

'Why are you going?' I asked, significantly, deliberately, and looking straight at him.

He did not answer at once.

'Business!' he muttered at last and dropped his eyes.

I realized how difficult he found it to lie to me, and in reply to such a frank question.

'Listen,' I said; you know what today is to me, how important for many reasons. If I question you, it is not to show an interest in your doings (you know that I have become intimate with you and fond of you) – I ask you this question, because I must know the answer. Why are you going?'

'It is very hard for me to tell you the true reason,' he said. 'During this week I have thought much about you and about myself, and have decided that I must go. You understand why; and if you care for me, you will ask no questions.' He put up a hand to rub his forehead and cover his eyes. 'I find it very difficult . . . But you will understand.'

My heart began to beat fast.

'I cannot understand you,' I said; 'I cannot! you must tell me; in God's name and for the sake of this day tell me what you please, and I shall hear it with calmness,' I said.

He changed his position, glanced at me, and again drew the lilac-twig towards him.

'Well!' he said, after a short silence and in a voice that tried in vain to seem steady, 'it's a foolish business and impossible to put into words, and I feel the difficulty, but I will try to explain it to you,' he added, frowning as if in bodily pain.

'Well?' I said.

'Just imagine the existence of a man – let us call him A – who has left youth far behind, and of a woman whom we may call B, who is young and happy and has seen nothing as yet of life or of the world. Family circumstances of various kinds brought them together, and he grew to love her as a daughter, and had no fear that his love would change its nature.'

He stopped, but I did not interrupt him.

'But he forgot that B was so young, that life was still all a May-game to her,' he went on with a sudden swiftness and determination and without looking at me, 'and that it was easy to fall in love with her in a different way, and that this would amuse her. He made a mistake and was suddenly aware of another feeling, as heavy as remorse, making its way into his heart, and he was afraid. He was afraid that their old friendly relations would be destroyed, and he made up his mind to go away before that happened.' As he said this, he began again to rub his eyes with a pretence of indifference, and to close them.

'Why was he afraid to love differently?' I asked very low; but I restrained my emotion and spoke in an even voice. He evidently thought that I was not serious; for he answered as if he were hurt.

'You are young, and I am not young. You want amusement, and I want something different. Amuse yourself, if you like, but not with me. If you do, I shall take it seriously; and then I shall be unhappy, and you will repent. That is what A said,' he added; 'however, this is all nonsense; but you understand why I am going. And don't let us continue this conversation. Please not!'

'No! no!' I said, 'we must continue it,' and tears began to tremble in my voice. 'Did he love her, or not?'

He did not answer.

'If he did not love her, why did he treat her as a child and pretend to love her?' I asked.

'Yes, A behaved badly,' he interrupted me quickly; 'but it all came to an end and they parted friends.'

'This is horrible! Is there no other ending?' I said with a great effort and then felt afraid of what I had said.

'Yes, there is,' he said, showing a face full of emotion and looking straight at me. 'There are two different endings. But, for God's sake, listen to me quietly and don't interrupt. Some say – ' here he stood up and smiled with a smile that was heavy with pain – 'some say that A went off his head, fell passionately in love with B, and told her so. But she only laughed. To her it was all a jest, but to him a matter of life and death.'

I shuddered and tried to interrupt him – tried to say that he must not dare to speak for me; but he checked me, laying his hand on mine.

'Wait!' he said, and his voice shook. 'The other story is that she took pity on him, and fancied, poor child, from her ignorance of the world, that she really could love hiim, and so consented to be his wife. And he, in his madness, believed it – believed that his whole life could begin anew; but she saw herself that she had deceived him and that he had deceived her . . . But let us drop the subject finally,' he ended, clearly unable to say more; and then he began to walk up and down in silence before me.

Though he had asked that subject should be dropped, I saw that his whole soul was hanging on my answer. I tried to speak, but the pain at my heart kept me dumb. I glanced at him – he was pale and his lower lip trembled. I felt sorry for him. With a sudden effort I broke the bonds of silence which had held me fast, and began to speak in a low inward voice, which I feared would break every moment.

'There is a third ending to the story,' I said, and then paused, but he said nothing; 'the third ending is that he did not love her, but hurt her, hurt her, and thought that he was right; and he left her and was actually proud of himself. You have been pretending, not I; I have loved you since the first day we met, loved you,' I repeated, and at the word 'loved' my low inward voice changed, without intention of mine, to a wild cry which frightened me myself.

He stood pale before me, his lip trembled more and more violently, and two tears came out upon his cheeks.

'It is wrong!' I almost screamed, feeling that I was choking with angry unshed tears. 'Why do you do it?' I cried and got up to leave him.

But he would not let me go. His head was resting on my knees, his lips were kissing my still trembling hands, and his tears were wetting them. 'My God! if I had only known!' he whispered.

'Why? Why?' I kept on repeating, but in my heart there was happiness, happiness which had now come back, after so nearly departing for ever.

Five minutes later Sonya was rushing upstairs to Katya and proclaiming all over the house that Masha intended to marry Sergey Mikhaylych.

Chapter 5

There were no reasons for putting off our wedding, and neither
he nor I wished for delay. Katya, it is true, thought we ought to
go to Moscow, to buy and order wedding clothes; and his mother
tried to insist that, before the wedding, he must set up a new
carriage, buy new furniture, and repaper the whole house. But
we two together carried our point, that all these things, if they
were really indispensable, should be done afterwards, and that we
should be married within a fortnight after my birthday, quietly,
without wedding clothes, without a party, without best men and
supper and champagne, and all the other conventional features of
a wedding. He told me how dissatisfied his mother was that there
should be no band, no mountain of luggage, no renovation of the
whole house – so unlike her own marriage which had cost thirty
thousand rubles; and he told of the solemn and secret confab-
ulations which she held in her store room with her housekeeper,
Maryushka, rummaging the chests and discussing carpets, curtains,
and salvers as indispensable conditions of our happiness. At our
house Katya did just the same with my old nurse, Kuzminichna. It
was impossible to treat the matter lightly with Katya. She was
firmly convinced that he and I, when discussing our future, were
merely talking the sentimental nonsense natural to people in our
position; and that our real future happiness depended on the
hemming of table cloths and napkins and the proper cutting out
and stitching of underclothing. Several times a day secret inform-
ation passed between the two houses, to communicate what was
going forward in each; and though the external relations between
Katya and his mother were most affectionate, yet a slightly hostile
though very subtle diplomacy was already perceptible in their
dealings. I now became more intimate with Tatyana Semyonovna,
the mother of Sergey Mikhaylych, an old-fashioned lady, strict and
formal in the management of her household. Her son loved her,
and not merely because she was his mother: he thought her the
best, cleverest, kindest, and most affectionate woman in the world.
She was always kind to us and to me especially, and was glad that
her son should be getting married; but when I was with her after
our engagement, I always felt that she wished me to understand
that, in her opinion, her son might have looked higher, and that it

would be as well for me to keep that in mind. I understood her meaning perfectly and thought her quite right.

During that fortnight he and I met every day. He came to dinner regularly and stayed on till midnight. But though he said – and I knew he was speaking the truth – that he had no life apart from me, yet he never spent the whole day with me, and tried to go on with his ordinary occupations. Our outward relations remained unchanged to the very day of our marriage: we went on saying 'you' and not 'thou' to each other; he did not even kiss my hand; he did not seek, but even avoided, opportunities of being alone with me. It was as if he feared to yield to the harmful excess of tenderness he felt. I don't know which of us had changed; but I now felt myself entirely his equal; I no longer found in him the pretence of simplicity which had displeased me earlier; and I often delighted to see in him, not a grown man inspiring respect and awe but a loving and wildly happy child. 'How mistaken I was about him!' I often thought; 'he is just such another human being as myself!' It seemed to me now, that his whole character was before me and that I thoroughly understood it. And how simple was every feature of his character, and how congenial to my own! Even his plans for our future life together were just my plans, only more clearly and better expressed in his words.

The weather was bad just then, and we spent most of our time indoors. The corner between the piano and the window was the scene of our best intimate talks. The candlelight was reflected on the blackness of the window near us; from time to time drops struck the glistening pane and rolled down. The rain pattered on the roof; the water splashed in a puddle under the spout; it felt damp near the window; but our corner seemed all the brighter and warmer and happier for that.

'Do you know, there is something I have long wished to say to you,' he began one night when we were sitting up late in our corner; 'I was thinking of it all the time you were playing.'

'Don't say it, I know all about it,' I replied.

'All right! mum's the word!'

'No! what is it?' I asked.

'Well, it is this. You remember the story I told you about A and B?'

'I should just think I did! What a stupid story! Lucky that it ended as it did!'

'Yes, I was very near destroying my happiness by my own act. You saved me. But the main thing is that I was always telling lies then, and I'm ashamed of it, and I want to have my say out now.'

'Please don't! You really mustn't!'

'Don't be frightened,' he said, smiling. 'I only want to justify myself. When I began then, I meant to argue.'

'It is always a mistake to argue,' I said.

'Yes, I argued wrong. After all my disappointments and mistakes in life, I told myself firmly when I came to the country this year, that love was no more for me, and that all I had to do was to grow old decently. So for a long time, I was unable to clear up my feeling towards you, or to make out where it might lead me. I hoped, and I didn't hope: at one time I thought you were trifling with me; at another I felt sure of you but could not decide what to do. But after that evening, you remember when we walked in the garden at night, I got alarmed: the present happiness seemed too great to be real. What if I allowed myself to hope and then failed? But of course I was thinking only of myself, for I am disgustingly selfish.'

He stopped and looked at me.

'But it was not all nonsense that I said then. It was possible and right for me to have fears. I take so much from you and can give so little. You are still a child, a bud that has yet to open; you have never been in love before, and I . . . '

'Yes, do tell me the truth . . . ' I began, and then stopped, afraid of his answer. 'No, never mind,' I added.

'Have I been in love before? Is that it?' he said, guessing my thoughts at once. 'That I can tell you. No, never before – nothing at all like what I feel now.' But a sudden painful recollection seemed to flash across his mind. 'No,' he said sadly; 'in this too I need your compassion, in order to have the right to love you. Well, was I not bound to think twice before saying that I loved you? What do I give you? Love, no doubt.'

'And is that little?' I asked, looking him in the face.

'Yes, my dear, it is little to give you,' he continued; 'you have youth and beauty. I often lie awake at night from happiness, and all the time I think of our future life together. I have lived through much, and now I think I have found what is needed for happiness. A quiet secluded life in the country, with the possibility of being useful to people to whom it is easy to do good, and who are not accustomed to have it done to them; then work which one hopes may be of some use; then rest, nature, books, music, love for one's neighbour – such is my idea of happiness. And then, on the top of all that, you for a mate, and children perhaps – what more can the hear of man desire?'

'It should be enough,' I said.

'Enough for me whose youth is over,' he went on, 'but not for you. Life is still before you, and you will perhaps seek happiness, and perhaps find it, in something different. You think now that this is happiness, because you love me.'

'You are wrong,' I said; 'I have always desired just that quiet domestic life and prized it. And you only say just what I have thought.'

He smiled.

'So you think, my dear; but that is not enough for you. You have youth and beauty,' he repeated thoughtfully.

But I was angry because he disbelieved me and seemed to cast my youth and beauty in my teeth.

'Why do you love me then?' I asked angrily; 'for my youth or for myself?'

'I don't know, but I love you,' he answered, looking at me with his attentive and attractive gaze.

I did not reply and involuntarily looked into his eyes. Suddenly a strange thing happened to me: first I ceased to see what was around me; then his face seemed to vanish till only the eyes were left, shining over against mine; next the eyes seemed to be in my own head, and then all became confused – I could see nothing and was forced to shut my eyes, in order to break loose from the feeling of pleasure and fear which his gaze was producing in me . . .

The day before our wedding day, the weather cleared up towards evening. The rains which had begun in summer gave place to clear weather, and we had our first autumn evening, bright and cold. It was a wet, cold, shining world, and the garden showed for the first time the spaciousness and colour and bareness of autumn. the sky was clear, cold, and pale. I went to bed happy in the thought that tomorrow, our wedding day, would be fine. I awoke with the sun, and the thought that this very day . . . seemed alarming and surprising. I went out into the garden. The sun had just risen and shone fitfully through the meagre yellow leaves of the lime avenue. The path was strewn with rustling leaves, clusters of mountain ash berries hung red and wrinkled on the boughs, with a sprinkling of frost-bitten crumpled leaves; the dahlias were black and wrinkled. The first rime lay like silver on the pale green of the grass and on the broken burdock plants round the house. In the clear cold sky there was not, and could not be, a single cloud.

'Can it possibly be today?' I asked myself, incredulous of my own happiness. 'Is it possible that I shall wake tomorrow, not here but in that strange house with the pillars? Is it possible that I shall never again wait for his coming and meet him, and sit up late with Katya to talk about him? Shall I never sit with him beside the piano in our drawing room? never see him off and feel uneasy about him on dark nights?' But I remembered that he promised yesterday to pay a last visit, and that Katya had insisted on my trying on my wedding dress, and had said 'For tomorrow'. I believed for a moment that it was all real, and then doubted again. 'Can it be that after today I shall be living there with a mother-inlaw, without Nadezhda or Grigori or Katya? Shall I go to bed without kissing my old nurse good night and hearing her say, while she signs me with the cross from old custom, 'Good night, Miss'? Shall I never again teach Sonya and play with her and knock through the wall to her in the morning and hear her hearty laugh? Shall I become from today someone that I myself do not know? and is a new world, that will realize my hopes and desires, opening before me? and will that new world last for ever?' Alone with these thoughts I was depressed and impatient for his arrival. He came early, and it required his presence to convince me that I should really be his wife that very day, and the prospect ceased to frighten me.

Before dinner we walked to our church, to attend a memorial service for my father.

'If only he were living now!' I thought as we were returning and I leant silently on the arm of him who had been the dearest friend of the object of my thoughts. During the service, while I pressed my forehead against the cold stone of the chapel floor, I called up my father so vividly; I was so convinced that he understood me and approved my choice, that I felt as if his spirit were still hovering over us and blessing me. And my recollections and hopes, my joy and sadness, made up one solemn and satisfied feeling which was in harmony with the fresh still air, the silence, the bare fields and pale sky, from which the bright but powerless rays, trying in vain to burn my cheek, fell over all the landscape. My companion seemed to understand and share my feeling. He walked slowly and silently; and his face, at which I glanced from time to time, expressed the same serious mood between joy and sorrow which I shared with nature.

Suddenly he turned to me, and I saw that he intended to speak. 'Suppose he starts some other subject than that which is in my mind?' I thought. But he began to speak of my father and did not even name him.

'He once said to me in jest, "you should marry my Masha",' he began.

'He would have been happy now,' I answered, pressing closer the arm which held mine.

'You were a child then,' he went on, looking into my eyes; 'I loved those eyes and used to kiss them only because they were like his, never thinking they would be so dear to me for their own sake. I used to call you Masha then.'

'I want you to say "thou" to me,' I said.

'I was just going to,' he answered; 'I feel for the first time that thou art entirely mine;' and his calm happy gaze that drew me to him rested on me.

We went on along the footpath over the beaten and trampled stubble; our voices and footsteps were the only sounds. On one side the brownish stubble stretched over a hollow to a distant leafless wood; across it at some distance a peasant was noiselessly ploughing a black strip which grew wider and wider. A drove of horses scattered under the hill seemed close to us. On the other side, as far as the garden and our house peeping through the trees, a field of winter corn, thawed by the sun, showed black with occasional patches of green. The winter sun shone over everything, and everything was covered with long gossamer spider's webs, which floated in the air round us, lay on the frost-dried stubble, and got into our eyes and hair and clothes. When we spoke, the sound of our voices hung in the motionless air above us, as if we two were alone in the whole world – alone under that azure vault, in which the beams of the winter sun played and flashed without scorching.

I too wished to say 'thou' to him, but I felt ashamed.

'Why dost thou walk so fast?' I said quickly and almost in a whisper; I could not help blushing.

He slackened his pace, and the gaze he turned on me was even more affectionate, gay, and happy.

At home we found that his mother and the inevitable guests had arrived already, and I was never alone with him again till we came out of church to drive to Nikolskoe.

The church was nearly empty: I just caught a glimpse of his mother standing up straight on a mat by the choir and of Katya wearing a cap with purple ribbons and with tears on her cheeks, and of two or three of our servants looking curiously at me. I did not look at him, but felt his presence there beside me. I attended to the words of the prayers and repeated them, but they found no echo in my heart. Unable to pray, I looked listlessly at the icons, the candles, the embroidered cross on the priest's cope, the screen, and the window, and took nothing in. I only felt that something strange was being done to me. At last the priest turned to us with the cross in his hand, congratulated us, and said, 'I christened you and by God's mercy have lived to marry you.' Katya and his mother kissed us, and Grigori's voice was heard, calling up the carriage. But I was only frightened and disappointed: all was over, but nothing extraordinary, nothing worthy of the Sacrament I had just received, had taken place in myself. He and I exchanged kisses, but the kiss seemed strange and not expressive of our feeling. 'Is this all?' I thought. We went out of church, the sound of wheels reverberated under the vaulted roof, the fresh air blew on my face, he put on his hat and handed me into the carriage. Through the window I could see a frosty moon with a halo round it. He sat down beside me and shut the door after him. I felt a sudden pang. The assurance of his proceedings seemed to me insulting. Katya called out that I should put something on my head; the wheels rumbled on the stone and then moved along the soft road, and we were off. Huddling in a corner, I looked out at the distant fields and the road flying past in the cold glitter of the moon. Without looking at him, I felt his presence beside me. 'Is this all I have got from the moment, of which I expected so much?' I thought; and still it seemed humiliating and insulting to be sitting alone with him, and so close. I turned to him, intending to speak; but the words would not come, as if my love had vanished, giving place to a feeling of mortification and alarm.

'Till this moment I did not believe it was possible,' he said in a low voice in answer to my look.

'But I am afraid somehow,' I said.

'Afraid of me, my dear?' he said, taking my hand and bending over it.

My hand lay lifeless in his, and the cold at my heart was painful. 'Yes,' I whispered.

But at that moment my heart began to beat faster, my hand trembled and pressed his, I grew hot, my eyes sought his in the half darkness, and all at once I felt that I did not fear him, that this fear was love – a new love still more tender and stronger than the old. I felt that I was wholly his, and that I was happy in his power over me.

PART 2

Chapter 1

Days, weeks, two whole months of seclusion in the country
slipped by unnoticed, as we thought then; and yet those two
months comprised feelings, emotions, and happiness, sufficient for
a lifetime. Our plans for the regulation of our life in the country
were not carried out at all in the way that we expected; but the
reality was not inferior to our ideal. There was none of that hard
work, performance of duty, self-sacrifice, and life for others, which
I had pictured to myself before our marriage; there was, on the
contrary, merely a selfish feeling of love for one another, a wish to
be loved, a constant causeless gaiety and entire oblivion of all the
world. It is true that my husband sometimes went to his study to
work, or drove to town on business, or walked about attending to
the management of the estate; but I saw what it cost him to tear
himself away from me. He confessed later that every occupation,
in my absence, seemed to him mere nonsense in which it was
impossible to take any interest. It was just the same with me. If I
read, or played the piano, or passed my time with his mother, or
taught in the school, I did so only because each of these occupations
was connected with him and won his approval; but whenever the
thought of him was not associated with any duty, my hands fell by
my sides and it seemed to me absurd to think that anything existed
apart from him. Perhaps it was a wrong and selfish feeling, but it
gave me happiness and lifted me high above all the world. He alone
existed on earth for me, and I considered him the best and most
faultless man in the world; so that I could not live for anything else
than for him, and my one object was to realize his conception of
me. And in his eyes I was the first and most excellent woman in the
world, the possessor of all possible virtues; and I strove to be that
woman in the opinion of the first and best of men.

He came to my room one day while I was praying. I looked round at him and went on with my prayers. Not wishing to interrupt me, he sat down at a table and opened a book. But I thought he was looking at me and looked round myself. He smiled, I laughed, and had to stop my prayers.

'Have you prayed already?' I asked.

'Yes. But you go on; I'll go away.'

'You do say your prayers, I hope?'

He made no answer and was about to leave the room when I stopped him.

'Darling, for my sake, please repeat the prayers with me!' He stood up beside me, dropped his arms awkwardly, and began, with a serious face and some hesitation. Occasionally he turned towards me, seeking signs of approval and aid in my face.

When he came to an end, I laughed and embraced him.

'I feel just as if I were ten! And you do it all!' he said, blushing and kissing my hands.

Our house was one of those old-fashioned country houses in which several generations have passed their lives together under one roof, respecting and loving one another. It was all redolent of good sound family traditions, which as soon as I entered it seemed to become mine too. The management of the household was carried on by Tatyana Semyonovna, my mother-in-law, on old-fashioned lines. Of grace and beauty there was not much; but, from the servants down to the furniture and food, there was abundance of everything, and a general cleanliness, solidity, and order, which inspired respect. The drawing room furniture was arranged symmetrically; there were portraits on the walls, and the floor was covered with home-made carpets and mats. In the morning-room there was an old piano, with chiffoniers of two different patterns, sofas, and little carved tables with bronze ornaments. My sitting room, specially arranged by Tatyana Semyonovna, contained the best furniture in the house, of many styles and periods, including an old pier-glass, which I was frightened to look into at first, but came to value as an old friend. Though Tatyana Semyonovna's voice was never heard, the whole household went like a clock. The number of servants was far too large (they all wore soft boots with no heels, because Tatyana Semyonovna had an intense dislike for stamping heels and creaking soles); but they all seemed proud of their calling, trembled before their old mistress, treated my husband and me with an affectionate air of patronage, and performed their duties, to all appearance, with extreme satisfaction. Every Saturday the floors were scoured and the carpets beaten without fail; on the first of every month there was a religious service in the house and holy water was sprinkled; on Tatyana Semyonovna's name day and on her son's (and on mine too, beginning from that autumn) an entertainment was regularly provided for the whole neighbourhood. and all this had gone on without a break ever since the beginning of Tatyana Semyonovna's life.

My husband took no part in the household management, he attended only to the farm-work and the labourers, and gave much time to this. Even in winter he got up so early that I often woke to find him gone. He generally came back for early tea, which we drank alone together; and at that time, when the worries and vexations of the farm were over, he was almost always in that state of high spirits which we called 'wild ecstasy'. I often made him tell me what he had been doing in the morning, and he gave such absurd accounts that we both laughed till we cried. Sometimes I insisted on a serious account, and he gave it, restraining a smile. I watched his eyes and moving lips and took nothing in: the sight of him and the sound of his voice was pleasure enough.

'Well, what have I been saying? Repeat it,' he would sometimes say. But I could repeat nothing. It seemed so absurd that he should talk to me of any other subject than ourselves. As if it mattered in the least what went on in the world outside! It was at a much later time that I began to some extent to understand and take an interest in his occupations. Tatyana Semyonovna never appeared before dinner: she breakfasted alone and said good morning to us by deputy. In our exclusive little world of frantic happiness a voice from the staid orderly region in which she dwelt was quite startling: I often lost self-control and could only laugh without speaking, when the maid stood before me with folded hands and made her formal report: 'The mistress bade me inquire how you slept after your walk yesterday evening; and about her I was to report that she had pain in her side all night, and a stupid dog barked in the village and kept her awake; and also I was to ask how you liked the bread this morning, and to tell you that it was not Taras who baked today, but Nikolashka who was trying his hand for the first time; and she says his baking is not at all bad, especially the cracknels: but the tea-rusks were over-baked.' Before dinner we saw little of each other: he wrote or went out again while I played the piano or read; but at four o'clock we all met in the drawing room before dinner. Tatyana Semyonovna sailed out of her own room, and certain poor and pious maiden ladies, of whom there were always two or three living in the house, made their appearance also. Every day without fail my husband by old habit offered his arm to his mother, to take her in to dinner; but she insisted that I should take the other, so that every day, without fail, we stuck in the doors and got in each other's way. She also presided at dinner, where the conversation, if rather solemn, was polite and sensible. The commonplace talk between my husband and me was a pleasant interruption to the formality of those entertainments. Sometimes there were squabbles between mother and son and they bantered one another; and I especially enjoyed the scenes, because they were the best proof of the strong and tender love which united the two. After dinner Tatyana Semyonovna went to the parlour, where she sat in an armchair and ground her snuff or cut the leaves of new books, while we read aloud or went off to the piano in the morning room. We read much together at this time, but music was our favourite and best enjoyment, always evoking fresh chords in our hearts and as it were revealing each afresh to the other. While I played his favourite pieces, he sat on a distant sofa where I could hardly see him. He was ashamed to betray the impression produced on him by the music; but often, when he was not expecting it, I rose from the piano, went up to him, and tried to detect on his face signs of emotion – the unnatural brightness and moistness of the eyes, which he tried in vain to conceal. Tatyana Semyonovna, though she often wanted to take a look at us there, was also anxious to put no constraint upon us. So she always passed through the room with an air of indifference and a pretence of being busy; but I knew that she had no real reason for going to her room and returning so soon. In the evening I poured out tea in the large drawing room, and all the household met again. This solemn ceremony of distributing cups and glasses before the solemnly shining samovar made me nervous for a long time. I felt myself still unworthy of such a distinction, too young and frivolous to turn the tap of such a big samovar, to put glasses on Nikita's salver, saying 'For Peter Ivanovich', 'For Marya Minichna', to ask 'Is it sweet enough?' and to leave out lumps of sugar for Nurse and other deserving persons. 'Capital! capital! Just like a grown-up person!' was a frequent comment from my husband, which only increased my confusion.

After tea Tatyana Semyonovna played patience or listened to Marya Minichna telling fortunes by the cards. Then she kissed us both and signed us with the cross, and we went off to our own rooms. But we generally sat up together till midnight, and that was our best and pleasantest time. He told me stories of his past life; we made plans and sometimes even talked philosophy; but we tried always to speak low, for fear we should be heard upstairs and reported to Tatyana Semyonovna, who insisted on our going to bed early. Sometimes we grew hungry; and then we stole off to the pantry, secured a cold supper by the good offices of Nikita, and ate it in my sitting room by the light of one candle. He and I lived like strangers in that big old house, where the uncompromising spirit of the past and of Tatyana Semyonovna ruled supreme. Not she only, but the servants, the old ladies, the furniture, even the pictures, inspired me with respect and a little alarm, and made me feel that he and I were a little out of place in that house and must always be very careful and cautious in our doings. Thinking it over now, I see that many things – the pressure of that unvarying routine, and that crowd of idle and inquisitive servants – were uncomfortable and oppressive; but at the time that very constraint made our love for one another still keener. Not I only, but he also, never grumbled openly at anything; on the contrary he shut his eyes to what was amiss. Dmitri Sidorov, one of the footmen, was a great smoker; and regularly every day, when we two were in the morning room after dinner, he went to my husband's study to take tobacco from the jar; and it was a sight to see Sergey Mikhaylych creeping on tiptoe to me with a face between delight and terror, and a wink and a warning forefinger, while he pointed at Dmitri Sidorov, who was quite unconscious of being watched. Then, when Dmitri Sidorov had gone away without having seen us, in his joy that all had passed off successfully, he declared (as he did on every other occasion) that I was a darling, and kissed me. At times his calm connivance and apparent indifference to everything annoyed me, and I took it for weakness, never noticing that I acted in the same way myself. 'It's like a child who dares not show his will,' I thought.

'My dear! my dear!' he said once when I told him that his weakness surprised me; 'how can a man, as happy as I am, be dissatisfied with anything? Better to give way myself than to put compulsion on others; of that I have long been convinced. There is no condition in which one cannot be happy; but our life is such bliss! I simply cannot be angry; to me now nothing seems bad, but only pitiful and amusing. Above all – *le mieux est l'ennemi du bien*. Will you believe it, when I hear a ring at the bell, or receive a letter, or even wake up in the morning, I'm frightened. Life must go on, something may change; and nothing can be better than the present.'

I believed him but did not understand him. I was happy; but I took that as a matter of course, the invariable experience of people in our position, and believed that there was somewhere, I knew not where, a different happiness, not greater but different.

So two months went by and winter came with its cold and snow; and, in spite of his company, I began to feel lonely, that life was repeating itself, that there was nothing new either in him or in myself, and that we were merely going back to what had been before. He began to give more time to business which kept him away from me, and my old feeling returned, that there was a special department of his mind into which he was unwilling to admit me. His unbroken calmness provoked me. I loved him as much as ever and was as happy as ever in his love; but my love, instead of increasing, stood still; and another new and disquieting sensation began to creep into my heart. To love him was not enough for me after the happiness I had felt in falling in love. I wanted movement and not a calm course of existence. I wanted excitement and danger and the chance to sacrifice myself for my love. I felt in myself a superabundance of energy which found no outlet in our quiet life. I had fits of depression which I was ashamed of and tried to conceal from him, and fits of excessive tenderness and high spirits which alarmed him. He realized my state of mind before I did, and proposed a visit to Petersburg; but I begged him to give this up and not to change our manner of life or spoil our happiness. Happy indeed I was; but I was tormented by the thought that this happiness cost me no effort and no sacrifice, though I was even painfully conscious of my power to face both. I loved him and saw that I was all in all to him; but I wanted everyone to see our love; I wanted to love him in spite of obstacles. My mind, and even my senses, were fully occupied; but there was another feeling of youth and craving for movement, which found no satisfaction in our quiet life. What made him say that, whenever I liked, we could go to town? Had he not said so I might have realized that my uncomfortable feelings were my own fault and dangerous nonsense, and that the sacrifice I desired was there before me, in the task of overcoming these feelings. I was haunted by the thought that I could escape from depression by a mere change from the country; and at the same time I felt ashamed and sorry to tear him away, out of selfish motives, from all he cared for. So time went on, the snow grew deeper, and there we remained together, all alone and just the same as before, while outside I knew there was noise and glitter and excitement, and hosts of people suffering or rejoicing without one thought of us and our remote existence. I suffered most from the feeling that custom was daily petrifying our lives into one fixed shape, that our minds were losing their freedom and becoming enslaved to the steady passionless course of time. The morning always found us cheerful; we were polite at dinner, and affectionate in the evening. 'It is all right,' I thought, 'to do good to others and lead upright lives, as he says; but there is time for that later; and there are other things, for which the time is now or never.' I wanted, not what I had got, but a life of struggle; I wanted feeling to be the guide of life, and not life to guide feeling. If only I could go with him to the edge of a precipice and say, 'One step, and I shall fall over – one movement, and I shall be lost!' then, pale with fear, he would catch me in his strong arms and hold me over the edge till my blood froze, and then carry me off whither he pleased.

This state of feeling even affected my health, and I began to suffer from nerves. One morning I was worse than usual. He had come beck from the estate office out of sorts, which was a rare thing with him. I noticed it at once and asked what was the matter. He would not tell me and said it was of no importance. I found out afterwards that the police inspector, out of spite against my husband, was summoning our peasants, making illegal demands on them, and using threats to them. My husband could not swallow this at once; he could not feel it merely 'pitiful and amusing'. He was provoked, and therefore unwilling to speak of it to me. But it seemed to me that he did not wish to speak to me about it because he considered me a mere child, incapable of understanding his concerns. I turned from him and said no more. I then told the servant to ask Marya Minichna, who was staying in the house, to join us at breakfast. I ate my breakfast very fast and took her to the morning room where I began to talk loudly to her about some trifle which did not interest me in he least. He walked about the room, glancing at us from time to time. This made me more and more inclined to talk and even to laugh; all that I said myself, and all that Marya Minichna said, seemed to me laughable. Without a word to me he went off to his study and shut the door behind him. When I ceased to hear him, all my high spirits vanished at once; indeed Marya Minichna was surprised and asked what was the matter. I sat down on a sofa without answering, and felt ready to cry. 'What has he got on his mind?' I wondered; 'some trifle which he thinks important; but, if he tried to tell it me, I should soon show him it was mere nonsense. But he must needs think that I won't understand, must humiliate me by his majestic composure, and always be in the right as against me. But I too am in the right when I find things tiresome and trivial,' I reflected; 'and I do well to want an active life rather than to stagnate in one spot and feel life flowing past me. I want to move forward, to have some new experience every day and every hour, whereas he wants to stand still and to keep me standing beside him. And how easy it would be for him to gratify me! He need not take me to town; he need only be like me and not put compulsion on himself and regulate his feelings, but live simply. That is the advice he gives me, but he is not simple himself. That is what is the matter.'

I felt the tears rising and knew that I was irritated with him. My irritation frightened me, and I went to his study. He was sitting at the table, writing. Hearing my step, he looked up for a moment and then went on writing; he seemed calm and unconcerned. His look vexed me: instead of going up to him, I stood beside his writing table, opened a book, and began to look at it. He broke off his writing again and looked at me.

'Masha, are you out of sorts?' he asked.

I replied with a cold look, as much as to say, 'You are very polite, but what is the use of asking?' He shook his head and smiled with a tender timid air; but his smile, for the first time, drew no answering smile from me.

'What happened to you today?' I asked; 'why did you not tell me?'

'Nothing much – a trifling nuisance,' he said. 'But I might tell you now. Two of our serfs went off to the town . . . '

But I would not let him go on.

'Why would you not tell me, when I asked you at breakfast?:

'I was angry then and should have said something foolish.'

'I wished to know then.'

'Why?'

'Why do you suppose that I can never help you in anything?'

'Not help me!' he said, dropping his pen. 'Why, I believe that without you I could not live. You not only help me in everything I do, but you do it yourself. You are very wide of the mark,' he said, and laughed. 'My life depends on you. I am pleased with things, only because you are there, because I need you . . . '

'Yes, I know; I am a delightful child who must be humoured and kept quiet,' I said in a voice that astonished him, so that he looked up as if this was a new experience; 'but I don't want to be quiet and calm; that is more in your line, and too much in your line,' I added.

'Well,' he began quickly, interrupting me and evidently afraid to let me continue, 'when I tell you the facts, I should like to know your opinion.'

'I don't want to hear them now,' I answered. I did want to hear the story, but I found it so pleasant to break down his composure. 'I don't want to play at life,' I said, 'but to live, as you do yourself.'

His face, which reflected every feeling so quickly and so vividly, now expressed pain and intense attention.

'I want to share your life, to . . . ,' but I could not go on – his face showed such deep distress. He was silent for a moment.

'But what part of my life do you not share?' he asked; 'is it because I, and not you, have to bother with the inspector and with tipsy labourers?'

'That's not the only thing,' I said.

'For God's sake try to understand me, my dear!' he cried. 'I know that excitement is always painful; I have learnt that from the experience of life. I love you, and I can't but wish to save you from excitement. My life consists of my love for you; so you should not make life impossible for me.'

'You are always in the right,' I said without looking at him.

I was vexed again by his calmness and coolness while I was conscious of annoyance and some feeling akin to penitence.

'Masha, what is the matter?' he asked. 'The question is not, which of us is in the right – not at all; but rather, what grievance have you against me? Take time before you answer, and tell me all that is in your mind. You are dissatisfied with me: and you are, no doubt, right; but let me understand what I have done wrong.'

But how could I put my feeling into words? That he understood me at once, that I again stood before him like a child, that I could do nothing without his understanding and foreseeing it – all this only increased my agitation.

'I have no complaint to make of you,' I said; 'I am merely bored and want not to be bored. But you say that it can't be helped, and, as always, you are right.'

I looked at him as I spoke. I had gained my object: his calmness had disappeared, and I read fear and pain in his face.

'Masha,' he began in a low troubled voice, 'this is no mere trifle: the happiness of our lives is at stake. Please hear me out without answering. why do you wish to torment me?'

But I interrupted him.

'Oh, I know you will turn out to be right. Words are useless; of course you are right.' I spoke coldly, as if some evil spirit were speaking with my voice.

'If you only knew what you are doing!' he said, and his voice shook.

I burst out crying and felt relieved. He sat down beside me and said nothing. I felt sorry for him, ashamed of myself, and annoyed at what I had done. I avoided looking at him. I felt that any look from him at that moment must express severity or perplexity. At last I looked up and saw his eyes: they were fixed on me with a tender gentle expression that seemed to ask for pardon. I caught his hand and said, 'Forgive me! I don't know myself what I have been saying.'

'But I do; and you spoke the truth.'

'What do you mean?' I asked.

'That we must go to Petersburg,' he said; 'there is nothing for us to do here just now.'

'As you please,' I said.

He took me in his arms and kissed me.

'You must forgive me,' he said; 'for I am to blame.'

That evening I played to him for a long time, while he walked about the room. He had a habit of muttering to himself; and when I asked him what he was muttering, he always thought for a moment and then told me exactly what it was. It was generally verse, and sometimes mere nonsense, but I could always judge of his mood by it. When I asked him now, he stood still, thought an instant, and then repeated two lines from Lermontov.

> He in his madness prays for storms,
> And dreams that storms will bring him peace.

'He is really more than human,' I thought; 'he knows everything. How can one help loving him?'

I got up, took his arm, and began to walk up and down with him, trying to keep step.

'Well?' he asked, smiling and looking at me.

'All right,' I whispered. And then a sudden fit of merriment came over us both: our eyes laughed, we took longer and longer steps, and rose higher and higher on tiptoe. Prancing in this manner, to the profound dissatisfaction of the butler and astonishment of my mother-in-law, who was playing patience in the parlour, we proceeded through the house till we reached the dining room; there we stopped, looked at one another, and burst out laughing.

A fortnight later, before Christmas, we were in Petersburg.

Chapter 2

The journey to Petersburg, a week in Moscow, visits to my own relations and my husband's, settling down in our new quarters, travel, new towns and new faces – all this passed before me like a dream. It was all so new, various, and delightful, so warmly and brightly lighted up by his presence and his love, that our quiet life in the country seemed to me something very remote and unimportant. I had expected to find people in society proud and cold; but to my great surprise, I was received everywhere with unfeigned cordiality and pleasure, not only by relations, but also by strangers. I seemed to be the one object of their thoughts, and my arrival the one thing they wanted, to complete their happiness. I was surprised too to discover in what seemed to me the very best society a number of people acquainted with my husband, though he had never spoken of them to me; and I often felt it odd and disagreeable to hear him now speak disapprovingly of some of these people who seemed to me so kind. I could not understand his coolness towards them or his endeavuors to avoid many acquaintances that seemed to me flattering. Surely, the more kind people one knows, the better; and here everyone was kind.

'This is how we must manage, you see,' he said to me before we left the country; 'here we are little Croesuses, but in town we shall not be at all rich. So we must not stay after Easter, or go into society, or we shall get into difficulties. For your sake too I should not wish it.'

'Why should we go into society?' I asked; 'we shall have a look at the theatres, see our relations, go to the opera, hear some good music, and be ready to come home before Easter.'

But these plans were forgotten the moment we got to Petersburg. I found myself at once in such a new and delightful world, surrounded by so many pleasures and confronted by such novel interests, that I instantly, though unconsciously, turned my back on my past life and its plans. 'All that was preparatory, a mere playing at life; but here is the real thing! And there is the future too!' Such were my thoughts. The restlessness and symptoms of depression which had troubled me at home vanished at once and entirely, as if by magic. My love for my husband grew calmer, and I ceased to wonder whether he loved me less. Indeed I could not doubt his love: every thought of mine was understood at once, every feeling shared, and every wish gratified by him. His composure, if it still existed, no longer provoked me. I also began to realize that he not only loved me but was proud of me. If we paid a call, or made some new acquaintance, or gave an evening party at which I, trembling inwardly from fear of disgracing myself, acted as hostess, he often said when it was over: 'Bravo, young woman! capital! you needn't be frightened; a real success!' And his praise gave me great pleasure. Soon after our arrival he wrote to his mother and asked me to add a postscript, but refused to let me see his letter; of course I insisted on reading it; and he had said: 'You would not know Masha again, I don't myself. Where does she get that charming graceful self-confidence and ease, such social gifts with such simplicity and charm and kindliness? Everybody is delighted with her. I can't admire her enough myself, and should be more in love with her than ever, if that were possible.'

'Now I know what I am like,' I thought. In my joy and pride I felt that I loved him more than before. My success with all our new acquaintances was a complete surprise to me. I heard on all sides, how this uncle had taken a special fancy for me, and that aunt was raving about me; I was told by one admirer that I had no rival among the Petersburg ladies, and assured by another, a lady, that I might, if I cared, lead the fashion in society. A cousin of my husband's, in particular, a Princess D., middle-aged and very much at home in society, fell in love with me at first sight and paid me compliments which turned my head. The first time that she invited me to a ball and spoke to my husband about it, he turned to me and asked if I wished to go; I could just detect a sly smile on his face. I nodded assent and felt that I was blushing.

'She looks like a criminal when confessing what she wishes,' he said with a good-natured laugh.

'But you said that we must not go into society, and you don't care for it yourself,' I answered, smiling and looking imploringly at him.

'Let us go, if you want to very much,' he said.

'Really, we had better not.'

'Do you want to? Very badly?' he asked again.

I said nothing.

'Society in itself is no great harm,' he went on; 'but unsatisfied social aspirations are a bad and ugly business. We must certainly accept, and we will.'

'To tell you the truth,' I said, 'I never in my life longed for anything as much as I do for this ball.'

So we went, and my delight exceeded all my expectations. It seemed to me, more than ever, that I was the centre round which everything revolved, that for my sake alone this great room was lighted up and the band played, and that this crowd of people had assembled to admire me. From the hairdresser and the lady's maid to my partners and the old gentlemen promenading the ball room, all alike seemed to make it plain that they were in love with me. The general verdict formed at the ball about me and reported by my cousin, came to this: I was quite unlike the other women and had a rural simplicity and charm of my own. I was so flattered by my success that I frankly told my husband I should like to attend two or three more balls during the season, and 'so get thoroughly sick of them', I added; but I did not mean what I said.

He agreed readily; and he went with me at first with obvious satisfaction. He took pleasure in my success, and seemed to have quite forgotten his former warning or to have changed his opinion.

But a time came when he was evidently bored and wearied by the life we were leading. I was too busy, however, to think about that. Even if I sometimes noticed his eyes fixed questioningly on me with a serious attentive gaze, I did not realize its meaning. I was utterly blinded by this sudden affection which I seemed to evoke in all our new acquaintances, and confused by the unfamiliar atmosphere of luxury, refinement, and novelty. It pleased me so much to find myself in these surroundings not merely his equal but his superior, and yet to love him better and more independently than before, that I could not understand what he could object to for me in society life. I had a new sense of pride and self-satisfaction when my entry at a ball attracted all eyes, while he, as if ashamed to confess his ownership of me in public, made haste to leave my side and efface himself in the crowd of black coats. 'Wait a little!' I often said in my heart, when I identified his obscure and some-times woebegone figure at the end of the room — 'Wait till we get home! Then you will see and understand for whose sake I try to be beautiful and brilliant, and what it is I love in all that surrounds me this evening!' I really believed that my success pleased me only because it enabled me to give it up for his sake. One danger I recognized as possible — that I might be carried away by a fancy for some new acquaintance, and that my husband might grow jealous. But he trusted me so absolutely, and seemed so undisturbed and indifferent, and all the young men were so inferior to him, that I was not alarmed by this one danger. Yet the attention of so many people in society gave me satisfaction, flattered my vanity, and made me think that there was some merit in my love for my husband. Thus I became more offhand and self-confident in my behaviour to him.

'Oh, I saw you this evening carrying on a most animated conversation with Mme N.,' I said one night on returning from a ball, shaking my finger at him. He had really been talking to this lady, who was a well-known figure in Petersburg society. He was more silent and depressed than usual, and I said this to rouse him up.

'What is the good of talking like that, for you especially, Masha?' he said with half-closed teeth and frowning as if in pain. 'Leave that to others; it does not suit you and me. Pretence of that sort may spoil the true relation between us, which I still hope may come back.'

I was ashamed and said nothing.

'Will it ever come back, Masha, do you think? he asked.

'It never was spoilt and never will be,' I said; and I really believed this then.

'God grant that you are right!' he said; 'if not, we ought to be going home.'

But he only spoke like this once – in general he seemed as satisfied as I was, and I was so gay and so happy! I comforted myself too by thinking, 'If he is bored sometimes, I endured the same thing for his sake in the country. If the relation between us has become a little different, everything will be the same again in summer, when we shall be alone in our house at Nikolskoye with Tatyana Semyonovna.'

So the winter slipped by, and we stayed on, in spite of our plans, over Easter in Petersburg. A week later we were preparing to start; our packing was all done; my husband who had bought things – plants for the garden and presents for people at Nikolskoye – was in a specially cheerful and affectionate mood. Just then Princess D. came and begged us to stay till the Saturday, in order to be present at a reception to be given by Countess R. The countess was very anxious to secure me, because a foreign prince, who was visiting Petersburg and had seen me already at a ball, wished to make my acquaintance; indeed this was his motive for attending the reception, and he declared that I was the most beautiful woman in Russia. All the world was to be there; and, in a word, it would really be too bad, if I did not go too.

My husband was talking to someone at the other end of the drawing room.

'So you will go, won't you, Mary?' said the Princess.

'We meant to start for the country the day after tomorrow,' I answered undecidedly, glancing at my husband. Our eyes met, and he turned away at once.

'I must persuade him to stay,' she said, 'and then we can go on Saturday and turn all heads. All right?'

'It would upset our plans; and we have packed,' I answered, beginning to give way.

'She had better go this evening and make her curtsey to the Prince,' my husband called out from the other end of the room; and he spoke in a tone of suppressed irritation which I had never heard from him before.

'I declare he's jealous, for the first time in his life,' said the lady, laughing. 'But it's not for the sake of the Prince I urge it, Sergey Mikhaylych, but for all our sakes. The Countess was so anxious to have her.'

'It rests with her entirely,' my husband said coldly, and then left the room.

I saw that he was much disturbed, and this pained me. I gave no positive promise. As soon as our visitor left, I went to my husband. He was walking up and down his room, thinking, and neither saw nor heard me when I came in on tiptoe.

Looking at him, I said to myself: 'He is dreaming already of his dear Nikolskoye, our morning coffee in the bright drawing room, the land and the labourers, our evenings in the music room, and our secret midnight suppers.' Then I decided in my own heart: 'Not for all the balls and all the flattering princes in the world will I give up his glad confusion and tender cares.' I was just about to say that I did not wish to go to the ball and would refuse, when he looked round, saw me, and frowned. His face, which had been gentle and thoughtful, changed at once to its old expression of sagacity, penetration, and patronizing composure. He would not show himself to me as a mere man, but had to be a demigod on a pedestal.

'Well, my dear?' he asked, turning towards me with an unconcerned air.

I said nothing. I ws provoked, because he was hiding his real self from me, and would not continue to be the man I loved.

'Do you want to go to this reception on Saturday?' he asked.

'I did, but you disapprove. Besides, our things are all packed,' I said.

Never before had I heard such coldness in his tone to me, and never before seen such coldness in his eye.

'I shall order the things to be unpacked,' he said, 'and I shall stay till Tuesday. So you can go to the party, if you like. I hope you will; but I shall not go.'

Without looking at me, he began to walk about the room jerkily, as his habit was when perturbed.

'I simply can't understand you,' I said, following him with my eyes from where I stood. 'You say that you never lose self-control' (he had never really said so); 'then why do you talk to me so strangely? I am ready on your account to sacrifice this pleasure, and then you, in a sarcastic tone which is new from you to me, insist that I should go.'

'So you make a sacrifice!' he threw special emphasis on the last word. 'Well, so do I. What could be better? We compete in generosity – what an example of family happiness!'

Such harsh and contemptuous language I had never heard from his lips before. I was not abashed, but mortified by his contempt; and his harshness did not frighten me but made me harsh too. How could he speak thus, he who was always so frank and simple and dreaded insincerity in our speech to one another? And what had I done that he should speak so? I really intended to sacrifice for his sake a pleasure in which I could see no harm; and a moment ago I loved him and understood his feelings as well as ever. We had changed parts: now he avoided direct and plain words, and I desired them.

'You are much changed,' I said, with a sigh. 'How am I guilty before you? It is not this party – you have something else, some old count against me. Why this insincerity? You used to be so afraid of it yourself. Tell me plainly what you complain of.'

'What will he say?' thought I, and reflected with some complacency that I had done nothing all winter which he could find fault with.

I went into the middle of the room, so that he had to pass close to me, and looked at him. I thought, 'He will come and clasp me in his arms, and there will be an end of it.' I was even sorry that I should not have the chance of proving him wrong. But he stopped at the far end of the room and looked at me.

'Do you not understand yet?' he asked.

'No, I don't.'

'Then I must explain. What I feel, and cannot help feeling, positively sickens me for the first time in my life.' He stopped, evidently startled by the harsh sound of his own voice.

'What do you mean?' I asked, with tears of indignation in my eyes.

'It sickens me that the Prince admired you, and you therefore run to meet him, forgetting your husband and yourself and womanly dignity; and you wilfully misunderstand what your want of self-respect makes your husband feel for you: you actually come to your husband and speak of the "sacrifice" you are making, by which you mean – "To show myself to His Highness is a great pleasure to me, but I sacrifice it." '

The longer he spoke, the more he was excited by the sound of his own voice, which was hard and rough and cruel. I had never seen him, had never thought of seeing him, like that. The blood rushed to my heart and I was frightened; but I felt that I had nothing to be ashamed of, and the excitement of wounded vanity made me eager to punish him.

'I have long been expecting this,' I said. 'Go on. Go on!'

'What you expected, I don't know,' he went on; 'but I might well expect the worst, when I saw you day after day sharing the dirtiness and idleness and luxury of this foolish society, and it has come at last. Never have I felt such shame and pain as now – pain for myself, when your friend thrusts her unclean fingers into my heart and speaks of my jealousy! – jealousy of a man whom neither you nor I know; and you refuse to understand me and offer to make a sacrifice for me – and what sacrifice? I am ashamed for you, for your degradation! . . . Sacrifice!' he repeated again.

'Ah, so this is a husband's power,' thought I: 'to insult and humiliate a perfectly innocent woman. Such may be a husband's rights, but I will not submit to them.' I felt the blood leave my face and a strange distension of my nostrils, as I said, 'No! I make no sacrifice on your account. I shall go to the party on Saturday without fail.'

'And I hope you may enjoy it. But all is over between us two!' he cried out in a fit of unrestrained fury. 'But you shall not torture me any longer! I was a fool, when I . . . ', but his lips quivered, and he refrained with a visible effort from ending the sentence.

I feared and hated him at that moment. I wished to say a great deal to him and punish him for all his insults; but if I had opened my mouth, I should have lost my dignity by bursting into tears. I said nothing and left the room. But as soon as I ceased to hear his footsteps, I was horrified at what we had done. I feared that the tie which had made all my happiness might really be snapped for ever; and I thought of going back. But then I wondered: 'Is he calm enough now to understand me, if I mutely stretch out my hand and look at him? Will he realize my generosity? What if he calls my grief a mere pretence? Or he may feel sure that he is right and accept my repentance and forgive me with unruffled pride. And why, oh why, did he whom I loved so well insult me so cruelly?'

I went not to him but to my own room, where I sat for a long time and cried. I recalled with horror each word of our conversation, and substituted different words, kind words, for those that we had spoken, and added others; and then again I remembered the reality with horror and a feeling of injury. In the evening I went down for tea and met my husband in the presence of a friend who was staying with us; and it seemed to me that a wide gulf had opened between us from that day. Our friend asked me when we were to start; and before I could speak, my husband answered.

'On Tuesday,' he said; 'we have to stay for Countess R.'s reception.' He turned to me: 'I believe you intend to go?' he asked.

His matter-of-fact tone frightened me, and I looked at him timidly. His eyes were directed straight at me with an unkind and scornful expression; his voice was cold and even.

'Yes,' I answered.

When we were alone that evening, he came up to me and held out his hand.

'Please forget what I said to you today,' he began.

As I took his hand, a smile quivered on my lips and the tears were ready to flow; but he took his hand away and sat down on an armchair at some distance, as if fearing a sentimental scene. 'Is it possible that he still thinks himself in the right?' I wondered; and, though I was quite ready to explain and to beg that we might not go to the party, the words died on my lips.

'I must write to my mother that we have put off our departure,' he said; 'otherwise she will be uneasy.'

'When do you think of going?' I asked.

'On Tuesday, after the reception,' he replied.

'I hope it is not on my account,' I said, looking into his eyes; but those eyes merely looked – they said nothing, and a veil seemed to cover them from me. His face seemed to me to have grown suddenly old and disagreeable.

We went to the reception, and good friendly relations between us seemed to have been restored, but these relations were quite different from what they had been.

At the party I was sitting with other ladies when the Prince came up to me, so that I had to stand up in order to speak to him. As I rose, my eyes involuntarily sought my husband. He was looking at me from the other end of the room, and now turned away. I was seized by a sudden sense of shame and pain; in my confusion I blushed all over my face and neck under the Prince's eye. But I was forced to stand and listen, while he spoke, eyeing me from his superior height. Our conversation was soon over: there was no room for him beside me, and he, no doubt, felt that I was uncomfortable with him. We talked of the last ball, of where I should spend the summer, and so on. As he left me, he expressed a wish to make the acquaintance of my husband, and I saw them meet and begin a conversation at the far end of the room. The Prince evidently said something about me; for he smiled in the middle of their talk and looked in my direction.

My husband suddenly flushed up. He made a low bow and turned away from the prince without being dismissed. I blushed too: I was ashamed of the impression which I and, still more, my husband must have made on the Prince. Everyone, I thought, must have noticed my awkward shyness when I was presented, and my husband's eccentric behaviour. 'Heaven knows how they will interpret such conduct? Perhaps they know already about my scene with my husband!'

Princess D. drove me home, and on the way I spoke to her about my husband. My patience was at an end, and I told her the whole story of what had taken place between us owing to this unlucky party. To calm me, she said that such differences were very common and quite unimportant, and that our quarrel would leave no trace behind. She explained to me her view of my husband's character – that he had become very stiff and unsociable. I agreed, and believed that I had learned to judge him myself more calmly and more truly.

But when I was alone with my husband later, the thought that I had sat in judgment upon him weighed like a crime upon my conscience; and I felt that the gulf which divided us had grown still greater.

Chapter 3

From that day there was a complete change in our life and our relations to each other. We were no longer as happy when we were alone together as before. To certain subjects we gave a wide berth, and conversation flowed more easily in the presence of a third person. When the talk turned on life in the country, or on a ball, we were uneasy and shrank from looking at one another. Both of us knew where the gulf between us lay, and seemed afraid to approach it. I was convinced that he was proud and irascible, and that I must be careful not to touch him on his weak point. He was equally sure that I disliked the country and was dying for social distraction, and that he must put up with this unfortunate taste of mine. We both avoided frank conversation on these topics, and each misjudged the other. We had long ceased to think each other the most perfect people in the world; each now judged the other in secret, and measured the offender by the standard of other people. I fell ill before we left Petersburg, and we went from there to a house near town, from which my husband went on alone, to join his mother at Nikolskoye. By that time I was well enough to have gone with him, but he urged me to stay on the pretext of my health. I knew, however, that he was really afraid we should be uncomfortable together in the country; so I did not insist much, and he went off alone. I felt it dull and solitary in his absence; but when he came back, I saw that he did not add to my life what he had added formerly. In the old days every thought and experience weighed on me like a crime till I had imparted it to him; every action and word of his seemed to me a model of perfection; we often laughed for joy at the mere sight of each other. But these relations had changed, so imperceptibly that we had not even noticed their disappearance. Separate interests and cares, which we no longer tried to share, made their appearance, and even the fact of our estrangement ceased to trouble us. The idea became familiar, and, before a year had passed, each could look at the other without confusion. His fits of boyish merriment with me had quite vanished; his mood of calm indulgence to all that passed, which used to provoke me, had disappeared; there was an end of those penetrating looks which used to confuse and delight me, an end of the ecstasies and prayers which we once shared in common. We did not even meet often: he was continually absent, with no fears or regrets for leaving me alone; and I was constantly in society, where I did not need him.

There were no further scenes or quarrels between us. I tried to satisfy him, he carried out all my wishes, and we seemed to love each other.

When we were by ourselves, which we seldom were, I felt neither joy nor excitement nor embarrassment in his company: it seemed like being alone. I realized that he was my husband and no mere stranger, a good man, and as familiar to me as my own self. I was convinced that I knew just what he would say and do, and how he would look; and if anything he did surprised me, I concluded that he had made a mistake. I expected nothing from him. In a word, he was my husband – and that was all. It seemed to me that things must be so, as a matter of course, and that no other relations between us had ever existed. When he left home, especially at first, I was lonely and frightened and felt keenly my need of support; when he came back, I ran to his arms with joy, though two hours later my joy was quite forgotten, and I found nothing to say to him. Only at moments which sometimes occurred between us of quiet undemonstrative affection, I felt something wrong and some pain at my heart, and I seemed to read the same story in his eyes. I was conscious of a limit to tenderness, which he seemingly would not, and I could not, overstep. This saddened me sometimes; but I had no leisure to reflect on any-thing, and my regret for a change which I vaguely realized I tried to drown in the distractions which were always within my reach. Fashionable life, which had dazzled me at first by its glitter and flattery of my self-love, now took entire command of my nature, became a habit, laid its fetters upon me, and monopolized my capacity for feeling. I could not bear solitude, and was afraid to reflect on my position. My whole day, from late in the morning till late at night, was taken up by the claims of society; even if I stayed at home, my time was not my own. This no longer seemed to me either gay or dull, but it seemed that so, and not otherwise, it always had to be.

So three years passed, during which our relations to one another remained unchanged and seemed to have taken a fixed shape which could not become either better or worse. Though two events of importance in our family life took place during that time, neither of them changed my own life. These were the birth of my first child and the death of Tatyana Semyonovna. At first the feeling of motherhood did take hold of me with such power, and produce in me such a passion of unanticipated joy, that I believed this would prove the beginning of a new life for me. But, in the course of two months, when I began to go out again, my feeling grew weaker and weaker, till it passed into mere habit and the lifeless performance of a duty. My husband, on the contrary, from the birth of our first boy, became his old self again – gentle, composed, and home-loving, and transferred to the child his old tenderness and gaiety. Many a night when I went, dressed for a ball, to the nursery, to sign the child with the cross before he slept, I found my husband there and felt his eyes fixed on me with something of reproof in their serious gaze. Then I was ashamed and even shocked by my own callousness, and asked myself if I was worse than other women. 'But it can't be helped,' I said to myself; 'I love my child, but to sit beside him all day long would bore me; and nothing will make me pretend what I do not really feel.'

His mother's death was a great sorrow to my husband; he said that he found it painful to go on living at Nikolskoye. For myself, although I mourned for her and sympathized with my husband's sorrow, yet I found life in that house easier and pleasanter after her death. Most of those three years we spent in town: I went only once to Nikolskoye for two months; and the third year we went abroad and spent the summer at Baden.

I was then twenty-one; our financial position was, I believed, satisfactory; my domestic life gave me all that I asked of it;

everyone I knew, it seemed to me, loved me; my health was good; I was the best-dressed woman in Baden; I knew that I was good looking; the weather was fine; I enjoyed the atmosphere of beauty and refinement; and, in short, I was in excellent spirits. They had once been even higher at Nikolskoye, when my happiness was in myself and came from the feeling that I deserved to be happy, and from the anticipation of still greater happiness to come. That was a different state of things; but I did very well this summer also. I had no special wishes or hopes of fears; it seemed to me that my life was full and my conscience easy. Among all the visitors at Baden that season there was no one man whom I preferred to the rest, or even to our old ambassador, Prince K., who was assiduous in his attentions to me. One was young, and another old; one was English and fair, another French and wore a beard – to me they were all alike, but all indispensable. Indistinguishable as they were, they together made up the atmosphere which I found so pleasant. But there was one, an Italian marquis, who stood out from the rest by reason of the boldness with which he expressed his admiration. He seized every opportunity of being with me – danced with me, rode with me, and met me at the casino; and everywhere he spoke to me of my charms. Several times I saw him from my windows loitering round our hotel, and the fixed gaze of his bright eyes often troubled me, and made me blush and turn away. He was young, handsome, and well-mannered; and above all, by his smile and the expression of his brow, he resembled my husband, though much handsomer than he. He struck me by this likeness, though in general, in his lips, eyes, and long chin, there was something coarse and animal which contrasted with my husband's charming expression of kindness and noble serenity. I supposed him to be passionately in love with me, and thought of him sometimes with proud commiseration. When I tried at times to soothe him and change his tone to one of easy, half-friendly confidence, he rejected the suggestion with vehemence, and continued to disquiet me by a smouldering passion which was ready at any moment to burst forth. Though I would not own it even to myself, I feared him and often thought of him against my will. My husband knew him, and greeted him – even more than other acquaintances of ours who regarded him only as my husband – with coldness and disdain.

Towards the end of the season I fell ill and stayed indoors for a fortnight. The first evening that I went out again to hear the band, I learnt that Lady S., an Englishwoman famous for her beauty, who had long been expected, had arrived in my absence. My return was welcomed, and a group gathered round me; but a more distinguished group attended the beautiful stranger. She and her beauty were the one subject of conversation around me. When I saw her, she was really beautiful, but her self-satisfied expression struck me as disagreeable, and I said so. That day everything that had formerly seemed amusing, seemed dull. Lady S. arranged an expedition to the ruined castle for the next day; but I declined to be of the party. Almost everyone else went; and my opinion of Baden underwent a complete change. Everything and everybody seemed to me stupid and tiresome; I wanted to cry, to break off my cure, to return to Russia. There was some evil feeling in my soul, but I did not yet acknowledge it to myself. Pretending that I was not strong, I ceased to appear at crowded parties; if I went out, it was only in the morning by myself, to drink the waters; and my only companion was Mme M., a Russian lady, with whom I sometimes took drives in the surrounding country. My husband was absent: he had gone to Heidelberg for a time, intending to return to Russia when my cure was over, and only paid me occasional visits at Baden.

One day when Lady S. had carried off all the company on a hunting expedition, Mme M. and I drove in the afternoon to the castle. While our carriage moved slowly along the winding road, bordered by ancient chestnut-trees and commanding a vista of the pretty and pleasant country round Baden, with the setting sun lighting it up, our conversation took a more serious turn than had ever happened to us before. I had known my companion for a long time; but she appeared to me now in a new light, as a well-principled and intelligent woman, to whom it was possible to speak without reserve, and whose friendship was worth having. We spoke of our private concerns, of our children, of the emptiness of life at Baden, till we felt a longing for Russia and the Russian countryside. When we entered the castle we were still under the impression of this serious feeling. Within the walls there was shade and coolness; the sunlight played from above upon the ruins. Steps and voices were audible. The landscape, charming enough but cold to a Russian eye, lay before us in the frame made by a doorway. We sat down to rest and watched the sunset in silence. The voices now sounded louder, and I thought I heard my own name. I listened and could not help overhearing every word. I recognized the voices: the speakers were the Italian marquis and a French friend of his whom I knew also. They were talking of me and of Lady S., and the Frenchman was comparing us as rival beauties. Though he said nothing insulting, his words made my pulse quicken. He explained in detail the good points of us both. I was already a mother, while Lady S. was only nineteen; though I had the advantage in hair, my rival had a better figure. 'Besides,' he added, 'Lady S. is a real *grande dame*, and the other is nothing in particular, only one of those obscure Russian princesses who turn up here nowadays in such numbers.' He ended by saying that I was wise in not attempting to compete with Lady S., and that I was completely buried as far as Baden was concerned.

'I am sorry for her – unless indeed she takes a fancy to console herself with you,' he added with a hard ringing laugh.

'If she goes away, I follow her' – the words were blurted out in an Italian accent.

'Happy man! he is still capable of a passion!' laughed the Frenchman.

'Passion!' said the other voice and then was still for a moment. 'It is a necessity to me: I cannot live without it. To make life a romance is the one thing worth doing. And with me romance never breaks off in the middle, and this affair I shall carry through to the end.'

'*Bonne chance, mon ami!*' said the Frenchman.

They now turned a corner, and the voices stopped. Then we heard them coming down the steps, and a few minutes later they came out upon us by a side door. They were much surprised to see us.

I blushed when the marquis approached me, and felt afraid when we left the castle and he offered me his arm. I could not refuse, and we set off for the carriage, walking behind Mme M. and his friend. I was mortified by what the Frenchman had said of me, though I secretly admitted that he had only put in words what I felt myself; but the plain speaking of the Italian had surprised and upset me by its coarseness. I was tormented by the thought that, though I had overheard him, he showed no fear of me. It was hateful to have him so close to me; and I walked fast after the other couple, not looking at him or answering him and trying to hold his arm in such a way as not to hear him. He spoke of the fine view, of the unexpected pleasure of our meeting, and so on; but I was not listening. My thoughts were with my husband, my child, my country; I felt ashamed, distressed, anxious; I was in a hurry to get back to my solitary room in the Hotel de Bade, there to think at leisure of the storm of feeling that had just risen in my heart. But Mme M. walked slowly, it was still a long way to the carriage, and my escort seemed to loiter on purpose as if he wished to detain me. 'None of that!' I thought, and resolutely quickened my pace. But it soon became unmistakable that he was detaining me and even pressing my arm. Mme M. turned a corner, and we were quite alone. I was afraid.

'Excuse me,' I said coldly and tried to free my arm; but the lace of my sleeve caught on a button of his coat. Bending towards me, he began to unfasten it, and his ungloved fingers touched my arm. A feeling new to me, half horror and half pleasure, sent an icy shiver down my back. I looked at him, intending by my coldness to convey all the contempt I felt for him; but my look expressed nothing but fear and excitement. His liquid blazing eyes, right up against my face, stared strangely at me, at my neck and breast; both his hands fingered my arm above the wrist; his parted lips were saying that he loved me, and that I was all the world to him; and those lips were coming nearer and nearer, and those hands were squeezing mine harder and harder and burning me. A fever ran through my veins, my sight grew dim, I trembled, and the words intended to check him died in my throat. Suddenly I felt a kiss on my cheek. Trembling all over and turning cold, I stood still and stared at him. Unable to speak or move, I stood there, horrified, expectant, even desirous. It was over in a moment, but the moment was horrible! In that short time I saw him exactly as he was – the low straight forehead (that forehead so like my husband's!) under the straw hat; the handsome regular nose and dilated nostrils; the long waxed moustache and short beard; the close-shaved cheeks and sunburned neck. I hated and feared him; he was utterly repugnant and alien to me. And yet the excitement and passion of this hateful strange man raised a powerful echo in my own heart; I felt an irresistible longing to surrender myself to the kisses of that coarse handsome mouth, and to the pressure of those white hands with their delicate veins and jewelled fingers; I was tempted to throw myself headlong into the abyss of forbidden delights that had suddenly opened up before me.

'I am so unhappy already,' I thought; 'let more and more storms of unhappiness burst over my head!'

He put one arm round me and bent towards my face. 'Better so!' I thought: 'let sin and shame cover me ever deeper and deeper!'

'*Je vous aime!*' he whispered in the voice which was so like my husband's. At once I thought of my husband and child, as creatures once precious to me who had now passed altogether out of my life. At that moment I heard Mme M.'s voice; she called to me from round the corner. I came to myself, tore my hand away without looking at him, and almost ran after her: I only looked at him after she and I were already seated in the carriage. Then I saw him raise his hat and ask some commonplace question with a smile. He little knew the inexpressible aversion I felt for him at that moment.

My life seemed so wretched, the future so hopeless, the past so black! When Mme M. spoke, her words meant nothing to me. I thought that she talked only out of pity, and to hide the contempt I aroused in her. In every word and every look I seemed to detect this contempt and insulting pity. The shame of that kiss burned my cheek, and the thought of my husband and child was more than I could bear. When I was alone in my own room, I tried to think over my position; but I was afraid to be alone. Without drinking the tea which was brought me, and uncertain of my own motives, I got ready with feverish haste to catch the evening train and join my husband at Heidelberg.

I found seats for myself and my maid in an empty carriage. When the train started and the fresh air blew through the window on my face, I grew more composed and pictured my past and future to myself more clearly. The course of our married life from the time of our first visit to Petersburg now presented itself to me in a new light, and lay like a reproach on my conscience. For the first time I clearly recalled our start at Nikolskoye and our plans for the future; and for the first time I asked myself what happiness had my husband had since then. I felt that I had behaved badly to him. 'But why', I asked myself, 'did he not stop me? Why did he make pretences? Why did he always avoid explanations? Why did he insult me? Why did he not use the power of his love to influence me? Or did he not love me?' But whether he was to blame or not, I still felt the kiss of that strange man upon my cheek. The nearer we got to Heidelberg, the clearer grew my picture of my husband, and the more I dreaded our meeting. 'I shall tell him all,' I thought, 'and wipe out everything with tears of repentance; and he will forgive me.' But I did not know myself what I meant by 'everything'; and I did not believe in my heart that he would forgive me.

As soon as I entered my husband's room and saw his calm though surprised expression, I felt at once that I had nothing to tell him, no confession to make, and nothing to ask forgiveness for. I had to suppress my unspoken grief and penitence.

'What put this into your head?' he asked. 'I meant to go to Baden tomorrow.' Then he looked more closely at me and seemed to take alarm. 'What's the matter with you? What has happened?' he said.

'Nothing at all,' I replied, almost breaking down. 'I am not going back. Let us go home, tomorrow if you like, to Russia.'

For some time he said nothing but looked at me attentively. Then he said, 'But do tell me what has happened to you.'

I blushed involuntarily and looked down. There came into his eyes a flash of anger and displeasure. Afraid of what he might imagine, I said with a power of pretence that surprised myself: 'Nothing at all has happened. It was merely that I grew weary and sad by myself; and I have been thinking a great deal of our way of life and of you. I have long been to blame towards you. Why do you take me abroad, when you can't bear it yourself? I have long been to blame. Let us go back to Nikolskoye and settle there for ever.'

'Spare us these sentimental scenes, my dear,' he said coldly. 'To go back to Nikolskoye is a good idea, for our money is running short; but the notion of stopping there for ever is fanciful. I know you would not settle down. Have some tea, and you will feel better,' and he rose to ring for the waiter.

I imagined all he might be thinking about me; and I was offended by the horrible thoughts which I ascribed to him when I encountered the dubious and shame-faced look he directed at me. 'He will not and cannot understand me.' I said I would go and look at the child, and I left the room. I wished to be alone, and to cry and cry and cry . . .

Chapter 4

The house at Nikolskoye, so long unheated and uninhabited, came to life again; but much of the past was dead beyond recall. Tatyana Semyonovna was no more, and we were now alone together. But far from desiring such close companionship, we even found it irksome. To me that winter was the more trying because I was in bad health, from which I only recovered after the birth of my second son. My husband and I were still on the same terms as during our life in Petersburg: we were coldly friendly to each other; but in the country each room and wall and sofa recalled what he had once been to me, and what I had lost. It was if some unforgiven grievance held us apart, as if he were punishing me and pretending not to be aware of it. But there was nothing to ask pardon for, no penalty to deprecate; my punishment was merely this, that he did not give his whole heart and mind to me as he used to do; but he did not give it to anyone or to anything; as though he had no longer a heart to give. Sometimes it occurred to me that he was only pretending to be like that, in order to hurt me, and that the old feeling was still alive in his breast; and I tried to call it forth. But I always failed: he always seemed to avoid frankness, evidently suspecting me of insincerity, and dreading the folly of any emotional display. I could read in his face and the tone of his voice, 'What is the good of talking? I know all the facts already, and I know what is on the tip of your tongue, and I know that you will say one thing and do another.' At first I was mortified by his dread of frankness, but I came later to think that it was rather the absence, on his part, of any need of frankness. It would never have occurred to me now, to tell him of a sudden that I loved him, or to ask him to repeat the prayers with me or listen while I played the piano. Our intercourse came to be regulated by a fixed code of good manners. We lived our separate lives: he had his own occupations in which I was not needed, and which I no longer wished to share, while I continued my idle life which no longer vexed or grieved him. The children were still too young to form a bond between us.

But spring came round and brought Katya and Sonya to spend the summer with us in the country. As the house at Nikolskoye was under repair, we went to live at my old home at Pokrovskoye. The old house was unchanged – the veranda, the folding table and the piano in the sunny drawing room, and my old bedroom with its white curtains and the dreams of my girlhood which I seemed to have left behind me there. In that room there were two beds: one had been mine, and in it now my plump little Kokosha lay sprawling, when I went at night to sign him with the cross; the other was a crib, in which the little face of my baby, Vanya, peeped out from his swaddling clothes. Often when I had made the sign over them and remained standing in the middle of the quiet room, suddenly there rose up from all the corners, from the walls and curtains, old forgotten visions of youth. Old voices began to sing the songs of my girlhood. Where were those visions now? Where were those dear old sweet songs? All that I had hardly dared to hope for had come to pass. My vague confused dreams had become a reality, and the reality had become an oppressive, difficult, and joyless life. All remained the same – the garden visible through the window, the grass, the path, the very same bench over there above the dell, the same song of the nightingale by the pond, the same lilacs in full bloom, the same moon shining above the house; and yet, in everything such a terrible inconceivable change! Such coldness in all that might have been near and dear! Just as in old times Katya and I sit quietly alone together in the parlour and talk, and talk of him. But Katya has grown wrinkled and pale; and her eyes no longer shine with joy and hope, but express only sympathy, sorrow, and regret. We do not go into raptures as we used to, we judge him coolly; we do not wonder what we have done to deserve such happiness, or long to proclaim our thoughts to all the world. No! we whisper together like conspirators and ask each other for the hundredth time why all has changed so sadly. Yet he was still the same man, save for the deeper furrow between his eyebrows and the whiter hair on his temples; but his serious attentive look was constantly veiled from me by a cloud. And I am the same woman, but without love or desire for love, with no longing for work and not content with myself. My religious ecstasies, my love for my husband, the fullness of my former life – all these now seem utterly remote and visionary. Once it seemed so plain and right that to live for others was happiness; but now it has become unintelligible. Why live for others, when life had no attraction even for oneself?

I had given up my music altogether since the time of our first visit to Petersburg; but now the old piano and the old music tempted me to begin again.

One day I was not well and stayed indoors alone. My husband had taken Katya and Sonya to see the new buildings at Nikolskoye. Tea was laid; I went downstairs and while waiting for them sat down at the piano. I opened the *Moonlight Sonata* and began to play. There was no one within sight or sound, the windows were open over the garden, and the familiar sounds floated through the room with a solemn sadness. At the end of the first movement I looked round instinctively to the corner where he used once to sit and listen to my playing. He was not there; his chair, long unmoved, was still in its place; through the window I could see a lilac bush against the light of the setting sun; the freshness of evening streamed in through the open windows. I rested my elbows on the piano and covered my face with both hands; and so I sat for a long time, thinking. I recalled with pain the irrevocable past, and timidly imagined the future. But for me there seemed to be no future, no desires at all and no hopes. 'Can life be over for me?' I thought with horror; then I looked up, and, trying to forget and not to think, I began playing the same movement over again. 'Oh, God!' I prayed, 'forgive me if I have sinned, or restore to me all that once blossomed in my heart, or teach me what to do and how to live now.' There was a sound of wheels on the grass and before the steps of the house; then I heard cautious and familiar footsteps pass along the veranda and cease; but my heart no longer replied to the sound. When I stopped playing the footsteps were behind me and a hand was laid on my shoulder.

'How clever of you to think of playing that!' he said.

I said nothing.

'Have you had tea?' he asked.

I shook my head without looking at him – I was unwilling to let him see the signs of emotion on my face.

'They'll be here immediately,' he said; 'the horse gave trouble, and they got out on the high road to walk home.'

'Let us wait for them,' I said, and went out to the veranda, hoping that he would follow; but he asked about the children and went upstairs to see them. Once more his presence and simple kindly voice made me doubt if I had really lost anything. What more could I wish? 'He is kind and gentle, a good husband, a good father; I don't know myself what more I want.' I sat down under the veranda awning on the very bench on which I had sat when we became engaged. The sun had set, it was growing dark, and a little spring rain cloud hung over the house and garden, and only behind the trees the horizon was clear, with the fading glow of twilight, in which one star had just begun to twinkle. The landscape, covered by the shadow of the cloud, seemed waiting for the light spring shower. There was not a breath of wind; not a single leaf or blade of grass stirred; the scent of lilac and bird cherry was so strong in the garden and veranda that it seemed as if all the air was in flower; it came in wafts, now stronger and now weaker, till one longed to shut both eyes and ears and drink in that fragrance only. The dahlias and rose bushes, not yet in flower, stood motionless on the black mould of the border, looking as if they were growing slowly upwards on their white-shaved props; beyond the dell, the frogs were making the most of their time before the rain drove them to the pond, croaking busily and loudly. Only the high continuous note of water falling at some distance rose above their croaking. From time to time the nightingales called to one another, and I could hear them flitting restlessly from bush to bush. Again this spring a nightingale had tried to build in a bush under the window, and I heard her fly off across the avenue when I went into the veranda. From there she whistled once and then stopped; she, too, was expecting the rain.

I tried in vain to calm my feelings: I had a sense of anticipation and regret.

He came downstairs again and sat down beside me.

'I am afraid they will get wet,' he said.

'Yes,' I answered; and we sat for long without speaking.

The cloud came down lower and lower with no wind. The air grew stiller and more fragrant. Suddenly a drop fell on the canvas awning and seemed to rebound from it; then another broke on the gravel path; soon there was a splash on the burdock leaves, and a fresh shower of big drops came down faster and faster. Nightingales and frogs were both dumb; only the high note of the falling water, though the rain made it seem more distant, still went on; and a bird, which must have sheltered among the dry leaves near the veranda, steadily repeated its two unvarying notes. My husband got up to go in.

'Where are you going?' I asked, trying to keep him; 'it is so pleasant here.'

'We must send them an umbrella and galoshes,' he replied.

'Don't trouble – it will soon be over.'

He thought I was right, and we remained together in the veranda. I rested one hand upon the wet slippery rail and put my head out. The fresh rain wetted my hair and neck in places. The cloud, growing lighter and thinner, was passing overhead; the steady patter of the rain gave place to occasional drops that fell from the sky or dripped from the trees. The frogs began to croak again in the dell; the nightingales woke up and began to call from the dripping bushes from one side and then from another. The whole prospect before us grew clear.

'How delightful!' he said, seating himself on the veranda rail and passing a hand over my wet hair.

This simple caress had on me the effect of a reproach: I felt inclined to cry.

'What more can a man need?' he said; 'I am so content now that I want nothing; I am perfectly happy!'

He told me a different story once, I thought. He had said that, however great his happiness might be, he always wanted more and more. Now he is calm and contented; while my heart is full of unspoken repentance and unshed tears.

'I think it delightful too,' I said; 'but I am sad just because of the beauty of it all. All is so fair and lovely outside me, while my own heart is confused and baffled and full of vague unsatisfied longing. Is it possible that there is no element of pain, no yearning for the past, in your enjoyment of nature?'

He took his hand off my head and was silent for a little.

'I used to feel that too,' he said, as though recalling it, 'especially in spring. I used to sit up all night too, with my hopes and fears for company, and good company they were! But life was all before me then. Now it is all behind me, and I am content with what I have. I find life capital,' he added with such careless confidence, that I believed, whatever pain it gave me to hear it, that it was the truth.

'But is there nothing you wish for?' I asked.

'I don't ask for impossibilities,' he said, guessing my thoughts. 'You go and get your head wet,' he added, stroking my head like a child's and again passing his hand over the wet hair; 'you envy the leaves and the grass their wetting from the rain, and you would like yourself to be the grass and the leaves and the rain. But I am contented to enjoy them and everything else that is good and young and happy.'

'And do you regret nothing of the past?' I asked, while my heart grew heavier and heavier.

Again he thought for a time before replying. I saw that he wished to reply with perfect frankness.

'Nothing,' he said shortly.

'Not true! not true!' I said, turning towards him and looking into his eyes. 'Do you really not regret the past?'

'No!' he repeated; 'I am grateful for it, but I don't regret it.'

'But would you not like to have it back?' I asked.

'No; I might as well wish to have wings. It is impossible.'

'And would you not alter the past? Do you not reproach yourself or me?'

'No, never! It was all for the best.'

'Listen to me!' I said touching his arm to make him look round. 'Why did you never tell me that you wished me to live as you really wished me to? Why did you give me a freedom for which I was unfit? Why did you stop teaching me? If you had wished it, if you had guided me differently, none of all this would have happened!' said I in a voice that increasingly expressed cold displeasure and reproach in place of the love of former days.

'What would not have happened?' he asked, turning to me in surprise. 'As it is, there is nothing wrong. Things are all right, quite all right,' he added with a smile.

'Does he really not understand?' I thought; 'or still worse, does he not wish to understand?'

Then I suddenly broke out. 'Had you acted differently, I should not now be punished, for no fault at all, by your indifference and even contempt, and you would not have taken from me unjustly all that I valued in life!'

'What do you mean, my dear one?' he asked – he seemed not to understand me.

'No! don't interrupt me! You have taken from me your confidence, your love, even your respect; for I cannot believe, when I think of the past, that you still love me. No! don't speak! I must once for all say out what has long been torturing me. Is it my fault that I knew nothing of life, and that you left me to learn experience for myself? Is it my fault that now, when I have gained the knowledge and have been struggling for nearly a year to come back to you, you push me away and pretend not to understand what I want? And you always do it so that it is impossible to reproach you, while I am guilty and unhappy. Yes, you wish to drive me out again to that life which might rob us both of happiness.'

'How did I show that!' he asked in evident alarm and surprise.

'No later than yesterday you said, and you constantly say, that I can never settle down here, and that we must spend this winter too at Petersburg; and I hate Petersburg!' I went on, 'Instead of supporting me, you avoid all plain speaking, you never say a single frank affectionate word to me. And then, when I fall utterly, you will reproach me and rejoice in my fall.'

'Stop!' he said with cold severity. 'You have no right to say that. It only proves that you are ill-disposed towards me, that you don't . . .'

'That I don't love you? Don't hesitate to say it!' I cried, and the tears began to flow. I sat down on the bench and covered my face with my handkerchief.

'So that is how he understood me!' I thought, trying to restrain the sobs which choked me. 'Gone, gone is our former love!' said a voice at my heart. He did not come close or try to comfort me. He was hurt by what I had said. When he spoke, his tone was cool and dry.

'I don't know what you reproach me with,' he began. 'If you mean that I don't love you as I once did . . .'

'Did love!' I said, with my face buried in the handkerchief, while the bitter tears fell still more abundantly.

'If so, time is to blame for that, and we ourselves. Each time of life has its own kind of love.' He was silent for a moment. 'Shall I tell you the whole truth, if you really wish for frankness? In that summer when I first knew you, I used to lie awake all night, thinking about you, and I made that love myself, and it grew and grew in my heart. So again, in Petersburg and abroad, in the course of horrible sleepless nights, I strove to shatter and destroy that love, which had come to torture me. I did not destroy it, but I destroyed that part of it which gave me pain. Then I grew calm; and I feel love still, but it is a different kind of love.'

'You call it love, but I call it torture!' I said. 'Why did you allow me to go into society, if you thought so badly of it that you ceased to love me on that account?'

'No, it was not society, my dear,' he said.

'Why did you not exercise your authority?' I went on: 'why did you not lock me up or kill me? That would have been better than the loss of all that formed my happiness. I should have been happy, instead of being ashamed.'

I began to sob again and hid my face.

Just then Katya and Sonya, wet and cheerful, came out to the veranda, laughing and talking loudly. They were silent as soon as they saw us, and went in again immediately.

We remained silent for a long time. I had had my cry out and felt relieved. I glanced at him. He was sitting with his head resting on his hand; he intended to make some reply to my glance, but only sighed deeply and resumed his former position.

I went up to him and removed his hand. His eyes turned thoughtfully to my face.

'Yes,' he began, as if continuing his thoughts aloud, 'all of us, and especially you women, must have personal experience of all the nonsense of life, in order to get back to life itself; the evidence of other people is no good. At that time you had not got near the end of that charming nonsense which I admired in you. So I let you go through it alone, feeling that I had no right to put pressure on you, though my own time for that sort of thing was long past.'

'If you loved me,' I said, 'how could you stand beside me and suffer me to go through it?'

'Because it was impossible for you to take my word for it, though you would have tried to. Personal experience was necessary, and now you have had it.'

'There was much calculation in all that,' I said, 'but little love.'

And again we were silent.

'What you said just now is severe, but it is true,' he began, rising suddenly and beginning to walk about the veranda. 'Yes, it is true. I was to blame,' he added, stopping opposite me; 'I ought either to have kept myself from loving you at all, or to have loved you in a simpler way.'

'Let us forget it all,' I said timidly.

'No,' he said; 'the past can never come back, never;' and his voice softened as he spoke.

'It is restored already,' I said, laying a hand on his shoulder.

He took my hand away and pressed it.

'I was wrong when I said that I did not regret the past. I do regret it; I weep for that past love which can never return. Who is to blame, I do not know. Love remains, but not the old love; its place remains, but it all wasted away and has lost all strength and substance; recollections are still left, and gratitude; but . . .'

'Do not say that!' I broke in. 'Let all be as it was before! Surely that is possible?' I asked, looking into his eyes; but their gaze was clear and calm, and did not look deeply into mine.

Even while I spoke, I knew that my wishes and my petition were impossible. He smiled calmly and gently; and I thought it the smile of an old man.

'How young you are still!' he said, 'and I am so old. What you seek in me is no longer there. Why deceive ourselves?' he added, still smiling.

I stood silent opposite to him, and my heart grew calmer.

'Don't let us try to repeat life,' he went on. 'Don't let us make pretences to ourselves. Let us be thankful that there is an end of the old emotions and excitements. The excitement of searching is over for us; our quest is done, and happiness enough has fallen to our lot. Now we must stand aside and make room – for him, if you like,' he said, pointing to the nurse who was carrying Vanya out and had stopped at the veranda door. 'that's the truth, my dear one,' he said, drawing down my head and kissing it, not a lover any longer but an old friend.

The fragrant freshness of the night rose ever stronger and sweeter from the garden; the sounds and the silence grew more solemn; star after star began to twinkle overhead. I looked at him, and suddenly my heart grew light; it seemed that the cause of my suffering had been removed like an aching nerve. Suddenly I realized clearly and calmly that the past feeling, like the past time itself, was gone beyond recall, and that it would be not only impossible but painful and uncomfortable to bring it back. And after all, was that time so good which seemed to me so happy? and it was all so long, long ago!

'Time for tea!' he said, and we went together to the parlour. At the door we met the nurse with the baby. I took him in my arms, covered his bare little red legs, pressed him to me, and kissed him with the lightest touch of my lips. Half asleep, he moved the parted fingers of one creased little hand and opened dim little eyes, as if he was looking for something or recalling something. All at once his eyes rested on me, a spark of consciousness shone in them, the little pouting lips, parted before, now met and opened in a smile. 'Mine, mine, mine!' I thought, pressing him to my breast with such an impulse of joy in every limb that I found it hard to restrain myself from hurting him. I fell to kissing the cold little feet, his stomach and hand and head with its thin covering of down. My husband came up to me, and I quickly covered the child's face and uncovered it again.

'Ivan Sergeich!' said my husband, tickling him under the chin. But I made haste to cover Ivan Sergeich up again. None but I had any business to look long at him. I glanced at my husband. His eyes smiled as he looked at me; and I looked into them with an ease and happiness which I had not felt for a long time.

That day ended the romance of our marriage; the old feeling became a precious irrecoverable remembrance; but a new feeling of love for my children and the father of my children laid the foundation of a new life and a quite different happiness; and that life and happiness have lasted to the present time.

THE COSSACKS

A Tale of 1852

Chapter 1

All is quiet in Moscow. The squeak of wheels is seldom heard in the snow-covered street. There are no lights left in the windows and the street lamps have been extinguished. Only the sound of bells, borne over the city from the church towers, suggests the approach of morning. The streets are deserted. At rare intervals a night-cabman's sledge kneads up the snow and sand in the street as the driver makes his way to another corner where he falls asleep while waiting for a fare. An old woman passes by on her way to church, where a few wax candles burn with a red light reflected on the gilt mountings of the icons. Workmen are already getting up after the long winter night and going to their work – but for the gentlefolk it is still evening.

From a window in Chevalier's Restaurant a light – illegal at that hour – is still to be seen through a chink in the shutter. At the entrance a carriage, a sledge, and a cabman's sledge, stand close together with their backs to the kerbstone. A three-horse sledge from the post-station is there also. A yard-porter muffled up and pinched with cold is sheltering behind the corner of the house.

'And what's the good of all this jawing?' thinks the footman who sits in the hall weary and haggard. 'This always happens when I'm on duty.' From the adjoining room are heard the voices of three young men, sitting there at a table on which are wine and the remains of supper. One, a rather plain, thin, neat little man, sits looking with tired kindly eyes at his friend, who is about to start on a journey. Another, a tall man, lies on a sofa beside a table on which are empty bottles, and plays with his watch-key. A third, wearing a short, fur-lined coat, is pacing up and down the room stopping now and then to crack an almond between his strong, rather thick, but well-tended fingers. He keeps smiling at something and his face and eyes are all aglow. He speaks warmly and gesticulates, but evidently does not find the words he wants and those that occur to him seem to him inadequate to express what has risen to his heart.

'Now I can speak out fully,' said the traveller. 'I don't want to defend myself, but I should like you at least to understand me as I understand myself, and not look at the matter superficially. You say I have treated her badly,' he continued, addressing the man with the kindly eyes who was watching him.

'Yes, you are to blame,' said the latter, and his look seemed to express still more kindliness and weariness.

'I know why you say that,' rejoined the one who was leaving. 'To be loved is in your opinion as great a happiness as to love, and if a man obtains it, it is enough for his whole life.'

'Yes, quite enough, my dear fellow, more than enough!' confirmed the plain little man, opening and shutting his eyes.

'But why shouldn't the man love too?' said the traveller thoughtfully, looking at his friend with something like pity. 'Why shouldn't one love? Because love doesn't come . . . No, to be beloved is a misfortune. It is a misfortune to feel guilty because you do not give something you cannot give. O my God!' he added, with a gesture of his arm. 'If it all happened reasonably, and not all topsy-turvy – not in our way but in a way of its own! Why, it's as if I had stolen that love! You think so too, don't deny it. You must think so. But will you believe it, of all the horrid and stupid things I have found time to do in my life – and there are many – this is one I do not and cannot repent of. Neither at the beginning nor afterwards did I lie to myself or to her. It seemed to me that I had at last fallen in love, but then I saw that it was an involuntary falsehood, and that that was not the way to love, and I could not go on, but she did. Am I to blame that I couldn't? What was I to do?'

'Well, it's ended now!' said his friend, lighting a cigar to master his sleepiness. 'The fact is that you have not yet loved and do not know what love is.'

The man in the fur-lined coat was going to speak again, and put his hands to his head, but could not express what he wanted to say.

'Never loved! . . . Yes, quite true, I never have! But after all, I have within me a desire to love, and nothing could be stronger than that desire! But then, again, does such love exist? There always remains something incomplete. Ah well! What's the use of talking? I've made an awful mess of life! But anyhow it's all over now; you are quite right. And I feel that I am beginning a new life.'

'Which you will again make a mess of,' said the man who lay on the sofa playing with his watch-key. But the traveller did not listen to him.

'I am sad and yet glad to go,' he continued. 'Why I am sad I don't know.'

And the traveller went on talking about himself, without noticing that this did not interest the others as much as it did him. A man is never such an egotist as at moments of spiritual ecstasy. At such times it seems to him that there is nothing on earth more splendid and interesting than himself.

'Dmitri Andreich! The coachman won't wait any longer!' said a young serf, entering the room in a sheepskin coat, with a scarf tied round his head. 'The horses have been standing since twelve, and it's now four o'clock!'

Dmitri Andreich looked at his serf, Vanyusha. The scarf round Vanyusha's head, his felt boots and sleepy face, seemed to be calling his master to a new life of labour, hardship, and activity.

'True enough! Goodbye!' said he, feeling for the unfastened hook and eye on his coat.

In spite of advice to mollify the coachman by another tip, he put on his cap and stood in the middle of the room. The friends kissed once, then again, and after a pause, a third time. The man in the fur-lined coat approached the table and emptied a champagne glass, then took the plain little man's hand and blushed.

'Ah well, I will speak out all the same . . . I must and will be frank with you because I am fond of you . . . Of course you love her – I always thought so – don't you?'

'Yes,' answered his friend, smiling still more gently.

'And perhaps . . . '

'Please sir, I have orders to put out the candles,' said the sleepy attendant, who had been listening to the last part of the conversation and wondering why gentlefolk always talk about one and the same thing. 'To whom shall I make out the bill? To you, sir?' he added, knowing whom to address and turning to the tall man.

'To me,' replied the tall man. 'How much?'

'Twenty-six rubles.'

The tall man considered for a moment, but said nothing and put the bill in his pocket.

The other two continued their talk.

'Goodbye, you are a capital fellow!' said the short plain man with the mild eyes. Tears filled the eyes of both. They stepped into the porch.

'Oh, by the by,' said the traveller, turning with a blush to the tall man, 'will you settle Chevalier's bill and write and let me know?'

'All right, all right!' said the tall man, pulling on his gloves. 'How I envy you!' he added quite unexpectedly when they were out in the porch.

The traveller got into his sledge, wrapped his coat about him, and said: 'Well then, come along!' He even moved a little to make room in the sledge for the man who said he envied him – his voice trembled.

'Goodbye, Mitya! I hope that with God's help you . . . ' said the tall one. But his wish was that the other would go away quickly, and so he could not finish the sentence.

They were silent a moment. Then someone again said, 'Goodbye,' and a voice cried, 'Ready,' and the coachman touched up the horses.

'Hy, Elisar!' one of the friends called out, and the other coachman and the sledge-drivers began moving, clicking their tongues and pulling at the reins. Then the stiffened carriage-wheels rolled squeaking over the frozen snow.

'A fine fellow, that Olenin!' said one of the friends. 'But what an idea to go to the Caucasus – as a cadet, too! I wouldn't do it for anything . . . Are you dining at the club tomorrow?'

'Yes.'

They separated.

The traveller felt warm, his fur coat seemed too hot. He sat on the bottom of the sledge and unfastened his coat, and the three shaggy post-horses dragged themselves out of one dark street into another, past houses he had never before seen. It seemed to Olenin that only travellers starting on a long journey went through those streets. All was dark and silent and dull around him, but his soul was full of memories, love, regrets, and a pleasant tearful feeling.

Chapter 2

'I'm fond of them, very fond! . . . First-rate fellows! . . . Fine!' he kept repeating, and felt ready to cry. But why he wanted to cry, who were the first-rate fellows he was so fond of – was more than he quite knew. Now and then he looked round at some house and wondered why it was so curiously built; sometimes he began wondering why the post-boy and Vanyusha, who were so different from himself, sat so near, and together with him were being jerked about and swayed by the tugs the side-horses gave at the frozen traces, and again he repeated: 'First rate . . . very fond!' and once he even said: 'And how it seizes one . . . excellent!' and wondered what made him say it. 'Dear me, am I drunk?' he asked himself. He had had a couple of bottles of wine, but it was not the wine alone that was having this effect on Olenin. He remembered all the words of friendship heartily, bashfully, spontaneously (as he believed) addressed to him on his departure. He remembered the clasp of hands, glances, the moments of silence, and the sound of a voice saying, 'Goodbye, Mitya!' when he was already in the sledge. He remembered his own deliberate frankness. And all this had a touching significance for him. Not only friends and relatives, not only people who had been indifferent to him, but even those who did not like him, seemed to have agreed to become fonder of him, or to forgive him, before his departure, as people do before confession or death. 'Perhaps I shall not return from the Caucasus,' he thought. And he felt that he loved his friends and someone besides. He was sorry for himself. But it was not love for his friends that so stirred and uplifted his heart that he could not repress the meaningless words that seemed to rise of themselves to his lips; nor was it love for a woman (he had never yet been in love) that had brought on this mood. Love for himself, love full of hope – warm young love for all that was good in his own soul (and at that moment it seemed to him that there was nothing but good in it) – compelled him to weep and to mutter incoherent words.

Olenin was a youth who had never completed his university course, never served anywhere (having only a nominal post in some government office or other), who had squandered half his fortune and had reached the age of twenty-four without having done anything or even chosen a career. He was what in Moscow society is termed *un jeune homme*.

At the age of eighteen he was free – as only rich young Russians in the 'forties who had lost their parents at an early age could be. Neither physical nor moral fetters of any kind existed for him; he could do as he liked, lacking nothing and bound by nothing. Neither relatives, nor fatherland, nor religion, nor wants, existed for him. He believed in nothing and admitted nothing. But although he believed in nothing he was not a morose or blasé young man, nor self-opinionated, but on the contrary continually let himself be carried away. He had come to the conclusion that there is no such thing as love, yet his heart always overflowed in the presence of any young and attractive woman. He had long been aware that honours and position were nonsense, yet involuntarily he felt pleased when at a ball Prince Sergius came up and spoke to him affably. But he yielded to his impulses only in so far as they did not limit his freedom. As soon as he had yielded to any influence and became conscious of its leading on to labour and struggle, he instinctively hastened to free himself from the feeling or activity into which he was being drawn and to regain his freedom. In this way he experimented with society-life, the civil service, farming, music – to which at one time he intended to devote his life – and even with the love of women in which he did not believe. He meditated on the use to which he should devote that power of youth which is granted to man only once in a lifetime: that force which gives a man the power of making himself, or even – as it seemed to him – of making the universe, into anything he wishes: should it be to art, to science, to love of woman, or to practical activities? It is true that some people are devoid of this impulse, and on entering life at once place their necks under the first yoke that offers itself and honestly labour under it for the rest of their lives. But Olenin was too strongly conscious of the presence of that all-powerful God of Youth – of that capacity to be entirely transformed into an aspiration or idea – the capacity to wish and to do – to throw oneself headlong into a bottomless abyss without knowing why or wherefore. He bore this consciousness within himself, was proud of it and, without knowing it, was happy in that consciousness. Up to that time he had loved only himself, and could not help loving himself, for he expected nothing but good of himself and had not yet had time to be disillusioned. On leaving Moscow he was in that happy state of mind in which a young man, conscious of past mistakes, suddenly says to himself, 'That was not the real thing.' All that had gone before was accidental and unimportant. Till then he had not really tried to live, but now with his departure from Moscow a new life was beginning – a life in which there would be no mistakes, no remorse, and certainly nothing but happiness.

It is always the case on a long journey that till the first two or three stages have been passed imagination continues to dwell on the place left behind, but with the first morning on the road it leaps to the end of the journey and there begins building castles in the air. So it happened to Olenin.

After leaving the town behind, he gazed at the snowy fields and felt glad to be alone in their midst. Wrapping himself in his fur coat, he lay at the bottom of the sledge, became tranquil, and fell into a doze. The parting with his friends had touched him deeply, and memories of that last winter spent in Moscow and images of the past, mingled with vague thoughts and regrets, rose unbidden in his imagination.

He remembered the friend who had seen him off and his relations with the girl they had talked about. The girl was rich. 'How could he love her knowing that she loved me?' thought he, and evil suspicions crossed his mind. 'There is much dishonesty in men when one comes to reflect.' Then he was confronted by the question: 'But really, how is it I have never been in love? Everyone tells me that I never have. Can it be that I am a moral monstrosity?' And he began to recall all his infatuations. He recalled his entry into society, and a friend's sister with whom he spent several evenings at a table with a lamp on it which lit up her slender fingers busy with needlework, and the lower part of her pretty delicate face. He recalled their conversations that dragged on like the game in which one passes on a stick which one keeps alight as long as possible, and the general awkwardness and restraint and his continual feeling of rebellion at all that conventionality. Some voice had always whispered: 'That's not it, that's not it,' and so it had proved. Then he remembered a ball and the mazurka he danced with the beautiful D— — . 'How much in love I was that night and how happy! And how hurt and vexed I was next morning when I woke and felt myself still free! Why does not love come and bind me hand and foot?' thought he. 'No, there is no such thing as love! That neighbour who used to tell me, as she told Dubrovin and the Marshal, that she loved the stars, was not *it* either.' And now his farming and work in the country recurred to his mind, and in those recollections also there was nothing to dwell on with pleasure. 'Will they talk long of my departure?' came into his head; but who 'they' were he did not quite know. Next came a thought that made him wince and mutter incoherently. It was the recollection of M. Cappele the tailor, and the six hundred and seventy-eight rubles he still owed him, and he recalled the words in which he had begged him to wait another year, and the look of perplexity and resignation which had appeared on the tailor's face. 'Oh, my God, my God!' he repeated, wincing and trying to drive away the intolerable thought. 'All the same and in spite of everything she loved me,' thought he of the girl they had talked about at the farewell supper. 'Yes, had I married her I should not now be owing anything, and as it is I am in debt to Vasilyev.' Then he remembered the last night he had played with Vasilyev at the club (just after leaving her), and he recalled his humiliating requests for another game and the other's cold refusal. 'A year's economizing and they will all be paid, and the devil take them!' . . . But despite this assurance he again began calculating his outstanding debts, their dates, and when he could hope to pay them off. 'And I owe something to Morell as well as to Chevalier,' thought he, recalling the night when he had run up so large a debt. It was at a carousel at the gipsies arranged by some fellows from Petersburg: Sashka B—, an aide-de-camp to the Tsar, Prince D—, and that pompous old — —. 'How is it those gentlemen are so self-satisfied?' thought he, 'and by what right do they form a clique to which they think others must be highly flattered to be admitted? Can it be because they are on the Emperor's staff? Why, it's awful what fools and scoundrels they consider other people to be! But I showed them that I at any rate, on the contrary, do not at all want their intimacy. All the same, I fancy Andrew, the steward, would be amazed to know that I am on familiar terms with a man like Sashka B—, a colonel and an aide-de-camp to the Tsar! Yes, and no one drank more than I did that evening, and I taught the gipsies a new song and everyone listened to it. Though I have done many foolish things, all the same I am a very good fellow,' thought he.

Morning found him at the third post-stage. He drank tea, and himself helped Vanyusha to move his bundles and trunks and sat down among them, sensible, erect, and precise, knowing where all his belongings were, how much money he had and where it was, where he had put his passport and the post-horse requisition and toll-gate papers, and it all seemed to him so well arranged that he grew quite cheerful and the long journey before him seemed an extended pleasure-trip.

All that morning and noon he was deep in calculations of how many versts he had travelled, how many remained to the next stage, how many to the next town, to the place where he would dine, to the place where he would drink tea, and to Stavropol, and what fraction of the whole journey was already accomplished. He also calculated how much money he had with him, how much would be left over, how much would pay off all his debts, and what proportion of his income he would spend each month. Towards evening, after tea, he calculated that to Stavropol there still remained seven-elevenths of the whole journey, that his debts would require seven months' economy and one-eighth of his whole fortune; and then, tranquillized, he wrapped himself up, lay down in the sledge, and again dozed off. His imagination was now turned to the future: to the Caucasus. All his dreams of the future were mingled with pictures of Amalat-Beks, Circassian women, mountains, precipices, terrible torrents, and perils. All these things were vague and dim, but the love of fame and the danger of death furnished the interest of that future. Now, with unprecedented courage and a strength that amazed everyone, he slew and subdued an innumerable host of hillsmen; now he was himself a hillsman and with them was maintaining their independence against the Russians. As soon as he pictured anything definite, familiar Moscow figures always appeared on the scene. Sashka B— fights with the Russians or the hillsmen against him. Even the tailor Cappele in some strange way takes part in the conqueror's triumph. Amid all this he remembered his former humiliations, weaknesses, and mistakes, and the recollection was not disagreeable. It was clear that there among the mountains, waterfalls, fair Circassians, and dangers, such mistakes could not recur. Having once made full confession to himself there was an end of it all. One other vision, the sweetest of them all, mingled with the young man's every thought of the future – the vision of a woman.

And there, among the mountains, she appeared to his imagination as a Circassian slave, a fine figure with a long plait of hair and deep submissive eyes. He pictured a lonely hut in the mountains, and on the threshold she stands awaiting him when, tired and covered with dust, blood, and fame, he returns to her. He is conscious of her kisses, her shoulders, her sweet voice, and her submissiveness. She is enchanting, but uneducated, wild, and rough. In the long winter evenings he begins her education. She is clever and gifted and quickly acquires all the knowledge essential. Why not? She can quite easily learn foreign languages, read the French masterpieces and understand them: *Nôtre Dame de Paris*, for instance, is sure to please her. She can also speak French. In a drawing-room she can show more innate dignity than a lady of the highest society. She can sing, simply, powerfully, and passionately . . . 'Oh, what nonsense!' said he to himself. But here they reached a post-station and he had to change into another sledge and give some tips. But his fancy again began searching for the 'nonsense' he had relinquished, and again fair Circassians, glory, and his return to Russia with an appointment as aide-de-camp and a lovely wife rose before his imagination. 'But there's no such thing as love,' said he to himself. 'Fame is all rubbish. But the six hundred and seventy-eight rubles? . . . And the conquered land that will bring me more wealth than I need for a lifetime? It will not be right though to keep all that wealth for myself. I shall have to distribute it. But to whom? Well, six hundred and seventy-eight rubles to Cappele and then we'll see.' . . . Quite vague visions now cloud his mind, and only Vanyusha's voice and the interrupted motion of the sledge break his healthy youthful slumber. Scarcely conscious, he changes into another sledge at the next stage and continues his journey.

Next morning everything goes on just the same: the same kind of post-stations and tea-drinking, the same moving horses' cruppers, the same short talks with Vanyusha, the same vague dreams and drowsiness, and the same tired, healthy, youthful sleep at night.

Chapter 3

The farther Olenin travelled from Central Russia the farther he left his memories behind, and the nearer he drew to the Caucasus the lighter his heart became. 'I'll stay away for good and never return to show myself in society,' was a thought that sometimes occurred to him. 'These people whom I see here are *not* people. None of them know me and none of them can ever enter the Moscow society I was in or find out about my past. And no one in that society will ever know what I am doing, living among these people.' And quite a new feeling of freedom from his whole past came over him among the rough beings he met on the road whom he did not consider to be *people* in the sense that his Moscow acquaintances were. The rougher the people and the fewer the signs of civilization the freer he felt. Stavropol, through which he had to pass, irked him. The signboards, some of them even in French, ladies in carriages, cabs in the marketplace, and a gentleman wearing a fur cloak and tall hat who was walking along the boulevard and staring at the passers by, quite upset him. 'Perhaps these people know some of my acquaintances,' he thought; and the club, his tailor, cards, society . . . came back to his mind. But after Stavropol everything was satisfactory – wild and also beautiful and warlike, and Olenin felt happier and happier. All the Cossacks, post-boys, and post-station masters seemed to him simple folk with whom he could jest and converse simply, without having to consider to what class they belonged. They all belonged to the human race which, without his thinking about it, all appeared dear to Olenin, and they all treated him in a friendly way.

Already in the province of the Don Cossacks his sledge had been exchanged for a cart, and beyond Stavropol it became so warm that Olenin travelled without wearing his fur coat. It was already spring – an unexpected joyous spring for Olenin. At night he was no longer allowed to leave the Cossack villages, and they said it was dangerous to travel in the evening. Vanyusha began to be uneasy, and they carried a loaded gun in the cart. Olenin became still happier. At one of the post-stations the post-master told of a terrible murder that had been committed recently on the high road. They began to meet armed men. 'So this is where it begins!' thought Olenin, and kept expecting to see the snowy mountains of which mention was so often made. Once, towards evening, the Nogay driver pointed with his whip to the mountains shrouded in clouds. Olenin looked eagerly, but it was dull and the mountains were almost hidden by the clouds. Olenin made out something grey and white and fleecy, but try as he would he could find nothing beautiful in the mountains of which he had so often read and heard. The mountains and the clouds appeared to him quite alike, and he thought the special beauty of the snow peaks, of which he had so often been told, was as much an invention as Bach's music and the love of women, in which he did not believe. So he gave up looking forward to seeing the mountains. But early next morning, being awakened in his cart by the freshness of the air, he glanced carelessly to the right. The morning was perfectly clear. Suddenly he saw, about twenty paces away as it seemed to him at first glance, pure white gigantic masses with delicate contours, the distinct fantastic outlines of their summits showing sharply against the far-off sky. When he had realized the distance between himself and them and the sky and the whole immensity of the mountains, and felt the infinitude of all that beauty, he became afraid that it was but a phantasm or a dream. He gave himself a shake to rouse himself, but the mountains were still the same.

'What's that! What is it?' he said to the driver.

'Why, the mountains,' answered the Nogay driver with indifference.

'And I too have been looking at them for a long while,' said Vanyusha. "Aren't they fine? They won't believe it at home."

The quick progress of the three-horsed cart along the smooth road caused the mountains to appear to be running along the horizon, while their rosy crests glittered in the light of the rising sun. At first Olenin was only astonished at the sight, then gladdened by it; but later on, gazing more and more intently at that snow-peaked chain that seemed to rise not from among other black mountains, but straight out of the plain, and to glide away into the distance, he began by slow degrees to be penetrated by their beauty and at length to *feel* the mountains. From that moment all he saw, all he thought, and all he felt, acquired for him a new character, sternly majestic like the mountains! All his Moscow reminiscences, shame, and repentance, and his trivial dreams about the Caucasus, vanished and did not return. 'Now it has begun,' a solemn voice seemed to say to him. The road and the Terek, just becoming visible in the distance, and the Cossack villages and the people, all no longer appeared to him as a joke. He looked at himself or Vanyusha, and again thought of the mountains . . . Two Cossacks ride by, their guns in their cases swinging rhythmically behind their backs, the white and bay legs of their horses mingling confusedly . . . and the mountains! Beyond the Terek rises the smoke from a Tartar village . . . and the mountains! The sun has risen and glitters on the Terek, now visible beyond the reeds . . . and the mountains! From the village comes a Tartar wagon, and women, beautiful young women, pass by . . . and the mountains! '*Abreks* canter about the plain, and here am I driving along and do not fear them! I have a gun, and strength, and youth . . . and the mountains!'

Chapter 4

That whole part of the Terek line (about fifty miles) along which lie the villages of the Grebensk Cossacks is uniform in character both as to country and inhabitants. The Terek, which separates the Cossacks from the mountaineers, still flows turbid and rapid though already broad and smooth, always depositing greyish sand on its low reedy right bank and washing away the steep, though not high, left bank, with its roots of century-old oaks, its rotting plane trees, and young brushwood. On the right bank lie the villages of pro-Russian, though still somewhat restless, Tartars. Along the left bank, back half a mile from the river and standing five or six miles apart from one another, are Cossack villages. In olden times most of these villages were situated on the banks of the river; but the Terek, shifting northward from the mountains year by year, washed away those banks, and now there remain only the ruins of the old villages and of the gardens of pear and plum trees and poplars, all overgrown with blackberry bushes and wild vines. No one lives there now, and one only sees the tracks of the deer, the wolves, the hares, and the pheasants, who have learned to love these places. From village to village runs a road cut through the forest as a cannon-shot might fly. Along the roads are cordons of Cossacks and watch-towers with sentinels in them. Only a narrow strip about seven hundred yards wide of fertile wooded soil belongs to the Cossacks. To the north of it begin the sand-drifts of the Nogay or Mozdok steppes, which fetch far to the north and run, Heaven knows where, into the Trukhmen, Astrakhan, and Kirghiz-Kaisatsk steppes. To the south, beyond the Terek, are the Great Chechnya river, the Kochkalov range, the Black Mountains, yet another range, and at last the snowy mountains, which can just be seen but have never yet been scaled. In this fertile wooded strip, rich in vegetation, has dwelt as far back as memory runs the fine warlike and prosperous Russian tribe belonging to the sect of Old Believers, and called the Grebensk Cossacks.

Long long ago their Old Believer ancestors fled from Russia and settled beyond the Terek among the Chechens on the Greben, the first range of wooded mountains of Chechnya. Living among the Chechens the Cossacks intermarried with them and adopted the manners and customs of the hill tribes, though they still retained the Russian language in all its purity, as well as their Old Faith. A tradition, still fresh among them, declares that Tsar Ivan the Terrible came to the Terek, sent for their Elders, and gave them the land on this side of the river, exhorting them to remain friendly to Russia and promising not to enforce his rule upon them nor oblige them to change their faith. Even now the Cossack families claim relationship with the Chechens, and the love of freedom, of leisure, of plunder and of war, still form their chief characteristics. Only the harmful side of Russian influence shows itself – by interference at elections, by confiscation of church bells, and by the troops who are quartered in the country or march through it. A Cossack is inclined to hate less the *dzhigit* hillsman who maybe has killed his brother, than the soldier quartered on him to defend his village, but who has defiled his hut with tobacco-smoke. He respects his enemy the hillsman and despises the soldier, who is in his eyes an alien and an oppressor. In reality, from a Cossack's point of view a Russian peasant is a foreign, savage, despicable creature, of whom he sees a sample in the hawkers who come to the country and in the Ukrainian immigrants whom the Cossack contemptuously calls 'woolbeaters'. For him, to be smartly dressed means to be dressed like a Circassian. The best weapons are obtained from the hillsmen and the best horses are bought, or stolen, from them. A dashing young Cossack likes to show off his knowledge of Tartar, and when carousing talks Tartar even to his fellow Cossack. In spite of all these things this small Christian clan stranded in a tiny corner of the earth, surrounded by half-savage Mohammedan tribes and by soldiers, considers itself highly advanced, acknowledges none but Cossacks as human beings, and despises everybody else. The Cossack spends most of his time in the cordon, in action, or in hunting and fishing. He hardly ever works at home. When he stays in the village it is an exception to the general rule and then he is holiday-making. All Cossacks make their own wine, and drunkenness is not so much a general tendency as a rite, the non-fulfilment of which would be considered apostasy. The Cossack looks upon a woman as an instrument for his welfare; only the unmarried girls are allowed to amuse themselves. A married woman has to work for her husband from youth to very old age: his demands on her are the Oriental ones of submission and labour. In consequence of this outlook women are strongly developed both physically and mentally, and though they are – as everywhere in the East – nominally in subjection, they possess far greater influence and importance in family life than Western women. Their exclusion from public life and inurement to heavy male labour give the women all the more power and importance in the household. A Cossack, who before strangers considers it improper to speak affectionately or needlessly to his wife, when alone with her is involuntarily conscious of her superiority. His house and all his property, in fact the entire homestead, has been acquired and is kept together solely by her labour and care. Though firmly convinced that labour is degrading to a Cossack and is only proper for a Nogay labourer or a woman, he is vaguely aware of the fact that all he makes use of and calls his own is the result of that toil, and that it is in the power of the woman (his mother or his wife) whom he considers his slave, to deprive him of all he possesses. Besides, the continuous performance of man's heavy work and the responsibilities entrusted to her have endowed the Grebensk women with a peculiarly independent masculine character and have remarkably developed their physical powers, common sense, resolution, and stability. The women are in most cases stronger, more intelligent, more developed, and handsomer than the men. A striking feature of a Grebensk woman's beauty is the combination of the purest Circassian type of face with the broad and powerful build of Northern women. Cossack women wear the Circassian dress –

a Tartar smock, *beshmet*, and soft slippers – but they tie their kerchiefs round their heads in the Russian fashion. Smartness, cleanliness and elegance in dress and in the arrangement of their huts, are with them a custom and a necessity. In their relations with men the women, and especially the unmarried girls, enjoy perfect freedom.

Novomlinsk village was considered the very heart of Grebensk Cossackdom. In it more than elsewhere the customs of the old Grebensk population have been preserved, and its women have from time immemorial been renowned all over the Caucasus for their beauty. A Cossack's livelihood is derived from vineyards, fruit-gardens, water melon and pumpkin plantations, from fishing, hunting, maize and millet growing, and from war plunder. Novomlinsk village lies about two and a half miles away from the Terek, from which it is separated by a dense forest. On one side of the road which runs through the village is the river; on the other, green vineyards and orchards, beyond which are seen the driftsands of the Nogay Steppe. The village is surrounded by earth-banks and prickly bramble hedges, and is entered by tall gates hung between posts and covered with little reed-thatched roofs. Beside them on a wooden gun-carriage stands an unwieldy cannon captured by the Cossacks at some time or other, and which has not been fired for a hundred years. A uniformed Cossack sentinel with dagger and gun sometimes stands, and sometimes does not stand, on guard beside the gates, and sometimes presents arms to a passing officer and sometimes does not. Below the roof of the gateway is written in black letters on a white board: 'Houses 266: male inhabitants 897: female 1012.' The Cossacks' houses are all raised on pillars two and a half feet from the ground. They are carefully thatched with reeds and have large carved gables. If not new they are at least all straight and clean, with high porches of different shapes; and they are not built close together but have ample space around them, and are all picturesquely placed along broad streets and lanes. In front of the large bright windows of many of the houses, beyond the kitchen gardens, dark green poplars and acacias with their delicate pale verdure and scented white blossoms overtop the houses, and beside them grow flaunting yellow sunflowers, creepers, and grape vines. In the broad open square are three shops where drapery, sunflower and pumpkin seeds, locust beans and gingerbreads are sold; and surrounded by a tall fence, loftier and larger than the other houses, stands the Regimental Commander's dwelling with its casement windows, behind a row of tall poplars. Few people are to be seen in the streets of the village on weekdays, especially in summer. The young men are on duty in the cordons or on military expeditions; the old ones are fishing or helping the women in the orchards and gardens. Only the very old, the sick, and the children, remain at home.

Chapter 5

It was one of those wonderful evenings that occur only in the Caucasus. The sun had sunk behind the mountains but it was still light. The evening glow had spread over a third of the sky, and against its brilliancy the dull white immensity of the mountains was sharply defined. The air was rarefied, motionless, and full of sound. The shadow of the mountains reached for several miles over the steppe. The steppe, the opposite side of the river, and the roads, were all deserted. If very occasionally mounted men appeared, the Cossacks in the cordon and the Chechens in their *aouls* (villages) watched them with surprised curiosity and tried to guess who those questionable men could be. At nightfall people from fear of one another flock to their dwellings, and only birds and beasts fearless of man prowl in those deserted spaces. Talking merrily, the women who have been tying up the vines hurry away from the gardens before sunset. The vineyards, like all the surrounding district, are deserted, but the villages become very animated at that time of the evening. From all sides, walking, riding, or driving in their creaking carts, people move towards the village. Girls with their smocks tucked up and twigs in their hands run chatting merrily to the village gates to meet the cattle that are crowding together in a cloud of dust and mosquitoes which they bring with them from the steppe. The well-fed cows and buffaloes disperse at a run all over the streets and Cossack women in coloured *beshmets* go to and fro among them. You can hear their merry laughter and shrieks mingling with the lowing of the cattle. There an armed and mounted Cossack, on leave from the cordon, rides up to a hut and, leaning towards the window, knocks. In answer to the knock the handsome head of a young woman appears at the window and you can hear caressing, laughing voices. There a tattered Nogay labourer, with prominent cheekbones, brings a load of reeds from the steppes, turns his creaking cart into the Cossack captain's broad and clean courtyard, and lifts the yoke off the oxen that stand tossing their heads while he and his master shout to one another in Tartar. Past a puddle that reaches nearly across the street, a barefooted Cossack woman with a bundle of firewood on her back makes her laborious way by clinging to the fences, holding her smock high and exposing her white legs. A Cossack returning from shooting calls out in jest: 'Lift it higher, shameless thing!' and points his gun at her. The woman lets down her smock and drops the wood. An old Cossack, returning home from fishing with his trousers tucked up and his hairy grey chest uncovered, has a net across his shoulder containing silvery fish that are still struggling; and to take a short cut climbs over his neighbour's broken fence and gives a tug to his coat which has caught on the fence. There a woman is dragging a dry branch along and from round the corner comes the sound of an axe. Cossack children, spinning their tops wherever there is a smooth place in the street, are shrieking; women are climbing over fences to avoid going round. From every chimney rises the odorous *kisyak* smoke. From every homestead comes the sound of increased bustle, precursor to the stillness of night.

Granny Ulitka, the wife of the Cossack cornet who is also teacher in the regimental school, goes out to the gates of her yard like the other women, and waits for the cattle which her daughter Maryanka is driving along the street. Before she has had time fully to open the wattle gate in the fence, an enormous buffalo cow surrounded by mosquitoes rushes up bellowing and squeezes in. Several well-fed cows slowly follow her, their large eyes gazing with recognition at their mistress as they swish their sides with their tails. The beautiful and shapely Maryanka enters at the gate and throwing away her switch quickly slams the gate to and rushes with all the speed of her nimble feet to separate and drive the cattle into their sheds. 'Take off your slippers, you devil's wench!' shouts her mother, 'you've worn them into holes!' Maryanka is not at all offended at being called a 'devil's wench', but accepting it as a term of endearment cheerfully goes on with her task. Her face is covered with a kerchief tied round her head. She is wearing a pink smock and a green *beshmet*. She disappears inside the lean-to shed in the yard, following the big fat cattle; and from the shed comes her voice as she speaks gently and persuasively to the buffalo: 'Won't she stand still? What a creature! Come now, come old dear!' Soon the girl and the old woman pass from the shed to the dairy carrying two large pots of milk, the day's yield. From the dairy chimney rises a thin cloud of *kisyak* smoke: the milk is being used to make into clotted cream. The girl makes up the fire while her mother goes to the gate. Twilight has fallen on the village. The air is full of the smell of vegetables, cattle, and scented *kisyak* smoke. From the gates and along the streets Cossack women come running, carrying lighted rags. From the yards one hears the snorting and quiet chewing of the cattle eased of their milk, while in the street only the voices of women and children sound as they call to one another. It is rare on a week-day to hear the drunken voice of a man.

One of the Cossack wives, a tall, masculine old woman, approaches Granny Ulitka from the homestead opposite and asks her for a light. In her hand she holds a rag.

'Have you cleared up, Granny?'

'The girl is lighting the fire. Is it fire you want?' says Granny Ulitka, proud of being able to oblige her neighbour.

Both women enter the hut, and coarse hands unused to dealing with small articles tremblingly lift the lid of a matchbox, which is a rarity in the Caucasus. The masculine-looking newcomer sits down on the doorstep with the evident intention of having a chat.

'And is your man at the school, Mother?' she asks.

'He's always teaching the youngsters, Mother. But he writes that he'll come home for the holidays,' said the cornet's wife.

'Yes, he's a clever man, one sees; it all comes useful.'

'Of course it does.'

'And my Lukashka is at the cordon; they won't let him come home,' said the visitor, though the cornet's wife had known all this long ago. She wanted to talk about her Lukashka whom she had lately fitted out for service in the Cossack regiment, and whom she wished to marry to the cornet's daughter, Maryanka.

'So he's at the cordon?'

'He is, Mother. He's not been home since last holidays. The

other day I sent him some shirts by Fomushkin. He says he's all right, and that his superiors are satisfied. He says they are looking out for *abreks* again. Lukashka is quite happy, he says.'

'Ah well, thank God,' said the cornet's wife. '"Snatcher" is certainly the only word for him.' Lukashka was surnamed 'the Snatcher' because of his bravery in snatching a boy from a watery grave, and the cornet's wife alluded to this, wishing in her turn to say something agreeable to Lukashka's mother.

'I thank God, Mother, that he's a good son! He's a fine fellow, everyone praises him,' says Lukashka's mother. 'All I wish is to get him married; then I could die in peace.'

'Well, aren't there plenty of young women in the village?' answered the cornet's wife slyly as she carefully replaced the lid of the matchbox with her horny hands.

'Plenty, Mother, plenty,' remarked Lukashka's mother, shaking her head. 'There's your girl now, your Maryanka – that's the sort of girl! You'd have to search through the whole place to find such another!' The cornet's wife knows what Lukashka's mother is after, but though she believes him to be a good Cossack she hangs back: first because she is a cornet's wife and rich, while Lukashka is the son of a simple Cossack and fatherless; secondly because she does not want to part with her daughter yet; but chiefly because propriety demands it.

'Well, when Maryanka grows up she'll be marriageable too,' she answers soberly and modestly.

'I'll send the matchmakers to you – I'll send them! Only let me get the vineyard done and then we'll come and make our bows to you,' says Lukashka's mother. 'And we'll make our bows to Elias Vasilich too.'

'Elias, indeed!' says the cornet's wife proudly. 'It's to me you must speak! All in its own good time.'

Lukashka's mother sees by the stern face of the cornet's wife that it is not the time to say anything more just now, so she lights her rag with the match and says, rising: 'Don't refuse us, think of my words. I'll go, it is time to light the fire.'

As she crosses the road swinging the burning rag, she meets Maryanka, who bows.

'Ah, she's a regular queen, a splendid worker, that girl!' she thinks, looking at the beautiful maiden. 'What need for her to grow any more? It's time she was married and to a good home; married to Lukashka!'

But Granny Ulitka had her own cares and she remained sitting on the threshold thinking hard about something, till the girl called her.

Chapter 6

The male population of the village spend their time on military expeditions and in the cordon – or 'at their posts', as the Cossacks say. Towards evening, that same Lukashka the Snatcher, about whom the old women had been talking, was standing on a watch-tower of the Nizhni-Prototsk post situated on the very banks of the Terek. Leaning on the railing of the tower and screwing up his eyes, he looked now far into the distance beyond the Terek, now down at his fellow Cossacks, and occasionally he addressed the latter. The sun was already approaching the snowy range that gleamed white above the fleecy clouds. The clouds undulating at the base of the mountains grew darker and darker. The clearness of evening was noticeable in the air. A sense of freshness came from the woods, though round the post it was still hot. The voices of the talking Cossacks vibrated more sonorously than before. The moving mass of the Terek's rapid brown waters contrasted more vividly with its motionless banks. The waters were beginning to subside and here and there the wet sands gleamed drab on the banks and in the shallows. The other side of the river, just opposite the cordon, was deserted; only an immense waste of low-growing reeds stretched far away to the very foot of the mountains. On the low bank, a little to one side, could be seen the flat-roofed clay houses and the funnel-shaped chimneys of a Chechen village. The sharp eyes of the Cossack who stood on the watch-tower followed, through the evening smoke of the pro-Russian village, the tiny moving figures of the Chechen women visible in the distance in their red and blue garments.

Although the Cossacks expected *abreks* to cross over and attack them from the Tartar side at any moment, especially as it was May when the woods by the Terek are so dense that it is difficult to pass through them on foot and the river is shallow enough in places for a horseman to ford it, and despite the fact that a couple of days

before a Cossack had arrived with a circular from the commander
of the regiment announcing that spies had reported the intention
of a party of some eight men to cross the Terek, and ordering
special vigilance – no special vigilance was being observed in the
cordon. The Cossacks, unarmed and with their horses unsaddled
just as if they were at home, spent their time some in fishing, some
in drinking, and some in hunting. Only the horse of the man on
duty was saddled, and with its feet hobbled was moving about
by the brambles near the wood, and only the sentinel had his
Circassian coat on and carried a gun and sword. The corporal, a tall
thin Cossack with an exceptionally long back and small hands and
feet, was sitting on the earth-bank of a hut with his *beshmet*
unbuttoned. On his face was the lazy, bored expression of a
superior, and having shut his eyes he dropped his head upon the
palm first of one hand and then of the other. An elderly Cossack
with a broad greyish-black beard was lying in his shirt, girdled
with a black strap, close to the river and gazing lazily at the waves
of the Terek as they monotonously foamed and swirled. Others,
also overcome by the heat and half naked, were rinsing clothes in
the Terek, plaiting a fishing line, or humming tunes as they lay on
the hot sand of the river bank. One Cossack, with a thin face much
burnt by the sun, lay near the hut evidently dead drunk, by a wall
which though it had been in shadow some two hours previously
was now exposed to the sun's fierce slanting rays.

Lukashka, who stood on the watch-tower, was a tall handsome
lad about twenty years old and very like his mother. His face and
whole build, in spite of the angularity of youth, indicated great
strength, both physical and moral. Though he had only lately
joined the Cossacks at the front, it was evident from the expression
of his face and the calm assurance of his attitude that he had already
acquired the somewhat proud and warlike bearing peculiar to
Cossacks and to men generally who continually carry arms, and
that he felt he was a Cossack and fully knew his own value. His
ample Circassian coat was torn in some places, his cap was on the
back of his head Chechen fashion, and his leggings had slipped
below his knees. His clothing was not rich, but he wore it with
that peculiar Cossack foppishness which consists in imitating the
Chechen brave. Everything on a real brave is ample, ragged, and
neglected, only his weapons are costly. But these ragged clothes

and these weapons are belted and worn with a certain air and matched in a certain manner, neither of which can be acquired by everybody and which at once strike the eye of a Cossack or a hillsman. Lukashka had this resemblance to a brave. With his hands folded under his sword, and his eyes nearly closed, he kept looking at the distant Tartar village. Taken separately his features were not beautiful, but anyone who saw his stately carriage and his dark-browed intelligent face would involuntarily say, 'What a fine fellow!'

'Look at the women, what a lot of them are walking about in the village,' said he in a sharp voice, languidly showing his brilliant white teeth and not addressing anyone in particular.

Nazarka who was lying below immediately lifted his head and remarked: 'They must be going for water.'

'Supposing one scared them with a gun?' said Lukashka, laughing, 'Wouldn't they be frightened?'

'It wouldn't reach.'

'What! Mine would carry beyond. Just wait a bit, and when their feast comes round I'll go and visit Girey Khan and drink *buza* there,' said Lukashka, angrily swishing away the mosquitoes which attached themselves to him.

A rustling in the thicket drew the Cossack's attention. A pied mongrel half-setter, searching for a scent and violently wagging its scantily furred tail, came running to the cordon. Lukashka recognized the dog as one belonging to his neighbour, Uncle Eroshka, a hunter, and saw, following it through the thicket, the approaching figure of the hunter himself.

Uncle Eroshka was a gigantic Cossack with a broad, snow-white beard and such broad shoulders and chest that in the wood, where there was no one to compare him with, he did not look particularly tall, so well proportioned were his powerful limbs. He wore a tattered coat and, over the bands with which his legs were swathed, sandals made of undressed deer's hide tied on with strings; while on his head he had a rough little white cap. He carried over one shoulder a screen to hide behind when shooting pheasants, and a bag containing a hen for luring hawks, and a small falcon; over the other shoulder, attached by a strap, was a wild cat he had killed; and stuck in his belt behind were some little bags containing bullets, gunpowder, and bread, a horse's tail to swish away the mosquitoes, a large dagger in a torn scabbard smeared with old bloodstains, and two dead pheasants. Having glanced at the cordon he stopped.

'Hy, Lyam!' he called to the dog in such a ringing bass that it awoke an echo far away in the wood; and throwing over his shoulder his big gun, of the kind the Cossacks call a 'flint', he raised his cap.

'Had a good day, good people, eh?' he said, addressing the Cossacks in the same strong and cheerful voice, quite without effort, but as loudly as if he were shouting to someone on the other bank of the river.

'Yes, yes, Uncle!' answered from all sides the voices of the young Cossacks.

'What have you seen? Tell us!' shouted Uncle Eroshka, wiping the sweat from his broad red face with the sleeve of his coat.

'Ah, there's a vulture living in the plane tree here, Uncle. As soon as night comes he begins hovering round,' said Nazarka, winking and jerking his shoulder and leg.

'Come, come!' said the old man incredulously.

'Really, Uncle! You must keep watch,' replied Nazarka with a laugh.

The other Cossacks began laughing.

The wag had not seen any vulture at all, but it had long been the custom of the young Cossacks in the cordon to tease and mislead Uncle Eroshka every time he came to them.

'Eh, you fool, always lying!' exclaimed Lukashka from the tower to Nazarka.

Nazarka was immediately silenced.

'It must be watched. I'll watch,' answered the old man to the great delight of all the Cossacks. 'But have you seen any boars?'

'Watching for boars, are you?' said the corporal, bending forward and scratching his back with both hands, very pleased at the chance of some distraction. 'It's *abreks* one has to hunt here and not boars! You've not heard anything, Uncle, have you?' he added, needlessly screwing up his eyes and showing his close-set white teeth.

'*Abreks*,' said the old man. 'No, I haven't. I say, have you any *chikhir*? Let me have a drink, there's a good man. I'm really quite done up. When the time comes I'll bring you some fresh meat, I really will. Give me a drink!' he added.

'Well, and are you going to watch?' inquired the corporal, as though he had not heard what the other said.

'I did mean to watch tonight,' replied Uncle Eroshka. 'Maybe, with God's help, I shall kill something for the holiday. Then you shall have a share, you shall indeed!'

'Uncle! Hallo, Uncle!' called out Lukashka sharply from above, attracting everybody's attention. All the Cossacks looked up at him. 'Just go to the upper water-course, there's a fine herd of boars there. I'm not inventing, really! The other day one of our Cossacks shot one there. I'm telling you the truth,' added he, readjusting the musket at his back and in a tone that showed he was not joking.

'Ah! Lukashka the Snatcher is here!' said the old man, looking up. 'Where has he been shooting?'

'Haven't you seen? I suppose you're too young!' said Lukashka. 'Close by the ditch,' he went on seriously with a shake of the head. 'We were just going along the ditch when all at once we heard something crackling, but my gun was in its case. Elias fired suddenly . . . But I'll show you the place, it's not far. You just wait a bit. I know every one of their footpaths . . . Daddy Mosev,' said he, turning resolutely and almost commandingly to the corporal, 'it's time to relieve guard!' and holding aloft his gun he began to descend from the watch-tower without waiting for the order.

'Come down!' said the corporal, after Lukashka had started, and glanced round. 'Is it your turn, Gurka? Then go . . . True enough your Lukashka has become very skilful,' he went on, addressing the old man. 'He keeps going about just like you, he doesn't stay at home. The other day he killed a boar.'

Chapter 7

The sun had already set and the shades of night were rapidly spreading from the edge of the wood. The Cossacks finished their task round the cordon and gathered in the hut for supper. Only the old man still stayed under the plane tree watching for the vulture and pulling the string tied to the falcon's leg, but though a vulture was really perching on the plane tree it declined to swoop down on the lure. Lukashka, singing one song after another, was leisurely placing nets among the very thickest brambles to trap pheasants. In spite of his tall stature and big hands every kind of work, both rough and delicate, prospered under Lukashka's fingers.

'Hallo, Luke!' came Nazarka's shrill, sharp voice calling him from the thicket close by. 'The Cossacks have gone in to supper.'

Nazarka, with a live pheasant under his arm, forced his way through the brambles and emerged on the footpath.

'Oh!' said Lukashka, breaking off in his song, 'where did you get that cock pheasant? I suppose it was in my trap?'

Nazarka was of the same age as Lukashka and had also only been at the front since the previous spring.

He was plain, thin and puny, with a shrill voice that rang in one's ears. They were neighbours and comrades. Lukashka was sitting on the grass crosslegged like a Tartar, adjusting his nets.

'I don't know whose it was – yours, I expect.'

'Was it beyond the pit by the plane tree? Then it is mine! I set the nets last night.'

Lukashka rose and examined the captured pheasant. After stroking the dark burnished head of the bird, which rolled its eyes and stretched out its neck in terror, Lukashka took the pheasant in his hands.

'We'll have it in a pilau tonight. You go and kill and pluck it.'

'And shall we eat it ourselves or give it to the corporal?'

'He has plenty!'

'I don't like killing them,' said Nazarka.

'Give it here!'

Lukashka drew a little knife from under his dagger and gave it a swift jerk. The bird fluttered, but before it could spread its wings the bleeding head bent and quivered.

'That's how one should do it!' said Lukashka, throwing down the pheasant. 'It will make a fat pilau.'

Nazarka shuddered as he looked at the bird.

'I say, Lukashka, that fiend will be sending us to the ambush again tonight,' he said, taking up the bird. (He was alluding to the corporal.) 'He has sent Fomushkin to get wine, and it ought to be his turn. He always puts it on us.'

Lukashka went whistling along the cordon.

'Take the string with you,' he shouted.

Nazarka obeyed.

'I'll give him a bit of my mind today, I really will,' continued Nazarka. 'Let's say we won't go; we're tired out and there's an end of it! No, really, you tell him, he'll listen to you. It's too bad!'

'Get along with you! What a thing to make a fuss about!' said Lukashka, evidently thinking of something else. 'What bosh! If he made us turn out of the village at night now, that would be annoying: there one can have some fun, but here what is there? It's all one whether we're in the cordon or in ambush. What a fellow you are!'

'And are you going to the village?'

'I'll go for the holidays.'

'Gurka says your Dunayka is carrying on with Fomushkin,' said Nazarka suddenly.

'Well, let her go to the devil,' said Lukashka, showing his regular white teeth, though he did not laugh. 'As if I couldn't find another!'

'Gurka says he went to her house. Her husband was out and there was Fomushkin sitting and eating pie. Gurka stopped awhile and then went away, and passing by the window he heard her say, "He's gone, the fiend . . . Why don't you eat your pie, my own? You needn't go home for the night," she says. And Gurka under the window says to himself, "That's fine!"'

'You're making it up.'

'No, quite true, by Heaven!'

'Well, if she's found another let her go to the devil,' said Lukashka, after a pause. 'There's no lack of girls and I was sick of her anyway.'

'Well, see what a devil you are!' said Nazarka. 'You should make up to the cornet's girl, Maryanka. Why doesn't she walk out with anyone?'

Lukashka frowned. 'What of Maryanka? They're all alike,' said he.

'Well, you just try . . . '

'What do you think? Are girls so scarce in the village?'

And Lukashka recommenced whistling, and went along the cordon pulling leaves and branches from the bushes as he went. Suddenly, catching sight of a smooth sapling, he drew the knife from the handle of his dagger and cut it down. 'What a ramrod it will make,' he said, swinging the sapling till it whistled through the air.

The Cossacks were sitting round a low Tartar table on the earthen floor of the clay-plastered outer room of the hut, when the question of whose turn it was to lie in ambush was raised. 'Who is to go tonight?' shouted one of the Cossacks through the open door to the corporal in the next room.

'Who is to go?' the corporal shouted back. 'Uncle Burlak has been and Fomushkin too,' said he, not quite confidently. 'You two had better go, you and Nazarka,' he went on, addressing Lukashka. 'And Ergushov must go too; surely he has slept it off?'

'You don't sleep it off yourself so why should he?' said Nazarka in a subdued voice.

The Cossacks laughed.

Ergushov was the Cossack who had been lying drunk and asleep near the hut. He had only that moment staggered into the room rubbing his eyes.

Lukashka had already risen and was getting his gun ready.

'Be quick and go! Finish your supper and go!' said the corporal; and without waiting for an expression of consent he shut the door, evidently not expecting the Cossack to obey. 'Of course,' thought he, 'if I hadn't been ordered to I wouldn't send anyone, but an officer might turn up at any moment. As it is, they say eight *abreks* have crossed over.'

'Well, I suppose I must go,' remarked Ergushov, 'it's the regulation. Can't be helped! The times are such. I say, we must go.'

Meanwhile Lukashka, holding a big piece of pheasant to his mouth with both hands and glancing now at Nazarka, now at Ergushov, seemed quite indifferent to what passed and only laughed at them both. Before the Cossacks were ready to go into ambush, Uncle Eroshka, who had been vainly waiting under the plane tree till night fell, entered the dark outer room.

'Well, lads,' his loud bass resounded through the low-roofed room drowning all the other voices, 'I'm going with you. You'll watch for Chechens and I for boars!'

Chapter 8

It was quite dark when Uncle Eroshka and the three Cossacks, in their cloaks and shouldering their guns, left the cordon and went towards the place on the Terek where they were to lie in ambush. Nazarka did not want to go at all, but Lukashka shouted at him and they soon started. After they had gone a few steps in silence the Cossacks turned aside from the ditch and went along a path almost hidden by reeds till they reached the river. On its bank lay a thick black log cast up by the water. The reeds around it had been recently beaten down.

'Shall we lie here?' asked Nazarka.

'Why not?' answered Lukashka. 'Sit down here and I'll be back in a minute. I'll only show Daddy where to go.'

'This is the best place; here we can see and not be seen,' said Ergushov, 'so it's here we'll lie. It's a first-rate place!'

Nazarka and Ergushov spread out their cloaks and settled down behind the log, while Lukashka went on with Uncle Eroshka.

'It's not far from here, Daddy,' said Lukashka, stepping softly in front of the old man; 'I'll show you where they've been – I'm the only one that knows, Daddy.'

'Show me! You're a fine fellow, a regular Snatcher!' replied the old man, also whispering.

Having gone a few steps Lukashka stopped, stooped down over a puddle, and whistled. 'That's where they come to drink, d'you see?' He spoke in a scarcely audible voice, pointing to fresh hoof-prints.

'Christ bless you,' answered the old man. 'The boar will be in the hollow beyond the ditch,' he added. I'll watch, and you can go.'

Lukashka pulled his cloak up higher and walked back alone, throwing swift glances now to the left at the wall of reeds, now to the Terek rushing by below the bank. 'I dare say he's watching or creeping along somewhere,' thought he of a possible Chechen hillsman. Suddenly a loud rustling and a splash in the water made him start and seize his musket. From under the bank a boar leapt up – his dark outline showing for a moment against the glassy surface of the water and then disappearing among the reeds. Lukashka pulled out his gun and aimed, but before he could fire the boar had disappeared in the thicket. Lukashka spat with vexation and went on. On approaching the ambuscade he halted again and whistled softly. His whistle was answered and he stepped up to his comrades.

Nazarka, all curled up, was already asleep. Ergushov sat with his legs crossed and moved slightly to make room for Lukashka.

'How jolly it is to sit here! It's really a good place,' said he. 'Did you take him there?'

'Showed him where,' answered Lukashka, spreading out his cloak. 'But what a big boar I roused just now close to the water! I expect it was the very one! You must have heard the crash?'

'I did hear a beast crashing through. I knew at once it was a beast. I thought to myself: "Lukashka has roused a beast,"' Ergushov said, wrapping himself up in his cloak. 'Now I'll go to sleep,' he added. 'Wake me when the cocks crow. We must have discipline. I'll lie down and have a nap, and then you will have a nap and I'll watch – that's the way.'

'Luckily I don't want to sleep,' answered Lukashka.

The night was dark, warm, and still. Only on one side of the sky the stars were shining, the other and greater part was overcast by one huge cloud stretching from the mountaintops. The black cloud, blending in the absence of any wind with the mountains, moved slowly onwards, its curved edges sharply defined against the deep starry sky. Only in front of him could the Cossack discern the Terek and the distance beyond. Behind and on both sides he was surrounded by a wall of reeds. Occasionally the reeds would sway and rustle against one another apparently without cause. Seen from down below, against the clear part of the sky, their waving tufts looked like the feathery branches of trees. Close in front at his very feet was the bank, and at its base the rushing torrent. A little farther on was the moving mass of glassy brown water which eddied rhythmically along the bank and round the shallows. Farther still, water, banks, and cloud all merged together in impenetrable gloom. Along the surface of the water floated black shadows, in which the experienced eyes of the Cossack detected trees carried down by the current. Only very rarely sheet-lightning, mirrored in the water as in a black glass, disclosed the sloping bank opposite. The rhythmic sounds of night – the rustling of the reeds, the snoring of the Cossacks, the hum of mosquitoes, and the rushing water, were every now and then broken by a shot fired in the distance, or by the gurgling of water when a piece of bank slipped down, the splash of a big fish, or the crashing of an animal breaking through the thick undergrowth in the wood. Once an owl flew past along the Terek, flapping one wing against the other rhythmically at every second beat. Just above the Cossack's head it turned towards the wood and then, striking its wings no longer after every other flap but at every flap, it flew to an old plane tree where it rustled about for a long time before settling down among the branches. At every one of these unexpected sounds the watching Cossack listened intently, straining his hearing, and screwing up his eyes while he deliberately felt for his musket.

The greater part of the night was past. The black cloud that had moved westward revealed the clear starry sky from under its torn edge, and the golden upturned crescent of the moon shone above the mountains with a reddish light. The cold began to be penetrating. Nazarka awoke, spoke a little, and fell asleep again. Lukashka feeling bored got up, drew the knife from his dagger-handle and began to fashion his stick into a ramrod. His head was full of the Chechens who lived over there in the mountains, and of how their brave lads came across and were not afraid of the Cossacks, and might even now be crossing the river at some other spot. He thrust himself out of his hiding-place and looked along the river but could see nothing. And as he continued looking out at intervals upon the river and at the opposite bank, now dimly distinguishable from the water in the faint moonlight, he no longer thought about the Chechens but only of when it would be time to wake his comrades, and of going home to the village. In the village he imagined Dunayka, his 'little soul', as the Cossacks call a man's mistress, and thought of her with vexation. Silvery mists, a sign of coming morning, glittered white above the water, and not far from him young eagles were whistling and flapping their wings. At last the crowing of a cock reached him from the distant village, followed by the long-sustained note of another, which was again answered by yet other voices.

'Time to wake them,' thought Lukashka, who had finished his ramrod and felt his eyes growing heavy. Turning to his comrades he managed to make out which pair of legs belonged to whom, when it suddenly seemed to him that he heard something splash on the other side of the Terek. He turned again towards the horizon beyond the hills, where day was breaking under the upturned crescent, glanced at the outline of the opposite bank, at the Terek, and at the now distinctly visible driftwood upon it. For one instant it seemed to him that he was moving and that the Terek with the drifting wood remained stationary. Again he peered out. One large black log with a branch particularly attracted his attention. The tree was floating in a strange way right down the middle of the stream, neither rocking nor whirling. It even appeared not to be floating altogether with the current, but to be crossing it in the direction of the shallows. Lukashka stretching out his neck watched it intently. The tree floated to the shallows, stopped, and shifted in a peculiar manner. Lukashka thought he saw an arm stretched out from beneath the tree. 'Supposing I killed an *abrek* all by myself!' he thought, and seized his gun with a swift, unhurried movement, putting up his gun-rest, placing the gun upon it, and holding it noiselessly in position. Cocking the trigger, with bated breath he took aim, still peering out intently. 'I won't wake them,' he thought. But his heart began beating so fast that he remained motionless, listening. Suddenly the trunk gave a plunge and again began to float across the stream towards our bank. 'Only not to miss . . . ' thought he, and now by the faint light of the moon he caught a glimpse of a Tartar's head in front of the floating wood. He aimed straight at the head which appeared to be quite near – just at the end of his rifle's barrel. He glanced across. 'Right enough it is an *abrek*! he thought joyfully, and suddenly rising to his knees he again took aim. Having found the sight, barely visible at the end of the long gun, he said: 'In the name of the Father and of the Son', in the Cossack way learnt in his childhood, and pulled the trigger. A flash of lightning lit up for an instant the reeds and the water, and the sharp, abrupt report of the shot was carried across the river, changing into a prolonged roll somewhere in the far distance. The piece of driftwood now floated not across, but with the current, rocking and whirling.

'Stop, I say!' exclaimed Ergushov, seizing his musket and raising himself behind the log near which he was lying.

'Shut up, you devil!' whispered Lukashka, grinding his teeth. '*Abreks*!'

'Whom have you shot?' asked Nazarka. 'Who was it, Lukashka?'

Lukashka did not answer. He was reloading his gun and watching the floating wood. A little way off it stopped on a sand-bank, and from behind it something large that rocked in the water came into view.

'What did you shoot? Why don't you speak?' insisted the Cossacks.

'*Abreks*, I tell you!' said Lukashka.

'Don't humbug! Did the gun go off? . . . '

'I've killed an *abrek*, that's what I fired at,' muttered Lukashka in a voice choked by emotion, as he jumped to his feet. 'A man was swimming . . . ' he said, pointing to the sandbank. 'I killed him. Just look there.'

'Have done with your humbugging!' said Ergushov again, rubbing his eyes.

'Have done with what? Look there,' said Lukashka, seizing him by the shoulders and pulling him with such force that Ergushov groaned.

He looked in the direction in which Lukashka pointed, and discerning a body immediately changed his tone.

'O Lord! But I say, more will come! I tell you the truth,' said he softly, and began examining his musket. 'That was a scout swimming across: either the others are here already or are not far off on the other side – I tell you for sure!'

Lukashka was unfastening his belt and taking off his Circassian coat.

'What are you up to, you idiot?' exclaimed Ergushov. 'Only show yourself and you've lost all for nothing, I tell you true! If you've killed him he won't escape. Let me have a little powder for my musket-pan – you have some? Nazarka, you go back to the cordon and look alive; but don't go along the bank or you'll be killed – I tell you true.'

'Catch me going alone! Go yourself!' said Nazarka angrily.

Having taken off his coat, Lukashka went down to the bank.

'Don't go in, I tell you!' said Ergushov, putting some powder on the pan. 'Look, he's not moving, I can see. It's nearly morning; wait till they come from the cordon. You go, Nazarka. You're afraid! Don't be afraid, I tell you.'

'Luke, I say, Lukashka! Tell us how you did it!' said Nazarka.

Lukashka changed his mind about going into the water just then. 'Go quick to the cordon and I will watch. Tell the Cossacks to send out the patrol. If the *abreks* are on this side they must be caught,' said he.

'That's what I say. They'll get off,' said Ergushov, rising. 'True, they must be caught!'

Ergushov and Nazarka rose and, crossing themselves, started off for the cordon – not along the riverbank but breaking their way through the brambles to reach a path in the wood.

'Now mind, Lukashka – they may cut you down here, so you'd best keep a sharp look-out, I tell you!'

'Go along; I know,' muttered Lukashka; and having examined his gun again he sat down behind the log.

He remained alone and sat gazing at the shallows and listening for the Cossacks; but it was some distance to the cordon and he was tormented by impatience. He kept thinking that the other *abreks* who were with the one he had killed would escape. He was vexed with the *abreks* who were going to escape just as he had been with the boar that had escaped the evening before. He glanced round and at the opposite bank, expecting every moment to see a man, and having arranged his gun-rest he was ready to fire. The idea that he might himself be killed never entered his head.

Chapter 9

It was growing light. The Chechen's body which was gently rocking in the shallow water was now clearly visible. Suddenly the reeds rustled not far from Luke and he heard steps and saw the feathery tops of the reeds moving. He set his gun at full cock and muttered: 'In the name of the Father and of the Son', but when the cock clicked the sound of steps ceased.

'Hallo, Cossacks! Don't kill your Daddy!' said a deep bass voice calmly; and moving the reeds apart Daddy Eroshka came up close to Luke.

'I very nearly killed you, by God I did!' said Lukashka.

'What have you shot?' asked the old man.

His sonorous voice resounded through the wood and downward along the river, suddenly dispelling the mysterious quiet of night around the Cossack. It was as if everything had suddenly become lighter and more distinct.

'There now, Uncle, you have not seen anything, but I've killed a beast,' said Lukashka, uncocking his gun and getting up with unnatural calmness.

The old man was staring intently at the white bank, now clearly visible, against which the Terek rippled.

'He was swimming with a log on his back. I spied him out! . . . Look there. There! He's got blue trousers, and a gun I think . . . Do you see?' inquired Luke.

'How can one help seeing?' said the old man angrily, and a serious and stern expression appeared on his face. 'You've killed a brave,' he said, apparently with regret.

'Well, I sat here and suddenly saw something dark on the other side. I spied him when he was still over there. It was as if a man had come there and fallen in. Strange! And a piece of drift-wood, a good-sized piece, comes floating, not with the stream but across it; and what do I see but a head appearing from under it! Strange! I stretched out of the reeds but could see nothing; then I rose and he must have heard, the beast, and crept out into the shallow and looked about. "No, you don't!" I said, as soon as he landed and looked round, "you won't get away!" Oh, there was something choking me! I got my gun ready but did not stir, and looked out. He waited a little and then swam out again; and when he came into the moonlight I could see his whole back. "In the name of the Father and of the Son and of the Holy Ghost" . . . and through the smoke I see him struggling. He moaned, or so it seemed to me. "Ah," I thought, "the Lord be thanked, I've killed him!" And when he drifted onto the sand-bank I could see him distinctly: he tried to get up but couldn't. He struggled a bit and then lay down. Everything could be seen. Look, he does not move − he must be dead! The Cossacks have gone back to the cordon in case there should be any more of them.'

'And so you got him!' said the old man. 'He is far away now, my lad! . . . ' And again he shook his head sadly.

Just then the sound reached them of breaking bushes and the loud voices of Cossacks approaching along the bank on horseback and on foot. 'Are you bringing the skiff?' shouted Lukashka.

'You're a trump, Luke! Lug it to the bank!' shouted one of the Cossacks.

Without waiting for the skiff Lukashka began to undress, keeping an eye all the while on his prey.

'Wait a bit, Nazarka is bringing the skiff,' shouted the corporal.

'You fool! Maybe he is alive and only pretending! Take your dagger with you!' shouted another Cossack.

'Get along,' cried Luke, pulling off his trousers. He quickly undressed and, crossing himself, jumped, plunging with a splash into the river. Then with long strokes of his white arms, lifting his back high out of the water and breathing deeply, he swam across the current of the Terek towards the shallows. A crowd of Cossacks stood on the bank talking loudly. Three horsemen rode off to patrol. The skiff appeared round a bend. Lukashka stood up on the sandbank, leaned over the body, and gave it a couple of shakes.

'Quite dead!' he shouted in a shrill voice.

The Chechen had been shot in the head. He had on a pair of blue trousers, a shirt, and a Circassian coat, and a gun and dagger were tied to his back. Above all these a large branch was tied, and it was this which at first had misled Lukashka.

'What a carp you've landed!' cried one of the Cossacks who had assembled in a circle, as the body, lifted out of the skiff, was laid on the bank, pressing down the grass.

'How yellow he is!' said another.

'Where have our fellows gone to search? I expect the rest of them are on the other bank. If this one had not been a scout he would not have swum that way. Why else should he swim alone?' said a third.

'Must have been a smart one to offer himself before the others; a regular brave!' said Lukashka mockingly, shivering as he wrung out his clothes that had got wet on the bank.

'His beard is dyed and cropped.'

'And he has tied a bag with a coat in it to his back.'

'That would make it easier for him to swim,' said someone.

'I say, Lukashka,' said the corporal, who was holding the dagger and gun taken from the dead man. 'Keep the dagger for yourself and the coat too; but I'll give you three rubles for the gun. You see it has a hole in it,' said he, blowing into the muzzle. 'I want it just for a souvenir.'

Lukashka did not answer. Evidently this sort of begging vexed him but he knew it could not be avoided.

'See, what a devil!' said he, frowning and throwing down the Chechen's coat. 'If at least it were a good coat, but it's a mere rag.'

'It'll do to fetch firewood in,' said one of the Cossacks.

'Mosev, I'll go home,' said Lukashka, evidently forgetting his vexation and wishing to get some advantage out of having to give a present to his superior.

'All right, you may go!'

'Take the body beyond the cordon, lads,' said the corporal, still examining the gun, 'and put a shelter over him from the sun. Perhaps they'll send from the mountains to ransom it.'

'It isn't hot yet,' said someone.

'And supposing a jackal tears him? Would that be well?' remarked another Cossack.

'We'll set a watch; if they should come to ransom him it won't do for him to have been torn.'

'Well, Lukashka, whatever you do you must stand a pail of vodka for the lads,' said the corporal gaily.

'Of course! That's the custom,' chimed in the Cossacks. 'See what luck God has sent you! Without ever having seen anything of the kind before, you've killed a brave!'

'Buy the dagger and coat and don't be stingy, and I'll let you have the trousers too,' said Lukashka. 'They're too tight for me; he was a thin devil.'

One Cossack bought the coat for a ruble and another gave the price of two pails of vodka for the dagger.

'Drink, lads! I'll stand you a pail!' said Luke. 'I'll bring it myself from the village.'

'And cut up the trousers into kerchiefs for the girls!' said Nazarka.

The Cossacks burst out laughing.

'Have done laughing!' said the corporal. 'And take the body away. Why have you put the nasty thing by the hut?'

'What are you standing there for? Haul him along, lads!' shouted Lukashka in a commanding voice to the Cossacks, who reluctantly took hold of the body, obeying him as though he were their chief. After dragging the body along for a few steps the Cossacks let fall the legs, which dropped with a lifeless jerk, and stepping apart they then stood silent for a few moments. Nazarka came up and straightened the head, which was turned to one side so that the round wound above the temple and the whole of the dead man's face were visible.

'See what a mark he has made right in the brain,' he said. 'He won't get lost. His owners will always know him!' No one answered, and again the Angel of Silence flew over the Cossacks.

The sun had risen high and its diverging beams were lighting up the dewy grass. Nearby, the Terek murmured in the awakened wood and, greeting the morning, the pheasants called to one another. The Cossacks stood still and silent around the dead man, gazing at him. The brown body, with nothing on but the wet blue trousers held by a girdle over the sunken stomach, was well shaped and handsome. The muscular arms lay stretched straight out by his sides; the blue, freshly shaven, round head with the clotted wound on one side of it was thrown back. The smooth tanned forehead contrasted sharply with the shaven part of the head. The open glassy eyes with lowered pupils stared upwards, seeming to gaze past everything. Under the red trimmed moustache the fine lips, drawn at the corners, seemed stiffened into a smile of good-natured subtle raillery. The fingers of the small hands covered with red hairs were bent inward, and the nails were dyed red.

Lukashka had not yet dressed. He was wet. His neck was redder and his eyes brighter than usual, his broad jaws twitched, and from his healthy body a hardly perceptible steam rose in the fresh morning air.

'He too was a man!' he muttered, evidently admiring the corpse.

'Yes, if you had fallen into his hands you would have had short shrift,' said one of the Cossacks.

The Angel of Silence had taken wing. The Cossacks began bustling about and talking. Two of them went to cut brushwood for a shelter, others strolled towards the cordon. Luke and Nazarka ran to get ready to go to the village.

Half an hour later they were both on their way homewards, talking incessantly and almost running through the dense woods which separated the Terek from the village.

'Mind, don't tell her I sent you, but just go and find out if her husband is at home,' Luke was saying in his shrill voice.

'And I'll go round to Yamka too,' said the devoted Nazarka. 'We'll have a spree, shall we?'

'When should we have one if not today?' replied Luke.

When they reached the village the two Cossacks drank, and lay down to sleep till evening.

Chapter 10

On the third day after the events above described, two companies of a Caucasian infantry regiment arrived at the Cossack village of Novomlinsk. The horses had been unharnessed and the companies' wagons were standing in the square. The cooks had dug a pit, and with logs gathered from various yards (where they had not been sufficiently securely stored) were now cooking the food; the pay-sergeants were settling accounts with the soldiers. The Service Corps men were driving piles in the ground to which to tie the horses, and the quartermasters were going about the streets just as if they were at home, showing officers and men to their quarters. Here were green ammunition boxes in a line, the company's carts, horses, and cauldrons in which buckwheat porridge was being cooked. Here were the captain and the lieutenant and the sergeant-major, Onisim Mikhaylovich, and all this was in the Cossack village where it was reported that the companies were ordered to take up their quarters: therefore they were at home here. But why they were stationed there, who the Cossacks were, and whether they wanted the troops to be there, and whether they were Old Believers or not – was all quite immaterial. Having received their pay and been dismissed, tired out and covered with dust, the soldiers noisily and in disorder, like a swarm of bees about to settle, spread over the squares and streets; quite regardless of the Cossacks' ill will, chattering merrily and with their muskets clinking, by twos and threes they entered the huts and hung up their accoutrements, unpacked their bags, and bantered the women. At their favourite spot, round the porridge-cauldrons, a large group of soldiers assembled and with little pipes between their teeth they gazed, now at the smoke which rose into the hot sky, becoming visible when it thickened into white clouds as it rose, and now at the camp fires which were quivering in the pure air like molten glass, and bantered and made fun of the Cossack men and women because they do not live at all like Russians. In all the yards one could see soldiers and hear their laughter and the exasperated and shrill cries of Cossack women defending their houses and refusing to give the soldiers water or cooking utensils. Little boys and girls, clinging to their mothers and to each other, followed all the movements of the troopers (never before seen by them) with frightened curiosity, or ran after them at a respectful distance. The old Cossacks came out silently and dismally and sat on the earthen embankments of their huts, and watched the soldiers' activity with an air of leaving it all to the will of God without understanding what would come of it.

Olenin, who had joined the Caucasian Army as a cadet three months before, was quartered in one of the best houses in the village, the house of the cornet, Elias Vasilich – that is to say at Granny Ulitka's.

'Goodness knows what it will be like, Dmitri Andreich,' said the panting Vanyusha to Olenin, who, dressed in a Circassian coat and mounted on a Kabarda horse which he had bought in Groznoe, was after a five-hours' march gaily entering the yard of the quarters assigned to him.

'Why, what's the matter?' he asked, caressing his horse and looking merrily at the perspiring, dishevelled, and worried Vanyusha, who had arrived with the baggage wagons and was unpacking.

Olenin looked quite a different man. In place of his clean-shaven lips and chin he had a youthful moustache and a small beard. Instead of a sallow complexion, the result of nights turned into day, his cheeks, his forehead, and the skin behind his ears were now red with healthy sunburn. In place of a clean new black suit he wore a dirty white Circassian coat with a deeply pleated skirt, and he bore arms. Instead of a freshly starched collar, his neck was tightly clasped by the red band of his silk *beshmet*. He wore Circassian dress but did not wear it well, and anyone would have known him for a Russian and not a Tartar brave. It was the thing – but not the real thing. But for all that, his whole person breathed health, joy, and satisfaction.

'Yes, it seems funny to you,' said Vanyusha, 'but just try to talk to these people yourself: they set themselves against one and there's an end of it. You can't get as much as a word out of them.' Vanyusha angrily threw down a pail on the threshold. 'Somehow they don't seem like Russians.'

'You should speak to the Chief of the Village!'

'But I don't know where he lives,' said Vanyusha in an offended tone.

'Who has upset you so?' asked Olenin, looking round.

'The devil only knows. Faugh! There is no real master here. They say he has gone to some kind of *kriga*, and the old woman is a real devil. God preserve us!' answered Vanyusha, putting his hands to his head. 'How we shall live here I don't know. They are worse than Tartars, I do declare – though they consider themselves Christians! A Tartar is bad enough, but all the same he is more noble. Gone to the *kriga* indeed! What this *kriga* they have invented is, I don't know!' concluded Vanyusha, and turned aside.

'It's not as it is in the serfs' quarters at home, eh?' chaffed Olenin without dismounting.

'Please sir, may I have your horse?' said Vanyusha, evidently perplexed by this new order of things but resigning himself to his fate.

'So a Tartar is more noble, eh, Vanyusha?' repeated Olenin, dismounting and slapping the saddle.

'Yes, you're laughing! You think it funny,' muttered Vanyusha angrily.

'Come, don't be angry, Vanyusha,' replied Olenin, still smiling. 'Wait a minute, I'll go and speak to the people of the house; you'll see I shall arrange everything. You don't know what a jolly life we shall have here. Only don't get upset.'

Vanyusha did not answer. Screwing up his eyes he looked contemptuously after his master, and shook his head. Vanyusha regarded Olenin as only his master, and Olenin regarded Vanyusha as only his servant; and they would both have been much surprised if anyone had told them that they were friends, as they really were without knowing it themselves. Vanyusha had been taken into his proprietor's house when he was only eleven and when Olenin was the same age. When Olenin was fifteen he gave Vanyusha lessons for a time and taught him to read French, of which the latter was inordinately proud; and when in specially good spirits he still let off French words, always laughing stupidly when he did so.

Olenin ran up the steps of the porch and pushed open the door of the hut. Maryanka, wearing nothing but a pink smock, as all Cossack women do in the house, jumped away from the door, frightened, and pressing herself against the wall covered the lower part of her face with the broad sleeve of her Tartar smock. Having opened the door wider, Olenin in the semi-darkness of the passage saw the whole tall, shapely figure of the young Cossack girl. With the quick and eager curiosity of youth he involuntarily noticed the firm maidenly form revealed by the fine print smock, and the beautiful black eyes fixed on him with childlike terror and wild curiosity. 'This is *she*,' thought Olenin. 'But there will be many others like her' came at once into his head, and he opened the inner door. Old Granny Ulitka, also dressed only in a smock, was stooping with her back turned to him, sweeping the floor.

'Good-day to you, Mother! I've come about my lodgings,' he began.

The Cossack woman, without unbending, turned her severe but still handsome face towards him.

'What have you come here for? Want to mock at us, eh? I'll teach you to mock; may the black plague seize you!' she shouted, looking askance from under her frowning brow at the newcomer.

Olenin had at first imagined that the way-worn, gallant Caucasian Army (of which he was a member) would be everywhere received joyfully, and especially by the Cossacks, our comrades in the war; and he therefore felt perplexed by this reception. Without losing presence of mind however he tried to explain that he meant to pay for his lodgings, but the old woman would not give him a hearing.

'What have you come for? Who wants a pest like you, with your scraped face? You just wait a bit; when the master returns he'll show you your place. I don't want your dirty money! A likely thing – just as if we had never seen any! You'll stink the house out with your beastly tobacco and want to put it right with money! Think we've never seen a pest! May you be shot in your bowels and your heart!' shrieked the old woman in a piercing voice, interrupting Olenin.

'It seems Vanyusha was right!' thought Olenin. '"A Tartar would be nobler",' and followed by Granny Ulitka's abuse he went out of the hut. As he was leaving, Maryanka, still wearing only her pink smock, but with her forehead covered down to her eyes by a white kerchief, suddenly slipped out from the passage past him. Pattering rapidly down the steps with her bare feet she ran from the porch, stopped, and looking round hastily with laughing eyes at the young man, vanished round the corner of the hut.

Her firm youthful step, the untamed look of the eyes glistening from under the white kerchief, and the firm stately build of the young beauty, struck Olenin even more powerfully than before. 'Yes, it must be *she*,' he thought, and troubling his head still less about the lodgings, he kept looking round at Maryanka as he approached Vanyusha.

'There you see, the girl too is quite savage, just like a wild filly!' said Vanyusha, who though still busy with the luggage wagon had now cheered up a bit. '*La fame!*' he added in a loud triumphant voice and burst out laughing.

Chapter 11

Towards evening the master of the house returned from his fishing, and having learnt that the cadet would pay for the lodging, pacified the old woman and satisfied Vanyusha's demands.

Everything was arranged in the new quarters. Their hosts moved into the winter hut and let their summer hut to the cadet for three rubles a month. Olenin had something to eat and went to sleep. Towards evening he woke up, washed and made himself tidy, dined, and having lit a cigarette sat down by the window that looked onto the street. It was cooler. The slanting shadow of the hut with its ornamental gables fell across the dusty road and even bent upwards at the base of the wall of the house opposite. The steep reed-thatched roof of that house shone in the rays of the setting sun. The air grew fresher. Everything was peaceful in the village. The soldiers had settled down and become quiet. The herds had not yet been driven home and the people had not returned from their work.

Olenin's lodging was situated almost at the end of the village. At rare intervals, from somewhere far beyond the Terek in those parts whence Olenin had just come (the Chechen or the Kumytsk plain), came muffled sounds of firing. Olenin was feeling very well contented after three months of bivouac life. His newly washed face was fresh and his powerful body clean (an unaccustomed sensation after the campaign) and in all his rested limbs he was conscious of a feeling of tranquillity and strength. His mind, too, felt fresh and clear. He thought of the campaign and of past dangers. He remembered that he had faced them no worse than other men, and that he was accepted as a comrade among valiant Caucasians. His Moscow recollections were left behind Heaven knows how far! The old life was wiped out and a quite new life had begun in which there were as yet no mistakes. Here as a new man among new men he could gain a new and good reputation. He was conscious of a youthful and unreasoning joy of life. Looking now out of the window at the boys spinning their tops in the shadow of the house, now round his neat new lodging, he thought how pleasantly he would settle down to this new Cossack village life. Now and then he glanced at the mountains and the blue sky, and an appreciation of the solemn grandeur of nature mingled with his reminiscences and dreams. His new life had begun, not as he imagined it would when he left Moscow, but unexpectedly well. 'The mountains, the mountains, the mountains!' they permeated all his thoughts and feelings.

'He's kissed his dog and licked the jug! . . . Daddy Eroshka has kissed his dog!' suddenly the little Cossacks who had been spinning their tops under the window shouted, looking towards the side street. 'He's drunk his bitch, and his dagger!' shouted the boys, crowding together and stepping backwards.

These shouts were addressed to Daddy Eroshka, who with his gun on his shoulder and some pheasants hanging at his girdle was returning from his shooting expedition.

'I have done wrong, lads, I have!' he said, vigorously swinging his arms and looking up at the windows on both sides of the street. 'I have drunk the bitch; it was wrong,' he repeated, evidently vexed but pretending not to care.

Olenin was surprised by the boys' behavior towards the old hunter, but was still more struck by the expressive, intelligent face and the powerful build of the man whom they called Daddy Eroshka.

'Here Daddy, here Cossack!' he called. 'Come here!'

The old man looked into the window and stopped.

'Good evening, good man,' he said, lifting his little cap off his cropped head.

'Good evening, good man,' replied Olenin. 'What is it the youngsters are shouting at you?'

Daddy Eroshka came up to the window. 'Why, they're teasing the old man. No matter, I like it. Let them joke about their old daddy,' he said with those firm musical intonations with which old and venerable people speak. 'Are you an army commander?' he added.

'No, I am a cadet. But where did you kill those pheasants?' asked Olenin.

'I dispatched these three hens in the forest,' answered the old man, turning his broad back towards the window to show the hen pheasants which were hanging with their heads tucked into his belt and staining his coat with blood. 'Haven't you seen any?' he asked. 'Take a brace if you like! Here you are,' and he handed two of the pheasants in at the window. 'Are you a sportsman yourself?' he asked.

'I am. During the campaign I killed four myself.'

'Four? What a lot!' said the old man sarcastically. 'And are you a drinker? Do you drink *chikhir*?'

'Why not? I like a drink.'

'Ah, I see you are a trump! We shall be *kunaks*, you and I,' said Daddy Eroshka.

'Step in,' said Olenin. 'We'll have a drop of *chikhir*.'

'I might as well,' said the old man, 'but take the pheasants.' The old man's face showed that he liked the cadet. He had seen at once that he could get free drinks from him, and that therefore it would be all right to give him a brace of pheasants.

Soon Daddy Eroshka's figure appeared in the doorway of the hut, and it was only then that Olenin became fully conscious of the enormous size and sturdy build of this man, whose red-brown face with its perfectly white broad beard was all furrowed by deep lines produced by age and toil. For an old man, the muscles of his legs, arms, and shoulders were quite exceptionally large and prominent. There were deep scars on his head under the short-cropped hair. His thick sinewy neck was covered with deep intersecting folds like a bull's. His horny hands were bruised and scratched. He stepped lightly and easily over the threshold, unslung his gun and placed it in a corner, and casting a rapid glance round the room noted the value of the goods and chattels deposited in the hut, and with out-turned toes stepped softly, in his sandals of raw hide, into the middle of the room. He brought with him a penetrating but not unpleasant smell of *chikhir* wine, vodka, gunpowder, and congealed blood.

Daddy Eroshka bowed down before the icons, smoothed his beard, and approaching Olenin held out his thick brown hand. '*Koshkildy*,' said he; That is Tartar for "Good-day" – "Peace be unto you", it means in their tongue.'

'*Koshkildy*, I know,' answered Olenin, shaking hands.

'Eh, but you don't, you won't know the right order! Fool!' said Daddy Eroshka, shaking his head reproachfully. 'If anyone says "*Koshkildy*" to you, you must say "*Allah rasi bo sun*", that is, "God save you." That's the way, my dear fellow, and not "*Koshkildy*". But I'll teach you all about it. We had a fellow here, Elias Mosevich, one of your Russians, he and I were *kunaks*. He was a trump, a drunkard, a thief, a sportsman – and what a sportsman! I taught him everything.'

'And what will you teach me?' asked Olenin, who was becoming more and more interested in the old man.

'I'll take you hunting and teach you to fish. I'll show you Chechens and find a girl for you, if you like – even that! That's the sort I am! I'm a wag!' – and the old man laughed. 'I'll sit down. I'm tired. *Karga*?' he added inquiringly.

'And what does "*Karga*" mean?' asked Olenin.

'Why, that means "All right" in Georgian. But I say it just so. It is a way I have, it's my favourite word. *Karga*, *Karga*. I say it just so; in fun I mean. Well, lad, won't you order the *chikhir*? You've got an orderly, haven't you? Hey, Ivan!' shouted the old man. 'All your soldiers are Ivans. Is yours Ivan?'

'True enough, his name is Ivan – Vanyusha. Here Vanyusha! Please get some *chikhir* from our landlady and bring it here.'

'Ivan or Vanyusha, that's all one. Why are all your soldiers Ivans? Ivan, old fellow,' said the old man, 'you tell them to give you some from the barrel they have begun. They have the best *chikhir* in the village. But don't give more than thirty kopeks for the quart, mind, because that witch would be only too glad . . . Our people are anathema people; stupid people,' Daddy Eroshka continued in a confidential tone after Vanyusha had gone out. 'They do not look upon you as on men, you are worse than a Tartar in their eyes. "Worldly Russians" they say. But as for me, though you are a soldier you are still a man, and have a soul in you. Isn't that right? Elias Mosevich was a soldier, yet what a treasure of a man he was! Isn't that so, my dear fellow?

That's why our people don't like me; but I don't care! I'm a merry fellow, and I like everybody. I'm Eroshka; yes, my dear fellow.'

And the old Cossack patted the young man affectionately on the shoulder.

Chapter 12

Vanyusha, who meanwhile had finished his housekeeping arrangements and had even been shaved by the company's barber and had pulled his trousers out of his high boots as a sign that the company was stationed in comfortable quarters, was in excellent spirits. He looked attentively but not benevolently at Eroshka, as at a wild beast he had never seen before, shook his head at the floor which the old man had dirtied and, having taken two bottles from under a bench, went to the landlady.

'Good evening, kind people,' he said, having made up his mind to be very gentle. 'My master has sent me to get some *chikhir*. Will you draw some for me, good folk?'

The old woman gave no answer. The girl, who was arranging the kerchief on her head before a little Tartar mirror, looked round at Vanyusha in silence.

'I'll pay money for it, honoured people,' said Vanyusha, jingling the coppers in his pocket. 'Be kind to us and we, too, will be kind to you,' he added.

'How much?' asked the old woman abruptly.

'A quart.'

'Go, my own, draw some for them,' said Granny Ulitka to her daughter. 'Take it from the cask that's begun, my precious.'

The girl took the keys and a decanter and went out of the hut with Vanyusha.

'Tell me, who is that young woman?' asked Olenin, pointing to Maryanka, who was passing the window. The old man winked and nudged the young man with his elbow.

'Wait a bit,' said he and reached out of the window. 'Khm,' he coughed, and bellowed, 'Maryanka dear. Hallo, Maryanka, my girlie, won't you love me, darling? I'm a wag,' he added in a whisper to Olenin. The girl, not turning her head and swinging her arms regularly and vigorously, passed the window with the peculiarly smart and bold gait of a Cossack woman and only turned her dark shaded eyes slowly towards the old man.

'Love me and you'll be happy,' shouted Eroshka, winking, and he looked questioningly at the cadet.

'I'm a fine fellow, I'm a wag!' he added. 'She's a regular queen, that girl. Eh?'

'She is lovely,' said Olenin. 'Call her here!'

'No, no,' said the old man. 'For that one a match is being arranged with Lukashka, Luke, a fine Cossack, a brave, who killed an *abrek* the other day. I'll find you a better one. I'll find you one that will be all dressed up in silk and silver. Once I've said it I'll do it. I'll get you a regular beauty!'

'You, an old man – and say such things,' replied Olenin. 'Why, it's a sin!'

'A sin? Where's the sin?' said the old man emphatically. 'A sin to look at a nice girl? A sin to have some fun with her? Or is it a sin to love her? Is that so in your parts? . . . No, my dear fellow, it's not a sin, it's salvation! God made you and God made the girl too. He made it all; so it is no sin to look at a nice girl. That's what she was made for; to be loved and to give joy. That's how I judge it, my good fellow.'

Having crossed the yard and entered a cool dark storeroom filled with barrels, Maryanka went up to one of them and repeating the usual prayer plunged a dipper into it. Vanyusha standing in the doorway smiled as he looked at her. He thought it very funny that she had only a smock on, close-fitting behind and tucked up in front, and still funnier that she wore a necklace of silver coins. He thought this quite un-Russian and that they would all laugh in the serfs' quarters at home if they saw a girl like that. '*La fille comme c'est très bien,* for a change,' he thought. 'I'll tell that to my master.'

'What are you standing in the light for, you devil!' the girl suddenly shouted. 'Why don't you pass me the decanter!'

Having filled the decanter with cool red wine, Maryanka handed it to Vanyusha.

'Give the money to Mother,' she said, pushing away the hand in which he held the money.

Vanyusha laughed.

'Why are you so cross, little dear?' he said good-naturedly, irresolutely shuffling with his feet while the girl was covering the barrel.

She began to laugh.

'And you! Are you kind?'

'We, my master and I, are very kind,' Vanyusha answered decidedly. 'We are so kind that wherever we have stayed our hosts were always very grateful. It's because he's generous.'

The girl stood listening.

'And is your master married?' she asked.

'No. The master is young and unmarried, because noble gentlemen can never marry young,' said Vanyusha didactically.

'A likely thing! See what a fed-up buffalo he is – and too young to marry! Is he the chief of you all?' she asked.

'My master is a cadet; that means he's not yet an officer, but he's more important than a general – he's an important man! Because not only our colonel, but the Tsar himself, knows him,' proudly explained Vanyusha. 'We are not like those other beggars in the line regiment, and our papa himself was a Senator. He had more than a thousand serfs, all his own, and they send us a thousand rubles at a time. That's why everyone likes us. Another may be a captain but have no money. What's the use of that?'

'Go away. I'll lock up,' said the girl, interrupting him.

Vanyusha brought Olenin the wine and announced that '*La fille c'est très joulie*,' and, laughing stupidly, at once went out.

Chapter 13

Meanwhile the tattoo had sounded in the village square. The people had returned from their work. The herd lowed as in clouds of golden dust it crowded at the village gate. The girls and the women hurried through the streets and yards, turning in their cattle. The sun had quite hidden itself behind the distant snowy peaks. One pale bluish shadow spread over land and sky. Above the darkened gardens stars just discernible were kindling, and the sounds were gradually hushed in the village. The cattle having been attended to and left for the night, the women came out and gathered at the corners of the streets and, cracking sunflower seeds with their teeth, settled down on the earthen embankments of the houses. Later on Maryanka, having finished milking the buffalo and the other two cows, also joined one of these groups.

The group consisted of several women and girls and one old Cossack man.

They were talking about the *abrek* who had been killed.

The Cossack was narrating and the women questioning him.

'I expect he'll get a handsome reward,' said one of the women.

'Of course. It's said that they'll send him a cross.'

'Mosev did try to wrong him. Took the gun away from him, but the authorities at Kizlyar heard of it.'

'A mean creature that Mosev is!'

'They say Lukashka has come home,' remarked one of the girls.

'He and Nazarka are merry-making at Yamka's.' (Yamka was an unmarried, disreputable Cossack woman who kept an illicit pot-house.) 'I heard say they had drunk half a pailful.'

'What luck that Snatcher has,' somebody remarked. 'A real snatcher. But there's no denying he's a fine lad, smart enough for anything, a right-minded lad! His father was just such another, Daddy Kiryak was: he takes after his father. When he was killed the whole village howled. Look, there they are,' added the speaker, pointing to the Cossacks who were coming down the street towards them.

'And Ergushov has managed to come along with them too! The drunkard!'

Lukashka, Nazarka, and Ergushov, having emptied half a pail of vodka, were coming towards the girls. The faces of all three, but especially that of the old Cossack, were redder than usual. Ergushov was reeling and kept laughing and nudging Nazarka in the ribs.

'Why are you not singing?' he shouted to the girls. 'Sing to our merry-making, I tell you!'

They were welcomed with the words, 'Had a good day? Had a good day?'

'Why sing? It's not a holiday,' said one of the women. 'You're tight, so you go and sing.'

Ergushov roared with laughter and nudged Nazarka. 'You'd better sing. And I'll begin too. I'm clever, I tell you.'

'Are you asleep, fair ones?' said Nazarka. 'We've come from the cordon to drink your health. We've already drunk Lukashka's health.'

Lukashka, when he reached the group, slowly raised his cap and stopped in front of the girls. His broad cheekbones and neck were red. He stood and spoke softly and sedately, but in his tranquillity and sedateness there was more of animation and strength than in all Nazarka's loquacity and bustle. He reminded one of a playful colt that with a snort and a flourish of its tail suddenly stops short and stands as though nailed to the ground with all four feet. Lukashka stood quietly in front of the girls, his eyes laughed, and he spoke but little as he glanced now at his drunken companions and now at the girls. When Maryanka joined the group he raised his cap with a firm deliberate movement, moved out of her way and then stepped in front of her with one foot a little forward and with his thumbs in his belt, fingering his dagger. Maryanka answered his greeting with a leisurely bow of her head, settled down on the earth-bank, and took some seeds out of the bosom of her smock. Lukashka, keeping his eyes fixed on Maryanka, slowly cracked seeds and spat out the shells. All were quiet when Maryanka joined the group.

'Have you come for long?' asked a woman, breaking the silence.

'Till tomorrow morning,' quietly replied Lukashka.

'Well, God grant you get something good,' said the Cossack; 'I'm glad of it, as I've just been saying.'

'And I say so too,' put in the tipsy Ergushov, laughing. 'What a lot of visitors have come,' he added, pointing to a soldier who was passing by. 'The soldiers' vodka is good – I like it.'

'They've sent three of the devils to us,' said one of the women. 'Grandad went to the village Elders, but they say nothing can be done.'

'Ah, ha! Have you met with trouble?' said Ergushov.

'I expect they have smoked you out with their tobacco?' asked another woman. 'Smoke as much as you like in the yard, I say, but we won't allow it inside the hut. Not if the Elder himself comes, I won't allow it. Besides, they may rob you. He's not quartered any of them on himself, no fear, that devil's son of an Elder.'

'You don't like it?' Ergushov began again.

'And I've also heard say that the girls will have to make the soldiers' beds and offer them *chikhir* and honey,' said Nazarka, putting one foot forward and tilting his cap like Lukashka.

Ergushov burst into a roar of laughter, and seizing the girl nearest to him, he embraced her. 'I tell you true.'

'Now then, you black pitch!' squealed the girl, 'I'll tell your old woman.'

'Tell her,' shouted he. 'That's quite right what Nazarka says; a circular has been sent round. He can read, you know. Quite true!' And he began embracing the next girl.

'What are you up to, you beast?' squealed the rosy, round-faced Ustenka, laughing and lifting her arm to hit him.

The Cossack stepped aside and nearly fell.

'There, they say girls have no strength, and you nearly killed me.'

'Get away, you black pitch, what devil has brought you from the cordon?' said Ustenka, and turning away from him she again burst out laughing. 'You were asleep and missed the *abrek*, didn't you? Suppose he had done for you it would have been all the better.'

'You'd have howled, I expect,' said Nazarka, laughing.

'Howled! A likely thing.'

'Just look, she doesn't care. She'd howl, Nazarka, eh? Would she?' said Ergushov.

Lukashka all this time had stood silently looking at Maryanka. His gaze evidently confused the girl.

'Well, Maryanka! I hear they've quartered one of the chiefs on you?' he said, drawing nearer.

Maryanka, as was her wont, waited before she replied, and slowly raising her eyes looked at the Cossack. Lukashka's eyes were laughing as if something special, apart from what was said, was taking place between himself and the girl.

'Yes, it's all right for them as they have two huts,' replied an old woman on Maryanka's behalf, 'but at Fomushkin's now they also have one of the chiefs quartered on them and they say one whole corner is packed full with his things, and the family have no room left. Was such a thing ever heard of as that they should turn a whole horde loose in the village?' she said. 'And what the plague are they going to do here?'

'I've heard say they'll build a bridge across the Terek,' said one of the girls.

'And I've been told that they will dig a pit to put the girls in because they don't love the lads,' said Nazarka, approaching Ustenka; and he again made a whimsical gesture which set everybody laughing, and Ergushov, passing by Maryanka, who was next in turn, began to embrace an old woman.

'Why don't you hug Maryanka? You should do it to each in turn,' said Nazarka.

'No, my old one is sweeter,' shouted the Cossack, kissing the struggling old woman.

'You'll throttle me,' she screamed, laughing.

The tramp of regular footsteps at the other end of the street interrupted their laughter. Three soldiers in their cloaks, with their muskets on their shoulders, were marching in step to relieve guard by the ammunition wagon.

The corporal, an old cavalry man, looked angrily at the Cossacks and led his men straight along the road where Lukashka and Nazarka were standing, so that they should have to get out of the way. Nazarka moved, but Lukashka only screwed up his eyes and turned his broad back without moving from his place.

'People are standing here, so you go round,' he muttered, half turning his head and tossing it contemptuously in the direction of the soldiers.

The soldiers passed by in silence, keeping step regularly along the dusty road.

Maryanka began laughing and all the other girls chimed in.

'What swells!' said Nazarka, 'Just like long-skirted choristers,' and he walked a few steps down the road imitating the soldiers.

Again everyone broke into peals of laughter.

Lukashka came slowly up to Maryanka.

'And where have you put up the chief?' he asked.

Maryanka thought for a moment.

'We've let him have the new hut,' she said.

'And is he old or young,' asked Lukashka, sitting down beside her.

'Do you think I've asked?' answered the girl. 'I went to get him some *chikhir* and saw him sitting at the window with Daddy Eroshka. Red-headed he seemed. They've brought a whole cart-load of things.'

And she dropped her eyes.

'Oh, how glad I am that I got leave from the cordon!' said Lukashka, moving closer to the girl and looking straight in her eyes all the time.

'And have you come for long?' asked Maryanka, smiling slightly.

'Till the morning. Give me some sunflower seeds,' he said, holding out his hand.

Maryanka now smiled outright and unfastened the neckband of her smock.

'Don't take them all,' she said.

'Really I felt so dull all the time without you, I swear I did,' he said in a calm, restrained whisper, helping himself to some seeds out of the bosom of the girl's smock, and stooping still closer over her he continued with laughing eyes to talk to her in low tones.

'I won't come, I tell you,' Maryanka suddenly said aloud, leaning away from him.

'No really . . . what I wanted to say to you, . . . ' whispered Lukashka. 'By the Heavens! Do come!'

Maryanka shook her head, but did so with a smile.

'Nursey Maryanka! Hallo Nursey! Mammy is calling! Supper time!' shouted Maryanka's little brother, running towards the group.

'I'm coming,' replied the girl. 'Go, my dear, go alone – I'll come in a minute.'

Lukashka rose and raised his cap.

'I expect I had better go home too, that will be best,' he said, trying to appear unconcerned but hardly able to repress a smile, and he disappeared behind the corner of the house.

Meanwhile night had entirely enveloped the village. Bright stars were scattered over the dark sky. The streets became dark and empty. Nazarka remained with the women on the earth-bank and their laughter was still heard, but Lukashka, having slowly moved away from the girls, crouched down like a cat and then suddenly started running lightly, holding his dagger to steady it: not homeward, however, but towards the cornet's house. Having passed two streets he turned into a lane and lifting the skirt of his coat sat down on the ground in the shadow of a fence. 'A regular cornet's daughter!' he thought about Maryanka. 'Won't even have a lark – the devil! But just wait a bit.'

The approaching footsteps of a woman attracted his attention. He began listening, and laughed all by himself. Maryanka with bowed head, striking the pales of the fences with a switch, was walking with rapid regular strides straight towards him. Lukashka rose. Maryanka started and stopped.

'What an accursed devil! You frightened me! So you have not gone home?' she said, and laughed aloud.

Lukashka put one arm round her and with the other hand raised her face. 'What I wanted to tell you, by Heaven!' his voice trembled and broke.

'What are you talking of, at night time!' answered Maryanka. 'Mother is waiting for me, and you'd better go to your sweetheart.'

And freeing herself from his arms she ran away a few steps. When she had reached the wattle fence of her home she stopped and turned to the Cossack who was running beside her and still trying to persuade her to stay a while with him.

'Well, what do you want to say, midnight-gadabout?' and she again began laughing.

'Don't laugh at me, Maryanka! By the Heaven! Well, what if I have a sweetheart? May the devil take her! Only say the word and now I'll love you – I'll do anything you wish. Here they are!' and he jingled the money in his pocket. 'Now we can live splendidly. Others have pleasures, and I? I get no pleasure from you, Maryanka dear!'

The girl did not answer. She stood before him breaking her switch into little bits with a rapid movement of her fingers.

Lukashka suddenly clenched his teeth and fists.

'And why keep waiting and waiting? Don't I love you, darling? You can do what you like with me,' said he suddenly, frowning angrily and seizing both her hands.

The calm expression of Maryanka's face and voice did not change.

'Don't bluster, Lukashka, but listen to me,' she answered, not pulling away her hands but holding the Cossack at arm's length. 'It's true I am a girl, but you listen to me! It does not depend on me, but if you love me I'll tell you this. Let go my hands, I'll tell you without. – I'll marry you, but you'll never get any nonsense from me,' said Maryanka without turning her face.

'What, you'll marry me? Marriage does not depend on us. Love me yourself, Maryanka dear,' said Lukashka, from sullen and furious becoming again gentle, submissive, and tender, and smiling as he looked closely into her eyes.

Maryanka clung to him and kissed him firmly on the lips.

'Brother dear!' she whispered, pressing him convulsively to her. Then, suddenly tearing herself away, she ran into the gate of her house without looking round.

In spite of the Cossack's entreaties to wait another minute to hear what he had to say, Maryanka did not stop.

'Go,' she cried, 'you'll be seen! I do believe that devil, our lodger, is walking about the yard.'

'Cornet's daughter,' thought Lukashka. 'She will marry me. Marriage is all very well, but you just love me!'

He found Nazarka at Yamka's house, and after having a spree with him went to Dunayka's house, where, in spite of her not being faithful to him, he spent the night.

Chapter 14

It was quite true that Olenin had been walking about the yard when Maryanka entered the gate, and had heard her say, 'That devil, our lodger, is walking about.' He had spent that evening with Daddy Eroshka in the porch of his new lodging. He had had a table, a samovar, wine, and a candle brought out, and over a cup of tea and a cigar he listened to the tales the old man told seated on the threshold at his feet. Though the air was still, the candle dripped and flickered: now lighting up the post of the porch, now the table and crockery, now the cropped white head of the old man. Moths circled round the flame and, shedding the dust of their wings, fluttered on the table and in the glasses, flew into the candle flame, and disappeared in the black space beyond. Olenin and Eroshka had emptied five bottles of *chikhir*. Eroshka filled the glasses every time, offering one to Olenin, drinking his health, and talking untiringly. He told of Cossack life in the old days: of his father, 'The Broad', who alone had carried on his back a boar's carcass weighing three hundredweight, and drank two pails of *chikhir* at one sitting. He told of his own days and his chum Girchik, with whom during the plague he used to smuggle felt cloaks across the Terek. He told how one morning he had killed two deer, and about his 'little soul' who used to run to him at the cordon at night. He told all this so eloquently and picturesquely that Olenin did not notice how time passed. 'Ah yes, my dear fellow, you did not know me in my golden days; then I'd have shown you things. Today it's "Eroshka licks the jug", but then Eroshka was famous in the whole regiment. Whose was the finest horse? Who had a Gurda sword? To whom should one go to get a drink? With whom go on the spree? Who should be sent to the mountains to kill Ahmet Khan? Why, always Eroshka! Whom did the girls love? Always Eroshka had to answer for it. Because I was a real brave: a drinker, a thief (I used to seize herds of horses in the mountains), a singer; I was a master of every art! There are no Cossacks like that nowadays. It's disgusting to look at them. When they're that high [Eroshka held his hand three feet from the ground] they put on idiotic boots and keep looking at them – that's all the pleasure they know. Or they'll drink themselves foolish, not like men but all wrong. And who was I? I was Eroshka, the thief; they knew me not only in this village but up in the mountains. Tartar princes, my *kunaks*, used to come to see me! I used to be everybody's *kunak*. If he was a Tartar – with a Tartar; an Armenian – with an Armenian; a soldier – with a soldier; an officer – with an officer! I didn't care as long as he was a drinker. He says you should cleanse yourself from intercourse with the world, not drink with soldiers, not eat with a Tartar.'

'Who says all that?' asked Olenin.

'Why, our teacher! But listen to a Mullah or a Tartar Cadi. He says, "You unbelieving Giaours, why do you eat pig?" That shows that everyone has his own law. But I think it's all one. God has made everything for the joy of man. There is no sin in any of it. Take example from an animal. It lives in the Tartar's reeds or in ours. Wherever it happens to go, there is its home! Whatever God gives it, that it eats! But our people say we have to lick red-hot plates in hell for that. And I think it's all a fraud,' he added after a pause.

'What is a fraud?' asked Olenin.

'Why, what the preachers say. We had an army captain in Chervlena who was my *kunak*: a fine fellow just like me. He was killed in Chechnya. Well, he used to say that the preachers invent all that out of their own heads. "When you die the grass will grow on your grave and that's all!"' The old man laughed. 'He was a desperate fellow.'

'And how old are you?' asked Olenin.

'The Lord only knows! I must be about seventy. When a Tsaritsa reigned in Russia I was no longer very small. So you can reckon it out. I must be seventy.'

'Yes you must, but you are still a fine fellow.'

'Well, thank Heaven I am healthy, quite healthy, except that a woman, a witch, has harmed me . . . .'

'How?'

'Oh, just harmed me.'

'And so when you die the grass will grow?' repeated Olenin.

Eroshka evidently did not wish to express his thought clearly. He was silent for a while.

'And what did you think? Drink!' he shouted suddenly, smiling and handing Olenin some wine.

Chapter 15

'Well, what was I saying?' he continued, trying to remember. 'Yes, that's the sort of man I am. I am a hunter. There is no hunter to equal me in the whole army. I will find and show you any animal and any bird, and what and where. I know it all! I have dogs, and two guns, and nets, and a screen and a hawk. I have everything, thank the Lord! If you are not bragging but are a real sportsman, I'll show you everything. Do you know what a man I am? When I have found a track – I know the animal. I know where he will lie down and where he'll drink or wallow. I make myself a perch and sit there all night watching. What's the good of staying at home? One only gets into mischief, gets drunk. And here women come and chatter, and boys shout at me – enough to drive one mad. It's a different matter when you go out at nightfall, choose yourself a place, press down the reeds and sit there and stay waiting, like a jolly fellow. One knows everything that goes on in the woods. One looks up at the sky: the stars move, you look at them and find out from them how the time goes. One looks round – the wood is rustling; one goes on waiting, now there comes a crackling – a boar comes to rub himself; one listens to hear the young eaglets screech and then the cocks give voice in the village, or the geese. When you hear the geese you know it is not yet midnight. And I know all about it! Or when a gun is fired somewhere far away, thoughts come to me. One thinks, who is that firing? Is it another Cossack like myself who has been watching for some animal? And has he killed it? Or only wounded it so that now the poor thing goes through the reeds smearing them with its blood all for nothing? I don't like that! Oh, how I dislike it! Why injure a beast? You fool, you fool! Or one thinks, "Maybe an *abrek* has killed some silly little Cossack." All this passes through one's mind. And once as I sat watching by the river I saw a cradle floating down. It was sound except for one corner which was broken off. Thoughts did come that time! I thought some of your soldiers, the devils, must have got into a Tartar village and seized the Chechen women, and one of the devils has killed the little one: taken it by its legs, and hit its head against a wall. Don't they do such things? Ah! men have no souls! And thoughts came to me that filled me with pity. I thought: they've thrown away the cradle and driven the wife out, and her brave has taken his gun and come across to our side to rob us. One watches and thinks. And when one hears a litter breaking through the thicket, something begins to knock inside one. Dear one, come this way! "They'll scent me," one thinks; and one sits and does not stir while one's heart goes dun! dun! dun! and simply lifts you. Once this spring a fine litter came near me, I saw something black. "In the name of the Father and of the Son," and I was just about to fire when she grunts to her pigs: "Danger, children," she says, "there's a man here," and off they all ran, breaking through the bushes. And she had been so close I could almost have bitten her.'

'How could a sow tell her brood that a man was there?' asked Olenin.

'What do you think? You think the beast's a fool? No, he is wiser than a man though you do call him a pig! He knows everything. Take this for instance. A man will pass along your track and not notice it; but a pig as soon as it gets onto your track turns and runs at once: that shows there is wisdom in him, since he scents your smell and you don't. And there is this to be said too: you wish to kill it and it wishes to go about the woods alive. You have one law and it has another. It is a pig, but it is no worse than you – it too is God's creature. Ah, dear! Man is foolish, foolish, foolish!' The old man repeated this several times and then, letting his head drop, he sat thinking.

Olenin also became thoughtful, and descending from the porch with his hands behind his back began pacing up and down the yard.

Eroshka, rousing himself, raised his head and began gazing intently at the moths circling round the flickering flame of the candle and burning themselves in it.

'Fool, fool!' he said. 'Where are you flying to? Fool, fool!' He rose and with his thick fingers began to drive away the moths.

'You'll burn, little fool! Fly this way, there's plenty of room.' He spoke tenderly, trying to catch them delicately by their wings with his thick ringers and then letting them fly again. 'You are killing yourself and I am sorry for you!'

He sat a long time chattering and sipping out of the bottle. Olenin paced up and down the yard. Suddenly he was struck by the sound of whispering outside the gate. Involuntarily holding his breath, he heard a woman's laughter, a man's voice, and the sound of a kiss. Intentionally rustling the grass under his feet he crossed to the opposite side of the yard, but after a while the wattle fence creaked. A Cossack in a dark Circassian coat and a white sheepskin cap passed along the other side of the fence (it was Luke), and a tall woman with a white kerchief on her head went past Olenin. 'You and I have nothing to do with one another' was what Maryanka's firm step gave him to understand. He followed her with his eyes to the porch of the hut, and he even saw her through the window take off her kerchief and sit down. And suddenly a feeling of lonely depression and some vague longings and hopes, and envy of someone or other, overcame the young man's soul.

The last lights had been put out in the huts. The last sounds had died away in the village. The wattle fences and the cattle gleaming white in the yards, the roofs of the houses and the stately poplars, all seemed to be sleeping the labourers' healthy peaceful sleep. Only the incessant ringing voices of frogs from the damp distance reached the young man. In the east the stars were growing fewer and fewer and seemed to be melting in the increasing light, but overhead they were denser and deeper than before. The old man was dozing with his head on his hand. A cock crowed in the yard opposite, but Olenin still paced up and down thinking of something. The sound of a song sung by several voices reached him and he stepped up to the fence and listened. The voices of several young Cossacks carolled a merry song, and one voice was distinguishable among them all by its firm strength.

'Do you know who is singing there?' said the old man, rousing himself. 'It is the Brave, Lukashka. He has killed a Chechen and now he rejoices. And what is there to rejoice at? . . . The fool, the fool!'

'And have you ever killed people?' asked Olenin.

'You devil!' shouted the old man. 'What are you asking? One must not talk so. It is a serious thing to destroy a human being . . . Ah, a very serious thing! Goodbye, my dear fellow. I've eaten my fill and am drunk,' he said rising. 'Shall I come tomorrow to go shooting?'

'Yes, come!'

'Mind, get up early; if you oversleep you will be fined!'

'Never fear, I'll be up before you,' answered Olenin.

The old man left. The song ceased, but one could hear footsteps and merry talk. A little later the singing broke out again but farther away, and Eroshka's loud voice chimed in with the other. 'What people, what a life!' thought Olenin with a sigh as he returned alone to his hut.

Chapter 16

Daddy Eroshka was a superannuated and solitary Cossack: twenty years ago his wife had gone over to the Orthodox Church and run away from him and married a Russian sergeant-major, and he had no children. He was not bragging when he spoke of himself as having been the boldest dare-devil in the village when he was young. Everybody in the regiment knew of his old-time prowess. The death of more than one Russian, as well as Chechen, lay on his conscience. He used to go plundering in the mountains, and robbed the Russians too; and he had twice been in prison. The greater part of his life was spent in the forests, hunting. There he lived for days on a crust of bread and drank nothing but water. But on the other hand, when he was in the village he made merry from morning to night. After leaving Olenin he slept for a couple of hours and awoke before it was light. He lay on his bed thinking of the man he had become acquainted with the evening before. Olenin's 'simplicity' (simplicity in the sense of not grudging him a drink) pleased him very much, and so did Olenin himself. He wondered why the Russians were all 'simple' and so rich, and why they were educated, and yet knew nothing. He pondered on these questions and also considered what he might get out of Olenin.

Daddy Eroshka's hut was of a good size and not old, but the absence of a woman was very noticeable in it. Contrary to the usual cleanliness of the Cossacks, the whole of this hut was filthy and exceedingly untidy. A blood-stained coat had been thrown on the table, half a dough-cake lay beside a plucked and mangled crow with which to feed the hawk. Sandals of raw hide, a gun, a dagger, a little bag, wet clothes, and sundry rags lay scattered on the benches. In a corner stood a tub with stinking water, in which another pair of sandals were being steeped, and nearby was a gun and a hunting-screen. On the floor a net had been thrown down and several dead pheasants lay there, while a hen tied by its leg was walking about near the table pecking among the dirt. In the unheated oven stood a broken pot with some kind of milky liquid. On the top of the oven a falcon was screeching and trying to break the cord by which it was tied, and a moulting hawk sat quietly on the edge of the oven, looking askance at the hen and occasionally bowing its head to right and left. Daddy Eroshka himself, in his shirt, lay on his back on a short bed rigged up between the wall and the oven, with his strong legs raised and his feet on the oven. He was picking with his thick fingers at the scratches left on his hands by the hawk, which he was accustomed to carry without wearing gloves. The whole room, especially near the old man, was filled with that strong but not unpleasant mixture of smells that he always carried about with him.

'*Uyde-ma*, Daddy?' (Is Daddy in?) came through the window in a sharp voice, which he at once recognized as Lukashka's.

'*Uyde, Uyde, Uyde.* I am in!' shouted the old man. 'Come in, neighbour Mark, Luke Mark. Come to see Daddy? On your way to the cordon?'

At the sound of his master's shout the hawk flapped his wings and pulled at his cord.

The old man was fond of Lukashka, who was the only man he excepted from his general contempt for the younger generation of Cossacks. Besides that, Lukashka and his mother, as near neighbours, often gave the old man wine, clotted cream, and other home produce which Eroshka did not possess. Daddy Eroshka, who all his life had allowed himself to get carried away, always explained his infatuations from a practical point of view. 'Well, why not?' he used to say to himself. 'I'll give them some fresh meat, or a bird, and they won't forget Daddy: they'll sometimes bring a cake or a piece of pie.'

'Good morning. Mark! I am glad to see you,' shouted the old man cheerfully, and quickly putting down his bare feet he jumped off his bed and walked a step or two along the creaking floor, looked down at his out-turned toes, and suddenly, amused by the appearance of his feet, smiled, stamped with his bare heel on the ground, stamped again, and then performed a funny dance-step. 'That's clever, eh?' he asked, his small eyes glistening. Lukashka smiled faintly. 'Going back to the cordon?' asked the old man.

'I have brought the *chikhir* I promised you when we were at the cordon.'

'May Christ save you!' said the old man, and he took up the extremely wide trousers that were lying on the floor, and his *beshmet*, put them on, fastened a strap round his waist, poured some water from an earthenware pot over his hands, wiped them on the old trousers, smoothed his beard with a bit of comb, and stopped in front of Lukashka. 'Ready,' he said.

Lukashka fetched a cup, wiped it and filled it with wine, and then handed it to the old man.

'Your health! To the Father and the Son!' said the old man, accepting the wine with solemnity. 'May you have what you desire, may you always be a hero, and obtain a cross.'

Lukashka also drank a little after repeating a prayer, and then put the wine on the table. The old man rose and brought out some dried fish which he laid on the threshold, where he beat it with a stick to make it tender; then, having put it with his horny hands on a blue plate (his only one), he placed it on the table.

'I have all I want. I have victuals, thank God!' he said proudly. 'Well, and what of Mosev?' he added.

Lukashka, evidently wishing to know the old man's opinion, told him how the officer had taken the gun from him.

'Never mind the gun,' said the old man. 'If you don't give the gun you will get no reward.'

'But they say, Daddy, it's little reward a fellow gets when he is not yet a mounted Cossack; and the gun is a fine one, a Crimean, worth eighty rubles.'

'Eh, let it go! I had a dispute like that with an officer, he wanted my horse. "Give it me and you'll be made a cornet," says he. I wouldn't, and I got nothing!'

'Yes, Daddy, but you see I have to buy a horse; and they say you can't get one the other side of the river under fifty rubles, and mother has not yet sold our wine.'

'Eh, we didn't bother,' said the old man; 'when Daddy Eroshka was your age he already stole herds of horses from the Nogay folk and drove them across the Terek. Sometimes we'd give a fine horse for a quart of vodka or a cloak.'

'Why so cheap?' asked Lukashka.

'You're a fool, a fool, Mark,' said the old man contemptuously. 'Why, that's what one steals for, so as not to be stingy! As for you, I suppose you haven't so much as seen how one drives off a herd of horses? Why don't you speak?'

'What's one to say, Daddy?' replied Lukashka. 'It seems we are not the same sort of men as you were.'

'You're a fool. Mark, a fool! "Not the same sort of men!" ' retorted the old man, mimicking the Cossack lad. 'I was not that sort of Cossack at your age.'

'How's that?' asked Lukashka.

The old man shook his head contemptuously.

'Daddy Eroshka was simple; he did not grudge anything! That's why I was *kunak* with all Chechnya. A *kunak* would come to visit me and I'd make him drunk with vodka and make him happy and put him to sleep with me, and when I went to see him I'd take him a present – a dagger! That's the way it is done, and not as you do nowadays: the only amusement lads have now is to crack seeds and spit out the shells!' the old man finished contemptuously, imitating the present-day Cossacks cracking seeds and spitting out the shells.

'Yes, I know,' said Lukashka; 'that's so!'

'If you wish to be a fellow of the right sort, be a brave and not a peasant! Because even a peasant can buy a horse – pay the money and take the horse.'

They were silent for a while.

'Well, of course it's dull both in the village and the cordon, Daddy: but there's nowhere one can go for a bit of sport. All our fellows are so timid. Take Nazarka. The other day when we went to the Tartar village, Girey Khan asked us to come to Nogay to take some horses, but no one went, and how was I to go alone?'

'And what of Daddy? Do you think I am quite dried up? . . . No, I'm not dried up. Let me have a horse and I'll be off to Nogay at once.'

'What's the good of talking nonsense!' said Luke. 'You'd better tell me what to do about Girey Khan. He says, "Only bring horses to the Terek, and then even if you bring a whole stud I'll find a place for them." You see he's also a shaven-headed Tartar – how's one to believe him?'

'You may trust Girey Khan, all his kin were good people. His father too was a faithful *kunak*. But listen to Daddy and I won't teach you wrong: make him take an oath, then it will be all right. And if you go with him, have your pistol ready all the same, especially when it comes to dividing up the horses. I was nearly killed that way once by a Chechen. I wanted ten rubles from him for a horse. Trusting is all right, but don't go to sleep without a gun.'

Lukashka listened attentively to the old man. 'I say, Daddy, have you any stone-break grass?' he asked after a pause.

'No, I haven't any, but I'll teach you how to get it. You're a good lad and won't forget the old man . . . Shall I tell you?'

'Tell me, Daddy.'

'You know a tortoise? She's a devil, the tortoise is!'

'Of course I know!'

'Find her nest and fence it round so that she can't get in. Well, she'll come, go round it, and then will go off to find the stone-break grass and will bring some along and destroy the fence. Anyhow next morning come in good time, and where the fence is broken there you'll find the stone-break grass lying. Take it wherever you like. No lock and no bar will be able to stop you.'

'Have you tried it yourself, Daddy?'

'As for trying, I have not tried it, but I was told of it by good people. I used only one charm: that was to repeat the Pilgrim rhyme when mounting my horse; and no one ever killed me!'

'What is the Pilgrim rhyme, Daddy?'

'What, don't you know it? Oh, what people! You're right to ask Daddy. Well, listen, and repeat after me:

> Hail! Ye, living in Sion,
> This is your King,
> Our steeds we shall sit on,

Sophonia is weeping,
Zacharias is speaking,
Father Mandrych,
Mankind ever loving.'

'Kind ever loving,' the old man repeated. 'Do you know it now? Try it.'

Lukashka laughed.

'Come, Daddy, was it that that hindered their killing you? Maybe it just happened so!'

'You've grown too clever! You learn it all, and say it. It will do you no harm. Well, suppose you have sung "Pilgrim", it's all right,' and the old man himself began laughing. 'But just one thing, Luke, don't you go to Nogay!'

'Why?'

'Times have changed. You are not the same men. You've become rubbishy Cossacks! And see how many Russians have come down on us! You'd get to prison. Really, give it up! Just as if you could! Now Girchik and I, we used . . .'

And the old man was about to begin one of his endless tales, but Lukashka glanced at the window and interrupted him.

'It is quite light, Daddy. It's time to be off. Look us up some day.'

'May Christ save you! I'll go to the officer; I promised to take him out shooting. He seems a good fellow.'

Chapter 17

From Eroshka's hut Lukashka went home. As he returned, the dewy mists were rising from the ground and enveloped the village. In various places the cattle, though out of sight, could be heard beginning to stir. The cocks called to one another with increasing frequency and insistence. The air was becoming more transparent, and the villagers were getting up. Not till he was close to it could Lukashka discern the fence of his yard, all wet with dew, the porch of the hut, and the open shed. From the misty yard he heard the sound of an axe chopping wood. Lukashka entered the hut. His mother was up, and stood at the oven throwing wood into it. His little sister was still lying in bed asleep.

'Well, Lukashka, had enough holiday-making?' asked his mother softly. 'Where did you spend the night?'

'I was in the village,' replied her son reluctantly, reaching for his musket, which he drew from its cover and examined carefully.

His mother swayed her head.

Lukashka poured a little gunpowder onto the pan, took out a little bag from which he drew some empty cartridge cases which he began filling, carefully plugging each one with a ball wrapped in a rag. Then, having tested the loaded cartridges with his teeth and examined them, he put down the bag.

'I say, Mother, I told you the bags wanted mending; have they been done?' he asked.

'Oh yes, our dumb girl was mending something last night. Why, is it time for you to be going back to the cordon? I haven't seen anything of you!'

'Yes, as soon as I have got ready I shall have to go,' answered Lukashka, tying up the gunpowder. 'And where is our dumb one? Outside?'

'Chopping wood, I expect. She kept fretting for you. "I shall not see him at all!" she said. She puts her hand to her face like this, and clicks her tongue and presses her hands to her heart as much as to say – "sorry". Shall I call her in? She understood all about the *abrek*.'

'Call her,' said Lukashka. 'And I had some tallow there; bring it: I must grease my sword.'

The old woman went out, and a few minutes later Lukashka's dumb sister came up the creaking steps and entered the hut. She was six years older than her brother and would have been extremely like him had it not been for the dull and coarsely changeable expression (common to all deaf and dumb people) of her face. She wore a coarse smock all patched; her feet were bare and muddy, and on her head she had an old blue kerchief. Her neck, arms, and face were sinewy like a peasant's. Her clothing and her whole appearance indicated that she always did the hard work of a man. She brought in a heap of logs which she threw down by the oven. Then she went up to her brother, and with a joyful smile which made her whole face pucker up, touched him on the shoulder and began making rapid signs to him with her hands, her face, and whole body.

'That's right, that's right, Stepka is a trump!' answered the brother, nodding. 'She's fetched everything and mended everything, she's a trump! Here, take this for it!' He brought out two pieces of gingerbread from his pocket and gave them to her.

The dumb woman's face flushed with pleasure, and she began making a weird noise for joy. Having seized the gingerbread she began to gesticulate still more rapidly, frequently pointing in one direction and passing her thick finger over her eyebrows and her face. Lukashka understood her and kept nodding, while he smiled slightly. She was telling him to give the girls dainties, and that the girls liked him, and that one girl, Maryanka – the best of them all – loved him. She indicated Maryanka by rapidly pointing in the direction of Maryanka's home and to her own eyebrows and face, and by smacking her lips and swaying her head. 'Loves' she expressed by pressing her hands to her breast, kissing her hand, and pretending to embrace someone. Their mother returned to the hut, and seeing what her dumb daughter was saying, smiled and shook her head. Her daughter showed her the gingerbread and again made the noise which expressed joy.

'I told Ulitka the other day that I'd send a matchmaker to them,' said the mother. 'She took my words well.'

Lukashka looked silently at his mother.

'But how about selling the wine, mother? I need a horse.'

'I'll cart it when I have time. I must get the barrels ready,' said the mother, evidently not wishing her son to meddle in domestic matters. 'When you go out you'll find a bag in the passage. I borrowed from the neighbours and got something for you to take back to the cordon; or shall I put it in your saddle-bag?'

'All right,' answered Lukashka. 'And if Girey Khan should come across the river send him to me at the cordon, for I shan't get leave again for a long time now; I have some business with him.'

He began to get ready to start.

'I will send him on,' said the old women. 'It seems you have been spreeing at Yamka's all the time. I went out in the night to see the cattle, and I think it was your voice I heard singing songs.'

Lukashka did not reply, but went out into the passage, threw the bags over his shoulder, tucked up the skirts of his coat, took his musket, and then stopped for a moment on the threshold.

'Goodbye, mother!' he said as he closed the gate behind him. 'Send me a small barrel with Nazarka. I promised it to the lads, and he'll call for it.'

'May Christ keep you, Lukashka. God be with you! I'll send you some, some from the new barrel,' said the old woman, going to the fence: 'But listen,' she added, leaning over the fence.

The Cossack stopped.

'You've been making merry here; well, that's all right. Why should not a young man amuse himself? God has sent you luck and that's good. But now look out and mind, my son. Don't you go and get into mischief. Above all, satisfy your superiors: one has to! And I will sell the wine and find money for a horse and will arrange a match with the girl for you.'

'All right, all right!' answered her son, frowning.

His deaf sister shouted to attract his attention. She pointed to her head and the palm of her hand, to indicate the shaved head of a Chechen. Then she frowned, and pretending to aim with a gun, she shrieked and began rapidly humming and shaking her head. This meant that Lukashka should kill another Chechen.

Lukashka understood. He smiled, and shifting the gun at his back under his cloak, stepped lightly and rapidly, and soon disappeared in the thick mist.

The old woman, having stood a little while at the gate, returned silently to the hut and immediately began working.

Chapter 18

Lukasha returned to the cordon and at the same time Daddy Eroshka whistled to his dogs and, climbing over his wattle fence, went to Olenin's lodging, passing by the back of the houses (he disliked meeting women before going out hunting or shooting). He found Olenin still asleep, and even Vanyusha, though awake, was still in bed and looking round the room considering whether it was not time to get up, when Daddy Eroshka, gun on shoulder and in full hunter's trappings, opened the door.

'A cudgel!' he shouted in his deep voice. 'An alarm! The Chechens are upon us! Ivan! get the samovar ready for your master, and get up yourself – quick,' cried the old man. 'That's

our way, my good man! Why even the girls are already up! Look
out of the window. See, she's going for water and you're still
sleeping!'

Olenin awoke and jumped up, feeling fresh and lighthearted at
the sight of the old man and at the sound of his voice.

'Quick, Vanyusha, quick!' he cried.

'Is that the way you go hunting?' said the old man. 'Others are
having their breakfast and you are asleep! Lyam! Here!' he called to
his dog. 'Is your gun ready?' he shouted, as loud as if a whole
crowd were in the hut.

'Well, it's true I'm guilty, but it can't be helped! The powder,
Vanyusha, and the wads!' said Olenin.

'A fine!' shouted the old man.

'*Du tay voulay vou?*' asked Vanyusha, grinning.

'You're not one of us – your gabble is not like our speech, you
devil!' the old man shouted at Vanyusha, showing the stumps of
his teeth.

'A first offence must be forgiven,' said Olenin playfully, drawing
on his high boots.

'The first offence shall be forgiven,' answered Eroshka, 'but if
you oversleep another time you'll be fined a pail of *chikhir*. When
it gets warmer you won't find the deer.'

'And even if we do find him he is wiser than we are,' said
Olenin, repeating the words spoken by the old man the evening
before, 'and you can't deceive him!'

'Yes, laugh away! You kill one first, and then you may talk.
Now then, hurry up! Look, there's the master himself coming to
see you,' added Eroshka, looking out of the window. 'Just see how
he's got himself up. He's put on a new coat so that you should see
that he's an officer. Ah, these people, these people!'

Sure enough Vanyusha came in and announced that the master
of the house wished to see Olenin.

'*L'arjan!*' he remarked profoundly, to forewarn his master of
the meaning of this visitation. Following him, the master of the
house in a new Circassian coat with an officer's stripes on the
shoulders and with polished boots (quite exceptional among
Cossacks) entered the room, swaying from side to side, and
congratulated his lodger on his safe arrival.

The cornet, Elias Vasilich, was an educated Cossack. He had

been to Russia proper, was a regimental schoolteacher, and above all he was noble. He wished to appear noble, but one could not help feeling beneath his grotesque pretence of polish, his affectation, his self-confidence, and his absurd way of speaking, he was just the same as Daddy Eroshka. This could also be clearly seen by his sunburnt face and his hands and his red nose. Olenin asked him to sit down.

'Good morning, Father Elias Vasilich,' said Eroshka, rising with (or so it seemed to Olenin) an ironically low bow.

'Good morning, Daddy. So you're here already,' said the cornet, with a careless nod.

The cornet was a man of about forty, with a grey pointed beard, skinny and lean, but handsome and very fresh-looking for his age. Having come to see Olenin he was evidently afraid of being taken for an ordinary Cossack, and wanted to let Olenin feel his importance from the first.

'That's our Egyptian Nimrod,' he remarked, addressing Olenin and pointing to the old man with a self-satisfied smile. 'A mighty hunter before the Lord! He's our foremost man on every hand. You've already been pleased to get acquainted with him.'

Daddy Eroshka gazed at his feet in their shoes of wet raw hide and shook his head thoughtfully at the cornet's ability and learning, and muttered to himself: 'Gyptian Nimvrod! What things he invents!'

'Yes, you see we mean to go hunting,' answered Olenin.

'Yes, sir, exactly,' said the cornet, 'but I have a small business with you.'

'What do you want?'

'Seeing that you are a gentleman,' began the cornet, 'and as I may understand myself to be in the rank of an officer too, and therefore we may always progressively negotiate, as gentlemen do.' (He stopped and looked with a smile at Olenin and at the old man.) 'But if you have the desire with my consent, then, as my wife is a foolish woman of our class, she could not quite comprehend your words of yesterday's date. Therefore my quarters might be let for six rubles to the Regimental Adjutant, without the stables; but I can always avert that from myself free of charge. But, as you desire, therefore I, being myself of an officer's rank, can come to an agreement with you in everything personally, as an inhabitant of this district, not according to our customs, but can maintain the conditions in every way . . . '

'Speaks clearly!' muttered the old man.

The cornet continued in the same strain for a long time. At last, not without difficulty, Olenin gathered that the cornet wished to let his rooms to him, Olenin, for six rubles a month. The latter gladly agreed to this, and offered his visitor a glass of tea. The cornet declined it.

'According to our silly custom we consider it a sort of sin to drink out of a "worldly" tumbler,' he said. 'Though, of course, with my education I may understand, but my wife from her human weakness . . . '

'Well then, will you have some tea?'

'If you will permit me, I will bring my own particular glass,' answered the cornet, and stepped out into the porch.

'Bring me my glass!' he cried.

In a few minutes the door opened and a young sunburnt arm in a print sleeve thrust itself in, holding a tumbler in the hand. The cornet went up, took it, and whispered something to his daughter. Olenin poured tea for the cornet into the latter's own 'particular' glass, and for Eroshka into a 'worldly' glass.

'However, I do not desire to detain you,' said the cornet, scalding his lips and emptying his tumbler. 'I too have a great liking for fishing, and I am here, so to say, only on leave of absence for recreation from my duties. I too have the desire to tempt fortune and see whether some Gifts of the Terek may not fall to my share. I hope you too will come and see us and have a drink of our wine, according to the custom of our village,' he added.

The cornet bowed, shook hands with Olenin, and went out. While Olenin was getting ready, he heard the cornet giving orders to his family in an authoritative and sensible tone, and a few minutes later he saw him pass by the window in a tattered coat with his trousers rolled up to his knees and a fishing net over his shoulder.

'A rascal!' said Daddy Eroshka, emptying his 'worldly' tumbler. 'And will you really pay him six rubles? Was such a thing ever heard of? They would let you the best hut in the village for two rubles. What a beast! Why, I'd let you have mine for three!'

'No, I'll remain here,' said Olenin.

'Six rubles! . . . Clearly it's a fool's money. Eh, eh, eh! answered the old man. 'Let's have some *chikhir*, Ivan!'

Having had a snack and a drink of vodka to prepare themselves for the road, Olenin and the old man went out together before eight o'clock.

At the gate they came up against a wagon to which a pair of oxen were harnessed. With a white kerchief tied round her head down to her eyes, a coat over her smock, and wearing high boots, Maryanka with a long switch in her hand was dragging the oxen by a cord tied to their horns.

'Mammy,' said the old man, pretending that he was going to seize her.

Maryanka flourished her switch at him and glanced merrily at them both with her beautiful eyes.

Olenin felt still more light-hearted.

'Now then, come on, come on,' he said, throwing his gun on his shoulder and conscious of the girl's eyes upon him.

'Gee up!' sounded Maryanka's voice behind them, followed by the creak of the moving wagon.

As long as their road lay through the pastures at the back of the village Eroshka went on talking. He could not forget the cornet and kept on abusing him.

'Why are you so angry with him?' asked Olenin.

'He's stingy. I don't like it,' answered the old man. 'He'll leave it all behind when he dies! Then who's he saving up for? He's built two houses, and he's got a second garden from his brother by a law-suit. And in the matter of papers what a dog he is! They come to him from other villages to fill up documents. As he writes it out, exactly so it happens. He gets it quite exact. But who is he saving for? He's only got one boy and the girl; when she's married who'll be left?'

'Well then, he's saving up for her dowry,' said Olenin.

'What dowry? The girl is sought after, she's a fine girl. But he's such a devil that he must yet marry her to a rich fellow. He wants to get a big price for her. There's Luke, a Cossack, a neighbour and a nephew of mine, a fine lad. It's he who killed the Chechen – he has been wooing her for a long time, but he hasn't let him have her. He's given one excuse, and another, and a third. "The girl's too young," he says. But I know what he is thinking. He wants to keep them bowing to him. He's been acting shamefully about that girl. Still, they will get her for Lukashka, because he is the best Cossack in the village, a brave, who has killed an *abrek* and will be rewarded with a cross.'

'But how about this? When I was walking up and down the yard last night, I saw my landlord's daughter and some Cossack kissing,' said Olenin.

'You're pretending!' cried the old man, stopping.

'On my word,' said Olenin.

'Women are the devil,' said Eroshka pondering. 'But what Cossack was it?'

'I couldn't see.'

'Well, what sort of a cap had he, a white one?'

'Yes.'

'And a red coat? About your height?'

'No, a bit taller.'

'It's he!' and Eroshka burst out laughing. 'It's himself, it's Mark. He is Luke, but I call him Mark for a joke. His very self! I love him. I was just such a one myself. What's the good of minding them? My sweetheart used to sleep with her mother and her sister-in-law, but I managed to get in. She used to sleep upstairs; that witch her mother was a regular demon; it's awful how she hated me. Well, I used to come with a chum, Girchik his name was. We'd come under her window and I'd climb on his shoulders, push up the window and begin groping about. She used to sleep just there on a bench. Once I woke her up and she nearly called out. She hadn't recognized me. "Who is there?" she said, and I could not answer. Her mother was even beginning to stir, but I took off my cap and shoved it over her mouth; and she at once knew it by a seam in it, and ran out to me. I used not to want anything then. She'd bring along clotted cream and grapes and everything,' added Eroshka (who always explained things practically), 'and she wasn't the only one. It was a life!'

'And what now?'

'Now we'll follow the dog, get a pheasant to settle on a tree, and then you may fire.'

'Would you have made up to Maryanka?'

'Attend to the dogs. I'll tell you tonight,' said the old man, pointing to his favourite dog, Lyam.

After a pause they continued talking, while they went about a hundred paces. Then the old man stopped again and pointed to a twig that lay across the path.

'What do you think of that?' he said. 'You think it's nothing? It's bad that this stick is lying so.'

'Why is it bad?'

He smiled.

'Ah, you don't know anything. Just listen to me. When a stick lies like that don't you step across it, but go round it or throw it off the path this way, and say "Father and Son and Holy Ghost," and then go on with God's blessing. Nothing will happen to you. That's what the old men used to teach me.'

'Come, what rubbish!' said Olenin. 'You'd better tell me more about Maryanka. Does she carry on with Lukashka?'

'Hush . . . be quiet now!' the old man again interrupted in a whisper: 'just listen, we'll go round through the forest.'

And the old man, stepping quietly in his soft shoes, led the way by a narrow path leading into the dense, wild, overgrown forest. Now and again with a frown he turned to look at Olenin, who rustled and clattered with his heavy boots and, carrying his gun carelessly, several times caught the twigs of trees that grew across the path.

'Don't make a noise. Step softly, soldier!' the old man whispered angrily.

There was a feeling in the air that the sun had risen. The mist was dissolving but it still enveloped the tops of the trees. The forest looked terribly high. At every step the aspect changed: what had appeared like a tree proved to be a bush, and a reed looked like a tree.

Chapter 19

The mist had partly lifted, showing the wet reed thatches, and was now turning into dew that moistened the road and the grass beside the fence. Smoke rose everywhere in clouds from the chimneys. The people were going out of the village, some to their work, some to the river, and some to the cordon. The hunters walked together along the damp, grass-grown path. The dogs, wagging their tails and looking at their masters, ran on both sides of them.

Myriads of gnats hovered in the air and pursued the hunters, covering their backs, eyes, and hands. The air was fragrant with the grass and with the dampness of the forest. Olenin continually looked round at the ox-cart in which Maryanka sat urging on the oxen with a long switch.

It was calm. The sounds from the village, audible at first, now no longer reached the sportsmen. Only the brambles cracked as the dogs ran under them, and now and then birds called to one another. Olenin knew that danger lurked in the forest, that *abreks* always hid in such places. But he knew too that in the forest, for a man on foot, a gun is a great protection. Not that he was afraid, but he felt that another in his place might be; and looking into the damp misty forest and listening to the rare and faint sounds with strained attention, he changed his hold on his gun and experienced a pleasant feeling that was new to him. Daddy Eroshka went in front, stopping and carefully scanning every puddle where an animal had left a double track, and pointing it out to Olenin. He hardly spoke at all and only occasionally made remarks in a whisper. The track they were following had once been made by wagons, but the grass had long overgrown it. The elm and plane-tree forest on both sides of them was so dense and overgrown with creepers that it was imposs-ible to see anything through it. Nearly every tree was enveloped from top to bottom with wild grape vines, and dark bramble bushes covered the ground thickly. Every little glade was overgrown with blackberry bushes and grey feathery reeds. In places, large hoof-prints and small funnel-shaped pheasant-trails led from the path into the thicket. The vigour of the growth of this forest, untrampled by cattle, struck Olenin at every turn, for he had never seen anything like it. This forest, the danger, the old man and his mysterious whispering, Maryanka with her virile upright bearing, and the mountains – all this seemed to him like a dream.

'A pheasant has settled,' whispered the old man, looking round and pulling his cap over his face – 'Cover your mug! A pheasant!' he waved his arm angrily at Olenin and pushed forward almost on all fours. 'He don't like a man's mug.'

Olenin was still behind him when the old man stopped and began examining a tree. A cock-pheasant on the tree clucked at the dog that was barking at it, and Olenin saw the pheasant; but at that moment a report, as of a cannon, came from Eroshka's enormous gun, the bird fluttered up and, losing some feathers, fell to the ground. Coming up to the old man Olenin disturbed another, and raising his gun he aimed and fired. The pheasant flew swiftly up and then, catching at the branches as he fell, dropped like a stone to the ground.

'Good man!' the old man (who could not hit a flying bird) shouted, laughing.

Having picked up the pheasants they went on. Olenin, excited by the exercise and the praise, kept addressing remarks to the old man.

'Stop! Come this way,' the old man interrupted. 'I noticed the track of deer here yesterday.'

After they had turned into the thicket and gone some three hundred paces they scrambled through into a glade overgrown with reeds and partly under water. Olenin failed to keep up with the old huntsman and presently Daddy Eroshka, some twenty paces in front, stooped down, nodding and beckoning with his arm. On coming up with him Olenin saw a man's footprint to which the old man was pointing.

'D'you see?'

'Yes, well?' said Olenin, trying to speak as calmly as he could. 'A man's footstep!'

Involuntarily a thought of Cooper's Pathfinder and of *abreks* flashed through Olenin's mind, but noticing the mysterious manner with which the old man moved on, he hesitated to question him and remained in doubt whether this mysteriousness was caused by fear of danger or by the sport.

'No, it's my own footprint,' the old man said quietly, and pointed to some grass under which the track of an animal was just perceptible.

The old man went on; and Olenin kept up with him.

Descending to lower ground some twenty paces farther on they came upon a spreading pear-tree, under which, on the black earth, lay the fresh dung of some animal.

The spot, all covered over with wild vines, was like a cosy arbour, dark and cool.

'He's been here this morning,' said the old man with a sigh; 'the lair is still damp, quite fresh.'

Suddenly they heard a terrible crash in the forest some ten paces from where they stood. They both started and seized their guns, but they could see nothing and only heard the branches breaking. The rhythmical rapid thud of galloping was heard for a moment and then changed into a hollow rumble which resounded farther and farther off, re-echoing in wider and wider circles through the forest. Olenin felt as though something had snapped in his heart. He peered carefully but vainly into the green thicket and then turned to the old man. Daddy Eroshka with his gun pressed to his breast stood motionless; his cap was thrust backwards, his eyes gleamed with an unwonted glow, and his open mouth, with its worn yellow teeth, seemed to have stiffened in that position.

'A horned stag!' he muttered, and throwing down his gun in despair he began pulling at his grey beard, 'Here it stood. We should have come round by the path . . . Fool! fool!' and he gave his beard an angry tug. Fool! Pig!' he repeated, pulling painfully at his own beard. Through the forest something seemed to fly away in the mist, and ever farther and farther off was heard the sound of the flight of the stag.

It was already dusk when, hungry, tired, but full of vigour, Olenin returned with the old man. Dinner was ready. He ate and drank with the old man till he felt warm and merry. Olenin then went out into the porch. Again, to the west, the mountains rose before his eyes. Again the old man told his endless stories of hunting, of *abreks*, of sweethearts, and of all that free and reckless life. Again the fair Maryanka went in and out and across the yard, her beautiful powerful form outlined by her smock.

Chapter 20

The next day Olenin went alone to the spot where he and the old man startled the stag. Instead of passing round through the gate he climbed over the prickly hedge, as everybody else did, and before he had had time to pull out the thorns that had caught in his coat, his dog, which had run on in front, started two pheasants. He had hardly stepped among the briers when the pheasants began to rise at every step (the old man had not shown him that place the day before as he meant to keep it for shooting from behind the screen). Olenin fired twelve times and killed five pheasants, but clambering after them through the briers he got so fatigued that he was drenched with perspiration. He called off his dog, uncocked his gun, put in a bullet above the small shot, and brushing away the mosquitoes with the wide sleeve of his Circassian coat he went slowly to the spot where they had been the day before. It was however impossible to keep back the dog, who found trails on the very path, and Olenin killed two more pheasants, so that after being detained by this it was getting towards noon before he began to find the place he was looking for.

The day was perfectly clear, calm, and hot. The morning moisture had dried up even in the forest, and myriads of mosquitoes literally covered his face, his back, and his arms. His dog had turned from black to grey, its back being covered with mosquitoes, and so had Olenin's coat through which the insects thrust their stings. Olenin was ready to run away from them and it seemed to him that it was impossible to live in this country in the summer. He was about to go home, but remembering that other people managed to endure such pain he resolved to bear it and gave himself up to be devoured. And strange to say, by noontime the feeling became actually pleasant. He even felt that without this mosquito-filled atmosphere around him, and that mosquito-paste mingled with perspiration which his hand smeared over his face, and that unceasing irritation all over his body, the forest would lose for him some of its character and charm. These myriads of insects were so well suited to that monstrously lavish wild vegetation, these multitudes of birds and beasts which filled the forest, this dark foliage, this hot scented air, these runlets filled with turbid water which everywhere soaked through from the Terek and gurgled here and there under the overhanging leaves, that the very thing which had at first seemed to him dreadful and intolerable now seemed pleasant. After going round the place where yesterday they had found the animal and not finding anything, he felt inclined to rest. The sun stood right above the forest and poured its perpendicular rays down on his back and head whenever he came out into a glade or onto the road. The seven heavy pheasants dragged painfully at his waist. Having found the traces of yesterday's stag he crept under a bush into the thicket just where the stag had lain, and lay down in its lair. He examined the dark foliage around him, the place marked by the stag's perspiration and yesterday's dung, the imprint of the stag's knees, the bit of black earth it had kicked up, and his own footprints of the day before. He felt cool and comfortable and did not think of or wish for anything. And suddenly he was overcome by such a strange feeling of causeless joy and of love for everything, that from an old habit of his childhood he began crossing himself and thanking someone. Suddenly, with extraordinary clearness, he thought: 'Here am I, Dmitri Olenin, a being quite distinct from every other being, now lying all alone Heaven only knows where – where a stag used to live – an old stag, a beautiful stag who perhaps had never seen a man, and in a place where no human being has ever sat or thought these thoughts. Here I sit, and around me stand old and young trees, one of them festooned with wild grape vines, and pheasants are fluttering, driving one another about and perhaps scenting their murdered brothers.' He felt his pheasants, examined them, and wiped the warm blood off his hand onto his coat. 'Perhaps the jackals scent them and with dissatisfied faces go off in another direction: above me, flying in among the leaves which to them seem enormous islands, mosquitoes hang in the air and buzz: one, two, three, four, a hundred, a thousand, a million mosquitoes, and all of them buzz something or other and each one of them is separate from all else and is just such a separate Dmitri Olenin as I am myself.' He vividly imagined what the mosquitoes buzzed: 'This way, this way, lads! Here's someone we can eat!' They buzzed and stuck to him. And it was clear to him that he was not a Russian nobleman, a member of Moscow society, the friend and relation of so-and-so and so-and-so, but just such a mosquito, or pheasant, or deer, as those that were now living all around him. 'Just as they, just as Daddy Eroshka, I shall live awhile and die, and as he says truly:

Grass will grow and nothing more.

'But what though the grass does grow?' he continued thinking. 'Still I must live and be happy, because happiness is all I desire. Never mind what I am – an animal like all the rest, above whom the grass will grow and nothing more; or a frame in which a bit of the one God has been set, – still I must live in the very best way. How then must I live to be happy, and why was I not happy before?' And he began to recall his former life and he felt disgusted with himself. He appeared to himself to have been terribly exacting and selfish, though he now saw that all the while he really needed nothing for himself. And he looked round at the foliage with the light shining through it, at the setting sun and the clear sky, and he felt just as happy as before. 'Why am I happy, and what used I to live for?' thought he. 'How much I exacted for myself; how I schemed and did not manage to gain anything but shame and sorrow! and, there now, I require nothing to be happy;' and suddenly a new light seemed to reveal itself to him. 'Happiness is this!' he said to himself. 'Happiness lies in living for others. That is evident. The desire for happiness is innate in every man; therefore it is legitimate. When trying to satisfy it selfishly – that is, by seeking for oneself riches, fame, comforts, or love – it may happen that circumstances arise which make it impossible to satisfy these desires. It follows that it is these desires that are illegitimate, but not the need for happiness. But what desires can always be satisfied despite external circumstances? What are they? Love, self-sacrifice.' He was so glad and excited when he had discovered this, as it seemed to him, new truth, that he jumped up and began impatiently seeking someone to sacrifice himself for, to do good to and to love. 'Since one wants nothing for oneself,' he kept thinking, 'why not live for others?' He took up his gun with the intention of returning home quickly to think this out and to find an opportunity of doing good. He made his way out of the thicket. When he had come out into the glade he looked around him; the sun was no longer visible above the tree-tops. It had grown cooler and the place seemed to him quite strange and not like the country round the village. Everything seemed changed – the weather and the character of the forest; the sky was wrapped in clouds, the wind was rustling in the tree-tops, and all around nothing was visible but reeds and dying broken-down trees. He called to his dog who had run away to follow some animal, and his voice came back as in a desert. And suddenly he was seized with a terrible sense of weirdness. He grew frightened. He remembered the *abreks* and the murders he had been told about, and he expected every moment that an *abrek* would spring from behind every bush and he would have to defend his life and die, or be a coward. He thought of God and of the future life as for long he had not thought about them. And all around was that same gloomy stern wild nature. 'And is it worth while living for oneself,' thought he, 'when at any moment you may die, and die without having done any good, and so that no one will know of it?' He went in the direction where he fancied the village lay. Of his shooting he had no further thought; but he felt tired to death and peered round at every bush and tree with particular attention and almost with terror, expecting every moment to be called to account for his life. After having wandered about for a considerable time he came upon a ditch down which was flowing cold sandy water from the Terek, and, not to go astray any longer, he decided to follow it. He went on without knowing where the ditch would lead him. Suddenly the reeds behind him crackled. He shuddered and seized his gun, and then felt ashamed of himself: the over-excited dog, panting hard, had thrown itself into the cold water of the ditch and was lapping it!

He too had a drink, and then followed the dog in the direction it wished to go, thinking it would lead him to the village. But despite the dog's company everything around him seemed still more dreary. The forest grew darker and the wind grew stronger and stronger in the tops of the broken old trees. Some large birds circled screeching round their nests in those trees. The vegetation grew poorer and he came oftener and oftener upon rustling reeds and bare sandy spaces covered with animal footprints. To the howling of the wind was added another kind of cheerless monotonous roar. Altogether his spirits became gloomy. Putting his hand behind him he felt his pheasants, and found one missing. It had broken off and was lost, and only the bleeding head and beak remained sticking in his belt. He felt more frightened than he had ever done before. He began to pray to God, and feared above all that he might die without having done anything good or kind; and he so wanted to live, and to live so as to perform a feat of self-sacrifice.

Chapter 21

Suddenly it was as though the sun had shone into his soul. He heard Russian being spoken, and also heard the rapid smooth flow of the Terek, and a few steps farther in front of him saw the brown moving surface of the river, with the dim-coloured wet sand of its banks and shallows, the distant steppe, the cordon watch-tower outlined above the water, a saddled and hobbled horse among the brambles, and then the mountains opening out before him. The red sun appeared for an instant from under a cloud and its last rays glittered brightly along the river over the reeds, on the watch-tower, and on a group of Cossacks, among whom Lukashka's vigorous figure attracted Olenin's involuntary attention.

Olenin felt that he was again, without any apparent cause, perfectly happy. He had come upon the Nizhni-Prototsk post on the Terek, opposite a pro-Russian Tartar village on the other side of the river. He accosted the Cossacks, but not finding as yet any excuse for doing anyone a kindness, he entered the hut; nor in the hut did he find any such opportunity. The Cossacks received him coldly. On entering the mud hut he lit a cigarette. The Cossacks paid little attention to him, first because he was smoking a cigarette, and secondly because they had something else to divert them that evening. Some hostile Chechens, relatives of the *abrek* who had been killed, had come from the hills with a scout to ransom the body; and the Cossacks were waiting for their Commanding Officer's arrival from the village. The dead man's brother, tall and well shaped with a short cropped beard which was dyed red, despite his very tattered coat and cap was calm and majestic as a king. His face was very like that of the dead *abrek*. He did not deign to look at anyone, and never once glanced at the dead body, but sitting on his heels in the shade he spat as he smoked his short pipe, and occasionally uttered some few guttural sounds of command, which were respectfully listened to by his companion. He was evidently a brave who had met Russians more than once before in quite other circumstances, and nothing about them could astonish or even interest him. Olenin was about to approach the dead body and had begun to look at it when the brother, looking up at him from under his brows with calm contempt, said something sharply and angrily. The scout hastened to cover the dead man's face with his coat. Olenin was struck by the dignified and stern expression of the brave's face. He began to speak to him, asking from what village he came, but the Chechen, scarcely giving him a glance, spat contemptuously and turned away. Olenin was so surprised at the Chechen not being interested in him that he could only put it down to the man's stupidity or ignorance of Russian; so he turned to the scout, who also acted as interpreter. The scout was as ragged as the other, but instead of being red-haired he was black-haired, restless, with extremely white gleaming teeth and sparkling black eyes. The scout willingly entered into conversation and asked for a cigarette.

'There were five brothers,' began the scout in his broken Russian. 'This is the third brother the Russians have killed, only two are left. He is a brave, a great brave!' he said, pointing to the Chechen. 'When they killed Ahmet Khan (the dead brave) this one was sitting on the opposite bank among the reeds. He saw it all. Saw him laid in the skiff and brought to the bank. He sat there till the night and wished to kill the old man, but the others would not let him.'

Lukashka went up to the speaker, and sat down. 'Of what village?' asked he.

'From there in the hills,' replied the scout, pointing to the misty bluish gorge beyond the Terek. 'Do you know Suuk-su? It is about eight miles beyond that.'

'Do you know Girey Khan in Suuk-su?' asked Lukashka, evidently proud of the acquaintance. 'He is my *kunak*.'

'He is my neighbour,' answered the scout.

'He's a trump!' and Lukashka, evidently much interested, began talking to the scout in Tartar.

Presently a Cossack captain, with the head of the village, arrived on horseback with a suite of two Cossacks. The captain – one of the new type of Cossack officers – wished the Cossacks 'Good health', but no one shouted in reply, 'Hail! Good health to your honour,' as is customary in the Russian Army, and only a few replied with a bow. Some, and among them Lukashka, rose and stood erect. The corporal replied that all was well at the outposts. All this seemed ridiculous: it was as if these Cossacks were playing at being soldiers. But these formalities soon gave place to ordinary ways of behaviour, and the captain, who was a smart Cossack just like the others, began speaking fluently in Tartar to the interpreter. They filled in some document, gave it to the scout, and received from him some money. Then they approached the body.

'Which of you is Luke Gavrilov?' asked the captain.

Lukashka took off his cap and came forward.

'I have reported your exploit to the Commander. I don't know what will come of it. I have recommended you for a cross; you're too young to be made a sergeant. Can you read?'

'I can't.'

'But what a fine fellow to look at!' said the captain, again playing the commander. 'Put on your cap. Which of the Gavrilovs does he come of? . . . the Broad, eh?'

'His nephew,' replied the corporal.

'I know, I know. Well, lend a hand, help them,' he said, turning to the Cossacks.

Lukashka's face shone with joy and seemed handsomer than usual. He moved away from the corporal, and having put on his cap sat down beside Olenin.

When the body had been carried to the skiff the brother Chechen descended to the bank. The Cossacks involuntarily stepped aside to let him pass. He jumped into the boat and pushed off from the bank with his powerful leg, and now, as Olenin noticed, for the first time threw a rapid glance at all the Cossacks and then abruptly asked his companion a question. The latter answered something and pointed to Lukashka. The Chechen looked at him and, turning slowly away, gazed at the opposite bank. That look expressed not hatred but cold contempt. He again made some remark.

'What is he saying?' Olenin asked of the fidgety scout.

'Yours kill ours, ours slay yours. It's always the same,' replied the scout, evidently inventing, and he smiled, showing his white teeth, as he jumped into the skiff.

The dead man's brother sat motionless, gazing at the opposite bank. He was so full of hatred and contempt that there was nothing on this side of the river that moved his curiosity. The scout, standing up at one end of the skiff and dipping his paddle now on one side now on the other, steered skilfully while talking incessantly. The skiff became smaller and smaller as it moved obliquely across the stream, the voices became scarcely audible, and at last, still within sight, they landed on the opposite bank where their horses stood waiting. There they lifted out the corpse and (though the horse shied) laid it across one of the saddles, mounted, and rode at a foot-pace along the road past a Tartar village from which a crowd came out to look at them. The Cossacks on the Russian side of the river were highly satisfied and jovial. Laughter and jokes were heard on all sides. The captain and the head of the village entered the mud hut to regale themselves. Lukashka, vainly striving to impart a sedate expression to his merry face, sat down with his elbows on his knees beside Olenin and whittled away at a stick.

'Why do you smoke?' he said with assumed curiosity. 'Is it good?'

He evidently spoke because he noticed Olenin felt ill at ease and isolated among the Cossacks.

'It's just a habit,' answered Olenin. 'Why?'

'H'm, if one of us were to smoke there would be a row! Look there now, the mountains are not far off,' continued Lukashka, 'yet you can't get there! How will you get back alone? It's getting dark. I'll take you, if you like. You ask the corporal to give me leave.'

'What a fine fellow!' thought Olenin, looking at the Cossack's bright face. He remembered Maryanka and the kiss he had heard by the gate, and he was sorry for Lukashka and his want of culture. 'What confusion it is,' he thought. 'A man kills another and is happy and satisfied with himself as if he had done something excellent. Can it be that nothing tells him that it is not a reason for any rejoicing, and that happiness lies not in killing, but in sacrificing oneself?'

'Well, you had better not meet him again now, mate!' said one of the Cossacks who had seen the skiff off, addressing Lukashka. 'Did you hear him asking about you?'

Lukashka raised his head.

'My godson?' said Lukashka, meaning by that word the dead Chechen.

'Your godson won't rise, but the red one is the godson's brother!'

'Let him thank God that he got off whole himself,' replied Lukashka.

'What are you glad about?' asked Olenin. 'Supposing your brother had been killed; would you be glad?'

The Cossack looked at Olenin with laughing eyes. He seemed to have understood all that Olenin wished to say to him, but to be above such considerations.

'Well, that happens too! Don't our fellows get killed sometimes?'

Chapter 22

The Captain and the head of the village rode away, and Olenin, to please Lukashka as well as to avoid going back alone through the dark forest, asked the corporal to give Lukashka leave, and the corporal did so. Olenin thought that Lukashka wanted to see Maryanka and he was also glad of the companionship of such a pleasant-looking and sociable Cossack. Lukashka and Maryanka he involuntarily united in his mind, and he found pleasure in thinking about them. 'He loves Maryanka,' thought Olenin, 'and I could love her,' and a new and powerful emotion of tenderness overcame him as they walked homewards together through the dark forest. Lukashka too felt happy; something akin to love made itself felt between these two very different young men. Every time they glanced at one another they wanted to laugh.

'By which gate do you enter?' asked Olenin.

'By the middle one. But I'll see you as far as the marsh. After that you have nothing to fear.'

Olenin laughed.

'Do you think I am afraid? Go back, and thank you. I can get on alone.'

'It's all right! What have I to do? And how can you help being afraid? Even we are afraid,' said Lukashka to set Olenin's self-esteem at rest, and he laughed too.

'Then come in with me. We'll have a talk and a drink and in the morning you can go back.'

'Couldn't I find a place to spend the night?' laughed Lukashka. 'But the corporal asked me to go back.'

'I heard you singing last night, and also saw you.'

'Everyone . . . ' and Luke swayed his head.

'Is it true you are getting married?' asked Olenin.

'Mother wants me to marry. But I have not got a horse yet.'

'Aren't you in the regular service?'

'Oh dear no! I've only just joined, and have not got a horse yet, and don't know how to get one. That's why the marriage does not come off.'

'And what would a horse cost?'

'We were bargaining for one beyond the river the other day and they would not take sixty rubles for it, though it is a Nogay horse.'

'Will you come and be my drabant?' (A drabant was a kind of orderly attached to an officer when campaigning.) 'I'll get it arranged and will give you a horse,' said Olenin suddenly. 'Really now, I have two and I don't want both.'

'How – don't want it?' Lukashka said, laughing. 'Why should you make me a present? We'll get on by ourselves by God's help.'

'No, really! Or don't you want to be a drabant?' said Olenin, glad that it had entered his head to give a horse to Lukashka, though, without knowing why, he felt uncomfortable and confused and did not know what to say when he tried to speak.

Lukashka was the first to break the silence.

'Have you a house of your own in Russia?' he asked.

Olenin could not refrain from replying that he had not only one, but several houses.

'A good house? Bigger than ours?' asked Lukashka good-naturedly.

'Much bigger; ten times as big and three storeys high,' replied Olenin.

'And have you horses such as ours?'

'I have a hundred horses, worth three or four hundred rubles each, but they are not like yours. They are trotters, you know . . . But still, I like the horses here best.'

'Well, and did you come here of your own free will, or were you sent?' said Lukashka, laughing at him. 'Look! that's where you lost your way,' he added, 'you should have turned to the right.'

'I came by my own wish,' replied Olenin. 'I wanted to see your parts and to join some expeditions.'

'I would go on an expedition any day,' said Lukashka. 'D'you hear the jackals howling?' he added, listening.

'I say, don't you feel any horror at having killed a man?' asked Olenin.

'What's there to be frightened about? But I should like to join an expedition. How I want to! How I want to!' Lukashka repeated.

'Perhaps we may be going together. Our company is going before the holidays, and your "hundred" too.'

'And what did you want to come here for? You've a house and horses and serfs. In your place I'd do nothing but make merry! And what is your rank?'

'I am a cadet, but have been recommended for a commission.'

'Well, if you're not bragging about your home, if I were you I'd never have left it! Yes, I'd never have gone away anywhere. Do you find it pleasant living among us?'

'Yes, very pleasant,' answered Olenin.

It had grown quite dark before, talking in this way, they approached the village. They were still surrounded by the deep gloom of the forest. The wind howled through the tree-tops. The jackals suddenly seemed to be crying close beside them, howling, chuckling, and sobbing; but ahead of them in the village the sounds of women's voices and the barking of dogs could already be heard; the outlines of the huts were clearly to be seen; lights gleamed and the air was filled with the peculiar smell of *kisyak* smoke. Olenin felt keenly, that night especially, that here in this village was his home, his family, all his happiness, and that he never had and never would live so happily anywhere as he did in this Cossack village. He was so fond of everybody and especially of Lukashka that night. On reaching home, to Lukashka's great surprise, Olenin with his own hands led out of the shed a horse he had bought in Groznoe – it was not the one he usually rode but another – not a bad horse though no longer young, and gave it to Lukashka.

'Why should you give me a present?' said Lukashka, 'I have not yet done anything for you.'

'Really it is nothing,' answered Olenin. 'Take it, and you will give me a present, and we'll go on an expedition against the enemy together.'

Lukashka became confused.

'But what d'you mean by it? As if a horse were of little value,' he said without looking at the horse.

'Take it, take it! If you don't you will offend me. Vanyusha! Take the grey horse to his house.'

Lukashka took hold of the halter.

'Well then, thank you! This is something unexpected, undreamt of.'

Olenin was as happy as a boy of twelve.

'Tie it up here. It's a good horse. I bought it in Groznoe; it gallops splendidly! Vanyusha, bring us some *chikhir*. Come into the hut.'

The wine was brought. Lukashka sat down and took the wine-bowl.

'God willing I'll find a way to repay you,' he said, finishing his wine. 'How are you called?'

'Dmitri Andreich.'

'Well, 'Mitry Andreich, God bless you. We will be *kunaks*. Now you must come to see us. Though we are not rich people still we can treat a *kunak*, and I will tell mother in case you need anything – clotted cream or grapes – and if you come to the cordon I'm your servant to go hunting or to go across the river, anywhere you like! There now, only the other day, what a boar I killed, and I divided it among the Cossacks, but if I had only known, I'd have given it to you.'

'That's all right, thank you! But don't harness the horse, it has never been in harness.'

'Why harness the horse? And there is something else I'll tell you if you like,' said Lukashka, bending his head. 'I have a *kunak*, Girey Khan. He asked me to lie in ambush by the road where they come down from the mountains. Shall we go together? I'll not betray you. I'll be your *murid*.'

'Yes, we'll go; we'll go some day.'

Lukashka seemed quite to have quieted down and to have understood Olenin's attitude towards him. His calmness and the ease of his behaviour surprised Olenin, and he did not even quite like it. They talked long, and it was late when Lukashka, not tipsy (he never was tipsy) but having drunk a good deal, left Olenin after shaking hands.

Olenin looked out of the window to see what he would do. Lukashka went out, hanging his head. Then, having led the horse out of the gate, he suddenly shook his head, threw the reins of the halter over its head, sprang onto its back like a cat, gave a wild shout, and galloped down the street. Olenin expected that Lukashka would go to share his joy with Maryanka, but though he did not do so Olenin still felt his soul more at ease than ever before in his life. He was as delighted as a boy, and could not refrain from telling Vanyusha not only that he had given Lukashka the horse, but also why he had done it, as well as his new theory of happiness. Vanyusha did not approve of his theory, and announced that '*l'argent il n'y a pas!*' and that therefore it was all nonsense.

Lukashka rode home, jumped off the horse, and handed it over to his mother, telling her to let it out with the communal Cossack herd. He himself had to return to the cordon that same night. His deaf sister undertook to take the horse, and explained by signs that when she saw the man who had given the horse, she would bow down at his feet. The old woman only shook her head at her son's story, and decided in her own mind that he had stolen it. She therefore told the deaf girl to take it to the herd before daybreak.

Lukashka went back alone to the cordon pondering over Olenin's action. Though he did not consider the horse a good one, yet it was worth at least forty rubles and Lukashka was very glad to have the present. But why it had been given him he could not at all understand, and therefore he did not experience the least feeling of gratitude. On the contrary, vague suspicions that the cadet had some evil intentions filled his mind. What those intentions were he could not decide, but neither could he admit the idea that a stranger would give him a horse worth forty rubles for nothing, just out of kindness; it seemed impossible. Had he been drunk one might understand it! He might have wished to show off. But the cadet had been sober, and therefore must have wished to bribe him to do something wrong. 'Eh, humbug!' thought Lukashka. 'Haven't I got the horse and we'll see later on. I'm not a fool myself and we shall see who'll get the better of the other,' he thought, feeling the necessity of being on his guard, and therefore arousing in himself unfriendly feelings towards Olenin. He told no one how he had got the horse. To some he said he had bought it, to others he replied evasively. However, the truth soon got about in the village, and Lukashka's mother and Maryanka, as well as Elias Vasilich and other Cossacks, when they heard of Olenin's unnecessary gift, were perplexed, and began to be on their guard against the cadet. But despite their fears his action aroused in them a great respect for his simplicity and wealth.

'Have you heard,' said one, 'that the cadet quartered on Elias Vasilich has thrown a fifty-ruble horse at Lukashka? He's rich! . . . '

'Yes, I heard of it,' replied another profoundly, 'he must have done him some great service. We shall see what will come of this cadet. Eh! what luck that Snatcher has!'

'Those cadets are crafty, awfully crafty,' said a third. 'See if he don't go setting fire to a building, or doing something!'

Chapter 23

Olenin's life went on with monotonous regularity. He had little intercourse with the commanding officers or with his equals. The position of a rich cadet in the Caucasus was peculiarly advantageous in this respect. He was not sent out to work, or for training. As a reward for going on an expedition he was recommended for a commission, and meanwhile he was left in peace. The officers regarded him as an aristocrat and behaved towards him with dignity. Cardplaying and the officers' carousals accompanied by the soldier-singers, of which he had had experience when he was with the detachment, did not seem to him attractive, and he also avoided the society and life of the officers in the village. The life of officers stationed in a Cossack village has long had its own definite form. Just as every cadet or officer when in a fort regularly drinks porter, plays cards, and discusses the rewards given for taking part in the expeditions, so in the Cossack villages he regularly drinks *chikhir* with his hosts, treats the girls to sweet-meats and honey, dangles after the Cossack women, and falls in love, and occasionally marries there. Olenin always took his own path and had an unconscious objection to the beaten tracks. And here, too, he did not follow the ruts of a Caucasian officer's life.

It came quite naturally to him to wake up at daybreak. After drinking tea and admiring from his porch the mountains, the morning, and Maryanka, he would put on a tattered ox-hide coat, sandals of soaked raw hide, buckle on a dagger, take a gun, put cigarettes and some lunch in a little bag, call his dog, and soon after five o'clock would start for the forest beyond the village. Towards seven in the evening he would return tired and hungry with five or six pheasants hanging from his belt (sometimes with some other animal) and with his bag of food and cigarettes untouched. If the thoughts in his head had lain like the lunch and cigarettes in the bag, one might have seen that during all those fourteen hours not a single thought had moved in it. He returned morally fresh, strong, and perfectly happy, and he could not tell what he had been thinking about all the time. Were they ideas, memories, or dreams that had been flitting through his mind? They were frequently all three. He would rouse himself and ask what he had been thinking about; and would see himself as a Cossack working in a vineyard with his Cossack wife, or an *abrek* in the mountains, or a boar running away from himself. And all the time he kept peering and watching for a pheasant, a boar, or a deer.

In the evening Daddy Eroshka would be sure to be sitting with him. Vanyusha would bring a jug of *chikhir*, and they would converse quietly, drink, and separate to go quite contentedly to bed. The next day he would again go shooting, again be healthily

weary, again they would sit conversing and drink their fill, and
again be happy. Sometimes on a holiday or day of rest Olenin
spent the whole day at home. Then his chief occupation was
watching Maryanka, whose every movement, without realizing it
himself, he followed greedily from his window or his porch. He
regarded Maryanka and loved her (so he thought) just as he loved
the beauty of the mountains and the sky, and he had no thought
of entering into any relations with her. It seemed to him that
between him and her such relations as there were between her and
the Cossack Lukashka could not exist, and still less such as often
existed between rich officers and other Cossack girls. It seemed to
him that if he tried to do as his fellow officers did, he would
exchange his complete enjoyment of contemplation for an abyss of
suffering, disillusionment, and remorse. Besides, he had already
achieved a triumph of self-sacrifice in connection with her which
had given him great pleasure, and above all he was in a way afraid
of Maryanka and would not for anything have ventured to utter a
word of love to her lightly.

Once during the summer, when Olenin had not gone out
shooting but was sitting at home, quite unexpectedly a Moscow
acquaintance, a very young man whom he had met in society,
came in.

'Ah, *mon cher*, my dear fellow, how glad I was when I heard that
you were here!' he began in his Moscow French, and he went on
intermingling French words in his remarks. 'They said, "Olenin".
What, Olenin? and I was so pleased . . . Fancy fate bringing us
together here! Well, and how are you? How? Why?' and Prince
Beletski told his whole story: how he had temporarily entered the
regiment, how the Commander-in-Chief had offered to take him
as an adjutant, and how he would take up the post after this
campaign although personally he felt quite indifferent about it.

'Living here in this hole one must at least make a career – get a
cross – or a rank – be transferred to the Guards. That is quite
indispensable, not for myself but for the sake of my relations and
friends. The prince received me very well; he is a very decent
fellow,' said Beletski, and went on unceasingly. 'I have been
recommended for the St Anna Cross for the expedition. Now I
shall stay here a bit until we start on the campaign. It's capital here.
What women! Well, and how are you getting on? I was told by

our captain, Startsev you know, a kind-hearted stupid creature . . .
Well, he said you were living like an awful savage, seeing no one!
I quite understand you don't want to be mixed up with the set of
officers we have here. I am so glad now you and I will be able to
see something of one another. I have put up at the Cossack
corporal's house. There is such a girl there. Ustenka! I tell you
she's just charming.'

And more and more French and Russian words came pouring
forth from that world which Olenin thought he had left for ever.
The general opinion about Beletski was that he was a nice, good-
natured fellow. Perhaps he really was; but in spite of his pretty,
good-natured face, Olenin thought him extremely unpleasant.
He seemed just to exhale that filthiness which Olenin had for-
sworn. What vexed him most was that he could not – had not the
strength – abruptly to repulse this man who came from that
world: as if that old world he used to belong to had an irresistible
claim on him. Olenin felt angry with Beletski and with himself,
yet against his wish he introduced French phrases into his own
conversation, was interested in the Commander-in-Chief and in
their Moscow acquaintances, and because in this Cossack village
he and Beletski both spoke French, he spoke contemptuously of
their fellow officers and of the Cossacks, and was friendly with
Beletski, promising to visit him and inviting him to drop in to
see him. Olenin however did not himself go to see Beletski.
Vanyusha for his part approved of Beletski, remarking that he was
a real gentleman.

Beletski at once adopted the customary life of a rich officer in a
Cossack village. Before Olenin's eyes, in one month he came to be
like an old resident of the village; he made the old men drunk,
arranged evening parties, and himself went to parties arranged by
the girls – bragged of his conquests, and even got so far that, for
some unknown reason, the women and girls began calling him
grandad, and the Cossacks, to whom a man who loved wine and
women was clearly understandable, got used to him and even liked
him better than they did Olenin, who was a puzzle to them.

Chapter 24

It was five in the morning. Vanyusha was in the porch heating the samovar, and using the leg of a long boot instead of bellows. Olenin had already ridden off to bathe in the Terek. (He had recently invented a new amusement: to swim his horse in the river.) His landlady was in her outhouse, and the dense smoke of the kindling fire rose from the chimney. The girl was milking the buffalo cow in the shed. 'Can't keep quiet, the damned thing!' came her impatient voice, followed by the rhythmical sound of milking.

From the street in front of the house horses' hoofs were heard clattering briskly, and Olenin, riding bareback on a handsome dark-grey horse which was still wet and shining, rode up to the gate. Maryanka's handsome head, tied round with a red kerchief, appeared from the shed and again disappeared. Olenin was wearing a red silk shirt, a white Circassian coat girdled with a strap which carried a dagger, and a tall cap. He sat his well-fed wet horse with a slightly conscious elegance and, holding his gun at his back, stooped to open the gate. His hair was still wet, and his face shone with youth and health. He thought himself handsome, agile, and like a brave; but he was mistaken. To any experienced Caucasian he was still only a soldier.

When he noticed that the girl had put out her head he stooped with particular smartness, threw open the gate and, tightening the reins, swished his whip and entered the yard. 'Is tea ready, Vanyusha?' he cried gaily, not looking at the door of the shed. He felt with pleasure how his fine horse, pressing down his flanks, pulling at the bridle and with every muscle quivering, and with each foot ready to leap over the fence, pranced on the hard clay of the yard. '*C'est prêt*,' answered Vanyusha. Olenin felt as if Maryanka's beautiful head was still looking out of the shed, but he did not turn to look at her. As he jumped down from his horse he made an awkward movement, and caught his gun against the porch and turned a frightened look towards the shed, where there was no one to be seen and whence the sound of milking could still be heard.

Soon after he had entered the hut he came out again and sat down with his pipe and a book on the side of the porch which was not yet exposed to the rays of the sun. He meant not to go anywhere before dinner that day, and to write some long-postponed letters;

but somehow he felt disinclined to leave his place in the porch, and he was as reluctant to go back into the hut as if it had been a prison. The housewife had heated her oven, and the girl, having driven the cattle, had come back and was collecting *kisyak* and heaping it up along the fence. Olenin went on reading but did not understand a word of what was written in the book that lay open before him. He kept lifting his eyes from it and looking st the powerful young woman who was moving about. Whether she stepped into the moist morning shadow thrown by the house, or went out into the middle of the yard lit up by the joyous young light so that the whole of her stately figure in its bright coloured garmnt gleamed in the sunshine and cast a black shadow – always he feared to lose any one of her movements. It delighted him to see how freely and gracefully her figure bent: into what folds her only garment, a pink smock, draped itself on her bosom and down her shapely legs; how she drew herself up and her tight-drawn smock showed the outline of her breathing bosom; how the soles of her narrow feet in her worn red slippers stood on the ground without altering their shape; how her strong arms with the sleeves rolled up, exerting the muscles, used the spade almost as if in anger, and how her deep dark eyes sometimes glanced at him. Though the delicate brows frowned, yet her eyes expressed pleasure and a knowledge of her own beauty.

'I say, Olenin, have you been up long?' said Beletski as he entered the yard dressed in the coat of a Caucasian officer.

'Ah, Beletski,' replied Olenin, holding out his hand. 'How is it you are out so early?'

'I had to. I was driven out; we are having a ball tonight. Maryanka, of course you'll come to Ustenka's?' he added, turning to the girl.

Olenin felt surprised that Beletski could address this woman so easily. But Maryanka, as though she had not heard him, bent her head, and throwing the spade across her shoulder went with her firm masculine tread towards the outhouse.

'She's shy, the wench is shy,' Beletski called after her. 'Shy of you,' he added as, smiling gaily, he ran up the steps of the porch.

'How is it you are having a ball and have been driven out?'

'It's at Ustenka's, at my landlady's, that the ball is, and you two are invited. A ball consists of a pie and a gathering of girls.'

'What should we do there?'

Beletski smiled knowingly and winked, jerking his head in the direction of the outhouse into which Maryanka had disappeared.

Olenin shrugged his shoulders and blushed.

'Well, really you are a strange fellow!' said he.

'Come now, don't pretend'

Olenin frowned, and Beletski noticing this smiled insinuatingly. 'Oh, come, what do you mean?' he said, 'living in the same house – and such a fine girl, a splendid girl, a perfect beauty.'

'Wonderfully beautiful! I never saw such a woman before,' replied Olenin.

'Well then?' said Beletski, quite unable to understand the situation.

'It may be strange,' replied Olenin, 'but why should I not say what is true? Since I have lived here women don't seem to exist for me. And it is so good, really! Now what can there be in common between us and women like these? Eroshka – that's a different matter! He and I have a passion in common – sport.'

'There now! In common! And what have I in common with Amalia Ivanovna? It's the same thing! You may say they're not very clean – that's another matter . . . *À la guerre, comme à la guerre!* . . . '

'But I have never known any Amalia Ivanovas, and have never known how to behave with women of that sort,' replied Olenin. 'One cannot respect them, but these I do respect.'

'Well, go on respecting them! Who wants to prevent you?'

Olenin did not reply. He evidently wanted to complete what he had begun to say. It was very near his heart.

'I know I am an exception . . . ' He was visibly confused. 'But my life has so shaped itself that I not only see no necessity to renounce my rules, but I could not live here, let alone live as happily as I am doing, were I to live as you do. Therefore I look for something quite different from what you look for.'

Beletski raised his eyebrows incredulously. 'Anyhow, come to me this evening; Maryanka will be there and I will make you acquainted. Do come, please! If you feel dull you can go away. Will you come?'

'I would come, but to speak frankly I am afraid of being seriously carried away.'

'Oh, oh, oh!' shouted Beletski. 'Only come, and I'll see that you aren't. Will you? On your word?'

'I would come, but really I don't understand what we shall do; what part we shall play!'

'Please, I beg of you. You will come?'

'Yes, perhaps I'll come,' said Olenin.

'Really now! Charming women such as one sees nowhere else, and to live like a monk! What an idea! Why spoil your life and not make use of what is at hand? Have you heard that our company is ordered to Vozdvizhensk?'

'Hardly. I was told the 8th Company would be sent there,' said Olenin.

'No. I have had a letter from the adjutant there. He writes that the Prince himself will take part in the campaign. I am very glad I shall see something of him. I'm beginning to get tired of this place.'

'I hear we shall start on a raid soon.'

'I have not heard of it; but I have heard that Krinovitsin has received the Order of St Anna for a raid. He expected a lieutenancy,' said Beletski laughing. 'He was let in! He has set off for headquarters.'

It was growing dusk and Olenin began thinking about the party. The invitation he had received worried him. He felt inclined to go, but what might take place there seemed strange, absurd, and even rather alarming. He knew that neither Cossack men nor older women, nor anyone besides the girls, were to be there. What was going to happen? How was he to behave? What would they talk about? What connection was there between him and those wild Cossack girls? Beletski had told him of such curious, cynical, and yet rigid relations. It seemed strange to think that he would be there in the same hut with Maryanka and perhaps might have to talk to her. It seemed to him impossible when he remembered her majestic bearing. But Beletski spoke of it as if it were all perfectly simple. 'Is it possible that Beletski will treat Maryanka in the same way? That is interesting,' thought he. 'No, better not go. It's all so horrid, so vulgar, and above all – it leads to nothing!' But again he was worried by the question of what would take place; and besides he felt as if bound by a promise. He went out without having made up his mind one way or the other, but he walked as far as Beletski's, and went in there.

The hut in which Beletski lived was like Olenin's. It was raised nearly five feet from the ground on wooden piles, and had two rooms. In the first (which Olenin entered by the steep flight of steps) feather beds, rugs, blankets, and cushions were tastefully and handsomely arranged, Cossack fashion, along the main wall. On the side wall hung brass basins and weapons, while on the floor, under a bench, lay watermelons and pumpkins. In the second room there was a big brick oven, a table, and sectarian icons. It was here that Beletski was quartered, with his camp-bed and his pack and trunks. His weapons hung on the wall with a little rug behind them, and on the table were his toilet appliances and some portraits. A silk dressing-gown had been thrown on the bench. Beletski himself, clean and good-looking, lay on the bed in his underclothing, reading *Les Trois Mousquetaires*.

He jumped up.

'There, you see how I have arranged things. Fine! Well, it's good that you have come. They are working furiously. Do you know what the pie is made of? Dough with a stuffing of pork and grapes. But that's not the point. You just look at the commotion out there!'

And really, on looking out of the window they saw an unusual bustle going on in the hut. Girls ran in and out, now for one thing and now for another.

'Will it soon be ready?' cried Beletski.

'Very soon! Why? Is Grandad hungry?' and from the hut came the sound of ringing laughter.

Ustenka, plump, small, rosy, and pretty, with her sleeves turned up, ran into Beletski's hut to fetch some plates.

'Get away or I shall smash the plates!' she squeaked, escaping from Beletski. 'You'd better come and help,' she shouted to Olenin, laughing. 'And don't forget to get some refreshments for the girls.' ('Refreshments' meaning spicebread and sweets.)

'And has Maryanka come?'

'Of course! She brought some dough.'

'Do you know,' said Beletski, 'if one were to dress Ustenka up and clean and polish her up a bit, she'd be better than all our beauties. Have you ever seen that Cossack woman who married a colonel; she was charming! Borsheva? What dignity! Where do they get it . . . .'

'I have not seen Borsheva, but I think nothing could be better than the costume they wear here.'

'Ah, I'm first-rate at fitting into any kind of life,' said Beletski with a sigh of pleasure. 'I'll go and see what they are up to.'

He threw his dressing-gown over his shoulders and ran out, shouting, 'And you look after the "refreshments".'

Olenin sent Beletski's orderly to buy spice-bread and honey; but it suddenly seemed to him so disgusting to give money (as if he were bribing someone) that he gave no definite reply to the orderly's question: 'How much spice-bread with peppermint, and how much with honey?'

'Just as you please.'

'Shall I spend all the money,' asked the old soldier impressively. 'The peppermint is dearer. It's sixteen kopeks.'

'Yes, yes, spend it all,' answered Olenin and sat down by the window, surprised that his heart was thumping as if he were preparing himself for something serious and wicked.

He heard screaming and shrieking in the girls' hut when Beletski went there, and a few moments later saw how he jumped out and ran down the steps, accompanied by shrieks, bustle, and laughter.

'Turned out,' he said.

A little later Ustenka entered and solemnly invited her visitors to come in: announcing that all was ready.

When they came into the room they saw that everything was really ready. Ustenka was rearranging the cushions along the wall. On the table, which was covered by a disproportionately small cloth, was a decanter of *chikhir* and some dried fish. The room smelt of dough and grapes. Some half dozen girls in smart tunics, with their heads not covered as usual with kerchiefs, were huddled together in a corner behind the oven, whispering, giggling, and spluttering with laughter.

'I humbly beg you to do honour to my patron saint,' said Ustenka, inviting her guests to the table.

Olenin noticed Maryanka among the group of girls, who without exception were all handsome, and he felt vexed and hurt that he met her in such vulgar and awkward circumstances. He felt stupid and awkward, and made up his mind to do what Beletski did. Beletski stepped to the table somewhat solemnly yet with confidence and ease, drank a glass of wine to Ustenka's health, and invited the others to do the same. Ustenka announced that girls don't drink. 'We might with a little honey,' exclaimed a voice from among the group of girls. The orderly, who had just returned with the honey and spice-cakes, was called in. He looked askance (whether with envy or with contempt) at the gentlemen, who in his opinion were on the spree; and carefully and conscientiously handed over to them a piece of honey-comb and the cakes wrapped up in a piece of greyish paper, and began explaining circumstantially all about the price and the change, but Beletski sent him away. Having mixed honey with wine in the glasses, and having lavishly scattered the three pounds of spice-cakes on the table, Beletski dragged the girls from their corners by force, made them sit down at the table, and began distributing the cakes among them. Olenin involuntarily noticed how Maryanka's sunburnt but small hand closed on two round peppermint nuts and one brown one, and that she did not know what to do with them. The conversation was halting and constrained, in spite of Ustenka's and Beletski's free and easy manner and their wish to enliven the company. Olenin faltered, and tried to think of something to say, feeling that he was exciting curiosity and perhaps provoking ridicule and infecting the others with his shyness. He blushed, and it seemed to him that Maryanka in particular was feeling uncomfortable. 'Most likely they are expecting us to give them some money,' thought he. 'How are we to do it? And how can we manage quickest to give it and get away?'

Chapter 25

'How is it you don't know your own lodger?' said Beletski, addressing Maryanka.

'How is one to know him if he never comes to see us?' answered Maryanka, with a look at Olenin.

Olenin felt frightened, he did not know of what. He flushed and, hardly knowing what he was saying, remarked: 'I'm afraid of your mother. She gave me such a scolding the first time I went in.'

Maryanka burst out laughing. 'And so you were frightened?' she said, and glanced at him and turned away.

It was the first time Olenin had seen the whole of her beautiful face. Till then he had seen her with her kerchief covering her to the eyes. It was not for nothing that she was reckoned the beauty of the village. Ustenka was a pretty girl, small, plump, rosy, with merry brown eyes, and red lips which were perpetually smiling and chattering. Maryanka on the contrary was certainly not pretty but beautiful. Her features might have been considered too masculine and almost harsh had it not been for her tall stately figure, her powerful chest and shoulders, and especially the severe yet tender expression of her long dark eyes which were darkly shadowed beneath their black brows, and for the gentle expression of her mouth and smile. She rarely smiled, but her smile was always striking. She seemed to radiate virginal strength and health. All the girls were good-looking, but they themselves and Beletski, and the orderly when he brought in the spice-cakes, all involuntarily gazed at Maryanka, and anyone addressing the girls was sure to address her. She seemed a proud and happy queen among them.

Beletski, trying to keep up the spirit of the party, chattered incessantly, made the girls hand round *chikhir*, fooled about with them, and kept making improper remarks in French about Maryanka's beauty to Olenin, calling her 'yours' (*la vôtre*), and advising him to behave as he did himself. Olenin felt more and more uncomfortable. He was devising an excuse to get out and run away when Beletski announced that Ustenka, whose saint's day it was, must offer *chikhir* to everybody with a kiss. She consented on condition that they should put money on her plate, as is the custom at weddings.

'What fiend brought me to this disgusting feast?' thought Olenin, rising to go away.

'Where are you off to?'

'I'll fetch some tobacco,' he said, meaning to escape, but Beletski seized his hand.

'I have some money,' he said to him in French.

'One can't go away, one has to pay here,' thought Olenin bitterly, vexed at his own awkwardness. 'Can't I really behave like Beletski? I ought not to have come, but once I am here I must not spoil their fun. I must drink like a Cossack,' and taking the wooden bowl (holding about eight tumblers) he almost filled it with *chikhir* and drank it almost all. The girls looked at him, surprised and almost frightened, as he drank. It seemed to them strange and not right. Ustenka brought them another glass each, and kissed them both. 'There girls, now we'll have some fun,' she said, clinking on the plate the four rubles the men had put there.

Olenin no longer felt awkward, but became talkative.

'Now, Maryanka, it's your turn to offer us wine and a kiss,' said Beletski, seizing her hand.

'Yes, I'll give you such a kiss!' she said playfully, preparing to strike at him.

'One can kiss Grandad without payment,' said another girl.

'There's a sensible girl,' said Beletski, kissing the struggling girl. 'No, you must offer it,' he insisted, addressing Maryanka. 'Offer a glass to your lodger.'

And taking her by the hand he led her to the bench and sat her down beside Olenin.

'What a beauty,' he said, turning her head to see it in profile.

Maryanka did not resist but proudly smiling turned her long eyes towards Olenin.

'A beautiful girl,' repeated Beletski.

'Yes, see what a beauty I am,' Maryanka's look seemed to endorse. Without considering what he was doing Olenin embraced Maryanka and was going to kiss her, but she suddenly extricated herself, upsetting Beletski and pushing the top off the table, and sprang away towards the oven. There was much shouting and laughter. Then Beletski whispered something to the girls and suddenly they all ran out into the passage and locked the door behind them.

'Why did you kiss Beletski and won't kiss me?' asked Olenin.

'Oh, just so. I don't want to, that's all!' she answered, pouting and frowning. 'He's Grandad,' she added with a smile. She went to the door and began to bang at it. 'Why have you locked the door, you devils?'

'Well, let them be there and us here,' said Olenin, drawing closer to her.

She frowned, and sternly pushed him away with her hand. And again she appeared so majestically handsome to Olenin that he came to his senses and felt ashamed of what he was doing. He went to the door and began pulling at it himself.

'Beletski! Open the door! What a stupid joke!'

Maryanka again gave a bright happy laugh. 'Ah, you're afraid of me?' she said.

'Yes, you know you're as cross as your mother.'

'Spend more of your time with Eroshka; that will make the girls love you!' And she smiled, looking straight and close into his eyes.

He did not know what to reply. 'And if I were to come to see you – ' he let fall.

'That would be a different matter,' she replied, tossing her head.

At that moment Beletski pushed the door open, and Maryanka sprang away from Olenin and in doing so her thigh struck his leg.

'It's all nonsense what I have been thinking about – love and self-sacrifice and Lukashka. Happiness is the one thing. He who is happy is right,' flashed through Olenin's mind, and with a strength unexpected to himself he seized and kissed the beautiful Maryanka on her temple and her cheek. Maryanka was not angry, but only burst into a loud laugh and ran out to the other girls.

That was the end of the party. Ustenka's mother, returned from her work, gave all the girls a scolding, and turned them all out.

Chapter 26

'Yes,' thought Olenin, as he walked home. 'I need only slacken the reins a bit and I might fall desperately in love with this Cossack girl.' He went to bed with these thoughts, but expected it all to blow over and that he would continue to live as before.

But the old life did not return. His relations to Maryanka were changed. The wall that had separated them was broken down. Olenin now greeted her every time they met.

The master of the house having returned to collect the rent, on hearing of Olenin's wealth and generosity invited him to his hut. The old woman received him kindly, and from the day of the party onwards Olenin often went in of an evening and sat with them till late at night. He seemed to be living in the village just as he used to, but within him everything had changed. He spent his days in the forest, and towards eight o'clock, when it began to grow dusk, he would go to see his hosts, alone or with Daddy Eroshka. They grew so used to him that they were surprised when he stayed away. He paid well for his wine and was a quiet fellow. Vanyusha would bring him his tea and he would sit down in a corner near the oven. The old woman did not mind him but went on with her work, and over their tea or their *chikhir* they talked about Cossack affairs, about the neighbours, or about Russia: Olenin relating and the others inquiring. Sometimes he brought a book and read to himself. Maryanka crouched like a wild goat with her feet drawn up under her, sometimes on the top of the oven, sometimes in a dark corner. She did not take part in the conversations, but Olenin saw her eyes and face and heard her moving or cracking sunflower seeds, and he felt that she listened with her whole being when he spoke, and was aware of his presence while he silently read to himself. Sometimes he thought her eyes were fixed on him, and meeting their radiance he involuntarily became silent and gazed at her. Then she would instantly hide her face and he would pretend to be deep in conversation with the old woman, while he listened all the time to her breathing and to her every movement and waited for her to look at him again. In the presence of others she was generally bright and friendly with him, but when they were alone together she was shy and rough. Sometimes he came in before Maryanka had returned home. Suddenly he would hear her firm footsteps and catch a glimmer of her blue cotton smock at the open door. Then she would step into the middle of the hut, catch sight of him, and her eyes would give a scarcely perceptible kindly smile, and he would feel happy and frightened.

He neither sought for nor wished for anything from her, but every day her presence became more and more necessary to him.

Olenin had entered into the life of the Cossack village so fully that his past seemed quite foreign to him. As to the future, especially a future outside the world in which he was now living, it did not interest him at all. When he received letters from home, from relatives and friends, he was offended by the evident distress with which they regarded him as a lost man, while he in his village considered those as lost who did not live as he was living. He felt sure he would never repent of having broken away from his former surroundings and of having settled down in this village to such a solitary and original life. When out on expeditions, and when quartered at one of the forts, he felt happy too; but it was here, from under Daddy Eroshka's wing, from the forest and from his hut at the end of the village, and especially when he thought of

Maryanka and Lukashka, that he seemed to see the falseness of his former life. That falseness used to rouse his indignation even before, but now it seemed inexpressibly vile and ridiculous. Here he felt freer and freer every day and more and more of a man. The Caucasus now appeared entirely different to what his imagination had painted it. He had found nothing at all like his dreams, nor like the descriptions of the Caucasus he had heard and read. 'There are none of all those chestnut steeds, precipices, Amalet Beks, heroes or villains,' thought he. 'The people live as nature lives: they die, are born, unite, and more are born – they fight, eat and drink, rejoice and die, without any restrictions but those that nature imposes on sun and grass, on animal and tree. They have no other laws.' Therefore these people, compared to himself, appeared to him beautiful, strong, and free, and the sight of them made him feel ashamed and sorry for himself. Often it seriously occurred to him to throw up everything, to get registered as a Cossack, to buy a hut and cattle and marry a Cossack woman (only not Maryanka, whom he conceded to Lukashka), and to live with Daddy Eroshka and go shooting and fishing with him, and go with the Cossacks on their expeditions. 'Why ever don't I do it? What am I waiting for?' he asked himself, and he egged himself on and shamed himself. 'Am I afraid of doing what I hold to be reasonable and right? Is the wish to be a simple Cossack, to live close to nature, not to injure anyone but even to do good to others, more stupid than my former dreams, such as those of becoming a minister of state or a colonel?' But a voice seemed to say that he should wait, and not take any decision. He was held back by a dim consciousness that he could not live altogether like Eroshka and Lukashka because he had a different idea of happiness – he was held back by the thought that happiness lies in self-sacrifice. What he had done for Lukashka continued to give him joy. He kept looking for occasions to sacrifice himself for others, but did not meet with them. Sometimes he forgot this newly discovered recipe for happiness and considered himself capable of identifying his life with Daddy Eroshka's, but then he quickly bethought himself and promptly clutched at the idea of conscious self-sacrifice, and from that basis looked calmly and proudly at all men and at their happiness.

Chapter 27

Just before the vintage Lukashka came on horseback to see Olenin. He looked more dashing than ever. 'Well? Are you getting married?' asked Olenin, greeting him merrily.

Lukashka gave no direct reply.

'There, I've exchanged your horse across the river. This is a horse! A Kabarda horse from the Lov stud. I know horses.'

They examined the new horse and made him caracole about the yard. The horse really was an exceptionally fine one, a broad and long gelding, with glossy coat, thick silky tail, and the soft fine mane and crest of a thoroughbred. He was so well fed that 'you might go to sleep on his back' as Lukashka expressed it. His hoofs, eyes, teeth, were exquisitely shaped and sharply outlined, as one only finds them in very pure-bred horses. Olenin could not help admiring the horse, he had not yet met with such a beauty in the Caucasus.

'And how it goes!' said Lukashka, patting its neck. 'What a step! And so clever – he simply runs after his master.'

'Did you have to add much to make the exchange?' asked Olenin.

'I did not count it,' answered Lukashka with a smile. 'I got him from a *kunak*.'

'A wonderfully beautiful horse! What would you take for it?' asked Olenin.

'I have been offered a hundred and fifty rubles for it, but I'll give it you for nothing,' said Lukashka, merrily. 'Only say the word and it's yours. I'll unsaddle it and you may take it. Only give me some sort of a horse for my duties.'

'No, on no account.'

'Well then, here is a dagger I've brought you,' said Lukashka, unfastening his girdle and taking out one of the two daggers which hung from it. 'I got it from across the river.'

'Oh, thank you!'

'And mother has promised to bring you some grapes herself.'

'That's quite unnecessary. We'll balance up some day. You see I don't offer you any money for the dagger!'

'How could you? We are *kunaks*. It's just the same as when Girey Khan across the river took me into his home and said, "Choose what you like!" So I took this sword. It's our custom.'

They went into the hut and had a drink.

'Are you staying here awhile?' asked Olenin.

'No, I have come to say goodbye. They are sending me from the cordon to a company beyond the Terek. I am going tonight with my comrade Nazarka.'

'And when is the wedding to be?'

'I shall be coming back for the betrothal, and then I shall return to the company again,' Lukashka replied reluctantly.

'What, and see nothing of your betrothed?'

'Just so – what is the good of looking at her? When you go on campaign ask in our company for Lukashka the Broad. But what a lot of boars there are in our parts! I've killed two. I'll take you. Well, goodbye! Christ save you.' Lukashka mounted his horse, and without calling on Maryanka, rode caracoling down the street, where Nazarka was already awaiting him.

'I say, shan't we call round?' asked Nazarka, winking in the direction of Yamka's house.

'That's a good one!' said Lukashka. 'Here, take my horse to her and if I don't come soon give him some hay. I shall reach the company by the morning anyway.'

'Hasn't the cadet given you anything more?'

'I am thankful to have paid him back with a dagger – he was going to ask for the horse,' said Lukashka, dismounting and handing over the horse to Nazarka.

He darted into the yard past Olenin's very window, and came up to the window of the cornet's hut. It was already quite dark. Maryanka, wearing only her smock, was combing her hair preparing for bed.

'It's I – ' whispered the Cossack.

Maryanka's look was severely indifferent, but her face suddenly brightened up when she heard her name. She opened the window and leant out, frightened and joyous.

'What – what do you want?' she said.

'Open!' uttered Lukashka. 'Let me in for a minute. I am so sick of waiting! It's awful!'

He took hold of her head through the window and kissed her.

'Really, do open!'

'Why do you talk nonsense? I've told you I won't! Have you come for long?'

He did not answer but went on kissing her, and she did not ask again.

'There, through the window one can't even hug you properly,' said Lukashka.

'Maryanka dear!' came the voice of her mother, 'who is that with you?'

Lukashka took off his cap, which might have been seen, and crouched down by the window.

'Go, be quick!' whispered Maryanka.

'Lukashka called round,' she answered; 'he was asking for Daddy.'

'Well then send him here!'

'He's gone; said he was in a hurry.'

In fact, Lukashka, stooping, as with big strides he passed under the windows, ran out through the yard and towards Yamka's house unseen by anyone but Olenin. After drinking two bowls of *chikhir* he and Nazarka rode away to the outpost. The night was warm, dark, and calm. They rode in silence, only the footfall of their horses was heard. Lukashka started a song about the Cossack, Mingal, but stopped before he had finished the first verse, and after a pause, turning to Nazarka, said: 'I say, she wouldn't let me in!'

'Oh?' rejoined Nazarka. 'I knew she wouldn't. D'you know what Yamka told me? The cadet has begun going to their house. Daddy Eroshka brags that he got a gun from the cadet for getting him Maryanka.'

'He lies, the old devil!' said Lukashka, angrily. 'She's not such a girl. If he does not look out I'll wallop that old devil's sides,' and he began his favourite song:

From the village of Izmaylov,
From the master's favourite garden,
A bright-eyed falcon from his cage once flew there,
And soon after him a huntsman young came riding.
With his hand he beckoned to the bright-eyed falcon.
The bright-eyed falcon then made answer:
'In a golden cage you knew not how to keep me,
On your right hand you knew not how to hold me,
So now I'll fly to the blue sea, far far away.
And there I will kill a white swan for myself,
And I will get my fill of the sweet swan-flesh.'

Chapter 28

The betrothal was taking place in the cornet's hut. Lukashka had returned to the village, but had not been to see Olenin, and Olenin had not gone to the betrothal though he had been invited. He was sad as he had never been since he settled in this Cossack village. He had seen Lukashka earlier in the evening and was worried by the question why Lukashka was so cold towards him. Olenin shut himself up in his hut and began writing in his diary as follows.

Many things have I pondered over lately and much have I changed, [wrote he] and I have come back to the copybook maxim: The one way to be happy is to love, to love self-denyingly, to love everybody and everything; to spread a web of love on all sides and to take all who come into it. In this way I caught Vanyusha, Daddy Eroshka, Lukashka, and Maryanka.

As Olenin was finishing this sentence Daddy Eroshka entered the room.

Eroshka was in the happiest frame of mind. A few evenings before this, Olenin had gone to see him and had found him with a proud and happy face deftly skinning the carcass of a boar with a small knife in the yard. The dogs (Lyam his pet among them) were lying close by watching what he was doing and gently wagging their tails. The little boys were respectfully looking at him through the fence and not even teasing him as was their wont. His women neighbours, who were as a rule not too gracious towards him, greeted him and brought him, one a jug of *chikhir*, another some clotted cream, and a third a little flour. The next day Eroshka sat in his store-room all covered with blood, and distributed pounds of boar-flesh, taking in payment money from some and wine from others. His face clearly expressed, 'God has sent me luck. I have killed a boar, so now I am wanted.' Consequently, he naturally began to drink, and had gone on for four days never leaving the village. Besides which he had had something to drink at the betrothal.

He came to Olenin quite drunk: his face red, his beard tangled, but wearing a new *beshmet* trimmed with gold braid; and he brought with him a balalayka which he had obtained beyond the river. He had long promised Olenin this treat, and felt in the mood for it, so that he was sorry to find Olenin writing.

'Write on, write on, my lad,' he whispered, as if he thought that a spirit sat between him and the paper and must not be frightened away, and he softly and silently sat down on the floor. When Daddy Eroshka was drunk his favourite position was on the floor. Olenin looked round, ordered some wine to be brought, and continued to write. Eroshka found it dull to drink by himself and he wished to talk.

'I've been to the betrothal at the cornet's. But there! They're shwine! – Don't want them! – Have come to you.'

'And where did you get your balalayka asked Olenin, still writing.

'I've been beyond the river and got it there, brother mine,' he answered, also very quietly. 'I'm a master at it. Tartar or Cossack, squire or soldiers' songs, any kind you please.'

Olenin looked at him again, smiled, and went on writing.

That smile emboldened the old man.

'Come, leave off, my lad, leave off!' he said with sudden firmness.

'Well, perhaps I will.'

'Come, people have injured you but leave them alone, spit at them! Come, what's the use of writing and writing, what's the good?'

And he tried to mimic Olenin by tapping the floor with his thick fingers, and then twisted his big face to express contempt.

'What's the good of writing quibbles. Better have a spree and show you're a man!'

No other conception of writing found place in his head except that of legal chicanery.

Olenin burst out laughing and so did Eroshka. Then, jumping up from the floor, the latter began to show off his skill on the balalayka and to sing Tartar songs.

'Why write, my good fellow! You'd better listen to what I'll sing to you. When you're dead you won't hear any more songs. Make merry now!'

First he sang a song of his own composing accompanied by a dance:

Ah, dee, dee, dee, dee, dee, dim,
Say where did they last see him?
In a booth, at the fair,
He was selling pins, there.

Then he sang a song he had learnt from his former sergeant-major.

Deep I fell in love on Monday,
Tuesday nothing did but sigh,
Wednesday I popped the question,
Thursday waited her reply.
Friday, late, it came at last,
Then all hope for me was past!
Saturday my life to take
I determined like a man,
But for my salvation's sake
Sunday morning changed my plan!

Then he sang again.

Oh dee, dee, dee, dee, dee, dim,
Say where did they last see him?

And after that, winking, twitching his shoulders, and footing it to the tune, he sang;

I will kiss you and embrace,
Ribbons red twine round you;
And I'll call you little Grace.
Oh, you little Grace now do
Tell me, do you love me true?

And he became so excited that with a sudden dashing movement he started dancing around the room accompanying himself the while.

Songs like 'Dee, dee, dee' – 'gentlemen's songs' – he sang for Olenin's benefit, but after drinking three more tumblers of *chikhir* he remembered old times and began singing real Cossack and Tartar songs. In the midst of one of his favourite songs his voice suddenly trembled and he ceased singing, and only continued strumming on the balalayka.

'Oh, my dear friend!' he said.

The peculiar sound of his voice made Olenin look round.

The old man was weeping. Tears stood in his eyes and one tear was running down his cheek.

'You are gone, my young days, and will never come back!' he said, blubbering and halting. 'Drink, why don't you drink!'

he suddenly shouted with a deafening roar, without wiping away his tears.

There was one Tartar song that specially moved him. It had few words, but its charm lay in the sad refrain. 'Ay day, dalalay!' Eroshka translated the words of the song: 'A youth drove his sheep from the *aoul* to the mountains: the Russians came and burnt the *aoul*, they killed all the men and took all the women into bondage. The youth returned from the mountains. Where the *aoul* had stood was an empty space; his mother not there, nor his brothers, nor his house; one tree alone was left standing. The youth sat beneath the tree and wept. "Alone like thee, alone am I left," ' and Eroshka began singing: 'Ay day, dalalay!' and the old man repeated several times this wailing, heart-rending refrain.

When he had finished the refrain Eroshka suddenly seized a gun that hung on the wall, rushed hurriedly out into the yard and fired off both barrels into the air. Then again he began, more dolefully, his 'Ay day, dalalay – ah, ah', and ceased.

Olenin followed him into the porch and looked up into the starry sky in the direction where the shots had flashed. In the cornet's house there were lights and the sound of voices. In the yard girls were crowding round the porch and the windows, and running backwards and forwards between the hut and the out-house. Some Cossacks rushed out of the hut and could not refrain from shouting, re-echoing the refrain of Daddy Eroshka's song and his shots.

'Why are you not at the betrothal?' asked Olenin.

'Never mind them! Never mind them!' muttered the old man, who had evidently been offended by something there. 'Don't like them, I don't. Oh, those people! Come back into the hut! Let them make merry by themselves and we'll make merry by ourselves.'

Olenin went in.

'And Lukashka, is he happy? Won't he come to see me?' he asked.

'What, Lukashka? They've lied to him and said I am getting his girl for you,' whispered the old man. 'But what's the girl? She will be ours if we want her. Give enough money – and she's ours. I'll fix it up for you. Really!'

'No, Daddy, money can do nothing if she does not love me. You'd better not talk like that!'

'We are not loved, you and I. We are forlorn,' said Daddy Eroshka suddenly, and again he began to cry.

Listening to the old man's talk Olenin had drunk more than usual. 'So now my Lukashka is happy,' thought he; yet he felt sad. The old man had drunk so much that evening that he fell down on the floor and Vanyusha had to call soldiers in to help, and spat as they dragged the old man out. He was so angry with the old man for his bad behaviour that he did not even say a single French word.

Chapter 29

It was August. For days the sky had been cloudless, the sun scorched unbearably and from early morning the warm wind raised a whirl of hot sand from the sand-drifts and from the road, and bore it in the air through the reeds, the trees, and the village. The grass and the leaves on the trees were covered with dust, the roads and dried-up salt marshes were baked so hard that they rang when trodden on. The water had long since subsided in the Terek and rapidly vanished and dried up in the ditches. The slimy banks of the pond near the village were trodden bare by the cattle and all day long you could hear the splashing of water and the shouting of girls and boys bathing. The sand-drifts and the reeds were already drying up in the steppes, and the cattle, lowing, ran into the fields in the day-time. The boars migrated into the distant reed-beds and to the hills beyond the Terek. Mosquitoes and gnats swarmed in thick clouds over the low lands and villages. The snow-peaks were hidden in grey mist. The air was rarefied and smoky. It was said that *abreks* had crossed the now shallow river and were prowling on this side of it. Every night the sun set in a glowing red blaze. It was the busiest time of the year. The villagers all swarmed in the melon-fields and the vineyards. The vineyards thickly overgrown with twining verdure lay in cool, deep shade. Everywhere between the broad translucent leaves, ripe, heavy, black clusters peeped out. Along the dusty road from the vineyards the creaking carts moved slowly, heaped up with black grapes. Clusters of them, crushed by the wheels, lay in the dirt. Boys and girls in smocks stained with grape-juice, with grapes in their hands and mouths, ran after their mothers. On the road you continually came across tattered labourers with baskets of grapes on their powerful shoulders; Cossack maidens, veiled with kerchiefs to their eyes, drove bullocks harnessed to carts laden high with grapes. Soldiers who happened to meet these carts asked for grapes, and the maidens, clambering up without stopping their carts, would take an armful of grapes and drop them into the skirts of the soldiers' coats. In some homesteads they had already begun pressing the grapes; and the smell of the emptied skins filled the air. One saw the blood-red troughs in the pent-houses in the yards and Nogay labourers with their trousers rolled up and their legs stained with the juice. Grunting pigs gorged themselves with the empty skins and rolled about in them. The flat roofs of the outhouses were all spread over with the dark amber clusters drying in the sun. Daws and magpies crowded round the roofs, picking the seeds and fluttering from one place to another.

The fruits of the year's labour were being merrily gathered in, and this year the fruit was unusually fine and plentiful.

In the shady green vineyards amid a sea of vines, laughter, songs, merriment, and the voices of women were to be heard on all sides, and glimpses of their bright-coloured garments could be seen.

Just at noon Maryanka was sitting in their vineyard in the shade of a peach-tree, getting out the family dinner from under an unharnessed cart. Opposite her, on a spread-out horse-cloth, sat the cornet (who had returned from the school) washing his hands by pouring water on them from a little jug. Her little brother, who had just come straight out of the pond, stood wiping his face with his wide sleeves, and gazed anxiously at his sister and his mother and breathed deeply, awaiting his dinner. The old mother, with her sleeves rolled up over her strong sunburnt arms, was arranging grapes, dried fish, and clotted cream on a little low, circular Tartar table. The cornet wiped his hands, took off his cap, crossed himself, and moved nearer to the table. The boy seized the jug and eagerly began to drink. The mother and daughter crossed their legs under them and sat down by the table. Even in the shade it was intolerably hot. The air above the vineyard smelt unpleasant: the strong warm wind passing amid the branches brought no coolness, but only monotonously bent the tops of the pear, peach, and mulberry trees with which the vineyard was sprinkled. The cornet, having crossed himself once more, took a little jug of *chikhir* that stood behind him covered with a vine-leaf, and having had a drink from the mouth of the jug passed it to the old woman. He had nothing on over his shirt, which was unfastened at the neck, and showing his shaggy muscular chest. His fine-featured cunning face looked cheerful; neithr in his attitude nor in his words was his usual wiliness to be seen; he was cheerful and natural.

'Shall we finish the bit beyond the shed tonight?' he asked, wiping his wet beard.

'We'll manage it,' replied his wife, 'if only the weather does not hinder us. The Demkins have not half finished yet,' she added. 'Only Ustenka is at work there, wearing herself out.'

'What can you expect of them?' said the old man proudly.

'Here, have a drink, Maryanka dear!' said the old woman, passing the jug to the girl. 'God willing, we'll have enough to pay for the wedding feast,' added the old woman.

'That's not yet awhile,' said the cornet with a slight frown.

The girl hung her head.

'Why shouldn't we mention it?' said the old woman; 'the affair is settled, and the time is drawing near too.'

'Don't make plans beforehand,' said the cornet. 'Now we have the harvest to get in.'

'Have you seen Lukashka's new horse?' asked the old woman. 'That which Dmitri Andreich Olenin gave him is gone – he's exchanged it.'

'No, I have not; but I spoke with the servant today,' said the teacher, 'and he said his master has again received a thousand rubles.'

'Rolling in riches, in short,' said the old woman.

The whole family felt cheerful and contented. The work was progressing successfully. The grapes were more abundant and finer than they had expected. After dinner Maryanka threw some grass to the oxen, folded her *beshmet* for a pillow, and lay down under the wagon on the juicy down-trodden grass. She had on only a red jerchief over her head, and a faded blue print smock; yet she felt unbearably hot. Her face was burning, and she did not know where to put her feet, her eyes were moist with sleepiness and weariness, her lips parted involuntarily, and her chest heaved heavily and deeply.

The busy time of year had begun a fortnight ago and the continuous heavy labour had filled the girl's life. At dawn she jumped up, washed her face with cold water, wrapped herself in a shawl, and ran out barefoot to see to the cattle. Then she hurriedly put on her shoes and her *beshmet* and, taking a small bundle of bread, she harnessed the bullocks and drove away to the vineyards for the whole day. There she cut the grapes and carried the baskets with only an hour's interval for rest, and in the evening she returned to the village, bright and not tired, dragging the bullocks by a rope or driving them with a long stick. After attending to the cattle, she took some sunflower seeds in the wide sleeve of her smock and went to the corner of the street to crack them and have some fun with the other girls. But as soon as it was dusk she returned home, and after having supper with her parents and her brother in the dark outhouse, she went into the hut, healthy and free from care, and climbed onto the oven, where half drowsing she listened to their lodger's conversation. As soon as he went away she would throw herself down on her bed and sleep soundly and quietly till morning. And so it went on day after day. She had not seen Lukashka since the day of their betrothal, but calmly awaited the wedding. She had got used to their lodger and felt his intent looks with pleasure.

Chapter 30

Although there was no escape from the heat and the mosquitoes swarmed in the cool shadow of the wagons, and her little brother tossing about beside her kept pushing her, Maryanka having drawn her kerchief over her head was just falling asleep, when suddenly their neighbour Ustenka came running towards her and, diving under the wagon, lay down beside her.

'Sleep, girls, sleep!' said Ustenka, making herself comfortable under the wagon. 'Wait a bit,' she exclaimed, 'this won't do!'

She jumped up, plucked some green branches, and stuck them through the wheels on both sides of the wagon and hung her *beshmet* over them.

'Let me in,' she shouted to the little boy as she again crept under the wagon. 'Is this the place for a Cossack – with the girls? Go away!'

When alone under the wagon with her friend, Ustenka suddenly put both her arms round her, and clinging close to her began kissing her cheeks and neck.

'Darling, sweetheart,' she kept repeating, between bursts of shrill, clear laughter.

'Why, you've learnt it from Grandad,' said Maryanka, struggling. 'Stop it!'

And they both broke into such peals of laughter that Maryanka's mother shouted to them to be quiet.

'Are you jealous?' asked Ustenka in a whisper.

'What humbug! Let me sleep. What have you come for?'

But Ustenka kept on, 'I say! But I wanted to tell you such a thing.'

Maryanka raised herself on her elbow and arranged the kerchief which had slipped off.

'Well, what is it?'

'I know something about your lodger!'

'There's nothing to know,' said Maryanka.

'Oh, you rogue of a girl!' said Ustenka, nudging her with her elbow and laughing. 'Won't tell anything. Does he come to you?'

'He does. What of that?' said Maryanka with a sudden blush.

'Now I'm a simple lass. I tell everybody. Why should I pretend?' said Ustenka, and her bright rosy face suddenly became pensive. 'Whom do I hurt? I love him, that's all about it.'

'Grandad, do you mean?'

'Well, yes!'

'And the sin?'

'Ah, Maryanka! When is one to have a good time if not while one's still free? When I marry a Cossack I shall bear children and shall have cares. There now, when you get married to Lukashka not even a thought of joy will enter your head: children will come, and work!'

'Well? Some who are married live happily. It makes no difference!' Maryanka replied quietly.

'Do tell me just this once what has passed between you and Lukashka?'

'What has passed? A match was proposed. Father put it off for a year, but now it's been settled and they'll marry us in autumn.'

'But what did he say to you?' Maryanka smiled.

'What should he say? He said he loved me. He kept asking me to come to the vineyards with him.'

'Just see what pitch! But you didn't go, did you? And what a dare-devil he has become: the first among the braves. He makes merry out there in the army too! The other day our Kirka came home; he says: "What a horse Lukashka's got in exchange!" But all the same I expect he frets after you. And what else did he say?'

'Must you know everything?' said Maryanka laughing. 'One night he came to my window tipsy, and asked me to let him in.'

'And you didn't let him?'

'Let him, indeed! Once I have said a thing I keep to it firm as a rock,' answered Maryanka seriously.

'A fine fellow! If he wanted her, no girl would refuse him.'

'Well, let him go to the others,' replied Maryanka proudly.

'You don't pity him?'

'I do pity him, but I'll have no nonsense. It is wrong.' Ustenka suddenly dropped her head on her friend's breast, seized hold of her, and shook with smothered laughter. 'You silly fool!' she exclaimed, quite out of breath. 'You don't want to be happy,' and she began tickling Maryanka. 'Oh, leave off!' said Maryanka, screaming and laughing. 'You've crushed Lazutka.'

'Hark at those young devils! Quite frisky! Not tired yet!' came the old woman's sleepy voice from the wagon.

'Don't want happiness,' repeated Ustenka in a whisper, insistently. 'But you are lucky, that you are! How they love you! You are so crusty, and yet they love you. Ah, if I were in your place I'd soon turn the lodger's head! I noticed him when you were at our house. He was ready to eat you with his eyes. What things Grandad has given me! And yours they say is the richest of the Russians. His orderly says they have serfs of their own.'

Maryanka raised herself, and after thinking a moment, smiled.

'Do you know what he once told me: the lodger I mean?' she said, biting a bit of grass. 'He said, "I'd like to be Lukashka the Cossack, or your brother Lazutka – " What do you think he meant?'

'Oh, just chattering what came into his head,' answered Ustenka. 'What does mine not say! Just as if he was possessed!'

Maryanka dropped her hand on her folded *beshmet*, threw her arm over Ustenka's shoulder, and shut her eyes.

'He wanted to come and work in the vineyard today: father invited him,' she said, and after a short silence she fell asleep.

Chapter 31

The sun had come out from behind the pear-tree that had shaded the wagon, and even through the branches that Ustenka had fixed up it scorched the faces of the sleeping girls. Maryanka woke up and began arranging the kerchief on her head. Looking about her, beyond the pear-tree she noticed their lodger, who with his gun on his shoulder stood talking to her father. She nudged Ustenka and smilingly pointed him out to her.

'I went yesterday and didn't find a single one,' Olenin was saying as he looked about uneasily, not seeing Maryanka through the branches.

'Ah, you should go out there in that direction, go right round as by compasses, there in a disused vineyard denominated as the Waste, hares are always to be found,' said the cornet, having at once changed his manner of speech.

'A fine thing to go looking for hares in these busy times! You had better come and help us, and do some work with the girls,' the old woman said merrily. 'Now then, girls, up with you!' she cried.

Maryanka and Ustenka under the cart were whispering and could hardly restrain their laughter.

Since it had become known that Olenin had given a horse worth fifty rubles to Lukashka, his hosts had become more amiable and the cornet in particular saw with pleasure his daughter's growing intimacy with Olenin. 'But I don't know how to do the work,' replied Olenin, trying not to look through the green branches under the wagon where he had now noticed Maryanka's blue smock and red kerchief.

'Come, I'll give you some peaches,' said the old woman.

'It's only according to the ancient Cossack hospitality. It's her old woman's silliness,' said the cornet, explaining and apparently correcting his wife's words. 'In Russia, I expect, it's not so much peaches as pineapple jam and preserves you have been accustomed to eat at your pleasure.'

'So you say hares are to be found in the disused vineyard?' asked Olenin. 'I will go there,' and throwing a hasty glance through the green branches he raised his cap and disappeared between the regular rows of green vines.

The sun had already sunk behind the fence of the vineyards, and its broken rays glittered through the translucent leaves when Olenin returned to his host's vineyard. The wind was falling and a cool freshness was beginning to spread around. By some instinct Olenin recognized from afar Maryanka's blue smock among the rows of vine, and, picking grapes on his way, he approached her. His highly excited dog also now and then seized a low-hanging cluster of grapes in his slobbering mouth. Maryanka, her face flushed, sleeves rolled up, and her kerchief down below her chin, was rapidly cutting the heavy clusters and laying them in a basket. Without letting go of the vine she had hold of, she stopped to smile pleasantly at him and resumed her work. Olenin drew near and threw his gun behind his back to have his hands free. 'Where are your people? May God aid you! Are you alone?' he meant to say but did not say, and only raised his cap in silence.

He was ill at ease alone with Maryanka, but as if purposely to torment himself he went up to her.

'You'll be shooting the women with your gun like that,' said Maryanka.

'No, I shan't shoot them.'

They were both silent. Then after a pause she said: 'You should help me.'

He took out his knife and began silently to cut off the clusters. He reached from under the leaves low down a thick bunch weighing about three pounds, the grapes of which grew so close that they flattened each other for want of space. He showed it to Maryanka.

'Must they all be cut? Isn't this one too green?'

'Give it here.'

Their hands touched. Olenin took her hand, and she looked at him smiling.

'Are you going to be married soon?' he asked.

She did not answer, but turned away with a stern look.

'Do you love Lukashka?'

'What's that to you?'

'I envy him!'

'Very likely!'

'No really. You are so beautiful!'

And he suddenly felt terribly ashamed of having said it, so commonplace did the words seem to him. He flushed, lost control of himself, and seized both her hands.

'Whatever I am, I'm not for you. Why do you make fun of me?' replied Maryanka, but her look showed how certainly she knew he was not making fun.

'Making fun? If you only knew how I —'

The words sounded still more commonplace, they accorded still less with what he felt, but yet he continued, 'I don't know what I would not do for you —'

'Leave me alone, you pitch!'

But her face, her shining eyes, her swelling bosom, her shapely legs, said something quite different. It seemed to him that she understood how petty were all things he had said, but that she was superior to such considerations. It seemed to him she had long known all he wished and was not able to tell her, but wanted to hear how he would say it. 'And how can she help knowing,' he thought, 'since I only want to tell her all that she herself is? But she does not wish to understand, does not wish to reply.'

'Hallo!' suddenly came Ustenka's high voice from behind the vine at no great distance, followed by her shrill laugh. 'Come and help me, Dmitri Andreich. I am all alone,' she cried, thrusting her round, naive little face through the vines.

Olenin did not answer nor move from his place.

Maryanka went on cutting and continually looked up at Olenin. He was about to say something, but stopped, shrugged his shoulders and, having jerked up his gun, walked out of the vineyard with rapid strides.

Chapter 32

He stopped once or twice, listening to the ringing laughter of Maryanka and Ustenka who, having come together, were shouting something. Olenin spent the whole evening hunting in the forest and returned home at dusk without having killed anything. When crossing the road he noticed her open the door of the outhouse, and her blue smock showed through it. He called to Vanyusha very loud so as to let her know that he was back, and then sat down in the porch in his usual place. His hosts now returned from the vineyard; they came out of the outhouse and into their hut, but did not ask him in. Maryanka went twice out of the gate. Once in the twilight it seemed to him that she was looking at him. He eagerly followed her every movement, but could not make up his mind to approach her. When she disappeared into the hut he left the porch and began pacing up and down the yard; but Maryanka did not again come out. Olenin spent the whole sleepless night out in the yard, listening to every sound in his hosts' hut. He heard them talking early in the evening, heard them having their supper, and pulling out their cushions, and going to bed. He heard Maryanka laughing at something, and then heard everything growing gradually quiet.

The cornet and his wife talked a while in whispers, and someone was breathing. Olenin re-entered his hut. Vanyusha lay asleep in his clothes. Olenin envied him, and again went out to pace the yard, always expecting something, but no one came, no one moved, and he only heard the regular breathing of three people. He knew Maryanka's brething and listened to it and the beating of his own heart. In the village everything was quiet. The waning moon rose late and the deep-breathing cattle in the yard became more visible as they lay down and slowly rose. Olenin angrily asked himself, 'What is it I want?' but could not tear himself away from the enchantment of the night. Suddenly he thought he distinctly heard the floor creak and the sound of footsteps in his hosts' hut. He rushed to the door, but all was silent again, except for the sound of regular breathing, and in the yard the buffalo-cow, after a deep sigh, again moved, rose on her front knees and then on her feet, swished her tail, and something splashed steadily on the dry clay ground, and then she lay down again in the dim moonlight. He asked himself, 'What am I to do?' and definitely decided to go to bed, but again he heard a sound, and in his imagination there rose the image of Maryanka coming out into this moonlit misty night, and again he rushed to her window, and again heard the sound of footsteps. Not till just before dawn did he go up to her window and push at the shutter and then run to the door, and this time he really heard Maryanka's deep breathing and her footsteps. He took hold of the latch and knocked. The floor hardly creaked under the bare cautious footsteps which approached the door. The latch clicked, the door creaked, and he noticed a faint smell of marjoram and pumpkin, and Maryanka's whole figure appeared in the doorway. He saw her only for an instant in the moonlight. She slammed the door and, muttering something, ran lightly back again. Olenin began rapping softly but nothing responded. He ran to the window and listened. Suddenly he was startled by a shrill, squeaky man's voice.

'Fine!' exclaimed a rather small young Cossack in a white cap, coming across the yard close to Olenin. 'I saw . . . fine!'

Olenin recognized Nazarka, and was silent, not knowing what to do or say.

'Fine! I'll go and tell them at the office, and I'll tell her father! That's a fine cornet's daughter! One's not enough for her.'

'What do you want of me, what are you after?' uttered Olenin.

'Nothing; only I'll tell them at the office.'

Nazarka spoke very loud, and evidently did so intentionally, adding: 'Just see what a clever cadet!'

Olenin trembled and grew pale.

'Come here, here!' He seized the Cossack firmly by the arm and drew him towards his hut.

'Nothing happened, she did not let me in, and I too mean no harm. She is an honest girl – '

'Eh, discuss – '

'Yes, but all the same I'll give you something now. Wait a bit!'

Nazarka said nothing. Olenin ran into his hut and brought out ten rubles, which he gave to the Cossack.

'Nothing happened, but still I was to blame, so I give this! – Only for God's sake don't let anyone know, for nothing happened . . . '

'I wish you joy,' said Nazarka laughing, and went away.

Nazarka had come to the village that night at Lukashka's bidding to find a place to hide a stolen horse, and now, passing by on his way home, had heard the sound of footsteps. When he returned next morning to his company he bragged to his chum, and told him how cleverly he had got ten rubles. Next morning Olenin met his hosts and they knew nothing about the events of the night. He did not speak to Maryanka, and she only laughed a little when she looked at him. Next night he also passed without sleep, vainly wandering about the yard. The day after he purposely spent shooting, and in the evening he went to see Beletski to escape from his own thoughts. He was afraid of himself, and promised himself not to go to his hosts' hut any more.

That night he was roused by the sergeant-major. His company was ordered to start at once on a raid. Olenin was glad this had happened, and thought he would not again return to the village.

The raid lasted four days. The commander, who was a relative of Olenin's, wished to see him and offered to let him remain with the staff, but this Olenin declined. He found that he could not live away from the village, and asked to be allowed to return to it. For having taken part in the raid he received a soldier's cross, which he had formerly greatly desired. Now he was quite indifferent about it, and even more indifferent about his promotion, the order for which had still not arrived. Accompanied by Vanyusha he rode back to the cordon without any accident several hours in advance of the rest of the company. He spent the whole evening in his porch watching Maryanka, and he again walked about the yard, without aim or thought, all night.

Chapter 33

It was late when he awoke the next day. His hosts were no longer in. He did not go shooting, but now took up a book, and now went out into the porch, and now again re-entered the hut and lay down on the bed. Vanyusha thought he was ill.

Towards evening Olenin got up, resolutely began writing, and wrote on till late at night. He wrote a letter, but did not post it because he felt that no one would have understood what he wanted to say, and besides it was not necessary that anyone but himself should understand it. This is what he wrote.

I receive letters of condolence from Russia. They are afraid that I shall perish, buried in these wilds. They say about me: 'He will become coarse; he will be behind the times in everything; he will take to drink, and who knows but that he may marry a Cossack girl.' It was not for nothing, they say, that Ermolov declared: 'Anyone serving in the Caucasus for ten years either becomes a confirmed drunkard or marries a loose woman.' How terrible! Indeed it won't do for me to ruin myself when I might have the great happiness of even becoming the Countess B——'s husband, or a Court chamberlain, or a *Maréchal de Noblesse* of my district. Oh, how repulsive and pitiable you all seem to me! You do not know what happiness is and what life is! One must taste life once in all its natural beauty, must see and understand what I see every day before me – those eternally unapproachable snowy peaks, and a majestic woman in that primitive beauty in which the first woman must have come from her creator's hands – and then it becomes clear who is ruining himself and who is living truly or falsely – you or I. If you only knew how despicable and pitiable you, in your delusions, seem to me! When I picture to myself – in place of my hut, my forests, and my love – those drawing-rooms, those women with their pomatum-greased hair eked out with false curls, those unnaturally grimacing lips, those hidden, feeble, distorted limbs, and that chatter of obligatory drawing-room conversation which has no right to the name – I feel unendurably revolted. I then see before me those obtuse faces, those rich eligible girls whose looks seem to say: 'It's all right, you may come near though I am rich and eligible' – and that arranging and rearranging of seats, that shameless match-making and that eternal tittle-tattle and pretence; those rules – with whom to shake hands, to whom only to nod, with whom to converse (and all this done deliberately with a conviction of its inevitability), that continual ennui in the blood passing on from generation to generation. Try to understand or believe just this one thing: you need only see and comprehend what truth and beauty are, and all that you now say and think and all your wishes for me and for yourselves will fly to atoms! Happiness is being with nature, seeing her, and conversing with her. 'He may even (God forbid) marry a common Cossack girl, and be quite lost socially,' I can imagine them saying of me with sincere pity! Yet the one thing I desire is to be quite 'lost' in your sense of the word. I wish to marry a Cossack girl, and dare not because it would be a height of happiness of which I am unworthy.

Three months have passed since I first saw the Cossack girl, Maryanka. The views and prejudices of the world I had left were still fresh in me. I did not then believe that I could love that

woman. I delighted in her beauty just as I delighted in the beauty
of the mountains and the sky, nor could I help delighting in her,
for she is as beautiful as they. I found that the sight of her beauty
had become a necessity of my life and I began asking myself
whether I did not love her. But I could find nothing within
myself at all like love as I had imagined it to be. Mine was not
the restlessness of loneliness and desire for marriage, nor was it
platonic, still less a carnal love such as I have experienced. I
needed only to see her, to hear her, to know that she was near –
and if I was not happy, I was at peace.

After an evening gathering at which I met her and touched
her, I felt that between that woman and myself there existed
an indissoluble though unacknowledged bond against which I
could not struggle, yet I did struggle. I asked myself: 'Is it
possible to love a woman who will never understand the
profoundest interests of my life? Is it possible to love a woman
simply for her beauty, to love the statue of a woman?' But I
was already in love with her, though I did not yet trust to
my feelings.

After that evening when I first spoke to her our relations
changed. Before that she had been to me an extraneous but
majestic object of external nature: but since then she has become
a human being. I began to meet her, to talk to her, and sometimes to go to work for her father and to spend whole evenings
with them, and in this intimate intercourse she remained still
in my eyes just as pure, inaccessible, and majestic. She always
responded with equal calm, pride, and cheerful equanimity.
Sometimes she was friendly, but generally her every look, every
word, and every movement expressed equanimity – not contemptuous, but crushing and bewitching. Every day with a
feigned smile on my lips I tried to play a part, and with torments
of passion and desire in my heart I spoke banteringly to her. She
saw that I was dissembling, but looked straight at me cheerfully
and simply. This position became unbearable. I wished not to
deceive her but to tell her all I thought and felt. I was extremely
agitated. We were in the vineyard when I began to tell her of my
love, in words I am now ashamed to remember. I am ashamed
because I ought not to have dared to speak so to her because she
stood far above such words and above the feeling they were

meant to express. I said no more, but from that day my position has been intolerable. I did not wish to demean myself by continuing our former flippant relations, and at the same time I felt that I had not yet reached the level of straight and simple relations with her. I asked myself despairingly, 'What am I to do?' In foolish dreams I imagined her now as my mistress and now as my wife, but rejected both ideas with disgust. To make her a wanton woman would be dreadful. It would be murder. To turn her into a fine lady, the wife of Dmitri Andreich Olenin, like a Cossack woman here who is married to one of our officers, would be still worse. Now could I turn Cossack like Lukashka, and steal horses, get drunk on *chikhir*, sing rollicking songs, kill people, and when drunk climb in at her window for the night without a thought of who and what I am, it would be different: then we might understand one another and I might be happy.

I tried to throw myself into that kind of life but was still more conscious of my own weakness and artificiality. I cannot forget myself and my complex, distorted past, and my future appears to me still more hopeless. Every day I have before me the distant snowy mountains and this majestic, happy woman. But not for me is the only happiness possible in the world; I cannot have this woman! What is most terrible and yet sweetest in my condition is that I feel that I understand her but that she will never understand me; not because she is inferior: on the contrary she ought not to understand me. She is happy, she is like nature: consistent, calm, and self-contained; and I, a weak distorted being, want her to understand my deformity and my torments! I have not slept at night, but have aimlessly passed under her windows not rendering account to myself of what was happening to me. On the 18th our company started on a raid, and I spent three days away from the village. I was sad and apathetic, the usual songs, cards, drinking-bouts, and talk of rewards in the regiment, were more repulsive to me than usual. Yesterday I returned home and saw her, my hut, Daddy Eroshka, and the snowy mountains, from my porch, and was seized by such a strong, new feeling of joy that I understood it all. I love this woman; I feel real love for the first and only time in my life. I know what has befallen me. I do not fear to be degraded by this feeling, I am not ashamed of my love, I am proud of it. It is not my fault that I love. It has come about against my will. I tried to escape from my love by self-renunciation, and tried to devise a joy in the Cossack Lukashka's and Maryanka's love, but thereby only stirred up my own love and jealousy. This is not the ideal, the so-called exalted love which I have known before; not that sort of attachment in which you admire your own love and feel that the source of your emotion is within yourself and do everything yourself. I have felt that too. It is still less a desire for enjoyment: it is something different. Perhaps in her I love nature: the personification of all that is beautiful in nature; but yet I am not acting by my own will, but some elemental force loves through me; the whole of God's world, all nature, presses this love into my soul and says, 'Love her.' I love her not with my mind or my imagination, but with my whole being. Loving her I feel myself to be an integral part of all God's joyous world. I wrote before about the new convictions to which my solitary life had brought me, but no one knows with what labour they shaped themselves within me and with what joy I realized them and saw a new way of life opening out before me; nothing was dearer to me than those convictions . . . Well! . . . love has come and neither they nor any regrets for them remain! It is even difficult for me to believe that I could prize such a one-sided, cold, and abstract state of mind. Beauty came and scattered to the winds all that laborious inward toil, and no regret remains for what has vanished! Self-renunciation is all nonsense and absurdity! That is pride, a refuge from well-merited unhappiness, and salvation from the envy of others' happiness: 'Live for others, and do good!' – Why? when in my soul there is only love for myself and the desire to love her and to live her life with her? Not for others, not for Lukashka, I now desire happiness. I do not now love those others. Formerly I should have told myself that this is wrong. I should have tormented myself with the questions: What will become of her, of me, and of Lukashka? Now I don't care. I do not live my own life, there is something stronger than me which directs me. I suffer; but formerly I was dead and only now do I live. Today I will go to their house and tell her everything.

Chapter 34

Late that evening, after writing this letter, Olenin went to his hosts' hut. The old woman was sitting on a bench behind the oven unwinding cocoons. Maryanka with her head uncovered sat sewing by the light of a candle. On seeing Olenin she jumped up, took her kerchief and stepped to the oven. 'Maryanka dear,' said her mother, 'won't you sit here with me a bit?' 'No, I'm bare-headed,' she replied, and sprang up on the oven. Olenin could only see a knee, and one of her shapely legs hanging down from the oven. He treated the old woman to tea. She treated her guest to clotted cream which she sent Maryanka to fetch. But having put a plateful on the table Maryanka again sprang on the oven from whence Olenin felt her eyes upon him. They talked about house-hold matters. Granny Ulitka became animated and went into raptures of hospitality. She brought Olenin preserved grapes and a grape tart and some of her best wine, and pressed him to eat and drink with the rough yet proud hospitality of country folk, only found among those who produce their bread by the labour of their own hands. The old woman, who had at first struck Olenin so much by her rudeness, now often touched him by her simple tenderness towards her daughter.

'Yes, we need not offend the Lord by grumbling! We have enough of everything, thank God. We have pressed sufficient *chikhir* and have preserved and shall sell three or four barrels of grapes and have enough left to drink. Don't be in a hurry to leave us. We will make merry together at the wedding.'

'And when is the wedding to be?' asked Olenin, feeling his blood suddenly rush to his face while his heart beat irregularly and painfully.

He heard a movement on the oven and the sound of seeds being cracked.

'Well, you know, it ought to be next week. We are quite ready,' replied the old woman, as simply and quietly as though Olenin did not exist. 'I have prepared and have procured everything for Maryanka. We will give her away properly. Only there's one thing not quite right. Our Lukashka has been running rather wild. He has been too much on the spree! He's up to tricks! The other day a Cossack came here from his company and said he had been to Nogay.'

'He must mind he does not get caught,' said Olenin.

'Yes, that's what I tell him. "Mind, Lukashka, don't you get into mischief. Well, of course, a young fellow naturally wants to cut a dash. But there's a time for everything. Well, you've captured or stolen something and killed an *abrek*! Well, you're a fine fellow! But now you should live quietly for a bit, or else there'll be trouble." '

'Yes, I saw him a time or two in the division, he was always merry-making. He has sold another horse,' said Olenin, and glanced towards the oven. A pair of large, dark, and hostile eyes glittered as they gazed severely at him.

He became ashamed of what he had said. 'What of it? He does no one any harm,' suddenly remarked Maryanka. 'He makes merry with his own money,' and lowering her legs she jumped down from the oven and went out banging the door.

Olenin followed her with his eyes as long as she was in the hut, and then looked at the door and waited, understanding nothing of what Granny Ulitka was telling him.

A few minutes later some visitors arrived: an old man, Granny Ulitka's brother, with Daddy Eroshka, and following them came Maryanka and Ustenka.

'Good evening,' squeaked Ustenka. 'Still on holiday?' she added, turning to Olenin.

'Yes, still on holiday,' he replied, and felt, he did not know why, ashamed and ill at ease.

He wished to go away but could not. It also seemed to him impossible to remain silent. The old man helped him by asking for a drink, and they had a drink. Olenin drank with Eroshka, with the other Cossack, and again with Eroshka, and the more he drank the heavier was his heart. But the two old men grew merry. The girls climbed onto the oven, where they sat whispering and looking at the men, who drank till it was late. Olenin did not talk, but drank more than the others. The Cossacks were shouting. The old woman would not let them have any more *chikhir*, and at last turned them out. The girls laughed at Daddy Eroshka, and it was past ten when they all went out into the porch. The old men invited themselves to finish their merry-making at Olenin's. Ustenka ran off home and Eroshka led the old Cossack to Vanyusha. The old woman went out to tidy up the shed. Maryanka remained alone in the hut. Olenin felt fresh and joyous, as if he had only just woke up. He noticed everything, and having let the old men pass ahead he turned back to the hut where Maryanka was preparing for bed. He went up to her and wished to say something, but his voice broke. She moved away from him, sat down cross-legged on her bed in the corner, and looked at him silently with wild and frightened eyes. She was evidently afraid of him. Olenin felt this. He felt sorry and ashamed of himself, and at the same time proud and pleased that he aroused even that feeling in her.

'Maryanka!' he said. 'Will you never take pity on me? I can't tell you how I love you.'

She moved still farther away.

'Just hear how the wine is speaking! . . . You'll get nothing from me!'

'No, it is not the wine. Don't marry Lukashka. I will marry you.' ('What am I saying,' he thought as he uttered these words. 'Shall I be able to say the same tomorrow?' 'Yes, I shall, I am sure I shall, and I will repeat them now,' replied an inner voice.)

'Will you marry me?'

She looked at him seriously and her fear seemed to have passed.

'Maryanka, I shall go out of my mind! I am not myself. I will do whatever you command,' and madly tender words came from his lips of their own accord.

'Now then, what are you drivelling about?' she interrupted, suddenly seizing the arm he was stretching towards her. She did not push his arm away but pressed it firmly with her strong hard fingers. 'Do gentlemen marry Cossack girls? Go away!'

'But will you? Everything . . .'

'And what shall we do with Lukashka?' said she, laughing.

He snatched away the arm she was holding and firmly embraced her young body, but she sprang away like a fawn and ran barefoot into the porch: Olenin came to his senses and was terrified at himself. He again felt himself inexpressibly vile compared to her, yet not repenting for an instant of what he had said he went home, and without even glancing at the old men who were drinking in his room he lay down and fell asleep more soundly than he had done for a long time.

Chapter 35

The next day was a holiday. In the evening all the villagers, their holiday clothes shining in the sunset, were out in the street. That season more wine than usual had been produced, and the people were now free from their labours. In a month the Cossacks were to start on a campaign and in many families preparations were being made for weddings.

Most of the people were standing in the square in front of the Cossack Government Office and near the two shops, in one of which cakes and pumpkin seeds were sold, in the other kerchiefs and cotton prints. On the earth-embankment of the office-building sat or stood the old men in sober grey, or black coats without gold trimmings or any kind of ornament. They conversed among themselves quietly in measured tones, about the harvest, about the young folk, about village affairs, and about old times, looking with dignified equanimity at the younger generation. Passing by them, the women and girls stopped and bent their heads. The young Cossacks respectfully slackened their pace and raised their caps, holding them for a while over their heads. The old men then stopped speaking. Some of them watched the passers-by severely, others kindly, and in their turn slowly took off their caps and put them on again.

The Cossack girls had not yet started dancing their *khorovods*, but having gathered in groups, in their bright coloured *beshmets* with white kerchiefs on their heads pulled down to their eyes, they sat either on the ground or on the earth-banks about the huts sheltered from the oblique rays of the sun, and laughed and chattered in their ringing voices. Little boys and girls playing in the square sent their balls high up into the clear sky, and ran about squealing and shouting. The half-grown girls had started dancing their *khorovods*, and were timidly singing in their thin shrill voices. Clerks, lads not in the service, or home for the holiday, bright-faced and wearing smart white or new red Circassian gold-trimmed coats, went about arm in arm in twos or threes from one group of women or girls to another, and stopped to joke and chat with the Cossack girls. The Armenian shopkeeper, in a gold-trimmed coat of fine blue cloth, stood at the open door through which piles of folded bright-coloured kerchiefs were visible and, conscious of his own importance and with the pride of an Oriental tradesman, waited for customers. Two red-bearded, barefooted Chechens, who had come from beyond the Terek to see the fête, sat on their heels outside the house of a friend, negligently smoking their little pipes and occasionally spitting, watching the villagers and exchanging remarks with one another in their rapid guttural speech. Occasionally a workaday-looking soldier in an old overcoat passed across the square among the bright-clad girls. Here and there the songs of tipsy Cossacks who were merry-making could already be heard. All the huts were closed; the porches had been scrubbed clean the day before. Even the old women were out in the street, which was everywhere sprinkled with pumpkin and melon seed-shells. The air was warm and still, the sky deep and clear. Beyond the roofs the dead-white mountain range, which seemed very near, was turning rosy in the glow of the evening sun. Now and then from the other side of the river came the distant roar of a cannon, but above the village, mingling with one another, floated all sorts of merry holiday sounds.

Olenin had been pacing the yard all that morning hoping to see Maryanka. But she, having put on holiday clothes, went to Mass at the chapel and afterwards sat with the other girls on an earth-embankment cracking seeds; sometimes again, together with her companions, she ran home, and each time gave the lodger a bright and kindly look. Olenin felt afraid to address her playfully or in the presence of others. He wished to finish telling her what he had begun to say the night before, and to get her to give him a definite answer. He waited for another moment like that of yesterday evening, but the moment did not come, and he felt that he could not remain any longer in this uncertainty. She went out into the street again, and after waiting awhile he too went out and without knowing where he was going he followed her. He passed by the corner where she was sitting in her shining blue satin *beshmet*, and with an aching heart he heard behind him the girls laughing.

Beletski's hut looked out onto the square. As Olenin was passing it he heard Beletski's voice calling to him, 'Come in', and in he went.

After a short talk they both sat down by the window and were soon joined by Eroshka, who entered dressed in a new *beshmet* and sat down on the floor beside them.

'There, that's the aristocratic party,' said Beletski, pointing with his cigarette to a brightly coloured group at the corner. 'Mine is there too. Do you see her? In red. That's a new *beshmet*. Why don't you start the *khorovod*?' he shouted, leaning out of the window. 'Wait a bit, and then when it grows dark let us go too. Then we will invite them to Ustenka's. We must arrange a ball for them!'

'And I will come to Ustenka's,' said Olenin in a decided tone. 'Will Maryanka be there?'

'Yes, she'll be there. Do come!' said Beletski, without the least surprise. 'But isn't it a pretty picture?' he added, pointing to the motley crowds.

'Yes, very!' Olenin assented, trying to appear indifferent.

'Holidays of this kind,' he added, 'always make me wonder why all these people should suddenly be contented and jolly. Today for instance, just because it happens to be the fifteenth of the month, everything is festive. Eyes and faces and voices and movements and garments, and the air and the sun, are all in a holiday mood. And we no longer have any holidays!'

'Yes,' said Beletski, who did not like such reflections.

'And why are you not drinking, old fellow?' he said, turning to Eroshka.

Eroshka winked at Olenin, pointing to Beletski. 'Eh, he's a proud one that *kunak* of yours,' he said.

Beletski raised his glass. *Allah birdy*' he said, emptying it. (*Allah birdy*, 'God has given!' – the usual greeting of Caucasians when drinking together.)

'*Sau bul*' ('Your health'), answered Eroshka smiling, and emptied his glass.

'Speaking of holidays!' he said, turning to Olenin as he rose and looked out of the window, 'What sort of holiday is that! You should have seen them make merry in the old days! The women used to come out in their gold-trimmed *sarafans*. Two rows of gold coins hanging round their necks and gold-cloth diadems on their heads, and when they passed they made a noise, "flu, flu", with their dresses. Every woman looked like a princess. Sometimes they'd come out, a whole herd of them, and begin singing songs so that the air seemed to rumble, and they went on making merry all night. And the Cossacks would roll out a barrel into the yards and sit down and drink till break of day, or they would go hand-in-hand sweeping the village. Whoever they met they seized and took along with them, and went from house to house. Sometimes they used to make merry for three days on end. Father used to come home – I still remember it – quite red and swollen, without a cap, having lost everything: he'd come and lie down. Mother knew what to do: she would bring him some fresh caviar and a little *chikhir* to sober him up, and would herself run about in the village looking for his cap. Then he'd sleep for two days! That's the sort of fellows they were then! But now what are they?'

'Well, and the girls in the *sarafans*, did they make merry all by themselves?' asked Beletski.

'Yes, they did! Sometimes Cossacks would come on foot or on horse and say, "Let's break up the *khorovods*," and they'd go, but the girls would take up cudgels. Carnival week, some young fellow would come galloping up, and they'd cudgel his horse and cudgel him too. But he'd break through, seize the one he loved, and carry her off. And his sweetheart would love him to his heart's content! Yes, the girls in those days, they were regular queens!'

Chapter 36

Just then two men rode out of the side street into the square. One of them was Nazarka. The other, Lukashka, sat slightly sideways on his well-fed bay Kabarda horse which stepped lightly over the hard road jerking its beautiful head with its fine glossy mane. The well-adjusted gun in its cover, the pistol at his back, and the cloak rolled up behind his saddle showed that Lukashka had not come from a peaceful place or from one nearby. The smart way in which he sat a little sideways on his horse, the careless motion with which he touched the horse under its belly with his whip, and especially his half-closed black eyes, glistening as he looked proudly around him, all expressed the conscious strength and self-confidence of youth. 'Ever seen as fine a lad?' his eyes, looking from side to side, seemed to say. The elegant horse with its silver ornaments and trappings, the weapons, and the handsome Cossack himself attracted the attention of everyone in the square. Nazarka, lean and short, was much less well dressed. As he rode past the old men, Lukashka paused and raised his curly white sheepskin cap above his closely cropped black head.

'Well, have you carried off many Nogay horses?' asked a lean old man with a frowning, lowering look.

'Have you counted them, Grandad, that you ask?' replied Lukashka, turning away.

'That's all very well, but you need not take my lad along with you,' the old man muttered with a still darker frown.

'Just see the old devil, he knows everything,' muttered Lukashka to himself, and a worried expression came over his face; but then, noticing a corner where a number of Cossack girls were standing, he turned his horse towards them.

'Good evening, girls!' he shouted in his powerful, resonant voice, suddenly checking his horse. 'You've grown old without me, you witches!' and he laughed.

'Good evening, Lukashka! Good evening, laddie!' the merry voices answered. 'Have you brought much money? Buy some sweets for the girls! . . . Have you come for long? True enough, it's long since we saw you . . . .'

'Nazarka and I have just flown across to make a night of it,' replied Lukashka, raising his whip and riding straight at the girls.

'Why, Maryanka has quite forgotten you,' said Ustenka, nudging Maryanka with her elbow and breaking into a shrill laugh.

Maryanka moved away from the horse and throwing back her head calmly looked at the Cossack with her large sparkling eyes.

'True enough, you have not been home for a long time! Why are you trampling us under your horse?' she remarked dryly, and turned away.

Lukashka had appeared particularly merry. His face shone with audacity and joy. Obviously staggered by Maryanka's cold reply he suddenly knitted his brow.

'Step up on my stirrup and I'll carry you away to the mountains, Mammy!' he suddenly exclaimed, and as if to disperse his dark thoughts he caracoled among the girls. Stooping down towards Maryanka, he said, 'I'll kiss, oh, how I'll kiss you! . . . '

Maryanka's eyes met his and she suddenly blushed and stepped back.

'Oh, bother you! you'll crush my feet,' she said, and bending her head looked at her well-shaped feet in their tightly fitting light blue stockings with clocks and her new red slippers trimmed with narrow silver braid.

Lukashka turned towards Ustenka, and Maryanka sat down next to a woman with a baby in her arms. The baby stretched his plump little hands towards the girl and seized a necklace string that hung down onto her blue *beshmet*. Maryanka bent towards the child and glanced at Lukashka from the corner of her eyes. Lukashka just then was getting out from under his coat, from the pocket of his black *beshmet*, a bundle of sweetmeats and seeds.

'There, I give them to all of you,' he said, handing the bundle to Ustenka and smiling at Maryanka.

A confused expression again appeared on the girl's face. It was as though a mist gathered over her beautiful eyes. She drew her kerchief down below her lips, and leaning her head over the fair-skinned face of the baby that still held her by her coin necklace she suddenly began to kiss it greedily. The baby pressed his little hands against the girl's high breasts, and opening his toothless mouth screamed loudly.

'You're smothering the boy!' said the little one's mother, taking him away; and she unfastened her *beshmet* to give him the breast. 'You'd better have a chat with the young fellow.'

'I'll only go and put up my horse and then Nazarka and I will come back; we'll make merry all night,' said Lukashka, touching his horse with his whip and riding away from the girls.

Turning into a side street, he and Nazarka rode up to two huts that stood side by side.

'Here we are all right, old fellow! Be quick and come soon!' called Lukashka to his comrade, dismounting in front of one of the huts; then he carefully led his horse in at the gate of the wattle fence of his own home.

'How d'you do, Stepka?' he said to his dumb sister, who, smartly dressed like the others, came in from the street to take his horse; and he made signs to her to take the horse to the hay, but not to unsaddle it.

The dumb girl made her usual humming noise, smacked her lips as she pointed to the horse and kissed it on the nose, as much as to say that she loved it and that it was a fine horse.

'How d'you do, Mother? How is it that you have not gone out yet?' shouted Lukashka, holding his gun in place as he mounted the steps of the porch.

His old mother opened the door.

'Dear me! I never expected, never thought, you'd come,' said the old woman. 'Why, Kirka said you wouldn't be here.'

'Go and bring some *chikhir*, Mother. Nazarka is coming here and we will celebrate the feast day.'

'Directly, Lukashka, directly!' answered the old woman. 'Our women are making merry. I expect our dumb one has gone too.'

She took her keys and hurriedly went to the outhouse. Nazarka, after putting up his horse and taking the gun off his shoulder, returned to Lukashka's house and went in.

Chapter 37

'Your health!' said Lukashka, taking from his mother's hands a cup filled to the brim with *chikhir* and carefully raising it to his bowed head.

'A bad business!' said Nazarka. 'You heard how Daddy Burlak said, "Have you stolen many horses?" He seems to know!'

'A regular wizard!' Lukashka replied shortly. 'But what of it!' he added, tossing his head. 'They are across the river by now. Go and find them!'

'Still it's a bad lookout.'

'What's a bad lookout? Go and take some *chikhir* to him tomorrow and nothing will come of it. Now let's make merry. Drink!' shouted Lukashka, just in the tone in which old Eroshka uttered the word. 'We'll go out into the street and make merry with the girls. You go and get some honey; or no, I'll send our dumb wench. We'll make merry till morning.'

Nazarka smiled. 'Are we stopping here long?' he asked.

'Till we've had a bit of fun. Run and get some vodka. Here's the money.'

Nazarka ran off obediently to get the vodka from Yamka's.

Daddy Eroshka and Ergushov, like birds of prey, scenting where the merry-making was going on, tumbled into the hut one after the other, both tipsy.

'Bring us another half-pail,' shouted Lukashka to his mother, by way of reply to their greeting.

'Now then, tell us where did you steal them, you devil?' shouted Eroshka. 'Fine fellow, I'm fond of you!'

'Fond indeed . . .' answered Lukashka laughing, 'carrying sweets from cadets to lasses! Eh, you old . . .'

'That's not true, not true! . . . Oh, Mark,' and the old man burst out laughing. 'And how that devil begged me. "Go," he said, "and arrange it." He offered me a gun! But no. I'd have managed it, but I feel for you. Now tell us where have you been?' And the old man began speaking in Tartar.

Lukashka answered him promptly.

Ergushov, who did not know much Tartar, only occasionally put in a word in Russian: 'What I say is he's driven away the horses. I know it for a fact,' he chimed in.

'Girey and I went together.' (His speaking of Girey Khan as 'Girey' was, to the Cossack mind, evidence of his boldness.) 'Just beyond the river he kept bragging that he knew the whole of the steppe and would lead the way straight, but we rode on and the night was dark, and my Girey lost his way and began wandering in a circle without getting anywhere: couldn't find the village, and there we were. We must have gone too much to the right. I believe we wandered about well – nigh till midnight. Then, thank goodness, we heard dogs howling.'

'Fools!' said Daddy Eroshka. 'There now, we too used to lose our way in the steppe. (Who the devil can follow it?) But I used to ride up a hillock and start howling like the wolves, like this!' He placed his hands before his mouth, and howled like a pack of wolves, all on one note. 'The dogs would answer at once . . . Well, go on – so you found them?'

'We soon led them away! Nazarka was nearly caught by some Nogay women, he was!'

'Caught indeed,' Nazarka, who had just come back, said in an injured tone.

'We rode off again, and again Girey lost his way and almost landed us among the sand-drifts. We thought we were just getting to the Terek but we were riding away from it all the time!'

'You should have steered by the stars,' said Daddy Eroshka.

'That's what I say,' interjected Ergushov,

'Yes, steer when all is black; I tried and tried all about . . . and at last I put the bridle on one of the mares and let my own horse go free – thinking he'll lead us out, and what do you think! he just gave a snort or two with his nose to the ground, galloped ahead, and led us straight to our village. Thank goodness! It was getting quite light. We barely had time to hide them in the forest. Nagim came across the river and took them away.'

Ergushov shook his head. 'It's just what I said. Smart. Did you get much for them?'

'It's all here,' said Lukashka, slapping his pocket.

Just then his mother came into the room, and Lukashka did not finish what he was saying.

'Drink!' he shouted.

'We too, Girich and I, rode out late one night . . . ' began Eroshka.

'Oh bother, we'll never hear the end of you!' said Lukashka. 'I am going.' And having emptied his cup and tightened the strap of his belt he went out.

Chapter 38

It was already dark when Lukashka went out into the street. The autumn night was fresh and calm. The full golden moon floated up behind the tall dark poplars that grew on one side of the square. From the chimneys of the outhouses smoke rose and spread above the village, mingling with the mist. Here and there lights shone through the windows, and the air was laden with the smell of *kisyak*, grape-pulp, and mist. The sounds of voices, laughter, songs, and the cracking of seeds mingled just as they had done in the daytime, but were now more distinct. Clusters of white kerchiefs and caps gleamed through the darkness near the houses and by the fences.

In the square, before the shop door which was lit up and open, the black and white figures of Cossack men and maids showed through the darkness, and one heard from afar their loud songs and laughter and talk. The girls, hand in hand, went round and round in a circle stepping lightly in the dusty square. A skinny girl, the plainest of them all, set the tune.

> From beyond the wood, from the forest dark,
> From the garden green and the shady park,
> There came out one day two young lads so gay.
> Young bachelors, hey! brave and smart were they!

And they walked and walked, then stood still, each man,
And they talked and soon to dispute began!
Then a maid came out; as she came along,
Said, 'To one of you I shall soon belong!'
'Twas the fair-faced lad got the maiden fair,
Yes, the fair-faced lad with the golden hair!
Her right hand so white in his own took he,
And he led her round for his mates to see!
And said, 'Have you ever in all your life
Met a lass as fair as my sweet little wife?'

The old women stood round listening to the songs. The little boys and girls ran about chasing one another in the dark. The men stood by, catching at the girls as the latter moved round, and sometimes breaking the ring and entering it. On the dark side of the doorway stood Beletski and Olenin, in their Circassian coats and sheepskin caps, and talked together in a style of speech unlike that of the Cossacks, in low but distinct tones, conscious that they were attracting attention. Next to one another in the *khorovod* circle moved plump little Ustenka in her red *beshmet* and the stately Maryanka in her new smock and beshmet. Olenin and Beletski were discussing how to snatch Ustenka and Maryanka out of the ring. Beletski thought that Olenin wished only to amuse himself, but Olenin was expecting his fate to be decided. He wanted at any cost to see Maryanka alone that very day and to tell her everything, and ask her whether she could and would be his wife. Although that question had long been answered in the negative in his own mind, he hoped he would be able to tell her all he felt, and that she would understand him.

'Why did you not tell me sooner?' said Beletski. 'I would have got Ustenka to arrange it for you. You are such a queer fellow! . . .'

'What's to be done! . . . Some day, very soon, I'll tell you all about it. Only now, for Heaven's sake, arrange so that she should come to Ustenka's.'

'All right, that's easily done! Well, Maryanka, will you belong to the "fair-faced lad", and not to Lukashka?' said Beletski, speaking to Maryanka first for propriety's sake, but having received no reply he went up to Ustenka and begged her to bring Maryanka home with her. He had hardly time to finish what he was saying before

the leader began another song and the girls started pulling each
other round in the ring by the hand.

They sang:

Past the garden, by the garden,
A young man came strolling down,
Up the street and through the town.
And the first time as he passed
He did wave his strong right hand.
As the second time he passed
Waved his hat with silken band.
But the third time as he went
He stood still: before her bent.

'How is it that thou, my dear,
My reproaches dost not fear?
In the park don't come to walk
That we there might have a talk?
Come now, answer me, my dear,
Dost thou hold me in contempt?
Later on, thou knowest, dear,
Thou'lt get sober and repent.
Soon to woo thee I will come,
And when we shall married be
Thou wilt weep because of me!'

'Though I knew what to reply,
Yet I dared not him deny,
No, I dared not him deny!
So into the park went I,
In the park my lad to meet,
There my dear one I did greet.'

'Maiden dear, I bow to thee!
Take this handkerchief from me.
In thy white hand take it, see!
Say I am beloved by thee.
I don't know at all, I fear,
What I am to give thee, dear!
To my dear I think I will
Of a shawl a present make –
And five kisses for it take.'

Lukashka and Nazarka broke into the ring and started walking about among the girls. Lukashka joined in the singing, taking seconds in his clear voice as he walked in the middle of the ring swinging his arms. 'Well, come in, one of you!' he said. The other girls pushed Maryanka, but she would not enter the ring. The sound of shrill laughter, slaps, kisses, and whispers mingled with the singing.

As he went past Olenin, Lukashka gave a friendly nod.

'Dmitri Andreich! Have you too come to have a look?' he said.

'Yes,' answered Olenin dryly.

Beletski stooped and whispered something into Ustenka's ear. She had not time to reply till she came round again, when she said:

'All right, we'll come.'

'And Maryanka too?'

Olenin stooped towards Maryanka. 'You'll come? Please do, if only for a minute. I must speak to you.'

'If the other girls come, I will.'

'Will you answer my question?' said he, bending towards her. 'You are in good spirits today.'

She had already moved past him. He went after her.

'Will you answer?'

'Answer what?'

'The question I asked you the other day,' said Olenin, stooping to her ear. 'Will you marry me?'

Maryanka thought for a moment.

'I'll tell you,' said she, 'I'll tell you tonight.'

And through the darkness her eyes gleamed brightly and kindly at the young man.

He still followed her. He enjoyed stooping closer to her. But Lukashka, without ceasing to sing, suddenly seized her firmly by the hand and pulled her from her place in the ring of girls into the middle. Olenin had only time to say, 'Come to Ustenka's', and stepped back to his companion.

The song came to an end. Lukashka wiped his lips, Maryanka did the same, and they kissed. 'No, no, kisses five!' said Lukashka. Chatter, laughter, and running about, succeeded to the rhythmic movements and sound. Lukashka, who seemed to have drunk a great deal, began to distribute sweetmeats to the girls.

'I offer them to everyone!' he said with proud, comically pathetic self-admiration. 'But anyone who goes after soldiers goes out of the ring!' he suddenly added, with an angry glance at Olenin.

The girls grabbed his sweetmeats from him, and, laughing, struggled for them among themselves. Beletski and Olenin stepped aside.

Lukashka, as if ashamed of his generosity, took off his cap and wiping his forehead with his sleeve came up to Maryanka and Ustenka.

'Answer me, my dear, dost thou hold me in contempt?' he said in the words of the song they had just been singing, and turning to Maryanka he angrily repeated the words: 'Dost thou hold me in contempt? When we shall married be thou wilt weep because of me!' he added, embracing Ustenka and Maryanka both together.

Ustenka tore herself away, and swinging her arm gave him such a blow on the back that she hurt her hand.

'Well, are you going to have another turn?' he asked.

'The other girls may if they like,' answered Ustenka, 'but I am going home and Maryanka was coming to our house too.'

With his arm still round her, Lukashka led Maryanka away from the crowd to the darker corner of a house.

'Don't go, Maryanka,' he said, 'let's have some fun for the last time. Go home and I will come to you!'

'What am I to do at home? Holidays are meant for merry-making. I am going to Ustenka's,' replied Maryanka.

'I'll marry you all the same, you know!'

'All right,' said Maryanka, 'we shall see when the time comes.'

'So you are going,' said Lukashka sternly, and, pressing her close, he kissed her on the cheek.

'There, leave off! Don't bother,' and Maryanka, wrenching herself from his arms, moved away.

'Ah my girl, it will turn out badly,' said Lukashka reproachfully and stood still, shaking his head. 'Thou wilt weep because of me . . . ' and turning away from her he shouted to the other girls. 'Now then! Play away!'

What he had said seemed to have frightened and vexed Maryanka. She stopped, 'What will turn out badly?'

'Why, that!'

'That what?'

230 of COSSACKS AND OTHER EARLY STORIES

'Why, that you keep company with a soldier-lodger and no longer care for me!'

'I'll care just as long as I choose. You're not my father, nor my mother. What do you want? I'll care for whom I like!'

'Well, all right . . . ' said Lukashka, 'but remember!' He moved towards the shop. 'Girls!' he shouted, 'why have you stopped? Go on dancing. Nazarka, fetch some more *chikhir*.'

'Well, will they come?' asked Olenin, addressing Beletski.

'They'll come directly,' replied Beletski. 'Come along, we must prepare the ball.'

Chapter 39

It was already late in the night when Olenin came out of Beletski's hut following Maryanka and Ustenka. He saw in the dark street before him the gleam of the girl's white kerchief. The golden moon was descending towards the steppe. A silvery mist hung over the village. All was still; there were no lights anywhere and one heard only the receding footsteps of the young women. Olenin's heart beat fast. The fresh moist atmosphere cooled his burning face. He glanced at the sky and turned to look at the hut he had just come out of: the candle was already out. Then he again peered through the darkness at the girls' retreating shadows. The white kerchief disappeared in the mist. He was afraid to remain alone, he was so happy. He jumped down from the porch and ran after the girls.

'Bother you, someone may see . . . ' said Ustenka.

'Never mind!'

Olenin ran up to Maryanka and embraced her.

Maryanka did not resist.

'Haven't you kissed enough yet?' said Ustenka. 'Marry and then kiss, but now you'd better wait.'

'Good-night, Maryanka. Tomorrow I will come to see your father and tell him. Don't you say anything.'

'Why should I!' answered Maryanka.

Both the girls started running. Olenin went on by himself thinking over all that had happened. He had spent the whole evening alone with her in a corner by the oven. Ustenka had not left the hut for a single moment, but had romped about with the other girls and with Beletski all the time. Olenin had talked in whispers to Maryanka.

'Will you marry me?' he had asked.

'You'd deceive me and not have me,' she replied cheerfully and calmly.

'But do you love me? Tell me for God's sake!'

'Why shouldn't I love you? You don't squint,' answered Maryanka, laughing and with her hard hands squeezing his . . .

'What whi-ite, whi-i-ite, soft hands you've got – so like clotted cream,' she said.

'I am in earnest. Tell me, will you marry me?'

'Why not, if father gives me to you?'

'Well then remember, I shall go mad if you deceive me. Tomorrow I will tell your mother and father. I shall come and propose.'

Maryanka suddenly burst out laughing.

'What's the matter?'

'It seems so funny!'

'It's true! I will buy a vineyard and a house and will enroll myself as a Cossack.'

'Mind you don't go after other women then. I am severe about that.'

Olenin joyfully repeated all these words to himself. The memory of them now gave him pain and now such joy that it took away his breath. The pain was because she had remained as calm as usual while talking to him. She did not seem at all agitated by these new conditions. It was as if she did not trust him and did not think of the future. It seemed to him that she only loved him for the present moment, and that in her mind there was no future with him. He was happy because her words sounded to him true, and she had consented to be his. 'Yes,' thought he to himself, 'we shall only understand one another when she is quite mine. For such love there are no words. It needs life – the whole of life. Tomorrow everything will be cleared up. I cannot live like this any longer; tomorrow I will tell everything to her father, to Beletski, and to the whole village.'

Lukashka, after two sleepless nights, had drunk so much at the fête that for the first time in his life his feet would not carry him, and he slept in Yamka's house.

Chapter 40

The next day Olenin awoke earlier than usual, and immediately remembered what lay before him, and he joyfully recalled her kisses, the pressure of her hard hands, and her words, 'What white hands you have!' He jumped up and wished to go at once to his hosts' hut to ask for their consent to his marriage with Maryanka. The sun had not yet risen, but it seemed that there was an unusual bustle in the street and side-street: people were moving about on foot and on horseback, and talking. He threw on his Circassian coat and hastened out into the porch. His hosts were not yet up. Five Cossacks were riding past and talking loudly together. In front rode Lukashka on his broad-backed Kabarda horse.

The Cossacks were all speaking and shouting so that it was impossible to make out exactly what they were saying.

'Ride to the Upper Post,' shouted one.

'Saddle and catch us up, be quick,' said another.

'It's nearer through the other gate!'

'What are you talking about?' cried Lukashka. 'We must go through the middle gates, of course.'

'So we must, it's nearer that way,' said one of the Cossacks who was covered with dust and rode a perspiring horse. Lukashka's face was red and swollen after the drinking of the previous night and his cap was pushed to the back of his head. He was calling out with authority as though he were an officer.

'What is the matter? Where are you going?' asked Olenin, with difficulty attracting the Cossacks' attention.

'We are off to catch *abreks*. They're hiding among the sanddrifts. We are just off, but there are not enough of us yet.'

And the Cossacks continued to shout, more and more of them joining as they rode down the street. It occurred to Olenin that it would not look well for him to stay behind; besides he thought he could soon come back. He dressed, loaded his gun with bullets, jumped onto his horse which Vanyusha had saddled more or less well, and overtook the Cossacks at the village gates. The Cossacks had dismounted, and filling a wooden bowl with *chikhir* from a little cask which they had brought with them, they passed the bowl round to one another and drank to the success of their expedition. Among them was a smartly dressed young cornet, who happened to be in the village and who took command of the group of nine Cossacks who had joined for the expedition. All these Cossacks were privates, and although the cornet assumed the airs of a commanding officer, they only obeyed Lukashka. Of Olenin they took no notice at all, and when they had all mounted and started, and Olenin rode up to the cornet and began asking him what was taking place, the cornet, who was usually quite friendly, treated him with marked condescension. It was with great difficulty that Olenin managed to find out from him what was happening. Scouts who had been sent out to search for *abreks* had come upon several hillsmen some six miles from the village. These *abreks* had taken shelter in pits and had fired at the scouts, declaring they would not surrender. A corporal who had been scouting with two Cossacks had remained to watch the *abreks*, and had sent one Cossack back to get help.

The sun was just rising. Three miles beyond the village the steppe spread out and nothing was visible except the dry, monotonous, sandy, dismal plain covered with the footmarks of cattle, and here and there with tufts of withered grass, with low reeds in the flats, and rare, little-trodden footpaths, and the camps of the nomad Nogay tribe just visible far away. The absence of shade and the austere aspect of the place were striking. The sun always rises and sets red in the steppe. When it is windy whole hills of sand are carried by the wind from place to place.

When it is calm, as it was that morning, the silence, uninterrupted by any movement or sound, is peculiarly striking. That morning in the steppe it was quiet and dull, though the sun had already risen. It all seemed specially soft and desolate. The air was hushed, the footfalls and the snorting of the horses were the only sounds to be heard, and even they quickly died away.

The men rode almost silently. A Cossack always carries his weapons so that they neither jingle nor rattle. Jingling weapons are a terrible disgrace to a Cossack. Two other Cossacks from the village caught the party up and exchanged a few words. Lukashka's horse either stumbled or caught its foot in some grass, and became restive – which is a sign of bad luck among the Cossacks, and at such a time was of special importance. The others exchanged glances and turned away, trying not to notice what had happened.

Lukaskha pulled at the reins, frowned sternly, set his teeth, and flourished his whip above his head. His good Kabarda horse, prancing from one foot to another not knowing with which to start, seemed to wish to fly upwards on wings. But Lukashka hit its well-fed sides with his whip once, then again, and a third time, and the horse, showing its teeth and spreading out its tail, snorted and reared and stepped on its hind legs a few paces away from the others.

'Ah, a good steed that!' said the cornet.

That he said steed instead of *horse* indicated special praise.

'A lion of a horse,' assented one of the others, an old Cossack.

The Cossacks rode forward silently, now at a footpace, then at a trot, and these changes were the only incidents that interrupted for a moment the stillness and solemnity of their movements.

Riding through the steppe for about six miles, they passed nothing but one Nogay tent, placed on a cart and moving slowly along at a distance of about a mile from them. A Nogay family was moving from one part of the steppe to another. Afterwards they met two tattered Nogay women with high cheekbones, who with baskets on their backs were gathering dung left by the cattle that wandered over the steppe. The cornet, who did not know their language well, tried to question them, but they did not understand him and, obviously frightened, looked at one another.

Lukashka rode up to them both, stopped his horse, and promptly uttered the usual greeting. The Nogay women were evidently relieved, and began speaking to him quite freely as to a brother.

'*Ay-ay, kop abrek!*' they said plaintively, pointing in the direction in which the Cossacks were going. Olenin understood that they were saying, 'Many *abreks*.'

Never having seen an engagement of that kind, and having formed an idea of them only from Daddy Eroshka's tales, Olenin wished not to be left behind by the Cossacks, but wanted to see it all. He admired the Cossacks, and was on the watch, looking and listening and making his own observations. Though he had brought his sword and a loaded gun with him, when he noticed that the Cossacks avoided him he decided to take no part in the action, as in his opinion his courage had already been sufficiently proved when he was with his detachment, and also because he was very happy.

Suddenly a shot was heard in the distance.

The cornet became excited, and began giving orders to the Cossacks as to how they should divide and from which side they should approach. But the Cossacks did not appear to pay any attention to these orders, listening only to what Lukashka said and looking to him alone. Lukashka's face and figure were expressive of calm solemnity. He put his horse to a trot with which the others were unable to keep pace, and screwing up his eyes kept looking ahead.

'There's a man on horseback,' he said, reining in his horse and keeping in line with the others.

Olenin looked intently, but could not see anything. The Cossacks soon distinguished two riders and quietly rode straight towards them.

'Are those the *abreks*?' asked Olenin.

The Cossacks did not answer his question, which appeared quite meaningless to them. The *abreks* would have been fools to venture across the river on horseback.

'That's friend Rodka waving to us, I do believe,' said Lukashka, pointing to the two mounted men who were now clearly visible. 'Look, he's coming to us.'

A few minutes later it became plain that the two horsemen were the Cossack scouts. The corporal rode up to Lukashka.

Chapter 41

'Are they far?' was all Lukashka said.

Just then they heard a sharp shot some thirty paces off. The corporal smiled slightly.

'Our Gurka is having shots at them,' he said, nodding in the direction of the shot.

Having gone a few paces farther they saw Gurka sitting behind a sand-hillock and loading his gun. To while away the time he was exchanging shots with the *abreks*, who were behind another sand-heap. A bullet came whistling from their side.

The cornet was pale and grew confused. Lukashka dismounted from his horse, threw the reins to one of the other Cossacks, and went up to Gurka. Olenin also dismounted and, bending down, followed Lukashka. They had hardly reached Gurka when two bullets whistled above them.

Lukashka looked around laughing at Olenin and stooped a little.
'Look out or they will kill you, Dmitri Andreich,' he said.
'You'd better go away – you have no business here.'

But Olenin wanted absolutely to see the *abreks*.

From behind the mound he saw caps and muskets some two
hundred paces off. Suddenly a little cloud of smoke appeared from
thence, and again a bullet whistled past. The *abreks* were hiding in
a marsh at the foot of the hill. Olenin was much impressed by the
place in which they sat. In reality it was very much like the rest of
the steppe, but because the *abreks* sat there it seemed to detach
itself from all the rest and to have become distinguished. Indeed it
appeared to Olenin that it was the very spot for *abreks* to occupy.
Lukashka went back to his horse and Olenin followed him.

'We must get a hay-cart,' said Lukashka, 'or they will be killing
some of us. There behind that mound is a Nogay cart with a load
of hay.'

The cornet listened to him and the corporal agreed. The cart of
hay was fetched, and the Cossacks, hiding behind it, pushed it
forward. Olenin rode up a hillock from whence he could see
everything. The hay-cart moved on and the Cossacks crowded
together behind it. The Cossacks advanced, but the Chechens,
of whom there were nine, sat with their knees in a row and did
not fire.

All was quiet. Suddenly from the Chechens arose the sound of a
mournful song, something like Daddy Eroshka's '*Ay day, dalalay.*'
The Chechens knew that they could not escape, and to prevent
themselves from being tempted to take to flight they had strapped
themselves together, knee to knee, had got their guns ready, and
were singing their death-song.

The Cossacks with their hay-cart drew closer and closer, and
Olenin expected the firing to begin at any moment, but the silence
was only broken by the *abreks*' mournful song. Suddenly the song
ceased; there was a sharp report, a bullet struck the front of the
cart, and Chechen curses and yells broke the silence and shot
followed on shot and one bullet after another struck the cart. The
Cossacks did not fire and were now only five paces distant.

Another moment passed and the Cossacks with a whoop rushed
out on both sides from behind the cart – Lukashka in front of them.
Olenin heard only a few shots, then shouting and moans. He

thought he saw smoke and blood, and abandoning his horse and quite beside himself he ran towards the Cossacks. Horror seemed to blind him. He could not make out anything, but understood that all was over. Lukashka, pale as death, was holding a wounded Chechen by the arms and shouting, 'Don't kill him. I'll take him alive!' The Chechen was the red-haired man who had fetched his brother's body away after Lukashka had killed him. Lukashka was twisting his arms. Suddenly the Chechen wrenched himself free and fired his pistol. Lukashka fell, and blood began to flow from his stomach. He jumped up, but fell again, swearing in Russian and in Tartar. More and more blood appeared on his clothes and under him. Some Cossacks approached him and began loosening his girdle. One of them, Nazarka, before beginning to help, fumbled for some time, unable to put his sword in its sheath: it would not go the right way. The blade of the sword was blood-stained.

The Chechens with their red hair and clipped moustaches lay dead and hacked about. Only the one we know of, who had fired at Lukashka, though wounded in many places was still alive. Like a wounded hawk all covered with blood (blood was flowing from a wound under his right eye), pale and gloomy, he looked about him with wide-open excited eyes and clenched teeth as he crouched, dagger in hand, still prepared to defend himself. The cornet went up to him as if intending to pass by, and with a quick movement shot him in the ear. The Chechen started up, but it was too late, and he fell.

The Cossacks, quite out of breath, dragged the bodies aside and took the weapons from them. Each of the red-haired Chechens had been a man, and each one had his own individual expression. Lukashka was carried to the cart. He continued to swear in Russian and in Tartar.

'No fear, I'll strangle him with my hands. *Anna seni!*' he cried, struggling. But he soon became quiet from weakness.

Olenin rode home. In the evening he was told that Lukashka was at death's door, but that a Tartar from beyond the river had undertaken to cure him with herbs.

The bodies were brought to the village office. The women and the little boys hastened to look at them.

It was growing dark when Olenin returned, and he could not collect himself after what he had seen. But towards night memories of the evening before came rushing to his mind. He looked out of the window, Maryanka was passing to and fro from the house to the cowshed, putting things straight. Her mother had gone to the vineyard and her father to the office. Olenin could not wait till she had quite finished her work, but went out to meet her. She was in the hut standing with her back towards him. Olenin thought she felt shy.

'Maryanka,' said he, 'I say, Maryanka! May I come in?'

She suddenly turned. There was a scarcely perceptible trace of tears in her eyes and her face was beautiful in its sadness. She looked at him in silent dignity.

Olenin again said:

'Maryanka, I have come –'

'Leave me alone!' she said. Her face did not change but the tears ran down her cheeks.

'What are you crying for? What is it?'

'What?' she repeated in a rough voice. 'Cossacks have been killed, that's what for.'

'Lukashka?' said Olenin.

'Go away! What do you want?'

'Maryanka!' said Olenin, approaching her.

'You will never get anything from me!'

'Maryanka, don't speak like that,' Olenin entreated.

'Get away. I'm sick of you!' shouted the girl, stamping her foot, and moved threateningly towards him. And her face expressed such abhorrence, such contempt, and such anger that Olenin suddenly understood that there was no hope for him, and that his first impression of this woman's inaccessibility had been perfectly correct.

Olenin said nothing more, but ran out of the hut.

Chapter 42

For two hours after returning home he lay on his bed motionless. Then he went to his company commander and obtained leave to visit the staff. Without taking leave of anyone, and sending Vanyusha to settle his accounts with his landlord, he prepared to leave for the fort where his regiment was stationed. Daddy Eroshka was the only one to see him off. They had a drink, and then a second, and then yet another. Again as on the night of his departure from

Moscow, a three-horsed conveyance stood waiting at the door. But Olenin did not confer with himself as he had done then, and did not say to himself that all he had thought and done here was 'not it'. He did not promise himself a new life. He loved Maryanka more than ever, and knew that he could never be loved by her.

'Well, goodbye, my lad!' said Daddy Eroshka. 'When you go on an expedition, be wise and listen to my words – the words of an old man. When you are out on a raid or the like (you know I'm an old wolf and have seen things), and when they begin firing, don't get into a crowd where there are many men. When you fellows get frightened you always try to get close together with a lot of others. You think it is merrier to be with others, but that's where it is worst of all! They always aim at a crowd. Now I used to keep farther away from the others and went alone, and I've never been wounded. Yet what things haven't I seen in my day?'

'But you've got a bullet in your back,' remarked Vanyusha, who was clearing up the room.

'That was the Cossacks fooling about,' answered Eroshka.

'Cossacks? How was that?' asked Olenin.

'Oh, just so. We were drinking. Vanka Sitkin, one of the Cossacks, got merry, and puff! he gave me one from his pistol just here.'

'Yes, and did it hurt?' asked Olenin. 'Vanyusha, will you soon be ready?' he added.

'Ah, where's the hurry! Let me tell you. When he banged into me, the bullet did not break the bone but remained here. And I say: "You've killed me, brother. Eh! What have you done to me? I won't let you off! You'll have to stand me a pailful!" '

'Well, but did it hurt?' Olenin asked again, scarcely listening to the tale.

'Let me finish. He stood a pailful, and we drank it, but the blood went on flowing. The whole room was drenched and covered with blood. Grandad Burlak, he says, "The lad will give up the ghost. Stand a bottle of the sweet sort, or we shall have you taken up!" They bought more drink, and boozed and boozed – '

'Yes, but did it hurt you much?' Olenin asked once more.

'Hurt, indeed! Don't interrupt: I don't like it. Let me finish. We boozed and boozed till morning, and I fell asleep on the top of the oven, drunk. When I woke in the morning I could not unbend myself anyhow – '

'Was it very painful?' repeated Olenin, thinking that now he would at last get an answer to his question.

'Did I tell you it was painful? I did not say it was painful, but I could not bend and could not walk.'

'And then it healed up?' said Olenin, not even laughing, so heavy was his heart.

'It healed up, but the bullet is still there. Just feel it!' And lifting his shirt he showed his powerful back, where just near the bone a bullet could be felt and rolled about.

'Feel how it rolls,' he said, evidently amusing himself with the bullet as with a toy. 'There now, it has rolled to the back.'

'And Lukashka, will he recover?' asked Olenin.

'Heaven only knows! There's no doctor. They've gone for one.'

'Where will they get one? From Groznoe?' asked Olenin.

'No, my lad. Were I the Tsar I'd have hung all your Russian doctors long ago. Cutting is all they know! There's our Cossack Baklashka, no longer a real man now that they've cut off his leg! That shows they're fools. What's Baklashka good for now? No, my lad, in the mountains there are real doctors. There was my chum, Vorchik, he was on an expedition and was wounded just here in the chest. Well, your doctors gave him up, but one of theirs came from the mountains and cured him! They understand herbs, my lad!'

'Come, stop talking rubbish,' said Olenin. 'I'd better send a doctor from head-quarters.'

'Rubbish!' the old man said mockingly. 'Fool, fool! Rubbish. You'll send a doctor! – If yours cured people, Cossacks and Chechens would go to you for treatment, but as it is your officers and colonels send to the mountains for doctors. Yours are all humbugs, all humbugs.'

Olenin did not answer. He agreed only too fully that all was humbug in the world in which he had lived and to which he was now returning.

'How is Lukashka? You've been to see him?' he asked.

'He just lies as if he were dead. He does not eat nor drink. Vodka is the only thing his soul accepts. But as long as he drinks vodka it's well. I'd be sorry to lose the lad. A fine lad – a brave, like me. I too lay dying like that once. The old women were already wailing. My head was burning. They had already laid me out under the holy icons. So I lay there, and above me on the oven little drummers, no bigger than this, beat the tattoo. I shout at them and they drum all the harder.' (The old man laughed.) 'The women brought our church elder. They were getting ready to bury me. They said, "He defiled himself with worldly unbelievers; he made merry with women; he ruined people; he did not fast, and he played the balalayka. Confess," they said. So I began to confess. "I've sinned!" I said. Whatever the priest said, I always answered "I've sinned." He began to ask me about the balalayka. "Where is the accursed thing," he says. "Show it me and smash it." But I say, "I've not got it." I'd hidden it myself in a net in the outhouse. I knew they could not find it. So they left me. Yet after all I recovered. When I went for my balalayka – What was I saying?' he continued. 'Listen to me, and keep farther away from the other men or you'll get killed foolishly. I feel for you, truly: you are a drinker – I love you! And fellows like you like riding up the mounds. There was one who lived here who had come from Russia, he always would ride up the mounds (he called the mounds so funnily, "hillocks"). Whenever he saw a mound, off he'd gallop. Once he galloped off that way and rode to the top quite pleased, but a Chechen fired at him and killed him! Ah, how well they shoot from their gun-rests, those Chechens! Some of them shoot even better than I do. I don't like it when a fellow gets killed so foolishly! Sometimes I used to look at your soldiers and wonder at them. There's foolishness for you! They go, the poor fellows, all in a clump, and even sew red collars to their coats! How can they help being hit! One gets killed, they drag him away and another takes his place! What foolishness!' the old man repeated, shaking his head. 'Why not scatter, and go one by one? So you just go like that and they won't notice you. That's what you must do.'

'Well, thank you! Goodbye, Daddy. God willing we may meet again,' said Olenin, getting up and moving towards the passage.

The old man, who was sitting on the floor, did not rise.

'Is that the way one says "Goodbye"? Fool, fool!' he began. 'Oh dear, what has come to people? We've kept company, kept company for well-nigh a year, and now "Goodbye!" and off he goes! Why, I love you, and how I pity you! You are so forlorn, always alone, always alone. You're somehow so unsociable. At times I can't sleep for thinking about you. I am so sorry for you. As the song has it:

> It is very hard, dear brother,
> In a foreign land to live.

So it is with you.'

'Well, goodbye,' said Olenin again.

The old man rose and held out his hand. Olenin pressed it and turned to go.

'Give us your mug, your mug!'

And the old man took Olenin by the head with both hands and kissed him three times with wet moustaches and lips, and began to cry.

'I love you, goodbye!'

Olenin got into the cart.

'Well, is that how you're going? You might give me something for a remembrance. Give me a gun! What do you want two for?' said the old man, sobbing quite sincerely.

Olenin got out a musket and gave it to him.

'What a lot you've given the old fellow,' murmured Vanyusha, 'he'll never have enough! A regular old beggar. They are all such irregular people,' he remarked, as he wrapped himself in his overcoat and took his seat on the box.

'Hold your tongue, swine!' exclaimed the old man, laughing. 'What a stingy fellow!'

Maryanka came out of the cowshed, glanced indifferently at the cart, bowed and went towards the hut.

'*La fille!*' said Vanyusha, with a wink, and burst out into a silly laugh.

'Drive on!' shouted Olenin, angrily.

'Goodbye, my lad! Goodbye. I won't forget you!' shouted Eroshka.

Olenin turned round. Daddy Eroshka was talking to Maryanka, evidently about his own affairs, and neither the old man nor the girl looked at Olenin.

ALBERT

A Tale

I

Five wealthy young men had come, after two in the morning, to amuse themselves at a small Petersburg party.

Much champagne had been drunk, most of the men were very young, the girls were pretty, the piano and violin indefatigably played one polka after another, and dancing and noise went on unceasingly: yet for some reason it was dull and awkward, and, as often happens, everybody felt that it was all unnecessary and was not the thing.

Several times they tried to get things going, but forced merriment was worse even than boredom.

One of the five young men, more dissatisfied than the others with himself, with the others, and with the whole evening, rose with a feeling of disgust, found his hat, and went out quietly, intending to go home.

There was no one in the ante-room, but in the adjoining room he heard two voices disputing. The young man stopped to listen.

'You can't, there are guests there,' said a woman's voice.

'Let me in, please. I'm all right!' a man's weak voice entreated.

'No, I won't let you in without Madame's permission,' said the woman. 'Where are you going? Ah! What a man you are!'

The door burst open and a strange figure of a man appeared on the threshold. The servant on seeing a visitor no longer protested, and the strange figure, bowing timidly, entered the room, swaying on his bent legs. He was of medium height, with a narrow, stooping back, and long tangled hair. He wore a short overcoat, and narrow torn trousers over a pair of rough uncleaned boots. A necktie, twisted into a cord, was fastened round his long white neck. A dirty shirt showed from under his coat and hung over his thin hands. Yet despite the extreme emaciation of his body, his face was white and delicate, and freshness and colour played on his cheeks above his scanty black beard and whiskers. His unkempt hair, thrown back, revealed a rather low and extremely clear forehead. His dark languid eyes looked softly, imploringly, and yet with dignity, before him. Their expression corresponded alluringly with that of the fresh lips, curved at the corners, which showed from under his thin moustache.

Having advanced a few steps he stopped, turned to the young man, and smiled. He seemed to smile with difficulty, but when the smile lit up his face the young man – without knowing why – smiled too.

'Who is that?' he whispered to the servant, when the strange figure had passed into the room from which came the sounds of a dance.

'A crazy musician from the theatre,' replied the maid. 'He comes sometimes to see the mistress.'

'Where have you been, Delesov?' someone just then called out, and the young man, who was named Delesov, returned to the ballroom.

The musician was standing at the door and, looking at the dancers, showed by his smile, his look, and the tapping of his foot, the satisfaction the spectacle afforded him.

'Come in and dance yourself,' said one of the visitors to him. The musician bowed and looked inquiringly at the hostess.

'Go, go . . . Why not, when the gentlemen ask you to?' she said.

The thin, weak limbs of the musician suddenly came into active motion, and winking, smiling, and twitching, he began to prance awkwardly and heavily about the room. In the middle of the quadrille a merry officer, who danced very vivaciously and well, accidentally bumped into the musician with his back. The latter's weak and weary legs did not maintain their balance and after a few stumbling steps aside, he fell full length on the floor. Notwithstanding the dull thud produced by his fall, at first nearly everyone burst out laughing. But the musician did not get up. The visitors grew silent and even the piano ceased. Delesov and the hostess were the first to run up to the fallen man. He was lying on his elbow, staring with dull eyes at the floor. When they lifted him and seated him on a chair, he brushed the hair back from his forehead with a quick movement of his bony hand and began to smile without answering their questions.

'Mr Albert! Mr Albert!' said the hostess. 'Have you hurt yourself? Where? There now, I said you ought not to dance. He is so weak,' she continued, addressing her guests, 'he can hardly walk. How could he dance?'

'Who is he?' they asked her.

'A poor man – an artist. A very good fellow, but pitiable, as you see.'

She said this unembarrassed by the presence of the musician. He suddenly came to himself and, as if afraid of something, shrank into a heap and pushed those around him away.

'It's all nothing!' he suddenly said, rising from his chair with an obvious effort.

And to show that he was not at all hurt he went into the middle of the room and tried to jump about, but staggered and would have fallen down again had someone not supported him.

Everyone felt awkward, and looking at him they all became silent.

The musician's eyes again grew dim, and evidently oblivious of everyone he began rubbing his knee with his hand. Suddenly he raised his head, advanced a trembling leg, threw back his hair with the same heedless movement as before, and going up to the violinist took his violin from him.

'It's nothing!' he said once more, flourishing the violin. 'Gentlemen, let's have some music!'

'What a strange person!' the visitors remarked to one another.

'Perhaps a fine talent is perishing in this unfortunate creature,' said one of the guests.

'Yes, he's pitiable, pitiable!' said a third.

'What a beautiful face! . . . There is something extraordinary about him,' said Delesov. 'Let us see . . . .'

2

Albert meanwhile, paying no attention to anyone, pressed the violin to his shoulder and paced slowly up and down by the piano tuning it. His lips took on an impassive expression, his eyes could not be seen, but his narrow bony back, his long white neck, his crooked legs and shaggy black head, presented a queer – but for some reason not at all ridiculous – spectacle. Having tuned the violin he briskly struck a chord, and throwing back his head turned to the pianist who was preparing to accompany him.

'*Mélancolie G-dur!*' he said, addressing the pianist with a gesture of command. Then, as if begging forgiveness for that gesture, he smiled meekly, and glanced around at the audience with that same smile. Having pushed back his hair with the hand in which he held the bow, he stopped at the corner of the piano, and with a smooth and easy movement drew the bow across the strings. A clear melodious sound was borne through the room and complete silence ensued.

After that first note the theme flowed freely and elegantly, suddenly illumining the inner world of every listener with an unexpectedly clear and tranquillizing light. Not one false or exaggerated sound impaired the acquiescence of the listeners: the notes were all clear, elegant, and significant. Everyone silently followed their development with tremulous expectation. From the state of dullness, noisy distraction and mental torpor in which they had been, these people were suddenly and imperceptibly carried into another quite different world that they had forgotten.

Now a calm contemplation of the past arose in their souls, now an impassioned memory of some past happiness, now a boundless desire for power and splendour, now a feeling of resignation, of unsatisfied love and sadness. Sounds now tenderly sad, now vehemently despairing, mingled freely, flowing and flowing one after the other so elegantly, so strongly, and so unconsciously, that the sounds themselves were not noticed, but there flowed of itself into the soul a beautiful torrent of poetry, long familiar but only now expressed. At each note Albert grew taller and taller. He was far from appearing misshapen or strange. Pressing the violin with his chin and listening to his notes with an expression of passionate attention, he convulsively moved his feet. Now he straightened himself to his full height, now he strenuously bent his back. His left arm seemed to have become set in the bent position to which he had strained it and only the bony fingers moved convulsively: the right arm moved smoothly, elegantly, and almost imperceptibly. His face shone with uninterrupted, ecstatic joy; his eyes burnt with a bright, dry brilliance, his nostrils expanded, his red lips opened with delight.

Sometimes his head bent closer to the violin, his eyes closed, and his face, half covered by his hair, lit up with a smile of mild rapture. Sometimes he drew himself up rapidly, advancing one foot, and his clear brow and the beaming look he cast round the room gleamed with pride, dignity, and a consciousness of power. Once the pianist blundered and struck a wrong chord. Physical suffering was apparent in the whole face and figure of the musician. He paused for an instant and stamping his foot with an expression of childish anger, cried: '*Moll, ce moll!*' The pianist recovered himself. Albert closed his eyes, smiled, and again forgetting himself, the others, and the whole world, gave himself up rapturously to his task.

All who were in the room preserved a submissive silence while Albert was playing, and seemed to live and breathe only in his music.

The merry officer sat motionless on a chair by a window, directing a lifeless gaze upon the floor and breathing slowly and heavily. The girls sat in complete silence along the walls, and only occasionally threw approving and bewildered glances at one another. The hostess's fat smiling face expanded with pleasure. The pianist riveted his eyes on Albert's face and, with a fear of blundering which expressed itself in his whole taut figure, tried to keep up with him. One of the visitors who had drunk more than the others lay prone on the sofa, trying not to move for fear of betraying his agitation. Delesov experienced an unaccustomed sensation. It was as if a cold circle, now expanding, now contracting, held his head in a vice. The roots of his hair became sensitive, cold shivers ran up his spine, something rising higher and higher in his throat pricked his nose and palate as if with fine needles, and tears involuntarily wetted his cheeks. He shook himself, tried to restrain them and wipe them unperceived, but others rose and ran down his cheeks. By some strange concatenation of impressions the first sounds of Albert's violin carried Delesov back to his early youth. Now no longer very young, tired of life and exhausted, he suddenly felt himself a self-satisfied, good-looking, blissfully foolish and unconsciously happy lad of seventeen.

He remembered his first love – for his cousin in a little pink dress; remembered his first declaration of love made in a linden avenue; remembered the warmth and incomprehensible delight of a spontaneous kiss, and the magic and undivined mystery of the

Nature that then surrounded him. In the memories that returned to him she shone out amid a mist of vague hopes, uncomprehended desires, and questioning faith in the possibility of impossible happiness. All the unappreciated moments of that time arose before him one after another, not as insignificant moments of a fleeting present, but as arrested, growing, reproachful images of the past. He contemplated them with joy, and wept – wept not because the time was past that he might have spent better (if he had it again he would not have undertaken to employ it better), but merely because it was past and would never return. Memories rose up of themselves, and Albert's violin repeated again and again: 'For you that time of vigour, love, and happiness has passed for ever, and will not return. Weep for it, shed all your tears, die weeping for that time – that is the best happiness left for you.'

Towards the end of the last variation Albert's face grew red, his eyes burnt and glowed, and large drops of perspiration ran down his cheeks. The veins of his forehead swelled up, his whole body came more and more into motion, his pale lips no longer closed, and his whole figure expressed ecstatic eagerness for enjoyment.

Passionately swaying his whole body and tossing back his hair he lowered the violin, and with a smile of proud dignity and happiness surveyed the audience. Then his back sagged, his head hung down, his lips closed, his eyes grew dim, and he timidly glanced round as if ashamed of himself, and made his way stumblingly into the other room.

3

Something strange occurred with everyone present and something strange was felt in the dead silence that followed Albert's playing. It was as if each would have liked to express what all this meant, but was unable to do so. What did it mean – this bright hot room, brilliant women, the dawn in the windows, excitement in the blood, and the pure impression left by sounds that had flowed past? But no one even tried to say what it all meant: on the contrary everyone, unable to dwell in those regions which the new impression had revealed to them, rebelled against it.

'He really plays well, you know!' said the officer.

'Wonderfully!' replied Delesov, stealthily wiping his cheek with his sleeve.

'However, it's time for us to be going,' said the man who was lying on the sofa, having somewhat recovered. 'We must give him something. Let's make a collection.'

Meanwhile Albert sat alone on a sofa in the next room. Leaning his elbows on his bony knees he stroked his face and ruffled his hair with his moist and dirty hands, smiling happily to himself.

They made a good collection, which Delesov offered to hand to Albert.

Moreover it had occurred to Delesov, on whom the music had made an unusual and powerful impression, to be of use to this man. It occurred to him to take him home, dress him, get him a place somewhere, and in general rescue him from his sordid condition.

'Well, are you tired?' he asked, coming up to him.

Albert smiled.

'You have real talent. You ought to study music seriously and give public performances.'

'I'd like to have something to drink,' said Albert, as if just awake.

Delesov brought some wine, and the musician eagerly drank two glasses.

'What excellent wine!' he said.

'What a delightful thing that *Mélancolie* is!' said Delesov.

'Oh, yes, yes!' replied Albert with a smile – 'but excuse me: I don't know with whom I have the honour of speaking, maybe you are a count, or a prince: could you, perhaps, lend me a little money?' He paused a little 'I have nothing . . . I am a poor man. I couldn't pay it back.'

Delesov flushed: he felt awkward, and hastily handed the musician the money that had been collected.

'Thank you very much!' said Albert, seizing the money. 'Now let's have some music. I'll play for you as much as you like – only let me have a drink of something, a drink . . . ' he added rising.

Delesov brought him some more wine and asked him to sit beside him.

'Excuse me if I am frank with you,' he said, 'your talent interests me so much. It seems to me you are not in good circumstances.'

Albert looked now at Delesov and now at his hostess who had entered the room.

'Allow me to offer you my services,' continued Delesov. 'If you are in need of anything I should be glad if you would stay with me for a time. I am living alone and could perhaps be of use to you.'

Albert smiled and made no reply.

'Why don't you thank him?' said the hostess. 'Of course it is a godsend for you. Only I should not advise you to,' she continued, turning to Delesov and shaking her head disapprovingly.

'I am very grateful to you!' said Albert, pressing Delesov's hand with his own moist ones – 'Only let us have some music now, please.'

But the other visitors were preparing to leave, and despite Albert's endeavours to persuade them to stay they went out into the hall. Albert took leave of the hostess, put on his shabby broad-brimmed hat and old summer cloak, which was his only winter clothing, and went out into the porch with Delesov.

When Delesov had seated himself with his new acquaintance in his carriage, and became aware of the unpleasant odour of drunkenness and uncleanness which emanated so strongly from the musician, he began to repent of his action and blamed himself for childish softheartedness and imprudence. Besides, everything Albert said was so stupid and trivial, and the fresh air suddenly made him so disgustingly drunk that Delesov was repelled. 'What am I to do with him?' he thought.

When they had driven for a quarter of an hour Albert grew silent, his hat fell down at his feet, and he himself tumbled into a corner of the carriage and began to snore. The wheels continued to creak monotonously over the frozen snow; the feeble light of dawn hardly penetrated the frozen windows.

Delesov turned and looked at his companion. The long body covered by the cloak lay lifelessly beside him. The long head with its big black nose seemed to sway on that body, but looking closer Delesov saw that what he had taken for nose and face was hair, and that the real face hung lower. He stooped and was able to distinguish Albert's features. Then the beauty of the forehead and calmly closed lips struck him again.

Under the influence of tired nerves, restlessness from lack of sleep at that hour of the morning, and of the music he had heard,

Delesov, looking at that face, let himself again be carried back to the blissful world into which he had glanced that night; he again recalled the happy and magnanimous days of his youth and no longer repented of what he had done. At that moment he was sincerely and warmly attached to Albert, and firmly resolved to be of use to him.

4

Next morning when he was awakened to go to his office, Delesov with a feeling of unpleasant surprise saw around him his old screen, his old valet, and his watch lying on the small side-table. 'But what did I expect to see if not what is always around me?' he asked himself. Then he remembered the musician's black eyes and happy smile, the motif of *Mélancolie*, and all the strange experiences of the previous night passed through his mind.

He had no time however to consider whether he had acted well or badly by taking the musician into his house. While dressing he mapped out the day, took his papers, gave the necessary household orders, and hurriedly put on his overcoat and over-shoes. Passing the dining-room door he looked in. Albert, after tossing about, had sunk his face in the pillow, and lay in his dirty ragged shirt, dead asleep on the leather sofa where he had been deposited unconscious the night before. 'There's something wrong!' thought Delesov involuntarily.

'Please go to Boryuzovski and ask him to lend me a violin for a couple of days,' he said to his manservant. 'When he wakes up, give him coffee and let him have some underclothing and old clothes of mine. In general, make him comfortable – please!'

On returning late in the evening Delesov was surprised not to find Albert.

'Where is he?' he asked his man.

'He went away immediately after dinner,' replied the servant. 'He took the violin and went away. He promised to be back in an hour, but he's not here yet.'

'Tut, tut! How provoking!' muttered Delesov. 'Why did you let him go, Zakhar?'

Zakhar was a Petersburg valet who had been in Delesov's service for eight years. Delesov, being a lonely bachelor, could not help confiding his ntentions to him, and liked to know his opinions about all his undertakings.

'How could I dare not to let him?' Zakhar replied, toying with the fob of his watch. 'If you had told me to keep him in I might have amused him at home. But you only spoke to me about clothes.'

'Pshaw! How provoking! Well, and what was he doing here without me?'

Zakhar smiled.

'One can well call him an "artist", sir. As soon as he woke he asked for Madeira, and then he amused himself with the cook and with the neighbour's manservant. He is so funny. However, he is good-natured. I gave him tea and brought him dinner. He would not eat anything himself, but kept inviting me to do so. But when it comes to playing the violin, even Izler has few artists like him. One may well befriend such a man. When he played *Down the Little Mother Volga* to us it was as if a man were weeping. It was too beautiful. Even the servants from all the flats came to our back entrance to hear him.'

'Well, and did you get him dressed?' his master interrupted him.

'Of course. I gave him a night-shirt of yours and put my own paletot on him. A man like that is worth helping – he really is a dear fellow!' Zakhar smiled.

'He kept asking me what your rank is, whether you have influential acquaintances, and how many serfs you own.'

'Well, all right, but now he must be found, and in future don't let him have anything to drink, or it'll be worse for him.'

'That's true,' Zakhar interjected. 'He is evidently feeble; our old master had a clerk like that . . . '

But Delesov who had long known the story of the clerk who took hopelessly to drink, did not let Zakhar finish, and telling him to get everything ready for the night, sent him out to find Albert and bring him back.

He then went to bed and put out the light, but could not fall asleep for a long time, thinking about Albert. 'Though it may seem strange to many of my acquaintances,' he thought, 'yet one so seldom does anything for others that one ought to thank God when such an opportunity presents itself, and I will not miss it. I will do anything – positively anything in my power – to help him. He may not be mad at all, but only under the influence of drink. It won't cost me very much. Where there's enough for one there's enough for two. Let him live with me awhile, then we'll find him a place or arrange a concert for him and pull him out of the shallows, and then see what happens.'

He experienced a pleasant feeling of self-satisfaction after this reflection. 'Really I'm not altogether a bad fellow,' he thought. 'Not at all bad even – when I compare myself with others.'

He was already falling asleep when the sound of opening doors and of footsteps in the hall roused him.

'Well, I'll be stricter with him,' he thought, 'that will be best; and I must do it.'

He rang.

'Have you brought him back?' he asked when Zakhar entered.

'A pitiable man, sir,' said Zakhar, shaking his head significantly and closing his eyes.

'Is he drunk?'

'He is very weak.'

'And has he the violin?'

'I've brought it back. The lady gave it me.'

'Well, please don't let him in here now. Put him to bed, and tomorrow be sure not to let him leave the house on any account.'

But before Zakhar was out of the room Albert entered it.

5

'Do you want to sleep already?' asked Albert with a smile. 'And I have been at Anna Ivanovna's and had a very pleasant evening. We had music, and laughed, and there was delightful company. Let me have a glass of something,' he added, taking hold of a water-bottle that stood on a little table, ' – but not water.'

Albert was just the same as he had been the previous evening: the same beautiful smile in his eyes and on his lips, the same bright inspired forehead, and the same feeble limbs. Zakhar's paletot fitted him well, and the clean wide unstarched collar of the nightshirt encircled his thin white neck picturesquely, giving him a particularly childlike and innocent look. He sat down on Delesov's bed and looked at him silently with a happy and grateful smile. Delesov looked into his eyes, and again suddenly felt himself captivated by that smile. He no longer wanted to sleep, he forgot that it was his duty to be stern: on the contrary he wished to make merry, to hear music, and to chat amicably with Albert till morning. He told Zakhar to bring a bottle of wine, some cigarettes, and the violin.

'There, that's splendid!' said Albert. 'It's still early, and we'll have some music. I'll play for you as much as you like.'

Zakhar, with evident pleasure, brought a bottle of Lafitte, two tumblers, some mild cigarettes such as Albert smoked, and the violin. But instead of going to bed as his master told him to, he himself lit a cigar and sat down in the adjoining room.

'Let us have a talk,' said Delesov to the musician, who was about to take up the violin.

Albert submissively sat down on the bed and again smiled joyfully.

'Oh yes!' said he, suddenly striking his forehead with his hand and assuming an anxiously inquisitive expression. (A change of expression always preceded anything he was about to say.) 'Allow me to ask – ' he made a slight pause – 'that gentleman who was there with you last night – you called him N—, isn't he the son of the celebrated N— ?'

'His own son,' Delesov answered, not at all understanding how that could interest Albert.

'Exactly!' said Albert with a self-satisfied smile. 'I noticed at once something particularly aristocratic in his manner. I love aristocrats: there is something particularly beautiful and elegant in an aristocrat. And that officer who dances so well?' he asked. 'I liked him very much too: he is so merry and so fine. Isn't he Adjutant N.N.?'

'Which one?' asked Delesov.

'The one who bumped against me when we were dancing. He must be an excellent fellow.'

'No, he's a shallow fellow,' Delesov replied.

'Oh, no!' Albert warmly defended him. 'There is something very, very pleasant about him. He is a capital musician,' he added. 'He played something there out of an opera. It's a long time since I took such a liking to anyone.'

'Yes, he plays well, but I don't like his playing,' said Delesov, wishing to get his companion to talk about music. 'He does not understand classical music – Donizetti and Bellini, you know, are not music. You think so too, no doubt?'

'Oh, no, no, excuse me!' began Albert with a gentle, pleading look. 'The old music is music, and the new music is music. There are extraordinary beauties in the new music too. *Sonnambula*, and the finale of *Lucia*, and Chopin, and *Robert*! I often think – ' he paused, evidently collecting his thoughts – 'that if Beethoven were alive he would weep with joy listening to *Sonnambula*. There is beauty everywhere. I heard *Sonnambula* for the first time when Viardot and Rubini were here. It was like this . . . ' he said, and his eyes glistened as he made a gesture with both arms as though tearing something out of his breast. 'A little more and it would have been impossible to bear it.'

'And what do you think of the opera at the present time?' asked Delesov.

'Bosio is good, very good,' he said, 'extraordinarily exquisite, but she does not touch one here,' pointing to his sunken chest. 'A singer needs passion, and she has none. She gives pleasure but does not torment.'

'How about Lablache?'

'I heard him in Paris in the *Barbier de Seville*. He was unique then, but now he is old: he cannot be an artist, he is old.'

'Well, what if he is old? He is still good in *morceaux d'ensemble*,' said Delesov, who was in the habit of saying that of Lablache.

'How "what if he is old?" ' rejoined Albert severely. 'He should not be old. An artist should not be old. Much is needed for art, but above all, fire!' said he with glittering eyes and stretching both arms upwards.

And a terrible inner fire really seemed to burn in his whole body.

'O my God!' he suddenly exclaimed. 'Don't you know Petrov, the artist?'

'No, I don't,' Delesov replied, smiling.

'How I should like you to make his acquaintance! You would enjoy talks with him. How well he understands art, too! I used often to meet him at Anna Ivanovna's, but now she is angry with him for some reason. I should very much like you to know him. He has great talent, great talent!'

'Does he paint now?' Delesov asked.

'I don't know, I think not, but he was an Academy artist. What ideas he has! It's wonderful when he talks sometimes. Oh, Petrov has great talent, only he leads a very gay life . . . that's a pity,'

Albert added with a smile. After that he got off the bed, took the violin, and began tuning it.

'Is it long since you were at the opera?' Delesov asked.

Albert looked round and sighed.

'Ah, I can't go there any more!' he said. 'I will tell you!' And clutching his head he again sat down beside Delesov and muttered almost in a whisper: 'I can't go there. I can't play there – I have nothing – nothing! No clothes, no home, no violin. It is a miserable life! A miserable life!' he repeated several times. And why should I go there? What for? No need!' he said, smiling. 'Ah! *Don Juan* . . .'

He struck his head with his hand.

'Then let us go there together some time,' said Delesov.

Without answering, Albert jumped up, seized the violin, and began playing the finale of the first act of *Don Juan*, telling the story of the opera in his own words.

Delesov felt the hair stir on his head as Albert played the voice of the dying commandant.

'No!' said Albert, putting down the violin. 'I cannot play today. I have had too much to drink.'

But after that he went up to the table, filled a tumbler with wine, drank it at a gulp, and again sat down on Delesov's bed.

Delesov looked at Albert, not taking his eyes off him. Occasionally Albert smiled, and so did Delesov. They were both silent; but their looks and smiles created more and more affectionate relations between them. Delesov felt himself growing fonder of the man, and experienced an incomprehensible joy.

'Have you ever been in love?' he suddenly asked.

Albert thought for a few seconds, and then a sad smile lit up his face. He leaned over to Delesov and looked attentively in his eyes.

'Why have you asked me that?' he whispered. 'I will tell you everything, because I like you,' he continued, after looking at him for a while and then glancing round. 'I won't deceive you, but will tell you everything from the beginning, just as it happened.' He stopped, his eyes wild and strangely fixed. 'You know that my mind is weak,' he suddenly said. 'Yes, yes,' he went on. 'Anna Ivanovna is sure to have told you. She tells everybody that I am mad! That is not true; she says it as a joke, she is a kindly woman, and I have really not been quite well for some time.'

He stopped again and gazed with fixed wide-open eyes at the dark doorway. 'You asked whether I have been in love? . . . Yes, I have been in love,' he whispered, lifting his brows. 'It happened long ago, when I still had my job in the theatre. I used to play second violin at the Opera, and she used to have the lower-tier box next the stage, on the left.'

He got up and leaned over to Delesov's ear.

'No, why should I name her?' he said. 'You no doubt know her – everybody knows her. I kept silent and only looked at her; I knew I was a poor artist, and she an aristocratic lady. I knew that very well. I only looked at her and planned nothing . . . '

Albert reflected, trying to remember.

'How it happened I don't remember; but I was once called in to accompany her on the violin . . . but what was I, a poor artist?' he said, shaking his head and smiling. 'But no, I can't tell it . . . ' he added, clutching his head. 'How happy I was!'

'Yes? And did you often go to her house?' Delesov asked.

'Once! Once only . . . but it was my own fault. I was mad! I was a poor artist, and she an aristocratic lady. I ought not to have said anything to her. But I went mad and acted like a fool. Since then all has been over for me. Petrov told the truth, that it would have been better for me to have seen her only at the theatre . . . '

'What was it you did?' asked Delesov.

'Ah, wait! Wait! I can't speak of that!'

With his face hidden in his hands he remained silent for some time.

'I came late to the orchestra. Petrov and I had been drinking that evening, and I was distracted. She was sitting in her box talking to a general. I don't know who that general was. She sat at the very edge of the box, with her arm on the ledge; she had on a white dress and pearls round her neck. She talked to him and looked at me. She looked at me twice. Her hair was done like this. I was not playing, but stood near the basses and looked at her. Then for the first time I felt strange. She smiled at the general and looked at me. I felt she was speaking about me, and I suddenly saw that I was not in the orchestra, but in the box beside her and holding her arm, just there . . . How was that?' Albert asked after a short silence.

'That was vivid imagination,' said Delesov.

'No, no! . . . but I don't know how to tell it,' Albert replied, frowning. 'Even then I was poor and had no lodging, and when I went to the theatre I sometimes stayed the night there.'

'What, at the theatre? In that dark, empty place?'

'Oh, I am not afraid of such nonsense. Wait a bit . . . When they had all gone away I would go to the box where she had been sitting and sleep there. That was my one delight. What nights I spent there! But once it began again. Many things appeared to me in the night, but I can't tell you much.' Albert glanced at Delesov with downcast eyes. 'What was it?' he asked.

'It is strange!' said Delesov.

'No, wait, wait!' he continued, whispering in Delesov's ear. 'I kissed her hand, wept there beside her, and talked much with her. I inhaled the scent of her perfume and heard her voice. She told me much in one night. Then I took my violin and played softly; and I played splendidly. But I felt frightened. I am not afraid of those foolish things and don't believe in them, but I was afraid for my head,' he said, touching his forehead with an amiable smile. 'I was frightened for my poor wits. It seemed to me that something had happened to my head. Perhaps it's nothing. What do you think?'

Both were silent for some minutes.

> Und wenn die Wolken sie verhullen
> Die Sonne bleibt doch ewig klar.

Albert sang with a soft smile. 'Is not that so?' he added.

> Ich auch habe gelebt und genossen . . .

'Ah, how well old Petrov would have explained it all to you!'

Delesov looked silently and in terror at the pale and agitated face of his companion.'Do you know the *Juristen-Waltzer*? Albert suddenly exclaimed, and without awaiting an answer he jumped up, seized the violin, and began to play the merry waltz tune, forgetting himself completely, and evidently imagining that a whole orchestra was playing with him. He smiled, swayed, shifted his feet, and played superbly.

'Eh! Enough of merrymaking!' he said when he had finished, and flourished the violin.

'I am going,' he said, after sitting silently for a while – 'won't you come with me?'

'Where to?' Delesov asked in surprise.

'Let's go to Anna Ivanovna's again. It's gay there – noise, people, music!'

At first Delesov almost consented, but bethinking himself he tried to persuade Albert not to go that night.

'Only for a moment.'

'No, really, you'd better not!'

Albert sighed and put down the violin.

'So, I must stay here?'

And looking again at the table (there was no wine left) he said goodnight and left the room.

Delesov rang.

'See that you don't let Mr Albert go anywhere without my permission,' he said to Zakhar.

6

The next day was a holiday.

Delesov was already awake and sitting in his drawing-room drinking coffee and reading a book. Albert had not yet stirred in the next room.

Zakhar cautiously opened the door and looked into the dining-room.

'Would you believe it, sir? He is asleep on the bare sofa! He wouldn't have anything spread on it, really. Like a little child. Truly an artist.'

Towards noon groaning and coughing were heard through the door.

Zakhar again went into the dining-room, and Delesov could hear his kindly voice and Albert's weak, entreating one.

'Well?' he asked, when Zakhar returned.

'He's fretting, sir, won't wash, and seems gloomy. He keeps asking for a drink.'

'No. Having taken this matter up I must show character,' said Delesov to himself.

He ordered that no wine should be given to Albert and resumed his book, but involuntarily listened to what was going on in the dining-room. There was no sound of movement there and an occasional deep cough and spitting was all that could be heard. Two hours passed. Having dressed, Delesov decided to look in at his visitor before going out. Albert was sitting motionless at the window, his head resting on his hand. He looked round. His face was yellow, wrinkled, and not merely sad but profoundly miserable. He tried to smile by way of greeting, but his face took on a still more sorrowful expression. He seemed ready to cry. He rose with difficulty and bowed.

'If I might just have a glass of simple vodka!' he said with a look of entreaty. 'I am so weak – please!'

'Coffee will do you more good. Have some of that instead.'

Albert's face suddenly lost its childlike expression; he looked coldly, dim-eyed, out of the window, and sank feebly onto his chair.

'Or would you like some lunch?'

'No thank you, I have no appetite.'

'If you wish to play the violin you will not disturb me,' said Delesov, laying the violin on the table.

Albert looked at the violin with a contemptuous smile.

'No,' he said. 'I am too weak, I can't play,' and he pushed the instrument away from him.

After that, whatever Delesov might say, offering to go for a walk with him, and to the theatre in the evening, he only bowed humbly and remained stubbornly silent. Delesov went out, paid several calls, dined with friends, and before going to the theatre returned home to change and to see what the musician was doing. Albert was sitting in the dark hall, leaning his head in his hands and looking at the heated stove. He was neatly dressed, washed, and his hair was brushed; but his eyes were dim and lifeless, and his whole figure expressed weakness and exhaustion even more than in the morning.

'Have you dined, Mr Albert?' asked Delesov.

Albert made an affirmative gesture with his head and, after a frightened look at Delesov, lowered his eyes. Delesov felt uncomfortable.

'I spoke to the director of the theatre about you today,' he said, also lowering his eyes. 'He will be very glad to receive you if you will let him hear you.'

'Thank you, I cannot play!' muttered Albert under his breath, and went into his room, shutting the door behind him very softly.

A few minutes later the door-knob was turned just as gently, and he came out of the room with the violin. With a rapid and hostile glance at Delesov he placed the violin on a chair and disappeared again.

Delesov shrugged his shoulders and smiled.

'What more am I to do? In what am I to blame?' he thought.

'Well, how is the musician?' was his first question when he returned home late that evening.

'Bad!' said Zakhar, briefly and clearly. 'He has been sighing and coughing and says nothing, except that he started begging for vodka four or five times. At last I gave him one glass – or else we might finish him off, sir. Just like the clerk . . .'

'Has he not played the violin?'

'Didn't even touch it. I took it to him a couple of times, but he just took it up gently and brought it out again,' Zakhar answered with a smile. 'So your orders are not to give him any drink?'

'No, we'll wait another day and see what happens. And what's he doing now?'

'He has locked himself up in the drawing-room.'

Delesov went into his study and chose several French books and a German Bible. 'Put these books in his room tomorrow, and see that you don't let him out,' he said to Zakhar.

Next morning Zakhar informed his master that the musician had not slept all night: he had paced up and down the rooms, and had been into the pantry, trying to open the cupboard and the door, but he (Zakhar) had taken care to lock everything up. He said that while he pretended to be asleep he had heard Albert in the dark muttering something to himself and waving his arms about.

Albert grew gloomier and more taciturn every day. He seemed to be afraid of Delesov, and when their eyes met his face expressed sickly fear. He did not touch the books or the violin, and did not reply to questions put to him.

On the third day of the musician's stay Delesov returned home late, tired and upset. He had been driving about all day attending to a matter that had promised to be very simple and easy but, as often happens, in spite of strenuous efforts he had been quite unable to advance a single step with it. Besides that he had called in at his club and had lost at whist. He was in bad spirits.

'Well, let him go his way!' he said to Zakhar, who told him of Albert's sad plight. 'Tomorrow I'll get a definite answer out of him, whether he wants to stay here and follow my advice, or not. If not, he needn't! It seems to me that I have done all I could.'

'There now, try doing good to people!' he thought to himself. 'I put myself out for him, I keep that dirty creature in my house, so that I can't receive a visitor in the morning. I bustle and run about, and he looks on me as if I were a villain who for his own pleasure has locked him up in a cage. And above all, he won't take a single step to help himself. They are all like that.' (The 'they' referred to people in general, and especially to those with whom he had had business that day.) 'And what is the matter with him now? What is he thinking about and pining for? Pining for the debauchery from which I have dragged him? For the humiliation in which he was? For the destitution from which I have saved him? Evidently he has fallen so low that it hurts him to see a decent life . . . '

'No, it was a childish act,' Delesov concluded. 'How can I improve others, when God knows whether I can manage myself?' He thought of letting Albert go at once, but after a little reflection put it off till the next day.

During the night he was roused by the sound of a table falling in the hall, and the sound of voices and footsteps. He lit a candle and listened in surprise.

'Wait a bit. I'll tell my master,' Zakhar was saying; Albert's voice muttered something incoherently and heatedly.

Delesov jumped up and ran into the hall with the candle.

Zakhar stood against the front door in his night attire, and Albert, with his hat and cloak on, was pushing him aside and shouting in a tearful voice: 'You can't keep me here! I have a passport, and have taken nothing of yours. You may search me. I shall go to the chief of police! . . . '

'Excuse me, sir!' Zakhar said, addressing his master while continuing to guard the door with his back. 'He got up during the night, found the key in my overcoat pocket, and drank a whole decanter of liqueur vodka. Is that right? And now he wants to go away. You ordered me not to let him out, so I dare not let him go.'

On seeing Delesov Albert made for Zakhar still more excitedly.

'No one dare hold me! No one has a right to!' he shouted, raising his voice more and more.

'Step aside, Zakhar!' said Delesov. I can't and don't want to keep you, but I advise you to stay till the morning,' he said to Albert.

'No one can keep me! I'll go to the chief of police!' Albert cried louder and louder, addressing himself to Zakhar alone and not looking at Delesov.

'Help!' he suddenly screamed in a furious voice.

'What are you screaming like that for? Nobody is keeping you!' said Zakhar, opening the door.

Albert stopped shouting. 'You didn't succeed, did you? Wanted to do for me – did you!' he muttered to himself, putting on his galoshes. Without taking leave, and continuing to mutter incoherently, he went out. Zakhar held a light for him as far as the gate, and then came back.

'Well, God be thanked, sir!' he said to his master. 'Who knows what might happen? As it is I must count the silver plate . . . '

Delesov merely shook his head and did not reply. He vividly recalled the first two evenings he had spent with the musician, and recalled the last sad days which by his fault Albert had spent there, and above all he recalled that sweet, mixed feeling of surprise, affection and pity, which that strange man had aroused in him at first sight, and he felt sorry for him. 'And what will become of him now?' he thought. 'Without money, without warm clothing, alone in the middle of the night . . . ' He was about to send Zakhar after him, but it was too late.

'Is it cold outside?' he inquired.

'A hard frost, sir,' replied Zakhar. 'I forgot to inform you, but we shall have to buy more wood for fuel before the spring.'

'How is that? You said that we should have some left over.'

7

It was indeed cold outside, but Albert, heated by the liquor he had drunk and by the dispute, did not feel it. On reaching the street he looked round and rubbed his hands joyfully.

The street was empty, but the long row of lamps still burned with ruddy light; the sky was clear and starry. 'There now!' he said, addressing the lighted window of Delesov's lodging, thrusting his hands into his trouser pockets under his cape, and stooping forward. He went with heavy, uncertain steps down the street to the right. He felt an unusual weight in his legs and stomach, something made a noise in his head, and some invisible force was throwing him from side to side, but he still went on in the direction of Anna Ivanovna's house.

Strange, incoherent thoughts passed through his mind. Now he remembered his last altercation with Zakhar, then for some reason the sea and his first arrival in Russia by steamboat, then a happy night he had passed with a friend in a small shop he was passing, then suddenly a familiar motif began singing itself in his imagination, and he remembered the object of his passion and the dreadful night in the theatre.

Despite their incoherence all these memories presented themselves so clearly to his mind that, closing his eyes, he did not know which was the more real: what he was doing, or what he was thinking. He did not realize or feel how his legs were moving, how he swayed and bumped against the wall, how he looked around him, or passed from street to street. He realized and felt only the things that, intermingling and fantastically following one another, rose in his imagination.

Passing along the Little Morskaya Street, Albert stumbled and fell. Coming to his senses for a moment he saw an immense and splendid building before him and went on. In the sky no stars, nor moon, nor dawn, were visible, nor were there any street lamps, but everything was clearly outlined. In the windows of the building that towered at the end of the street lights were shining, but those lights quivered like reflections. The building stood out nearer and nearer and clearer and clearer before him. But the lights disappeared directly he entered the wide portals. All was dark within. Solitary footsteps resounded under the vaulted ceiling, and some shadows slid rapidly away as he approached.

'Why have I come here?' thought he; but some irresistible force drew him on into the depths of the immense hall. There was some kind of platform, around which some small people stood silently.

'Who is going to speak?' asked Albert. No one replied, except that someone pointed to the platform. A tall thin man with bristly hair and wearing a parti-coloured dressing-gown was already standing there, and Albert immediately recognized his friend Petrov.

'How strange that he should be here!' thought he.

'No, brothers!' Petrov was saying, pointing to someone. 'You did not understand a man living among you; you have not understood him! He is not a mercenary artist, not a mechanical performer, not a lunatic or a lost man. He is a genius – a great musical genius who has perished among you unnoticed and unappreciated!'

Albert at once understood of whom his friend was speaking, but not wishing to embarrass him he modestly lowered his head.

'The holy fire that we all serve has consumed him like a blade of straw!' the voice went on, 'but he has fulfilled all that God implanted in him and should therefore be called a great man. You could despise, torment, humiliate him,' the voice continued, growing louder and louder – 'but he was, is, and will be, immeasurably higher than you all. He is happy, he is kind. He loves or despises all alike, but serves only that which was implanted in him from above. He loves but one thing – beauty, the one indubitable blessing in the world. Yes, such is the man! Fall prostrate before him, all of you! On your knees!' he cried aloud.

But another voice came mildly from the opposite corner of the hall: 'I do not wish to bow my knees before him,' said the voice, which Albert immediately recognized as Delesov's. 'Wherein is he great? Why should we bow before him? Did he behave honourably and justly? Has he been of any use to society? Don't we know how he borrowed money and did not return it, and how he carried away his fellow-artist's violin and pawned it? . . .'

('Oh God, how does he know all that?' thought Albert, hanging his head still lower.)

'Do we not know how he flattered the most insignificant people, flattered them for the sake of money?' Delesov continued – 'Don't we know how he was expelled from the theatre? And how Anna Ivanovna wanted to send him to the police?'

('O God! That is all true, but defend me, Thou who alone knowest why I did it!' muttered Albert.)

'Cease, for shame!' Petrov's voice began again. 'What right have you to accuse him? Have you lived his life? Have you experienced his rapture?' ('True, true!' whispered Albert.)

'Art is the highest manifestation of power in man. It is given to a few of the elect, and raises the chosen one to such a height as turns the head and makes it difficult for him to remain sane. In Art, as in every struggle, there are heroes who have devoted themselves entirely to its service and have perished without having reached the goal.'

Petrov stopped, and Albert raised his head and cried out: 'True, true!' but his voice died away without a sound.

'It does not concern you,' said the artist Petrov, turning to him severely. 'Yes, humiliate and despise him,' he continued, 'but yet he is the best and happiest of you all.'

Albert, who had listened to these words with rapture in his soul, could not restrain himself, and went up to his friend wishing to kiss him.

'Go away! I do not know you!' Petrov said, 'Go your way, or you won't get there.'

'Just see how the drink's got hold of you! You won't get there,' shouted a policeman at the crossroad.

Albert stopped, collected his strength and, trying not to stagger, turned into the side street.

Only a few more steps were left to Anna Ivanovna's door. From the hall of her house the light fell on the snow in the courtyard, and sledges and carriages stood at the gate.

Holding onto the banister with his numbed hands, he ran up the steps and rang. The sleepy face of a maid appeared in the opening of the doorway, and she looked angrily at Albert. 'You can't!' she cried. 'The orders are not to let you in,' and she slammed the door to.

The sound of music and of women's voices reached the steps. Albert sat down, leaned his head against the wall, and closed his eyes. Immediately a throng of disconnected but kindred visions beset him with renewed force, engulfed him in their waves, and bore him away into the free and beautiful realm of dreams. 'Yes, he was the best and happiest!' ran involuntarily through his imagination. The sounds of a polka came through the door. These sounds also told him that he was the best and happiest. The bells in the nearest church rang out for early service, and these bells also said: 'Yes, he is the best and happiest!' . . . 'I will go back to the hall,' thought Albert. 'Petrov must tell me much more.'

But there was no one in the hall now, and instead of the artist Petrov, Albert himself stood on the platform and played on the violin all that the voice had said before. But the violin was of strange construction; it was made of glass and it had to be held in both hands and slowly pressed to the breast to make it produce sounds. The sounds were the most delicate and delightful Albert had ever heard. The closer he pressed the violin to his breast the more joyful and tender he felt. The louder the sounds grew the faster the shadows dispersed and the brighter the walls of the hall were lit up by transparent light. But it was necessary to play the violin very warily so as not to break it. He played the glass instrument very carefully and well. He played such things as he felt no one would ever hear again.

He was beginning to grow tired when another distant, muffled sound distracted his attention. It was the sound of a bell, but it spoke words: 'Yes,' said the bell, droning somewhere high up and far away, 'he seems to you pitiful, you despise him, yet he is the best and happiest of men! No one will ever again play that instrument.'

These familiar words suddenly seemed so wise, so new, and so true to Albert that he stopped playing and, trying not to move, raised his arms and eyes to heaven. He felt that he was beautiful and happy. Although there was no one else in the hall he expanded his chest and stood on the platform with head proudly erect so that all might see him. Suddenly someone's hand lightly touched his shoulder; he turned and saw a woman in the faint light. She looked at him sadly and shook her head deprecatingly. He immediately realized that what he was doing was bad, and felt ashamed of himself. 'Whither?' he asked her. She again gave him a long fixed look and sadly inclined her head. It was she – none other than she whom he loved, and her garments were the same; on her full white neck a string of pearls, and her superb arms bare to above the elbow. She took his hand and led him out of the hall. 'The exit is on the other side,' said Albert, but without replying she smiled and led him out.

At the threshold of the hall Albert saw the moon and some water. But the water was not below as it usually is, nor was the moon a white circle in one place up above as it usually is. Moon and water were together and everywhere – above, below, at the sides, and all around them both. Albert threw himself with her into the moon and the water, and realized that he could now embrace her, whom he loved more than anything in the world. He embraced her and felt unutterable happiness. 'Is this not a dream?' he asked himself. But no! It was more than reality: it was reality and recollection combined. Then he felt that the unutterable bliss he had at that moment enjoyed had passed and would never return. 'What am I weeping for?' he asked her. She looked at him silently and sadly. Albert understood what she meant by that. 'But how can it be, since I am alive?' he muttered. Without replying or moving she looked straight before her. 'This is terrible! How can I explain to her that I am alive?' he thought with horror. 'O Lord! I am alive, do understand me!' he whispered.

'He is the best and happiest!' a voice was saying. But something was pressing more and more heavily on Albert. Whether it was the moon and the water, her embraces, or his tears, he did not know, but he felt he would not be able to say all that was necessary, and that soon all would be over.

Two visitors, leaving Anna Ivanovna's house, stumbled over Albert, who lay stretched out on the threshold. One of them went back and called the hostess.

'Why, this is inhuman!' he said. 'You might let a man freeze like that!'

'Ah, that is Albert! I'm sick to death of him!' replied the hostess. 'Annushka, lay him down somewhere in a room,' she said to the maid.

'But I am alive – why bury me?' muttered Albert, as they carried him insensible into the room.

LUCERNE

from Prince Nekhlyudov's Memoirs

Lucerne

8th July, 1857

Last night I arrived at Lucerne, and put up at the Schweizerhof, the best hotel.

Lucerne, an ancient town and the capital of the canton, situated on the shore of the Lake of Lucerne, says Murray, is one of the most romantic places in Switzerland: here three important high roads meet, and it is only one hour by steam-boat to Mount Rigi, from which one of the most magnificent views in the world can be seen.

Whether this be right or not, other guide-books say the same, and so tourists of all nationalities, especially the English, flock there.

The magnificent five-storeyed Schweizerhof Hotel has been recently erected on the quay, close to the lake at the very place where of old there was a roofed and crooked bridge with chapels at its corners and carvings on its beams. Now, thanks to the enormous influx of English people, their needs, their tastes, and their money, the old bridge has been torn down and a granite quay, as straight as a stick, erected, on which straight, rectangular, five-storeyed houses have been built, in front of which two rows of little lindens with stakes to them have been planted, between which the usual small green benches have been placed. This is a promenade, and here Englishwomen wearing Swiss straw hats, and Englishmen in stout and comfortable clothes, walk about enjoying the work they have inspired. Perhaps such quays and houses and lime trees and Englishmen are all very well in some places, but not here amid this strangely majestic and yet inexpressibly genial and harmonious Nature.

When I went up to my room and opened the window facing the lake I was at first literally blinded and shaken by the beauty of that water, those mountains, and the sky. I felt an inward restlessness and a need to find expression for the emotion that filled my soul to overflowing. At that moment I felt a wish to embrace someone, to hug him closely, to tickle and pinch him – in a word to do something extraordinary to myself and to him.

It was past six and had rained all day, but was now beginning to clear up. The lake, light-blue like burning sulphur, and dotted with little boats which left vanishing tracks behind them, spread out before my windows motionless, smooth, and apparently convex between its variegated green shores, then passed into the distance where it narrowed between two enormous promontories, and, darkening, leaned against and disappeared among the pile of mountains, clouds, and glaciers, that towered one above the other. In the foreground were the moist, fresh-green, far-stretching shores with their reeds, meadows, gardens, and chalets; further off were dark-green wooded promontories crowned by ruined castles; in the background was the rugged, purple-white distance with its fantastic, rocky, dull-white, snow-covered mountain crests, the whole bathed in the delicate, transparent azure of the air and lit up by warm sunset rays that pierced the torn clouds. Neither on the lake nor on the mountains, nor in the sky, was there a single precise line, or one precise colour, or one unchanging moment: everywhere was motion, irregularity, fantastic shapes, an endless intermingling and variety of shades and lines, and over it all lay tranquillity, softness, unity, and inevitable beauty. And here, before my very window, amid this undefined, confused, unfettered beauty, the straight white line of the quay stretched stupidly and artificially, with its lime trees, their supports, and the green benches – miserable, vulgar human productions which did not blend with the general harmony and beauty as did the distant chalets and ruins, but on the contrary clashed coarsely with it. My eyes continually encountered that dreadfully straight quay, and I felt a desire to push it away or demolish it, as one would wipe off a black smudge that disfigured the nose just under one's eye. But the embankment with the English people walking about on it remained where it was, and I instinctively tried to find a point of view from which it would not be visible. I found a way to do this, and sat till dinner-time all alone, enjoying the incomplete, but all the more tormentingly sweet feeling one experiences when one gazes in solitude on the beauty of Nature.

At half-past seven I was called to dinner. In the large, splendidly decorated room on the ground floor two tables were laid for at least a hundred persons. For about three minutes the silent movement of assembling visitors continued – the rustle of women's dresses, light footsteps, whispered discussions with the very polite and elegant waiters – but at last all the seats were occupied by men and women very well and even richly and generally most immaculately dressed. As usual in Switzerland the majority of the visitors were English, and therefore the chief characteristic of the common table was the strict decorum they regard as an obligation – a reserve not based on pride, but on the absence of any necessity for social intercourse, and on content with the comfortable and agreeable satisfaction of their requirements. On all sides gleamed the whitest of laces, the whitest of collars, the whitest of teeth – natural or artificial – and the whitest of complexions and hands. But the faces, many of them very handsome, expressed only a consciousness of their own well-being and a complete lack of interest in all that surrounded them unless it directly concerned themselves; and the whitest of hands in rings and mittens moved only to adjust a collar, to cut up beef, or to lift a wine glass: no mental emotion was reflected in their movements. Occasionally families would exchange a few words among themselves in subdued voices about the pleasant flavour of this or that dish or wine, or the lovely view from Mount Rigi. Individual tourists, men and women, sat beside one another not even exchanging a look. If occasionally some two among these hundred people spoke to one another it was sure to be about the weather and the ascent of Mount Rigi. Knives and forks moved on the plates with scarcely any sound, food was taken a little at a time, peas and other vegetables were invariably eaten with a fork. The waiters, involuntarily subdued by the general silence, asked in a whisper what wine you would take. At such dinners I always feel depressed, uncomfortable, and at last melancholy. I always feel as if I were guilty of something and am being punished, as I used to be when, as a child, I was put in a chair when I had been naughty, and ironically told: 'Rest yourself, my dear!' while my youthful blood surged in my veins and I heard the merry shouts of my brothers in the next room. Formerly I tried to rebel against the feeling of oppression I experienced during such dinners, but in vain: all those inanimate countenances have an insuperable effect on me and I become similarly inanimate myself. I wish nothing, think nothing, and cease even to observe what is going on. At first I used to try to talk to my neighbours; but except for phrases apparently repeated a hundred thousand times in the same place and by the same people I got no response. And yet not all these frozen people are stupid and unfeeling, on the contrary many of them, no doubt, have an inner life just such as my own, and in many of them it may be much more complex and interesting. Then why do they deprive themselves of one of life's greatest pleasures – the enjoyment that comes from the intercourse of man with man?

How different it was in our Paris *pension*, where some twenty of us, of various nationalities, professions, and dispositions, under the influence of French sociability used to meet at the common table as at a game! There, from one end of the table to the other, conversation, interspersed with jests and puns, even if in broken language, at once became general. There everyone, not troubling how it would sound, said anything that came into his head. There we had our philosopher, our debater, our *bel esprit*, and our butt, all in common. There immediately after dinner we pushed away the table and, in time and out, danced the polka on the dusty carpet till late in the evening. There, even if we were inclined to flirt and were not very clever or respectable, we were human beings. The Spanish countess with her romantic adventures, the Italian abbé who declaimed the *Divine Comedy* after dinner, the American doctor who had the entrée to the Tuileries, the young playwright with long hair, and the pianist who, according to her account, had composed the best polka in the world, the unhappy widow who was a beauty and had three rings on every finger – we all treated one another like human beings, in a friendly if superficial manner, and carried away, some of us light, and others sincere and cordial, memories. But of these English at the *table d'hôte*, I often think as I look at all these silk dresses, laces, ribbons, rings, and pommaded locks, how many live women would be happy and make others happy with these adornments. It is strange to think how many potential friends and lovers – very happy friends and lovers – may be sitting there side by side without knowing it, and, God knows why, will never know it and never give one another the happiness they desire so much and which they might so easily give.

I began to feel depressed, as always after such a dinner, and without finishing my dessert went in very low spirits to stroll about the town. The narrow, dirty, unlighted streets, the shops closing, the encounters I had with tipsy workmen and with women going bareheaded to fetch water, or others wearing hats who flitted along the walls of the side-streets and continually glanced round, not only did not dispel my ill-humour but even increased it. It had already grown quite dark in the streets when, without looking around me and without any thought in my head, I turned back to the hotel hoping by sleep to rid myself of my dismal frame of mind. I was feeling terribly chilled at heart, lonely and depressed, as sometimes happens without cause to those who have just arrived at a new place.

Looking at nothing but the ground at my feet I walked along the quay towards the Schweizerhof, when I was suddenly struck by the sound of some strange but exceedingly sweet and agreeable music. These sounds had an immediately vivifying effect on me, as if a bright cheerful light had penetrated my soul. I felt myself happy and cheerful. My dormant attention was again alive to all the objects surrounding me. The beauty of the night and of the lake, to which I had been feeling indifferent, suddenly struck me joyfully like a novelty. In an instant I involuntarily noticed both the heavy grey patches of cloud on the dark blue of the sky lit up by the rising moon, the smooth dark-green lake with the little lights reflected on it, and the mist-covered mountains in the distance; I heard the croaking of the frogs from Freschenburg, and the fresh limpid whistle of quails on the opposite shore. But directly in front of me, on the spot whence the sounds to which my attention was chiefly directed came, I saw amid the semi-darkness a throng of people collected in a half-circle in the middle of the road, and at some short distance from them a tiny man in black clothes. Behind the people and the man the black poplars in the garden were gracefully silhouetted on the dark grey and blue ragged sky, and the severe spires on each side of the ancient cathedral towered majestically.

I drew nearer, the sounds became more distinct, and at some distance I could clearly distinguish the full chords of a guitar which vibrated sweetly in the evening air and several voices, which intercepting one another did not actually sing the melody but indicated it by chiming in at the chief passages. The tune was something in the nature of a charming and graceful mazurka. The voices sometimes seemed nearer and sometimes farther away; now you could hear a tenor, now a bass, and now a guttural falsetto with a warbling Tyrolese yodel. It was not a song, but the light, masterly sketch of a song. I could not make out what it was, but it was beautiful. The passionate soft chords of the guitar, that sweet gentle melody, and the lonely little figure of the man in black against the fantastic background of the dark lake, the gleaming moon, the two tall spires silently stretching upwards, and the black poplars in the garden, were all strangely but inexpressibly beautiful, or so it seemed to me.

All the confused and arbitrary impressions of life suddenly received meaning and charm. It was as if a fresh and fragrant flower had bloomed within me. Instead of the weariness, dullness, and indifference towards everything in the world that I had felt a moment before, I suddenly experienced a need of love, a fullness of hope, and a spontaneous joy in life. 'What can I possibly want, what desire?' I involuntarily thought. 'Here it is all around me – beauty, poetry. Inhale full deep draughts of it with all the strength that is in you, enjoying it. What more do you need? It is all yours, and all good . . . '

I went nearer. The little man seemed to be an itinerant singer from the Tyrol. He stood before the windows of the hotel with one foot advanced, his head thrown back, and while thrumming his guitar was singing his graceful song in those different voices. I immediately felt an affection for him, and gratitude for the change he had brought about in me. As far as I could see, he was dressed in an old black coat, had short black hair, and wore a very ordinary old cap on his head. There was nothing artistic about his attire, but his jaunty, childishly merry pose and movements, with his diminutive stature, produced a touching yet amusing effect. On the steps, at the windows, and on the balconies of the brilliantly lighted hotel, stood ladies resplendent in full-skirted dresses, gentlemen with the whitest of collars, a porter and footmen in gold-embroidered liveries; in the street, in the semicircle of the crowd, and farther along the boulevard among the lime-trees, elegantly dressed waiters, cooks in the whitest of caps and blouses, girls with their arms around one another, and passers-by, had gathered and stopped. They all seemed to experience the same sensation that I did, and stood in silence round the singer, listening attentively. All were quiet, only at intervals in the singing, from far away across the water came the rhythmic sound of a hammer, and from the Freschenburg shore the staccato trills of the frogs intermingling with the fresh, monotonous whistle of the quails.

In the darkness of the street the little man warbled like a nightingale, couplet after couplet and song after song. Though I had drawn close to him, his singing continued to give me great pleasure. His small voice was extremely pleasing, and the delicacy, the taste, and the sense of proportion with which he managed that voice were extraordinary, and showed immense natural gifts. He sang the refrain differently after each couplet and it was evident that all these graceful variations came to him freely and instantaneously.

Among the throng, above in the Schweizerhof and below on the boulevard, appreciative whispers could often be heard, and a respectful silence reigned. The balconies and windows kept filling, and by the hotel lights more and more elegantly dressed men and women could be seen leaning out picturesquely. The passers-by stopped and everywhere in the shadows on the embankment groups of men and women stood under the lime-trees. Near me, separated from the rest of the crowd and smoking cigars, stood an aristocratic waiter and the chef. The chef seemed to feel the charm of the music strongly and at every high falsetto note rapturously winked, nodded, and nudged the waiter in ecstatic perplexity, with a look that said: 'How he sings, eh?' The waiter, by whose broad smile I detected the pleasure the singing gave him, replied to the chef's nudgings by shrugging his shoulders to show that it was hard to surprise him, and that he had heard much better things than this.

In an interval of the singing, while the singer was clearing his throat, I asked the waiter who the man was and whether he came there often.

'Well, he comes about twice a summer,' replied the waiter. 'He is from Aargau – just a beggar.'

'And are there many like him about?' I asked.

'Oh, yes,' replied the man not having at first understood what I was asking, but having afterwards made it out, he added: 'Oh no, he is the only one I know of. There are no others.'

Just then the little man, having finished his first song, briskly turned his guitar over and said something in his German patois, which I could not understand but which caused the crowd to laugh.

'What did he say?' I asked.

'He says his throat is dry and he would like some wine,' replied the waiter near me.

'Well, I suppose he is fond of drink.'

'Yes, such people are all like that,' answered the waiter with a depreciatory gesture of his hand.

The singer raised his cap and with a flourish of the guitar went up to the hotel. Throwing back his head he addressed the gentlefolk at the windows and on the balconies: '*Messieurs et Mesdames*,' he said with a half-Italian and half-German accent and the intonation conjurors employ when addressing their audience: '*Si vous croyez que je gagne quelque chose, vous vous trompez; je ne suis qu'un pauvre tiable.*' He paused and waited a moment in silence, but as no one gave him anything, he again jerked his guitar and said: '*A présent, messieurs et mesdames, je vous chanterais l'air du Righi.*'

The audience up above kept silent, but continued to stand in expectation of the next song; below, among the throng, there was laughter, probably because he expressed himself so queerly and because no one had given him anything. I gave him a few centimes, which he threw nimbly from one hand to the other, and put into his waistcoat pocket. Then putting on his cap again he began to sing a sweet and graceful Tyrolese song which he called '*l'air du Righi.*' This song, which he had left to the last, was even better than the others, and on all sides among the now increased crowd one heard sounds of appreciation. He finished the song. Again he flourished his guitar, took off his cap, held it out, made two steps towards the windows, and again repeated his incomprehensible phrase: '*Messieurs et Mesdames, si vous croyez que je gagne quelque chose –* ' which he evidently considered very smart and witty, but in his voice and movements I now detected a certain hesitation and childlike timidity which were the more noticeable on account of his small figure. The elegant audience still stood just as picturesquely grouped in the windows and on the balconies, the lights shining on their rich attire. A few of them talked in decorously subdued voices, apparently about the singer who was standing before them with outstretched hand, others looked with attentive curiosity down at the little black figure; on one balcony could be heard a young girl's merry laughter.

In the crowd below the talking and laughter grew louder and louder. The singer repeated his phrase a third time, in a still feebler voice, and this time he did not even finish it, but again held out his cap, and then drew it back immediately. And for the second time not one of those hundreds of brilliantly dressed people who had come to hear him threw him a single penny. The crowd laughed unmercifully. The little singer seemed to me to shrink still more into himself. He took the guitar in his other hand, lifted his cap above his head, and said: '*Messieurs et Mesdames, je vous remercie, et je vous souhaite une bonne nuit.*' Then he replaced his cap. The crowd roared with merry laughter. The handsome men and women, quietly conversing, gradually disappeared from the balconies. The strolls on the boulevard were resumed. The street that had been quiet during the singing again became animated, only a few persons looked at the singer from a distance and laughed. I heard the little man mutter something to himself. He turned and, seeming to grow still smaller, went quickly towards the town. The merry strollers, still watching him, followed him at a certain distance, and laughed.

My mind was in a whirl. I was at a loss to understand what it all meant, and without moving from the spot where I had been, I senselessly gazed into the darkness after the tiny retreating figure of the man as he went striding rapidly towards the town and at the laughing strollers who followed him. I felt pained, grieved, and above all ashamed for the little man, for the crowd, and for myself, as if it were I who had been asking for money and had received nothing, and had been laughed at. I, too, without looking back and with an aching heart, moved off with rapid steps and went to the entrance of the Schweizerhof. I could not yet account for my emotions, but only knew that something heavy and unsolved filled my heart and oppressed me.

At the brilliantly lit entrance I met the hall porter who politely stepped aside, and an English family. A tall, portly, handsome man with black side-whiskers worn in the English fashion, a black hat on his head, a plaid over his arm, and an expensive cane in his hand, was walking with lazy self-confidence arm in arm with a lady in a grey silk gown, and a cap trimmed with bright ribbons and exquisite lace. Beside them walked a pretty, fresh-complexioned girl wearing a graceful Swiss hat trimmed with a feather *à la Mousquetaire*, and with charming long soft flaxen curls that fell over her fair face. In front of them skipped a ten-year-old girl with rosy cheeks, and plump white knees showing from under the finest embroideries.

'A lovely night!' said the lady in a tender, happy voice, just as I passed them.

'Ohe!' lazily muttered the Englishman, for whom life was so comfortable that he did not even feel like talking. To all of them life in this world was so comfortable, convenient, clean, and easy; their movements and faces expressed such indifference to any other kind of life than their own, such assurance that the porter would step aside for them and bow, and that on returning they would find comfortable rooms and beds, that it all must be so and that they had a right to it all, that I involuntarily contrasted them with the vagrant singer who, tired and perhaps hungry, was escaping ashamed from the laughing crowd, and I realized what it was that weighed on my heart like a stone, and I felt indescribable anger against these people. Twice I walked to and fro past the Englishman, and each time with inexpressible pleasure avoided making way for him and pushed him with my elbow; then darting down the steps I hastened through the darkness in the direction of the town, where the little man had disappeared.

Having overtaken three men who were walking together, I asked them where the singer was. They laughed and pointed straight ahead. He was walking quickly, by himself. No one went near him, and he seemed to me to be angrily muttering something to himself. I caught him up and proposed to him to go somewhere and drink a bottle of wine. He went on walking just as fast and looked disconsolately at me, but when he had made out what I wanted, he stopped.

'Well, I won't refuse it, if you are so kind,' he said. 'There is a small café here, we could go in there. It's a plain place,' he added, pointing to a drink shop which was still open.

The word 'plain' involuntarily suggested to me the idea of not going to the plain café but to the Schweizerhof, where the people were who had listened to him. Though in timid agitation he several times declined to go to the Schweizerhof, saying that it was too fine there, I insisted on it and he walked back along the quay with me pretending not to be at all abashed, and gaily swinging his guitar. Several idle strollers drew near as soon as I went up to the singer and listened to what I was saying: and now, after arguing among themselves, they followed us to the hotel entrance, probably expecting some further performance from the Tyrolese.

I met a waiter in the vestibule and asked him for a bottle of wine, but he merely looked at us with a smile and ran past. The head waiter, to whom I addressed the same request, listened to me seriously, and having scanned the tiny figure of the timid singer from head to foot, sternly told the porter to take us to the room on the left. This room was a bar for common people, the whole furniture consisted of bare wooden tables and benches, and a hunchbacked woman was washing up dishes in a corner. The waiter who came to take our order looked at us with a mildly supercilious smile and, thrusting his hands in his pockets, exchanged remarks with the hunchbacked dish-washer. He evidently wished to let us know that, feeling himself immeasurably superior to the singer in social standing as well as on his own merits, he was not at all offended, but even quite amused, to be waiting on us.

'Will you have *vin ordinaire*?' he asked with a knowing look, winking towards my companion and shifting his napkin from one arm to the other.

'Champagne, and your very best!' said I, trying to assume a haughty and imposing air. But neither the champagne nor my endeavour to look haughty and imposing had any effect on the waiter: he grinned, stood awhile gazing at us, looked deliberately at his gold watch, and went leisurely and with soft steps out of the room as if he were out for a stroll. He soon returned with the wine and with two other waiters. The two waiters sat down near the dish-washer and gazed at us with the amused attention and bland smiles with which parents watch their dear children when they play nicely. Only the hunchbacked dish-washer seemed to look at us with sympathy rather than irony. Though I felt it very uncomfortable and awkward to talk with the singer and entertain him under the fire of those eyes, I tried to do my part with as little constraint as possible. In the lighted room I could see him better.

He was a tiny, well-proportioned, wiry man, almost a midget, with bristly black hair, large tearful black eyes without lashes, and a thoroughly pleasant and attractively shaped little mouth. He had short side-whiskers, rather short hair, and his clothes were simple and poor. He was dingy, tattered, sunburnt, and had in general the look of a labourer. He was more like a poor pedlar than an artist. Only in his humid, shining eyes and puckering mouth was there something original and touching. Judging by his appearance he might have been anything from twenty-five to forty years old; he was really thirty-eight.

This is what he told me, with good-natured readiness and evident sincerity, about his life. He was from Aargau. While still a child he had lost his father and mother and had no other relations. He had never had any means of his own. He had been apprenticed to a joiner, but twenty-two years ago a bone of his finger had begun to decay, which made it impossible for him to work. He had been fond of music from his childhood, and began to go round singing. Foreigners occasionally gave him money. He made a profession of it, bought a guitar, and for eighteen years had wandered through Switzerland and Italy singing in front of hotels. His whole belongings were the guitar and a purse, in which he now had only a franc and a half, which he would have to spend that night on food and lodging. He had gone every year to all the best and most frequented places in Switzerland: Zurich, Lucerne, Interlaken, Chamonix, and so on; and was now going round for the eighteenth time. He passed over the St Bernard into Italy and returned by St Gotthard or through Savoy. It was getting hard for him to walk now, because a pain in his feet which he called *Gliederzucht* (rheumatism) got worse every year when he caught cold, and his eyes and his voice were growing weaker. In spite of this he was now on his way to Interlaken, Aix-les-Bains, and over the little St Bernard to Italy, of which country he was particularly fond; in general he seemed to be very well satisfied with his life. When I asked him why he was going home and whether he had any relations there, or a house and land, his mouth puckered into a merry smile and he replied: '*Oui, le sucre est bon, il est doux pour les enfants!*' and winked at the waiters.

I did not understand what he meant, but the group of waiters burst out laughing.

'I've got nothing, or would I be going about like this?' he explained. 'I go home because, after all, something draws me back to my native land.'

And he again repeated, with a sly self-satisfied smile, the phrase: '*Oui, le sucre est bon!*' and laughed good-naturedly. The waiters were very pleased and laughed heartily. Only the hunchbacked dish-washer looked at the little man seriously with her large kindly eyes and picked up the cap he had dropped from the bench during our conversation. I had noticed that wandering singers, acrobats, and even jugglers, like to call themselves artists, and so I hinted several times to my companion that he was an artist; but he did not at all acknowledge that quality in himself, and considered his occupation simply as a means of subsistence. When I asked him whether he did not himself compose the songs he sang, he was surprised at so strange a question, and answered: 'How could I? They are all old Tyrolese songs.'

'But what about the Rigi song – that is not old, is it?' I said.

'No, that was composed about fifteen years ago,' he said. 'There was a German in Basle, a very clever man. He composed it. It's a splendid song! You see, he composed it for the tourists.'

And, translating them into French as he went along, he began repeating to me the words of the Rigi song, which he liked so much:

> If you would go up the Rigi
> You need no shoes as far as Weggis
>   (Because you go that far by steamer)
> But in Weggis take a big stick,
> And upon your arm a maiden.
> Drink a glass of wine at starting,
>   Only do not drink too much.
> For he who wants to have a drink
>   Should first have earned . . .

'Oh, it's a splendid song' he said, as he finished.

The waiters, too, probably considered the song very good, for they came nearer to us.

'Yes, but who composed the music?' I asked.

'Oh, nobody! It comes of itself, you know – one must have something new to sing to the foreigners.'

When the ice was brought and I had poured out a glass of champagne for my companion, he seemed to feel ill at ease, and glancing round at the waiters shifted uneasily in his seat. We clinked glasses to the health of artists; he drank half a glass, and then found it necessary to raise his eyebrows in profound thought.

'It's a long time since I drank such wine, *je ne vous dis que ça*. In Italy the d'Asti wine is good, but this is better still. Ah, Italy! It's splendid to be there!' he added.

'Yes, there they know how to appreciate music and artists,' I said, wishing to lead him back to the subject of his failure that evening before the Schweizerhof.

'No,' he replied. 'There, as far as music is concerned, I cannot give anyone pleasure. The Italians are themselves musicians like none others in the world: I sing only Tyrolese songs – that at any rate is a novelty for them.'

'And are the gentlefolk more generous there?' I went on, wishing to make him share my resentment against the guests at the Schweizerhof. 'It couldn't happen there, could it, as it did here, that in an immense hotel frequented by rich people, out of a hundred who listen to an artist not one gives him anything?'

My question had quite a different effect on him from what I had expected. It did not enter his head to be indignant with them: on the contrary he detected in my remark a reflection on his talent, which had failed to elicit any reward, and he tried to justify himself to me.

'One does not get much every time,' he replied. 'Sometimes my voice fails or I am tired. Today, you know, I have been walking for nine hours and singing almost all the time. That is hard. And the great people, the aristocrats, don't always care to hear Tyrolese songs.'

'But still, how could they give nothing at all?' I insisted.

He did not understand my remark.

'It's not that,' he said, 'the chief thing here is, *on est très serré pour la police*, that's where the trouble is. Here under their republican laws you are not allowed to sing, but in Italy you may go about as much as you please, and no one will say a word to you. Here they allow it only when they please, and if they don't please, they may put you in prison.'

'How is that? Is it possible?'

'Yes, if they caution you once and you sing again they may imprison you. I was there for three months,' he said smiling, as though this were one of his pleasantest recollections.

'Oh, that's dreadful!' I said. 'What for?'

'That is so under the new republican laws,' he continued, growing animated. 'They don't want to understand that a poor fellow must live somehow. If I were not a cripple, I would work. But does my singing hurt anyone? What does it mean? The rich can live as they please, but *un pauvre tiable* like myself mayn't even live. Are these the laws a republic should have? If so, we don't want a republic – isn't that so, dear sir? We don't want a republic, but we want – we simply want . . . we want' – he hesitated a while – 'we want natural laws.'

I filled up his glass.

'You are not drinking,' I said to him.

He took the glass in his hand and bowed to me.

'I know what you want,' he said, screwing up his eyes and shaking his finger at me. 'You want to make me drunk, so as to see what will happen to me; but no, you won't succeed!'

'Why should I want to make you drunk?' I said. 'I only want to give you pleasure.'

Probably he was sorry to have offended me by interpreting my intention wrongly, for he grew confused, got up, and pressed my elbow.

'No, no, I was only joking!' he said, looking at me with a beseeching expression in his moist eyes.

Then he uttered some fearfully intricate, complicated sentence intended to imply that I was a good fellow after all.

'*Je ne vous dis que ça!*' he concluded.

So we continued drinking and talking and the waiters continued to watch us unceremoniously and, as it seemed, to make fun of us. Despite my interest in our conversation I could not help noticing them and, I confess, I grew more and more angry. One of them got up, came over to the little man, looked down on the crown of his head, and began to smile. I had accumulated a store of anger for the guests at the Schweizerhof which I had not yet been able to vent on anyone, and I own that this audience of waiters irritated me beyond endurance. Then the porter came in and, leaning his elbows on the table without taking off his hat, sat down beside me.

This last circumstance stung my self-esteem or vanity, and finally caused the oppressive rage that had been smouldering in me all the evening to explode. 'Why when I was alone at the entrance did he humbly bow to me, and now that I am sitting with an itinerant singer, sprawls near me so rudely?' I was filled with a boiling rage of indignation which I like in myself and even stimulate when it besets me, because it has a tranquillizing effect, and gives, at least for a short time, an unusual suppleness, energy, and power to all my physical and mental faculties.

I jumped up.

'What are you laughing at?' I shouted at the waiter, feeling that I was growing pale and that my lips were involuntarily twitching.

'I am not laughing; it's nothing!' said the waiter stepping back.

'No, you are laughing at this gentleman . . . And what right have you to be here and to be sitting down, when there are visitors here? Don't dare to sit here!' I cried turning to the porter.

He got up with a growl and moved towards the door.

'What right have you to laugh at this gentleman and to sit near him, when he is a visitor and you are a lackey? Why didn't you laugh at me or sit beside me at dinner this evening? Is it because he is poorly dressed and sings in the street? Is it? While I wear good clothes? He is poor, but I am convinced that he is a thousand times better than you, for he insults no one, while you are insulting him!'

'But I am not doing anything!' replied my enemy the waiter, timidly. 'Do I prevent his sitting here?'

The waiter did not understand me and my German speech was lost on him. The rude porter tried to take the waiter's part, but I attacked him so vehemently that he pretended that he, too, did not understand me, and waved his arm. The hunch-backed dish-washer, either noticing my heated condition and afraid of a scandal, or because she really shared my views, took my part and, trying to interpose between me and the porter, began to persuade him to be quiet, saying that I was right and asking me to calm myself. '*Der Herr hat recht; Sie haben recht!*' she said firmly. The singer presented a most piteous, frightened appearance and, evidently without understanding why I was excited or what I was aiming at, begged me to go away quickly. But my angry loquacity burned stronger and stronger in me. I recalled everything: the crowd that had laughed at him, and the audience that had given him nothing – and I would not quiet down on any account. I think that if the waiters and the porter had not been so yielding I should have enjoyed a fight with them, or could have whacked the defenceless young English lady on the head with a stick. Had I been at Sevastopol at that moment I would gladly have rushed into an English trench to hack and slash at them.

'And why did you show me and this gentleman into this room, and not the other, eh?' I asked the porter, seizing his arm to prevent his going away. 'What right had you to decide from his appearance that this gentleman must be in this and not in the other room? Are not all who pay on an equal footing in an hotel – not only in a republic, but all over the world? Yours is a scurvy republic! . . . This is your equality! You dare not show those English people into this room – the very Englishmen who listened to this gentleman without paying him – that is, who each stole from him the few centimes they ought to have given him. How dared you show us in here?'

'The other room is closed,' replied the porter.

'No!' I cried. 'That's not true – it's not closed.'

'You know better then.'

'I know! I know that you are lying.'

The porter turned his shoulder towards me. 'What is the use of talking?' he muttered.

'No, not "what is the use . . . " ' I shouted. 'Take us to the other room at once!'

Despite the hunchbacked woman's and the singer's entreaties that we should go away, I had the head waiter called and went into the other room with my companion. When the head waiter heard my angry voice and saw my excited face he did not argue with me, but told me with contemptuous civility that I might go where I liked. I could not convict the porter of his lie, as he had disappeared before I went into the other room.

The room was really open and lighted up, and at one of the tables the Englishman with the lady was having supper. Though we were shown to another table, I sat down with the dirty singer close to the Englishman, and ordered the unfinished bottle to be brought me.

The Englishman and the lady looked first with surprise and then with anger at the little man who sat beside me more dead than alive. They exchanged some words, and the lady pushed away her plate, and rustled her silk dress as they went away. Through the panes in the door I could see the Englishman speaking angrily to the waiter, pointing in our direction all the time. The waiter thrust his head in at the door and looked towards us. I waited with pleasure for them to come to turn us out, and to be able at last to vent my whole indignation on them – but fortunately, though I then regretted it, they left us in peace.

The singer, who had before refused the wine, now hastened to empty the bottle in order to get away as soon as possible. However, he thanked me, feelingly I thought, for his entertainment. His moist eyes became still more tearful and shining, and he expressed his gratitude in a most curious and confused little speech. But that speech, in which he said that if everyone respected artists as I did he would be well off, and that he wished me all happiness, was very pleasant to me. We went out into the vestibule. The waiters were there and my enemy the porter who seemed to be complaining of me to them. They all looked on me, I think, as insane. I let the little man come up to them all, and then, with all the respect I could show, I took off my hat and pressed his hand with its ossified and withered finger. The waiters made a show of not taking any notice of me, but one of them burst into a sardonic laugh.

After bowing to me, the singer disappeared into the darkness, and I went up to my room, wishing to sleep off all these impressions and the foolish, childish anger which had so unexpectedly beset me. Feeling too agitated however for sleep, I went out again into the street to walk about till I should have calmed down, and also I must admit with a vague hope of finding an opportunity to come across the porter, the waiter, or the Englishman, to prove to them how cruel and above all how unjust they had been. But I met no one except the porter, who turned his back on seeing me, and I paced up and down the embankment all alone.

'This is the strange fate of art!' I reflected, having grown a little calmer. 'All seek it and love it – it is the one thing everybody wants and tries to find in life, yet nobody acknowledges its power, nobody values this greatest blessing in the world, nor esteems or is grateful to those who give it to mankind. Ask any one you like of all these guests at the Schweizerhof what is the greatest blessing in the world, and everyone, or ninety-nine out of a hundred, assuming a sardonic expression, will say that the best thing in the world is money! "Maybe this idea does not please you and does not conform to your lofty ideas," he will tell you, "but what is to be done if human life is so constituted that money alone gives people happiness? I cannot help letting my reason see the world as it is," he will add, "that is – see the truth."

'Pitiful is your reason, pitiful the happiness you desire, and you are a miserable being who does not know what you want . . . Why have you all left your country, your relations, your occupations, and your financial affairs, and congregated here in this small Swiss town of Lucerne? Why did you all come out onto the balcony this evening and listen in respectful silence to the songs of that poor little mendicant? And had he chosen to go on singing you would still have remained silent and listened. What money, even millions of it, could have driven you all from your country and assembled you in this little corner, Lucerne? Could money have gathered you all on those balconies and made you stand for half an hour silent and motionless? No! One thing alone causes you to act, and will always influence you more strongly than any other motive power in life, and that is the need for art, which you do not acknowledge, but which you feel and will always feel as long as there is anything human left in you. The word "art" seems ridiculous to you. You use it as a scornful reproach; you perhaps allow love of the poetic in children and in silly girls, but even then you laugh at them; but for yourselves you require something positive. But children see life healthily, they love and know what men should love, and what gives happiness, but life has so enmeshed and depraved you that you laugh at the one thing you love, and seek only that which you hate and which causes you unhappiness. You are so enmeshed that you do not understand your obligation to this poor Tyrolese who has afforded you a pure enjoyment, yet you feel yourselves bound to humble yourselves gratuitously before a lord, without advantage or pleasure, and for some reason sacrifice for him your comfort and convenience. What nonsense! What incomprehensible sense-lessness! But it was not this that struck me most this evening. This ignorance of what gives happiness, this unconsciousness of poetic enjoyment, I almost understand, or have become used to, having often met it in my life; nor was the coarse, unconscious cruelty of the crowd new to me. Whatever the advocates of the popular spirit may say, a crowd is a combination possibly of good people, but of people who have come in touch merely on their base, animal sides, and it expresses only the weakness and cruelty of human nature. How could you, children of a free, humane nation, as Christians or simply as human beings, respond with coldness and ridicule to the pleasure afforded you by an unfortunate mendicant? But no, in your country there are institutions for the needy. There are no beggars and must be none, nor must there be any compassion, on which mendicancy is based. But this man had laboured, he gave you pleasure, he implored you to give him something from your superabundance for his pains, of which you availed yourselves. But you, from your lofty, brilliant palace, regarded him with a cold smile and there was not one among you hundred, happy, rich people who threw him anything. He went away humiliated, and the senseless crowd followed him laughing, and insulted not you but him, because you were cold, cruel, and dishonest; because you stole the pleasure he had afforded you, they insulted *him*.'

'*On the seventh of July 1857, in Lucerne, in front of the Hotel Schweizerhof in which the richest people stay, an itinerant beggar singer sang and played the guitar for half an hour. About a hundred people listened to him. The singer asked them all three times to give him something. Not one of them gave him anything, and many people laughed at him.*'

This is not fiction, but a positive fact, which can be verified by anyone who likes from the permanent residents at the Hotel Schweizerhof, after ascertaining from the papers who the foreigners were who were staying at the Schweizerhof on the 7th of July.

Here is an occurrence the historians of our time ought to record in indelible letters of fire. This incident is more significant, more serious, and has a profounder meaning, than the facts usually printed in newspapers and histories. That the English have killed another thousand Chinamen because the Chinese buy nothing for money while their country absorbs metal coins, that the French have killed another thousand Arabs because corn grows easily in Africa and constant warfare is useful for training armies; that the Turkish Ambassador in Naples must not be a Jew, and that the Emperor Napoleon walks on foot at Plombières and assures the people in print that he reigns only by the will of the whole nation – all these are words that conceal or reveal what has long been known; but what happened at Lucerne on July the 7th appears to me to be something quite new and strange, and relates not to the eternally evil side of human nature, but to a certain epoch in social evolution. This is a fact not for the history of human actions, but for the history of progress and civilization.

Why is this inhuman occurrence, which would be impossible in any German, French, or Italian village, possible here where civilization, liberty, and equality have been brought to the highest point, and where the most civilized travellers from the most civilized nations congregate? Why have these developed, humane people, who collectively are capable of any honourable and humane action, no human, cordial inclination to perform a kindly personal action? Why do these people – who in their parliaments, meetings, and societies are warmly concerned about the condition of the celibate Chinese in India, about propagating Christianity and education in Africa, about the establishment of societies for the betterment of the whole human race – not find in their souls the simple elemental feeling of human sympathy? Is it possible that they do not possess that feeling, and that its place has been occupied by the vanity, ambition, and cupidity governing these men in their parliaments, meetings, and societies? Can it be that the spread of the sensible and selfish association of men called civilization, destroys and contradicts the need for instinctive, loving association? And is it possible that this is the equality for which so much innocent blood has been shed and so many crimes committed? Is it possible that nations, like children, can be made happy by the mere sound of the word equality?

'Equality before the law?' But does the whole life of man take place in the sphere of law? Only a thousandth part of it depends on law, the rest takes place outside, in the sphere of social customs and conceptions. In this society the waiter is better dressed than the singer and insults him with impunity. I am better dressed than the waiter and insult him with impunity. The porter regards me as superior, and the singer as inferior, to himself; when I joined the singer he considered himself our equal and became rude. I grew insolent to the porter and he felt himself inferior to me. The waiter was insolent to the singer and the latter felt himself inferior to him. Can this be a free country – 'positively free' as people say – in which there is a single citizen who, without having caused harm to anyone, is put in prison for doing the only thing he can do to save himself from starvation?

What an unfortunate, pitiful creature is man, with his desire for positive decisions, thrown into this ever-moving, limitless ocean of good and evil, of facts, conceptions, and contradictions! For ages men have struggled and laboured to place good on one side and evil on the other. Centuries pass, and whenever an impartial mind places good and evil on the scales, the balance remains even, and the proportion of good and evil remains unaltered. If only man would learn not to judge, not to think sharply and positively, and not to answer questions presented to him only because they are for ever unanswerable! If only he understood that every thought is both false and true! False by one-sidedness resulting from man's inability to embrace the whole of truth, and true as an expression of one fact of human endeavour.

Men have made subdivisions for themselves in this eternally moving, unending, intermingled chaos of good and evil; they have traced imaginary lines on that ocean, and expect the ocean to divide itself accordingly, as if there were not millions of other subdivisions made from quite other points of view on another plane. It is true that fresh subdivisions are worked out from century to century, but millions of centuries have passed and millions more will pass. 'Civilization is good, barbarianism is bad. Freedom is good, subjection is bad.' This imaginary knowledge destroys the instinctive, beatific, primitive demand for kindliness in human nature. And who will define for me what is freedom, what is despotism, what is civilization, and what barbarianism? Where does the boundary lie between the one and the other? Whose soul possesses so absolute a standard of good and evil that he can measure all the confused and fleeting facts? Whose mind is so great that it can comprehend and measure even the facts of the stationary past? And who has seen a condition in which good and evil did not exist together? And how do I know that it is not my point of view which decides whether I see more of the one than of the other? Who is capable, even for a moment, of severing himself so completely from life as to look down on it with complete detachment? We have one unerring guide, and only one – the universal Spirit which inspiring each and all of us, implants in every individual a craving for what ought to be; that same Spirit which causes the tree to grow towards the sun, the flower to shed its seeds in the autumn, and bids us instinctively draw closer together.

And it is that one blissful and impeccable voice that the noisy, hasty development of civilization stifles. Who is more a man and less a barbarian: that lord who, seeing the threadbare clothes of the singer, angrily left the table, and for his efforts did not give him a millionth part of his wealth, and who now sits, well fed, in a bright comfortable room, calmly discussing the affairs in China and finding the massacres committed there quite justified – or the little singer, who risking imprisonment and with a franc in his pocket has for twenty years been going over mountains and valleys doing no one any harm, but bringing consolation to them by his singing, and who was today insulted and almost driven out and, tired, hungry, and humiliated, has gone to sleep somewhere on rotting straw?

At that moment, in the dead stillness of the night, I heard somewhere in the far distance the little man's guitar and voice.

'No,' I said to myself involuntarily, 'you have no right to pity him and to be indignant at the lord's well-being. Who has weighed the inner happiness to be found in the soul of each of them? He is now sitting somewhere on a dirty door-step, gazing at the gleaming moonlit sky and gaily singing in the calm of the fragrant night; in his heart there is no reproach, or malice, or regret. And who knows what is now going on in the souls of all the people within these palatial walls? Who can tell whether among them all there is as much carefree benign joy in life and harmony with the world as lives in the soul of that little man? Endless is the mercy and wisdom of Him who has allowed and ordained that all these contradictions should exist. Only to you, insignificant worm, who rashly and wrongly try to penetrate His laws and His intentions – only to you do they seem contradictions. He looks down benignly from His bright immeasurable height and rejoices in the infinite harmony into which all your endless contradictory movements resolve themselves.

'In your pride you thought you could separate yourself from the universal law. But you, too, with your mean and petty indignation at the waiters, have been playing your necessary part in the eternal and infinite harmony.'

TWO HUSSARS
A Story

Jomini and Jomini —
Not half a word of vodka.

— D. Davydov

Early in the nineteenth century, when there were as yet no railways or macadamized roads, no gaslight, no stearine candles, no low couches with sprung cushions, no unvarnished furniture, no disillusioned youths with eye glasses, no liberalizing women philosophers, nor any charming *dames aux camélias* of whom there are so many in our times, in those naive days, when leaving Moscow for Petersburg in a coach or carriage provided with a kitchenful of home-made provisions one travelled for eight days along a soft, dusty or muddy road and believed in chopped cutlets, sledge-bells, and plain rolls; when in the long autumn evenings the tallow candles, around which family groups of twenty or thirty people gathered, had to be snuffed; when ball-rooms were illuminated by candelabra with wax or spermaceti candles, when furniture was arranged symmetrically, when our fathers were still young and proved it not only by the absence of wrinkles and grey hair but by fighting duels for the sake of a woman and rushing from the opposite corner of a room to pick up a bit of handkerchief purposely or accidentally dropped; when our mothers wore short-waisted dresses and enormous sleeves and decided family affairs by drawing lots, when the charming *dames aux camélias* hid from the light of day – in those naïve days of Masonic lodges, Martinists, and Tugenbunds, the days of Miloradoviches and Davydovs and Pushkins – a meeting of landed proprietors was held in the Government town of K—, and the nobility elections were being concluded.

I

'Well, never mind, the saloon will do,' said a young officer in a fur cloak and hussar's cap, who had just got out of a post-sledge and was entering the best hotel in the town of K—.

'The assembly, your Excellency, is enormous,' said the boots, who had already managed to learn from the orderly that the hussar's name was Count Turbin, and therefore addressed him as 'your Excellency.'

'The proprietress of Afremovo with her daughters has said she is leaving this evening, so No. 11 will be at your disposal as soon as they go,' continued the boots, stepping softly before the count along the passage and continually looking round.

In the general saloon at a little table under the dingy full-length portrait of the Emperor Alexander the First, several men, probably belonging to the local nobility, sat drinking champagne, while at another side of the room sat some travellers – tradesmen in blue, fur-lined cloaks.

Entering the room and calling in Blücher, a gigantic grey mastiff he had brought with him, the count threw off his cloak, the collar of which was still covered with hoar-frost, called for vodka, sat down at the table in his blue-satin Cossack jacket, and entered into conversation with the gentlemen there.

The handsome open countenance of the newcomer immediately predisposed them in his favour and they offered him a glass of champagne. The count first drank a glass of vodka and then ordered another bottle of champagne to treat his new acquaintances. The sledge-driver came in to ask for a tip.

'Sashka!' shouted the count. 'Give him something!'

The driver went out with Sashka but came back again with the money in his hand. 'Look here, y'r 'xcellence, haven't I done my very best for y'r honour? Didn't you promise me half a ruble, and he's only given me a quarter!'

'Give him a ruble, Sashka.'

Sashka cast down his eyes and looked at the driver's feet.

'He's had enough!' he said, in a bass voice. 'And besides, I have no more money.'

The count drew from his pocket-book the two five-ruble notes which were all it contained and gave one of them to the driver, who kissed his hand and went off.

'I've run it pretty close!' said the count. 'These are my last five rubles.'

'Real hussar fashion, Count,' said one of the nobles who from his moustache, voice, and a certain energetic freedom about his legs, was evidently a retired cavalryman. 'Are you staying here some time, Count?'

'I must get some money. I shouldn't have stayed here at all but for that. And there are no rooms to be had, devil take them, in this accursed pub.'

'Permit me, Count,' said the cavalryman. 'Will you not join me? My room in No. 7 . . . . If you do not mind just for the night. And then you'll stay a couple of days with us? It happens that the *Maréchal de la Noblesse* is giving a ball tonight. You would make him very happy by going.'

'Yes, Count, do stay,' said another, a handsome young man. 'You have surely no reason to hurry away! You know this only comes once in three years – the elections, I mean. You should at least have a look at our young ladies, Count!'

'Sashka, get my clean linen ready. I am going to the bath,' said the count, rising, 'and from there perhaps I may look in at the Marshal's.'

Then, having called the waiter and whispered something to him to which the latter replied with a smile, 'That can all be arranged,' he went out.

'So I'll order my trunk to be taken to your room, old fellow,' shouted the count from the passage.

'Please do, I shall be most happy,' replied the cavalryman, running to the door. 'No. 7 – don't forget.'

When the count's footsteps could no longer be heard the cavalryman returned to his place and sitting close to one of the group – a government official – and looking him straight in the face with smiling eyes, said: 'It is the very man, you know!'

'No!'

'I tell you it is! It is the very same duellist hussar – the famous Turbin. He knew me – I bet you anything he knew me. Why, he and I went on the spree for three weeks without a break when I was at Lebedyani for remounts. There was one thing he and I did together . . . . He's a fine fellow, eh?'

'A splendid fellow. And so pleasant in his manner! Doesn't show a grain of – what d'you call it?' answered the handsome young man. 'How quickly we became intimate . . . He's not more than twenty-five, is he?'

'Oh no, that's what he looks but he is more than that. One has to get to know him, you know. Who abducted Migunova? He. It was he who killed Sablin. It was he who dropped Matnev out of the window by his legs. It was he who won three hundred thousand rubles from Prince Nestorov. He is a regular daredevil, you know: a gambler, a duellist, a seducer, but a jewel of an hussar — a real jewel. The rumours that are afloat about us are nothing to the reality — if anyone knew what a true hussar is! Ah yes, those were times!'

And the cavalryman told his interlocutor of such a spree with the count in Lebedyani as not only never had, but never even could have, taken place.

It could not have done so, first because he had never seen the count till that day and had left the army two years before the count entered it; and secondly because the cavalryman had never really served in the cavalry at all but had for four years been the humblest of cadets in the Belevski regiment and retired as soon as ever he became ensign. But ten years ago he had inherited some money and had really been in Lebedyani where he squandered seven hundred rubles with some officers who were there buying remounts. He had even gone so far as to have an uhlan uniform made with orange facings, meaning to enter an uhlan regiment. This desire to enter the cavalry, and the three weeks spent with the remount officers at Lebedyani, remained the brightest and happiest memories of his life, so he transformed the desire first into a reality and then into a reminiscence and came to believe firmly in his past as a cavalry officer — all of which did not prevent his being, as to gentleness and honesty, a most worthy man.

'Yes, those who have never served in the cavalry will never understand us fellows.'

He sat astride a chair and thrusting out his lower jaw began to speak in a bass voice. 'You ride at the head of your squadron, not a horse but the devil incarnate prancing about under you, and you just sit in devil-may-care style. The squadron commander rides up to review: "Lieutenant," he says. "We can't get on without you — please lead the squadron to parade." "All right," you say, and there you are: you turn round, shout to your moustached fellows . . . Ah, devil take it, those were times!'

The count returned from the bath-house very red and with wet hair, and went straight to No. 7, where the cavalryman was already sitting in his dressing-gown smoking a pipe and considering with pleasure, and not without some apprehension, the happiness that had befallen him of sharing a room with the celebrated Turbin. 'Now suppose,' he thought, 'that he suddenly takes me, strips me naked, drives me to the town gates, and sets me in the snow, or . . . tars me, or simply . . . But no,' he consoled himself, 'He wouldn't do that to a comrade.'

'Sashka, feed Blücher!' shouted the count.

Sashka, who had taken a tumbler of vodka to refresh himself after the journey and was decidedly tipsy, came in.

'What, already! You've been drinking, you rascal! . . . Feed Blücher!'

'He won't starve anyway: see how sleek he is!' answered Sashka, stroking the dog.

'Silence! Be off and feed him!'

'You want the dog to be fed, but when a man drinks a glass you reproach him.'

'Hey! I'll thrash you!' shouted the count in a voice that made the window-panes rattle and even frightened the cavalryman a bit.

'You should ask if Sashka has had a bite today! Yes, beat me if you think more of a dog than of a man,' muttered Sashka.

But here he received such a terrible blow in the face from the count's fist that he fell, knocked his head against the partition, and clutching his nose fled from the room and fell on a settee in the passage.

'He's knocked my teeth out,' grunted Sashka, wiping his bleeding nose with one hand while with the other he scratched the back of Blücher, who was licking himself. 'He's knocked my teeth out, Blüchy, but still he's my count and I'd go through fire for him – I would! Because he – is my count. Do you understand, Blüchy? Want your dinner, eh?'

After lying still for a while he rose, fed the dog and then, almost sobered, went in to wait on his count and to offer him some tea.

'I shall really feel hurt,' the cavalryman was saying meekly, as he stood before the count who was lying on the other's bed with his legs up against the partition. 'You see I also am an old army man and, if I may say so, a comrade. Why should you borrow from anyone else when I shall be delighted to lend you a couple of hundred rubles? I haven't got them just now – only a hundred rubles – but I'll get the rest today. You would really hurt my feelings, Count.'

'Thank you, old man,' said the count, instantly discerning what kind of relations had to be established between them, and slapping the cavalryman on the shoulder. 'Thanks! Well then, we'll go to the ball if it must be so. But what are we to do now? Tell me what you have in your town. What pretty girls? What men fit for a spree? What gaming?'

The cavalryman explained that there would be an abundance of pretty creatures at the ball, that Kolkov, who had been re-elected captain of police, was the best hand at a spree, only he lacked the true hussar go – otherwise he was a good sort of chap, that the Ilyushin gipsy chorus had been singing in the town since the elections began, Streshka leading, and that everybody meant to go to hear them after leaving the marshal's that evening.

'And there's a devilish lot of card-playing too,' he went on. Lukhnov plays. He has money and is staying here to break his journey, and Ilyin, an uhlan cornet who has room No. 8, has lost a lot. They have already begun in his room. They play every evening. And what a fine fellow that Ilyin is! I tell you, Count, he's not mean – he'll let his last shirt go.'

'Well then, let us go to his room. Let's see what sort of people they are,' said the count.

'Yes do – pray do. They'll be devilish glad.'

2

The uhlan cornet, Ilyin, had not long been awake. The evening before he had sat down to cards at eight o'clock and had lost pretty steadily for fifteen hours on end – till eleven in the morning. He had lost a considerable sum but did not know exactly how much, because he had about three thousand rubles of his own, and fifteen thousand of Crown money which had long since got mixed up with his own, and he feared to count lest his fears that some of the Crown money was already gone should be confirmed. It was nearly noon when he fell asleep and he had slept that heavy dreamless sleep which only very young men sleep after a heavy loss. Waking at six o'clock (just when Count Turbin arrived at the hotel), and seeing the floor all around strewn with cards and bits of chalk, and the chalk-marked tables in the middle of the room, he recalled with horror last night's play, and the last card – a knave on which he lost five hundred rubles; but not yet quite convinced of the reality of all this, he drew his money from under the pillow and began to count it. He recognized some notes which had passed from hand to hand several times with 'corners' and 'transports' and he recalled the whole course of the game. He had none of his own three thousand rubles left, and some two thousand five hundred of the government money was also gone.

Ilyin had been playing for four nights running.

He had come from Moscow where the crown money had been entrusted to him and at K— had been detained by the super-intendent of the post-house on the pretext that there were no horses, but really because the superintendent had an agreement with the hotel-keeper to detain all travellers for a day. The uhlan, a bright young lad who had just received three thousand rubles from his parents in Moscow for his equipment on entering his regiment, was glad to spend a few days in the town of K— during the elections and hoped to enjoy himself thoroughly. He knew one of the landed gentry there who had a family, and he was thinking of looking them up and flirting with the daughters, when the cavalryman turned up to make his acquaintance. Without any evil intention the cavalryman introduced him that same evening, in the general saloon or common room of the hotel, to his acquaintances, Lukhnov and other gamblers. And ever since then the uhlan had been playing cards, not asking at the post-station for horses, much less going to visit his acquaintance the landed proprietor, and not even leaving his room for four days on end.

Having dressed and drunk tea he went to the window. He felt that he would like to go for a stroll to get rid of the recollections that haunted him, and he put on his cloak and went out into the street. The sun was already hidden behind the white houses with the red roofs and it was getting dusk. It was warm for winter. Large wet snowflakes were falling slowly into the muddy street. Suddenly at the thought that he had slept all through the day now ending, a feeling of intolerable sadness overcame him.

'This day, now past, can never be recovered,' he thought.

'I have ruined my youth!' he suddenly said to himself, not because he really thought he had ruined his youth – he did not even think about it – but because the phrase happened to occur to him.

'And what am I to do now?' thought he. 'Borrow from someone and go away?' A lady passed him along the pavement. 'There's a stupid woman,' thought he for some reason. 'There's no one to borrow from . . . I have ruined my youth!' He came to the bazaar. A tradesman in a fox-fur cloak stood at the door of his shop touting for customers. 'If I had not withdrawn that eight I should have recovered my losses.' An old beggar-woman followed him whimpering. 'There's no one to borrow from.' A man drove past in a bearskin cloak; a policeman was standing at his post. 'What unusual thing could I do? Fire at them? No, it's dull . . . I have ruined my youth! . . . Ah, if only I could drive in a troyka: Gee-up, beauties! . . . I'll go back. Lukhnov will come soon, and we'll play.'

He returned to the hotel and again counted his money. No, he had made no mistake the first time: there were still two thousand five hundred rubles of Crown money missing. 'I'll stake twenty-five rubles, than make a "corner" . . . seven-fold it, fifteen-fold thirty, sixty . . . three thousand rubles. Then I'll buy the horse-collars and be off. He won't let me, the rascal! I have ruined my youth!'

That is what was going on in the uhlan's head when Lukhnov actually entered the room.

'Have you been up long, Michael Vasilich?' asked Lukhnov, slowly removing the gold spectacles from his skinny nose and carefully wiping them with a red silk handkerchief.

'No, I've only just got up – I slept uncommonly well.'

'Some hussar or other has arrived. He has put up with Zaval-shevski – had you heard?'

'No, I hadn't. But how is it no one else is here yet?'

'They must have gone to Pryakhin's. They'll be here directly.'

And sure enough a little later there came into the room a garrison officer who always accompanied Lukhnov, a Greek merchant with an enormous brown hooked nose and sunken black eyes, and a fat puffy landowner, the proprietor of a distillery, who played whole nights, always staking 'simples' of half a ruble each. Everybody wished to begin playing as soon as possible, but the principal gamesters, especially Lukhnov who was telling about a robbery in Moscow in an exceedingly calm manner, did not refer to the subject.

'Just fancy,' he said, 'a city like Moscow, the historic capital, a metropolis, and men dressed up as devils go about there with crooks, frighten stupid people, and rob the passers-by — and that's the end of it! What are the police about? That's the question.'

The uhlan listened attentively to the story about the robbers, but when a pause came he rose and quietly ordered cards to be brought. The fat landowner was the first to speak out.

'Well, gentlemen, why lose precious time? If we mean business let's begin.'

'Yes, you walked off with a pile of half-rubles last night so you like it,' said the Greek.

'I think we might start,' said the garrison officer.

Ilyin looked at Lukhnov. Lukhnov looking him in the eye quietly continued his story about robbers dressed up like devils with claws.

'Will you keep the bank?' asked the uhlan.

'Isn't it too early?'

'Belov!' shouted the uhlan, blushing for some unknown reason, 'bring me some dinner — I haven't had anything to eat yet, gentlemen — and a bottle of champagne and some cards.'

At this moment the count and Zavalshevski entered the room. It turned out that Turbin and Ilyin belonged to the same division. They took to one another at once, clinked glasses, drank champagne together, and were on intimate terms in five minutes. The count seemed to like Ilyin very much; he looked smilingly at him and teased him about his youth.

'There's an uhlan of the right sort!' he said. 'What moustaches! Dear me, what moustaches!'

Even what little down there was on Ilyin's lip was quite white.

'I suppose you are going to play?' said the count. 'Well, I wish you luck, Ilyin! I should think you are a master at it,' he added with a smile.

'Yes, they mean to start,' said Lukhnov, tearing open a bundle of a dozen packs of cards, 'and you'll joint in too, Count, won't you?'

'No, not today. I should clear you all out if I did. When I begin "cornering" in earnest the bank begins to crack! But I have nothing to play with — I was cleaned out at a station near Volo-chok. I met some infantry fellow there with rings on his fingers — a sharper I should think — and he plucked me clean.'

'Why, did you stay at that station long?' asked Ilyin.

'I sat there for twenty-two hours. I shan't forget that accursed station! And the superintendent won't forget me either . . . '

'How's that?'

'I drive up, you know; out rushes the superintendent looking a regular brigand. "No horses!" says he. Now I must tell you that it's my rule, if there are no horses I don't take off my fur cloak but go into the superintendent's own room – not into the public room but into his private room – and I have all the doors and windows opened on the ground that it's smoky. Well, that's just what I did there. You remember what frosts we had last month? About twenty degrees! The superintendent began to argue; I punched his head. There was an old woman there, and girls and other women; they kicked up a row, snatched up their pots and pans, and were rushing off to the village . . . I went to the door and said, "Let me have horses and I'll be off. If not, no one shall go out: I'll freeze you all."'

'That's an infernally good plan!' said the puffy squire, rolling with laughter. 'It's the way they freeze out cockroaches . . . '

'But I didn't watch carefully enough and the superintendent got away with the women. Only one old woman remained in pawn on the top of the stove; she kept sneezing and saying prayers. Afterwards we began negotiating: the superintendent came and from a distance began persuading me to let the old woman go, but I set Blücher at him a bit. Blücher's splendid at tackling superintendents! But still the rascal didn't let me have horses until the next morning. Meanwhile that infantry fellow came along. I joined him in another room, and we began to play. You have seen Blücher? . . . Blücher! . . . ' and he gave a whistle.

Blücher rushed in, and the players condescendingly paid some attention to him though it was evident that they wished to attend to quite other matters.

'But why don't you play, gentlemen? Please don't let me prevent you. I am a chatterbox, you see,' said Turbin. 'Play is play whether one likes it or not.'

3

Lukhnov drew two candles nearer to him, took out a large brown pocket-book full of paper money, and slowly, as if performing some rite, opened it on the table, took out two one-hundred rubles notes and placed them under the cards.

'Two hundred for the bank, the same as yesterday,' said he, adjusting his spectacles and opening a pack of cards.

'Very well,' said Ilyin, continuing his conversation with Turbin without looking at Lukhnov.

The game started. Lukhnov dealt the cards with machine-like precision, stopping now and then and deliberately jotting something down, or looking sternly over his spectacles and saying in low tones, 'Pass up!' The fat landowner spoke louder than anyone else, audibly deliberating with himself and wetting his plump fingers when he turned down the corner of a card. The garrison officer silently and neatly noted the amount of his stake on his card and bent down small corners under the table. The Greek sat beside the banker, watching the game attentively with his sunken black eyes, and seemed to be waiting for something. Zavalshevski, standing by the table, would suddenly begin to fidget all over, take a red or blue bank-note out of his trouser pocket, lay a card on it, slap it with his palm, and say, 'Little seven, pull me through!' Then he would bite his moustache, shift from foot to foot, and keep fidgeting till his card was dealt. Ilyin sat eating veal and pickled cucumbers, which were placed beside him on the horse-hair sofa, and hastily wiping his hands on his coat laid down one card after another. Turbin, who at first was sitting on the sofa, quickly saw how matters stood. Lukhnov did not look at or speak to Ilyin, only now and then his spectacles would turn for a moment towards the latter's hand, but most of Ilyin's cards lost.

'There now, I'd like to beat that card,' said Lukhnov of a card the fat landowner, who was staking half-rubles, had put down.

'You beat Ilyin's, never mind me!' remarked the squire.

And indeed Ilyin's cards lost more often than any of the others. He would tear up the losing card nervously under the table and choose another with trembling fingers. Turbin rose from the sofa and asked the Greek to let him sit by the banker. The Greek moved to another place; the count took his chair and began watching Lukhnov's hands attentively, not taking his eyes off them.

'Ilyin!' he suddenly said in his usual voice, which quite unintentionally drowned all the others. 'Why do you keep to a routine? You don't know how to play.'

'It's all the same how one plays.'

'But you're sure to lose that way. Let me play for you.'

'No, please excuse me. I always do it myself. Play for yourself if you like.'

'I said I should not play for myself, but I should like to play for you. I am vexed that you are losing.'

'I suppose it's my fate.'

The count was silent, but leaning on his elbows he again gazed intently at the banker's hands.

'Abominable!' he suddenly said in a loud, long-drawn tone.

Lukhnov glanced at him.

'Abominable, quite abominable!' he repeated still louder, looking straight into Lukhnov's eyes.

The game continued.

'It is not right!' Turbin remarked again, just as Lukhnov beat a heavily backed card of Ilyin's.

'What is it you don't like, Count?' inquired the banker with polite indifference.

'This! – that you let Ilyin win his simples and beat his corners. That's what's bad.'

Lukhnov made a slight movement with his brows and shoulders, expressing the advisability of submitting to fate in everything, and continued to play.

'Blücher!' shouted the count, rising and whistling to the dog. 'At him!' he added quickly.

Blücher, bumping his back against the sofa as he leapt from under it and nearly upsetting the garrison officer, ran to his master and growled, looking around at everyone and moving his tail as if asking, 'Who is misbehaving here, eh?'

Lukhnov put down his cards and moved his chair to one side.

'One can't play like that,' he said. 'I hate dogs. What kind of a game is it when you bring a whole pack of hounds in here?'

'Especially a dog like that. I believe they are called "leeches",' chimed in the garrison officer.

'Well, are we going to play or not, Michael Vasilich?' said Lukhnov to their host.

'Please don't interfere with us, Count,' said Ilyin, turning to Turbin.

'Come here a minute,' said Turbin, taking Ilyin's arm and going behind the partition with him.

The count's words, spoken in his usual tone, were distinctly audible from there. His voice always carried across three rooms.

'Are you daft, eh? Don't you see that that gentleman in spectacles is a sharper of the first water?'

'Come now, enough! What are you saying?'

'No enough about it! Stop playing, I tell you. It's nothing to me. Another time I'd pluck you myself, but somehow I'm sorry to see you fleeced. And maybe you have Crown money too?'

'No . . . why do you imagine such things?'

'Ah, my lad, I've been that way myself so I know all those sharpers' tricks. I tell you the one in spectacles is a sharper. Stop playing! I ask you as a comrade.'

'Well then, I'll only finish this one deal.'

'I know what "one deal" means. Well, we'll see.'

They went back. In that one deal Ilyin put down so many cards and so many of them were beaten that he lost a large amount.

Turbin put his hands in the middle of the table 'Now stop it! Come along.'

'No, I can't. Leave me alone, do!' said Ilyin, irritably shuffling some bent cards without looking at Turbin.

'Well, go to the devil! Go on losing for certain, if that pleases you. It's time for me to be off. Let's go to the Marshal's, Savalshevski.'

They went out. All remained silent and Lukhnov dealt no more cards until the sound of their steps and of Blücher's claws on the passage floor had died away.

'What a devil of a fellow!' said the landowner, laughing.

'Well, he won't interfere now,' remarked the garrison officer hastily, and still in a whisper.

And the play continued.

4

The band, composed of some of the marshal's serfs standing in the pantry – which had been cleared out for the occasion – with their coat-sleeves turned up already, had at a given signal struck up the old polonaise, 'Alexander, 'Lizabeth', and under the bright soft light of the wax-candles a Governor-General of Catherine's days, with a star on his breast, arm-in-arm with the marshal's skinny wife, and the rest of the local grandees with their partners, had begun slowly gliding over the parquet floor of the large dancing-room in various combinations and variations, when Zavalshevski entered, wearing stockings and pumps and a blue swallow-tail coat with an immense and padded collar, and exhaling a strong smell of the frangipane with which the facings of his coat, his handkerchief, and his moustaches, were abundantly sprinkled. The handsome hussar who came with him wore tight-fitting light-blue riding-breeches and a gold-embroidered scarlet on which a Vladimir cross and an 1812 medal were fastened. The count was not tall but remarkably well built. His clear blue and exceedingly brilliant eyes, and thick, closely curling, dark-brown hair, gave a remarkable character to his beauty. His arrival at the ball was expected, for the handsome young man who had seen him at the hotel had already prepared the Marshal for it. Various impressions had been produced by the news, for the most part not altogether pleasant.

'It's not unlikely that this youngster will hold us up to ridicule,' was the opinion of the men and of the older women. 'What if he should run away with me?' was more or less in the minds of the younger ladies, married or unmarried.

As soon as the polonaise was over and the couples after bowing to one another had separated – the women into one group and the men into another – Zavalshevski, proud and happy, introduced the count to their hostess.

The marshal's wife, feeling an inner trepidation lest this hussar should treat her in some scandalous manner before everybody, turned away haughtily and contemptuously as she said, 'Very pleased, I hope you will dance,' and then gave him a distrustful look that said, 'Now, if you offend a woman it will show me that you are a perfect villain.' The count however soon conquered her prejudices by his amiability, attentive manner, and handsome gay appearance, so that five minutes later the expression on the face of the Marshal's wife told the company: 'I know how to manage such gentlemen. He immediately understood with whom he had to deal, and now he'll be charming to me for the rest of the evening.' Moreover at that moment the governor of the town, who had known the count's father, came up to him and very affably took him aside for a talk, which still further calmed the provincial public and raised the count in its estimation. After that Zavalshevski introduced the count to his sister, a plump young widow whose large black eyes had not left the count from the moment he entered. The count asked her to dance the waltz the band had just commenced, and the general prejudice was finally dispersed by the masterly way in which he danced.

'What a splendid dancer!' said a fat landed proprietress, watching his legs in their blue riding-breeches as they flitted across the room, and mentally counting 'one, two, three – one, two, three – splendid!'

'There he goes – jig, jig, jig,' said another, a visitor in the town whom local society did not consider genteel. 'How does he manage not to entangle his spurs? Wonderfully clever!'

The count's artistic dancing eclipsed the three best dancers of the province: the tall fair-haired adjutant of the governor, noted for the rapidity with which he danced and for holding his partner very close to him; the cavalryman, famous for the graceful swaying motion with which he waltzed and for the frequent but light tapping of his heels; and a civilian, of whom everybody said that thought he was not very intellectual he was a first-rate dancer and the soul of every ball. In fact, from its very commencement this civilian would ask all the ladies in turn to dance, in the order in which they were sitting, and never stopped for a moment except occasionally to wipe the perspiration from his weary but cheerful face with a very wet cambric handkerchief. The count eclipsed them all and danced with the three principal ladies: the tall one, rich, handsome, stupid; the one of middle height, thin and not very pretty but splendidly dressed; and the little one, who was plain but very clever. He danced with others too – with all the pretty ones, and there were many of these – but it was Zaval-shevski's sister, the little widow, who pleased him best. With her he danced a quadrille, and *écossaise*, and a mazurka. When they were sitting down during the quadrille he began paying her many compliments; comparing her to Venus and Diana, to a rose, and to some other flower. But all these compliments only made the widow bend her white neck, lower her eyes and look at her white muslin dress, or pass her fan from hand to hand. But when she said 'Don't, you're only joking, Count,' and other words to that effect, there was a note of such naïve simplicity and amusing silliness in her slightly guttural voice that looking at her it really seemed that this was not a woman but a flower, and not a rose, but some gorgeous scentless rosy-white wild flower that had grown all alone out of a snowdrift in some very remote land.

This combination of naïveté and unconventionality with her fresh beauty created such a peculiar impression on the count that several times during the intervals of conversation, when gazing silently into her eyes or at the beautiful outline of her neck and arms, the desire to seize her in his arms and cover her with kisses assailed him with such force that he had to make a serious effort to resist it. The widow noticed with pleasure the effect she was producing, yet something in the count's behaviour began to frighten and excite her, though the young hussar, despite his insinuating amiability, was respectful to a degree that in our days would be considered cloying. He ran to fetch almond-milk for her, picked up her handkerchief, snatched a chair from the hands of a scrofulous young squire who danced attendance on her to hand it her more quickly, and so forth.

When he noticed that the society attentions of the day had little effect on the lady he tried to amuse her by telling her funny stories and assured her that he was ready to stand on his head, to crow like a cock, to jump out of the window or plunge into the water through a hole in the ice, if she ordered him to do so. This proved quite a success. The widow brightened up and burst into peals of laughter, showing her lovely white teeth, and was quite satisfied with her cavalier. The count liked her more and more every minute, so that by the end of the quadrille he was seriously in love with her.

When, after the quadrille, her eighteen-year-old adorer of long standing came up to the widow (he was the same scrofulous young man from whom Turbin had snatched the chair – a son of the richest local landed proprietor and not yet in government service) she received him with extreme coolness and did not show one-tenth of the confusion she had experienced with the count.

'Well, you are a fine fellow!' she said, looking all the time at Turbin's back and unconsciously considering how many yards of gold cord it had taken to embroider his whole jacket. 'You are a good one! You promised to call and fetch me for a drive and bring me some comfits.'

'I did come, Anna Fedorovna, but you had already gone, and I left some of the very best comfits for you,' said the young man, who – despite his tallness – spoke in a very high-pitched voice.

'You always find excuses! . . . I don't want your bon-bons. Please don't imagine – '

'I see, Anna Fedorovna, that you have changed towards me and I know why. But it's not right,' he added, evidently unable to finish his speech because a strong inward agitation caused his lips to quiver in a very strange and rapid manner.

Anna Fedorovna did not listen to him but continued to follow Turbin with her eyes.

The master of the house, the stout, toothless, stately old marshal, came up to the count, took him by the arm, and invited him into the study for a smoke and a drink. As soon as Turbin left the room Anna Fedorovna felt that there was absolutely nothing to do there and went out into the dressing-room arm-in-arm with a friend of hers, a bony, elderly, maiden lady.

'Well, is he nice?' asked the maiden lady.

'Only he bothers so!' Anna Fedorovna replied walking up to the mirror and looking at herself.

Her face brightened, her eyes laughed, she even blushed, and suddenly imitating the ballet-dancers she had seen during the elections, she twirled round on one foot, then laughed her guttural but pleasant laugh and even bent her knees and gave a jump.

'Just fancy, what a man! He actually asked me for a keepsake,' she said to her friend, 'but he will get no-o-o-thing.' She sang the last word and held up one finger in her kid glove which reached to her elbow.

In the study, where the marshal had taken Turbin, stood bottles of different sorts of vodka, liqueurs, champagne, and *zakuska*. The nobility, walking about or sitting in a cloud of tobacco smoke, were talking about the elections.

'When the whole worshipful society of our nobility has honoured him by their choice,' said the newly elected Captain of Police who had already imbibed freely, 'he should on no account transgress in the face of the whole society – he ought never . . .'

The count's entrance interrupted the conversation. Everybody wished to be introduced to him, and the Captain of Police especially kept pressing the count's hand between his own for a long time and repeatedly asked him not to refuse to accompany him to the new restaurant where he was going to treat the gentlemen after the ball, and where the gipsies were going to sing. The count promised to come without fail, and drank some glasses of champagne with him.

'But why are you not dancing, gentlemen?' said the count, as he was about to leave the room.

'We are not dancers,' replied the Captain of Police, laughing. 'Wine is more in our line, Count . . . And besides, I have seen all those young ladies grow up, Count! But I can walk through an *écossaise* now and then, Count . . . I can do it, Count.'

'Then come and walk through one now,' said Turbin. 'It will brighten us up before going to hear the gipsies.'

'Very well, gentlemen! Let's come and gratify our host.'

And three or four of the noblemen who had been drinking in the study since the commencement of the ball, put on gloves of black kid or knitted silk and with red faces were just about to follow the count into the ball-room when they were stopped by the scrofulous young man who, pale and hardly able to restrain his tears, accosted Turbin.

'You think that because you are a count you can jostle people about as if you were in the market-place,' he said, breathing with difficulty, 'but that is impolite . . .'

And again, do what he would, his quivering lips checked the flow of his words.

'What?' cried Turbin, suddenly frowning. 'What? . . . You brat!' he cried, seizing him by the arms and squeezing them so that the blood rushed to the young man's head not so much from vexation as from fear. 'What? Do you want to fight? I am at your service!'

Hardly had Turbin released the arms he had been squeezing so hard than two nobles caught hold of them and dragged the young man towards the back door.

'What! Are you out of your mind? You must be tipsy! Suppose we were to tell your papa! What's the matter with you?' they said to him.

'No, I'm not tipsy, but he jostles one and does not apologize. He's a swine, that's what he is!' squealed the young man, now quite in tears.

But they did not listen to him and someone took him home.

On the other side the Captain of Police and Zavalshevski were exhorting Turbin: 'Never mind him, Count, he's only a child. He still gets whipped, he's only sixteen . . . What can have happened to him? What bee has stung him? And his father such a respectable man – and our candidate.'

'Well, let him go to the devil if he does not wish . . . '

And the count returned to the ball-room and danced the *écossaise* with the pretty widow as gaily as before, laughed with all his heart as he watched the steps performed by the gentlemen who had come with him out of the study, and burst into peals of laughter than rang across the room when the Captain of Police slipped and measured his full length in the midst of the dancers.

5

While the count was in the study Anna Fedorovna had approached her brother, and supposing that she ought to pretend to be very little interested in the count, began by asking: 'Who is that hussar who was dancing with me? Can you tell me, brother?'

The cavalryman explained to his sister as well as he could what a great man the hussar was and told her at the same time that the count was only stopping in the town because his money had been stolen on the way, and that he himself had lent him a hundred rubles, but that that was not enough, so that perhaps 'sister' would lend another couple of hundred. Only Zavalshevski asked her on no account to mention the matter to anyone – especially not to the count. Anna Fedorovna promised to send her brother the money that very day and to keep the affair secret, but somehow during the *écossaise* she felt a great longing in herself to offer the count as much money as he wanted. She took a long time making up her mind, and blushed, but at last with a great effort broached the subject as follows.

'My brother tells me that a misfortune befell you on the road, Count, and that you have no money by you. If you need any, won't you take it from me? I should be so glad.'

But having said this, Anna Fedorovna suddenly felt frightened of something and blushed. All gaiety instantly left the count's face.

'Your brother is a fool!' he said abruptly. 'You know when a man insults another man they fight; but when a woman insults a man, what does he do then – do you know?'

Poor Anna Fedorovna's neck and ears grew red with confusion. She lowered her eyes and said nothing.

'He kisses the woman in public,' said the count in a low voice, leaning towards her ear. 'Allow me at least to kiss your little hand,' he added in a whisper after a prolonged silence, taking pity on his partner's confusion.

'But not now!' said Anna Fedorovna, with a deep sigh.

'When then? I am leaving early tomorrow and you owe it me.'

'Well then it's impossible,' said Anna Fedorovna with a smile.

'Only allow me a chance to meet you tonight to kiss your hand. I shall not fail to find an opportunity.'

'How can you find it?'

'That is not your business. In order to see you everything is possible . . . It's agreed?'

'Agreed.'

The *écossaise* ended. After that they danced a mazurka and the count was quite wonderful: catching handkerchiefs, kneeling on one knee, striking his spurs together in a quite special Warsaw manner, so that all the old people left their game of boston and flocked into the ball-room to see, and the cavalryman, their best dancer, confessed himself eclipsed. Then they had supper after which they danced the 'Grandfather', and the ball began to break up. The count never took his eyes off the little widow. It was not pretence when he said he was ready to jump through a hole in the ice for her sake. Whether it was whim, or love, or obstinacy, all his mental powers that evening were concentrated on the one desire – to meet and love her. As soon as he noticed that Anna Fedorovna was taking leave of her hostess he ran out to the footmen's room, and thence – without his fur cloak – into the courtyard to the place where the carriages stood.

'Anna Fedorovna Zaytseva's carriage!' he shouted.

A high four-seated closed carriage with lamps burning moved from its place and approached the porch.

'Stop!' he called to the coachman and plunging knee-deep into the snow ran to the carriage.

'What do you want?' said the coachman.

'I want to get into the carriage,' replied the count, opening the door and trying to get in while the carriage was moving. 'Stop, I tell you, you fool!'

'Stop, Vaska!' shouted the coachman to the postilion and pulled up the horses. 'What are you getting into other people's carriages for? This carriage belongs to my mistress, to Anna Fedorovna, and not to your honour.'

'Shut up, you blockhead! Here's a ruble for you; get down and close the door,' said the count. But as the coachman did not stir he lifted the steps himself and, lowering the window, managed somehow to close the door. In the carriage, as in all old carriages, especially in those in which yellow galloon is used, there was a musty odour something like the smell of decayed and burnt bristles. The count's legs were wet with snow up to the knees and felt very cold in his thin boots and riding-breeches; in fact the winter cold penetrated his whole body. The coachman grumbled on the box and seemed to be preparing to get down. But the count neither heard nor felt anything. His face was aflame and his heart beat fast. In his nervous tension he seized the yellow window strap and leant out of the side window, and all his being merged into one feeling of expectation.

This expectancy did not last long. Someone called from the porch: 'Zaytseva's carriage!' The coachman shook the reins, the body of the carriage swayed on its high springs, and the illuminated windows of the house ran one after another past the carriage windows.

'Mind, fellow,' said the count to the coachman, putting his head out of the front window, 'if you tell the footman I'm here, I'll thrash you, but hold your tongue and you shall have another ten rubles.'

Hardly had he time to close the window before the body of the carriage shook more violently and then stopped. He pressed close into the corner, held his breath, and even shut his eyes, so terrified was he lest anything should baulk his passionate expectation. The door opened, the carriage steps fell noisily one after the other, he heard the rustle of a woman's dress, a smell of frangipane perfume filled the musty carriage, quick little feet ran up the carriage steps, and Anna Fedorovna, brushing the count's leg with the skirt of her cloak which had come open, sank silently onto the seat behind him breathing heavily.

Whether she saw him or not no one could tell, not even Anna Fedorovna herself, but when he took her hand and said, 'Well, now I will kiss your little hand,' she showed very little fear, gave no reply, but yielded her arm to him, which he covered much higher than the top of her glove with kisses. The carriage started.

'Say something! Art thou angry?' he said.

She silently pressed into her corner, but suddenly something caused her to burst into tears and of her own accord she let her head fall on his breast.

6

The newly elected Captain of Police and his guests the cavalryman and other nobles had long been listening to the gipsies and drinking in the new restaurant when the count, wearing a blue cloth cloak lined with bearskin which had belonged to Anna Fedorovna's late husband, joined them.

'Sure, your excellency, we have been awaiting you impatiently!' said a dark cross-eyed gipsy, showing his white teeth, as he met the count at the very entrance and rushed to help him off with his cloak. 'We have not seen you since the fair at Lebedyani . . . Steshka is quite pining away for you.'

Steshka, a young, graceful little gipsy with a brick-red glow on her brown face and deep, sparkling black eyes shaded by long lashes, also ran out to meet him.

'Ah, little Count! Dearest! Jewel! This is a joy!' she murmured between her teeth, smiling merrily.

Ilyushka himself ran out to greet him, pretending to be very glad to see him. The old women, matrons, and maids jumped from their places and surrounded the guest, some claiming him as a fellow godfather, some as brother by baptism.

Turbin kissed all the young gipsy girls on their lips; the old women and the men kissed him on his shoulder or hand. The noblemen were also glad of their visitor's arrival, especially as the carousal, having reached its zenith, was beginning to flag, and everyone was beginning to feel satiated. The wine having lost its stimulating effect on the nerves merely weighed on the stomach. Each one had already let off his store of swagger, and they were getting tired of one another; the songs had all been sung and had got mixed in everyone's head, leaving a noisy, dissolute impression behind. No matter what strange or dashing thing anyone did, it began to occur to everyone that there was nothing agreeable or funny in it. The Captain of Police who lay in a shocking state on the floor at the feet of an old woman, began wriggling his legs and shouting: 'Champagne . . . The Count's come! . . . Champagne! . . . He's come . . . now then, champagne! . . . I'll have a champagne bath and bathe in it! Noble gentlemen! . . . I love the society of our brave old nobility . . . Steshka, sing *The Pathway*.'

The cavalryman was also rather tipsy, but in another way. He sat on a sofa in the corner very close to a tall handsome gipsy girl, Lyubasha; and feeling his eyes misty with drink he kept blinking and shaking his head and, repeating the same words over and over again in a whisper, besought the gypsy to fly with him somewhere. Lyubasha, smiling and listening as if what he said were very amusing and yet rather sad, glanced occasionally at her husband – the cross-eyed Sashka who was standing behind the chair opposite her – and in reply to the cavalryman's declarations of love, stooped and whispering his he ear asked him to buy her some scent and ribbons on the quiet so that the others should not notice.

'Hurrah!' cried the cavalryman when the count entered.

The handsome young man was pacing up and down the room with laboriously steady steps and a careworn expression on his face, warbling an air from *Il Seraglio*.

An elderly paterfamilias, who had been tempted by the persistent entreaties of the nobles to come and hear the gipsies, as they said that without him the thing would be worthless and it would be better not to go at all, was lying on a sofa where he had sunk as soon as he arrived, and no one was taking any notice of him. Some official or other who was also there had taken off his swallow-tail coat and was sitting up on the table, feet and all, ruffling his hair, and thereby showing that he was very much on the spree. As soon as the count entered, this official unbuttoned the collar of his shirt and got still farther onto the table. In general, on Turbin's arrival the carousal revived.

The gipsy girls, who had been wandering about the room, again gathered and sat down in a circle. The count took Steshka, the leading singer, on his knee, and ordered more champagne.

Ilyushka came and stood in front of Steshka with his guitar, and the 'dance' commenced – that is, the gipsy songs, *When you go along the Street, O Hussars!*, *Do you hear, do you know?*, and so on in a definite order. Steshka sang admirably. The flexible sonorous contralto that flowed from her very chest, her smiles while singing, her laughing passionate eyes, and her foot that moved involuntarily in measure with the song, her wild shriek at the commencement of the chorus – all touched some powerful but rarely-reached chord. It was evident that she lived only in the song she was singing. Ilyushka accompanied her on the guitar – his back, legs, smile, and whole being expressing sympathy with the song – and eagerly watching her, raised and lowered his head as attentive and engrossed as though he heard the song for the first time. Then at the last melodious note he suddenly drew himself up and, as if feeling himself superior to everyone in the world, proudly and resolutely threw up his guitar with his foot, twirled it about, stamped, tossed back his hair, and looked round at the choir with a frown. His whole body from neck to heels began dancing in every muscle – and twenty energetic, powerful voices each trying to chime in more strongly and more strangely than the rest, rang through the air. The old women bobbed up and down on their chairs waving their handkerchiefs, showing their teeth, and vying with one another in their harmonious and measured shouts. The basses with strained necks and heads bent to one side boomed while standing behind the chairs.

When Steshka took a high note Ilyushka brought his guitar closer to her as if wishing to help her, and the handsome young man screamed with rapture, saying that now they were beginning the *bemols*.

When a dance was struck up and Dunyasha, advancing with quivering shoulders and bosom, twirled round in front of the count and glided onwards, Turbin leapt up, threw off his jacket, and in his red shirt stepped jauntily with her in precise and measured step, accomplishing such things with his legs that the gipsies smiled with approval and glanced at one another.

The Captain of Police sat down like a Turk, beat his breast with his fist and cried 'Vivat!' and then, having caught hold of the count's leg, began to tell him that of two thousand rubles he now had only five hundred left, but that he could do anything he liked if only the count would allow it. The elderly paterfamilias awoke and wished to go away but was not allowed to do so. The handsome young man began persuading a gipsy to waltz with him. The cavalryman, wishing to show off his intimacy with the count, rose and embraced Turbin. 'Ah, my dear fellow,' he said, 'why didst thou leave us, eh?' The count was silent, evidently thinking of something else. 'Where did you go to? Ah, you rogue of a count, I know where you went to!'

For some reason this familiarity displeased Turbin. Without a smile he looked silently into the cavalryman's face and suddenly launched at him such a terrible and rude abuse that the cavalryman was pained and for a while could not make up his mind whether to take the offence as a joke or seriously. At last he decided to take it as a joke, smiled, and went back to his gipsy, assuring her that he would certainly marry her after Easter. They sang another song and another, danced again, and 'hailed the guests', and everyone continued to imagine that he was enjoying it. There was no end to the champagne. The count drank a great deal. His eyes seemed to grow moist, but he was not unsteady. He danced even better than before, spoke firmly, even joined in the chorus extremely well, and chimed in when Steshka sang *Friendship's Tender Emotions*. In the midst of a dance the landlord came in to ask the guests to return to their homes as it was getting on for three in the morning.

The count seized the landlord by the scruff of his neck and ordered him to dance the Russian dance. The landlord refused. The count snatched up a bottle of champagne and having stood the landlord on his head and had him held in that position, amidst general laughter, slowly emptied the bottle over him.

It was beginning to dawn. Everyone looked pale and exhausted except the count.

'Well, I must be starting for Moscow,' said he, suddenly rising. 'Come along, all of you! Come and see me off . . . and we'll have some tea together.'

All agreed except the paterfamilias (who was left behind asleep), and crowding into the three large sledges that stood at the door, they all drove off to the hotel.

7

'Get horses ready!' cried the count as he entered the saloon of his hotel, followed by the guests and gipsies. 'Sashka! – not gipsy Sashka but my Sashka – tell the superintendent I'll thrash him if he gives me bad horses. And get us some tea. Zavalshevski, look after the tea: I'm going to have a look at Ilyin and see how he's getting on . . . ' added Turbin and went along the passage towards the uhlan's room.

Ilyin had just finished playing and having lost his last kopek was lying face downwards on the sofa, pulling one hair after another from its torn horsehair cover, putting them in his mouth, biting them in two and spitting them out again.

Two tallow candles, one of which had burnt down to the paper in the socket, stood on the card-strewn table and feebly wrestled with the morning light that crept in through the window. There were no ideas in Ilyin's head: a dense mist of gambling passion shrouded all his faculties; he did not even feel penitent. He made one attempt to think of what he should do now: how being penniless he could get away, how he could repay the fifteen thousand rubles of Crown money, what his regimental commander would say, what his mother and his comrades would say, and he felt such terror and disgust with himself that wishing to forget himself he rose and began pacing up and down the room trying to step only where the floor-boards joined, and began, once more, vividly to recall every slightest detail of the course of play. He vividly imagined how he had begun to win back his money, how he withdrew a nine and placed the king of spades over two thousand rubles. A queen was dealt to the right, an ace to the left, then the king of diamonds to the right and all was lost; but if, say, a six had been dealt to the right and the king of diamonds to the left, he would have won everything back, would have played once more double or quits, would have won fifteen thousand rubles, and would then have bought himself an ambler from his regimental commander and another pair of horses besides, and a phaeton. Well, and what then? Well, it would have been a splendid, splendid thing!

And he lay down on the sofa again and began chewing the horse-hair.

'Why are they singing in No. 7?' thought he. 'There must be a spree on at Turbin's. Shall I go in and have a good drink?'

At this moment the count entered.

'Well, old fellow, cleaned out, are you? Eh?' cried he.

'I'll pretend to be asleep,' thought Ilyin, 'or else I shall have to speak to him, and I want to sleep.'

Turbin, however, came up and stroked his head.

'Well, my dear friend, cleaned out – lost everything? Tell me.'

Ilyin gave no answer.

The count pulled his arm.

'I have lost. But what is that to you?' muttered Ilyin in a sleepy, indifferent, discontented voice, without changing his position.

'Everything?'

'Well – yes. What of it? Everything. What is it to you?'

'Listen. Tell me the truth as to a comrade,' said the count, inclined to tenderness by the influence of the wine he had drunk and continuing to stroke Ilyin's hair. 'I have really taken a liking to you. Tell me the truth. If you have lost Crown money I'll get you out of your scrape: it will soon be too late . . . Had you Crown money?'

Ilyin jumped up from the sofa.

'Well then, if you wish me to tell you, don't speak to me, because . . . please don't speak to me . . . To shoot myself is the only thing!' said Ilyin, with real despair, and his head fell on his hands and he burst into tears, though but a moment before he had been calmly thinking about amblers.

'What pretty girlishness! Where's the man who has not done the like? It's not such a calamity; perhaps we can mend it. Wait for me here.'

The count left the room.

'Where is Squire Lukhnov's room?' he asked the boots.

The boots offered to show him the way. In spite of the valet's remark that his master had only just returned and was undressing, the count went in. Lukhnov was sitting at a table in his dressing-gown counting several packets of paper money that lay before him. A bottle of Rhine wine, of which he was very fond, stood on the table. After winning he permitted himself that pleasure. Lukhnov looked coldly and sternly through his spectacles at the count as though not recognizing him.

'You don't recognize me, I think?' said the count, resolutely stepping up to the table.

'Lukhnov made a gesture of recognition, and said, 'What is it you want?'

'I should like to play with you,' said Turbin, sitting down on the sofa.

'Now?'

'Yes.'

'Another time with pleasure, Count! But now I am tired and am going to bed. Won't you have a glass of wine? It is famous wine.'

'But I want to play a little – now.'

'I don't intend to play any more tonight. Perhaps some of the other gentlemen will, but I won't. You must please excuse me, Count.'

'Then you won't?'

'Lukhnov shrugged his shoulders to express his regret at his inability to comply with the count's desire.

'Not on any account?'

The same shrug.

'But I particularly request it . . . Well, will you play?'

Silence.

'Will you play?' the count asked again. 'Mind!'

The same silence and a rapid glance over the spectacles at the count's face which was beginning to frown.

'Will you play?' shouted the count very loud, striking the table with his hand so that the bottle toppled over and the wine was spilt. 'You know you did not win fairly . . . Will you play? I ask you for the third time.'

'I said I would not. This is really strange, Count! And it is not at all proper to come and hold a knife to a man's throat,' remarked Lukhnov, not raising his eyes. A momentary silence followed during which the count's face grew paler and paler. Suddenly a terrible blow on the head stupefied Lukhnov. He fell on the sofa trying to seize the money and uttered such a piercingly despairing cry as no one could have expected from so calm and imposing a person. Turbin gathered up what money lay on the table, pushed aside the servant who ran in to his master's assistance, and left the room with rapid strides.

'If you want satisfaction I am at your service! I shall be in my room for another half-hour,' said the count, returning to Lukhnov's door.

'Thief! Robber! I'll have the law on you . . .' was all that was audible from the room.

Ilyin, who had paid no attention to the count's promise to help him, still lay as before on the sofa in his room choking with tears of despair. Consciousness of what had really happened, which the count's caresses and sympathy had evoked from behind the strange tangle of feelings, thoughts, and memories filling his soul, did not leave him. His youth, rich with hope, his honour, the respect of society, his dreams of love and friendship – all were utterly lost. The source of his tears began to run dry, a too passive feeling of hopelessness overcame him more and more, and thoughts of suicide, no longer arousing revulsion or horror, claimed his attention with increasing frequency. Just then the count's firm footsteps were heard.

In Turbin's face traces of anger could still be seen, his hands shook a little, but his eyes beamed with kindly merriment and self-satisfaction.

'Here you are, it's won back!' he said, throwing several bundles of paper money on the table. 'See if it's all there and then make haste and come into the saloon. I am just leaving,' he added, as though not noticing the joy and gratitude and extreme agitation on Ilyin's face, and whistling a gipsy song he left the room.

8

Sashka, with a sash tied round his waist, announced that the horses were ready but insisted that the count's cloak, which, he said, with its fur collar was worth three hundred rubles, should be recovered, and the shabby blue one returned to the rascal who had changed it for the count's at the Marshal's; but Turbin told him there was no need to look for the cloak, and went to his room to change his clothes.

The cavalryman kept hiccoughing as he sat silent beside his gipsy girl. The Captain of Police called for vodka and invited everyone to come at once and have breakfast with him, promising that his wife would certainly dance with the gipsies. The handsome young man was profoundly explaining to Ilyushka that there is more soulfulness in pianoforte music and that it is not possible to play *bemols* on a guitar. The official sat in a corner sadly drinking his tea and in the daylight seemed ashamed of his debauchery. The gipsies were disputing among themselves in their own tongue as to 'hailing the guests' again, which Steshka opposed, saying that the *baroray* (in gipsy language, count or prince or, more literally, 'great gentleman') would be angry. In general the last embers of the debauch were dying down in everyone.

'Well, one farewell song, and then off home!' said the count, entering the parlour in travelling dress, fresh, merry, and handsomer than ever.

The gipsies again formed their circle and were just ready to begin when Ilyin entered with a packet of paper money in his hand and took the count aside.

'I had only fifteen thousand rubles of Crown money and you have given me sixteen thousand three hundred,' he said, 'so this is yours.'

'That's a good thing. Give it here!'

Ilyin gave him the money and, looking timidly at the count, opened his lips to say something, but only blushed till tears came into his eyes and seizing the count's hand began to press it.

'You be off! . . . Ilyushka! Listen! Here's some money for you, but you must accompany me out of the town with songs!' and he threw onto the guitar the thirteen hundred rubles Ilyin had brought him. But the count quite forgot to repay the hundred rubles he had borrowed of the cavalryman the day before.

It was already ten o'clock in the morning. The sun had risen above the roofs of the houses. People were moving about in the streets. The tradesmen had long since opened their shops. Noblemen and officials were driving through the streets and ladies were shopping in the bazaar, when the whole gipsy band, with the Captain of Police, the cavalryman, the handsome young man, Ilyin, and the count in the blue bearskin cloak came out into the hotel porch.

It was a sunny day and a thaw had set in. The large post-sledges, each drawn by three horses with their tails tied up tight, drove up to the porch splashing through the mud and the whole lively party took their places. The count, Ilyin, Steshka, and Ilyushka, with Sashka the count's orderly, got into the first sledge. Blücher was beside himself and wagged his tail, barking at the shaft-horse. The other gentlemen got into the two other sledges with the rest of the gipsy men and women. The troykas got abreast as they left the hotel and the gipsies struck up in chorus. The troykas with their songs and bells – forcing every vehicle they met right onto the pavements – dashed through the whole town right to the town gates.

The tradesmen and passers-by who did not know them, and especially those who did, were not a little astonished when they saw the noblemen driving through the streets in broad daylight with gipsy girls and tipsy gipsy men, singing.

When they had passed the town gates the troykas stopped and everyone began bidding the count farewell.

Ilyin, who had drunk a good deal at the leave-taking and had himself been driving the sledge all the way, suddenly became very sad, begged the count to stay another day, and, when he found that this was not possible, rushed quite unexpectedly at his new friend, kissed him, and promised with tears to try to exchange into the hussar regiment the count was serving in as soon as he got back. The count was particularly gay; he tumbled the cavalryman, who had become very familiar in the morning, into a snowdrift, set Blücher at the Captain of Police, took Steshka in his arms and wished to carry her off to Moscow, and finally jumped into his sledge and made Blücher, who wanted to stand up in the middle, sit down by his side. Sashka jumped on the box after having again asked the cavalryman to recover the count's cloak from *them* and to send it on. The count cried, 'Go!,' took off his cap, waved it over his head, and whistled to the horses like a post-boy. The troykas drove off in their different directions.

A monotonous snow-covered plain stretched far in front with a dirty yellowish road winding through it. The bright sunshine – playfully sparkling on the thawing snow which was coated with a transparent crust of ice – was pleasantly warm to one's face and back. Steam rose thickly from the sweating horses. The bell tinkled merrily. A peasant, with a loaded sledge that kept gliding to the side of the road, got hurriedly out of the way, jerking his rope reins and plashing with his wet bast shoes as he ran along the thawing road. A fat red-faced peasant woman, with a baby wrapped in the bosom of her sheepskin cloak, sat in another laden sledge, urging on a thin-tailed, jaded white horse with the ends of the reins. The count suddenly thought of Anna Fedorovna.

'Turn back!' he shouted.

The driver did not at once understand.

'Turn back! Back to town! Be quick!'

The troyka passed the town gates once more, and drove briskly up to the wooden porch of Anna Fedorovna's house. The count ran quickly up the steps, passed through the vestibule and the drawing-room, and having found the widow still asleep, took her in his arms, lifted her out of bed, kissed her sleepy eyes, and ran quickly back. Anna Fedorovna, only half awake, licked her lips and asked, 'What has happened?' The count jumped into his sledge, shouted to the driver, and with no further delay and without even a thought of Lukhnov, or the widow, or Steshka, but only of what awaited him in Moscow, left the town of K— forever.

9

More than twenty years had gone by. Much water had flowed away, many people had died, many been born, many had grown up or grown old; still more ideas had been born and had died, much that was old and beautiful and much that was old and bad had perished; much that was beautiful and new had grown up and still more that was immature, monstrous, and new, had come into God's world.

Count Fedor Turbin had been killed long ago in a duel by some foreigner he had horse-whipped in the street. His son, physically as like him as one drop of water to another, was a handsome young man already twenty-three years old and serving in the Horse Guards. But morally the young Turbin did not in the least resemble his father. There was not a shade of the impetuous, passionate, and, to speak frankly, depraved propensities of the past age. Together with his intelligence, culture, and the gifted nature he had inherited a love of propriety and the comforts of life; a practical way of looking at men and affairs, reasonableness, and prudence were his distinguishing characteristics. The young count had got on well in the service and at twenty-three was already a lieutenant. At the commencement of the war he made up his mind that he would be more likely to secure promotion if he exchanged into the active army, and so he entered an hussar regiment as captain and was soon in command of a squadron.

In May 1848 the S— hussar regiment was marching to the campaign through the province of K— and the very squadron young Count Turbin commanded had to spend the night in the village of Morozovka, Anna Fedorovna's estate.

Ann Fedorovna was still living but was already so far from young that she did not even consider herself young, which means a good deal for a woman. She had grown very fat, which is said to make a woman look younger, but deep soft wrinkles were apparent on her white plumpness. She never went to town now, it was an effort for her even to get into her carriage, but she was still just as kind-hearted and as silly as ever (now that her beauty no longer biases one, the truth may be told). With her lived her twenty-three-year-old daughter Lisa, a Russian country belle, and her brother – our acquaintance the cavalryman – who had good-naturedly squandered the whole of his small fortune and had found a home for his old age with Anna Fedorovna. His hair was quite grey and his upper lip had fallen in, but the moustache above it was still carefully blackened. His back was bent, and not only his forehead and cheeks but even his nose and neck were wrinkled, yet in the movements of his feeble crooked legs the manner of a cavalryman was still perceptible.

The family and household sat in the small drawing-room of the old house, with an open door leading out onto the verandah, and open windows overlooking the ancient star-shaped garden with its lime trees. Grey-haired Anna Fedorovna, wearing a lilac jacket, sat on the sofa laying out cards on a round mahogany table. Her old brother in his clean white trousers and a blue coat had settled himself by the window and was plaiting a cord out of white cotton with the aid of a wooden fork – a pastime his niece had taught him and which he liked very much, as he could no longer do anything and his eyes were too weak for newspaper reading, his favourite occupation. Pimochka, Anna Fedorovna's ward, sat by him learning a lesson – Lisa helping her and at the same time making a goat's-wool stocking for her uncle with wooden knitting needles. The last rays of the setting sun, as usual at that hour, shone through the lime-tree avenue and threw slanting gleams on the farthest window and the what-not standing near it. It was so quiet in the garden and the room that one could hear the swift flutter of a swallow's wings outside the window and Anna Fedorovna's soft sigh or the old man's slight groan as he crossed his legs.

'How do they go? Show me, Lisa! I always forget,' said Anna Fedorovna, at a standstill in laying out her cards for patience.

Without stopping her work Lisa went to her mother and glanced at the cards.

'Ah, you've muddled them all, mamma dear!' she said, re-arranging them. 'That's the way they should go. And what you are trying your fortune about will still come true,' she added, withdrawing a card so that it was not noticed.

'Ah yes, you always deceive me and say it has come out.'

'No, really, it means . . . you'll succeed. It has come out.'

'All right, all right, you sly puss! But isn't it time we had tea?'

'I have ordered the samovar to be lit. I'll see to it at once. Do you want to have it here? . . . Be quick and finish your lesson Pimochka, and let's have a run.'

And Lisa went to the door.

'Lisa, Lizzie!' said her uncle, looking intently at his fork. 'I think I've dropped a stitch again – pick it up for me, there's a dear.'

'Directly, directly. But I must give out a loaf of sugar to be broken up.'

And really, three minutes later she ran back, went to her uncle and pinched his ear.

'That's for dropping your stitches!' she said, laughing, and you haven't done your task!'

'Well, well, never mind, never mind. Put it right – there's a little knot or something.'

Lisa took the fork, drew a pin out of her tippet – which thereupon the breeze coming in at the door blew slightly open – and managing somehow to pick up the stitch with the pin, pulled two loops through, and returned the fork to her uncle.

'Now give me a kiss for it,' she said, holding out her rosy cheek to him and pinning up her tippet. 'You shall have rum with your tea today. It's Friday, you know.'

And she again went into the tea-room.

'Come here and look, uncle, the hussars are coming!' she called from there in her clear voice.

Anna Fedorovna came with her brother into the tea-room, the windows of which overlooked the village, to see the hussars. Very little was visible from the windows – only a crowd moving in a cloud of dust.

'It's a pity we have so little room, sister, and that the wing is not yet finished,' said the old man to Anna Fedorovna. 'We might have invited the officers. Hussar officers are such splendid, gay young fellows, you know. It would have been good to see something of them.'

'Why of course, I should have been only too glad, brother; but you know yourself we have no room. There's my bedroom, Lisa's room, the drawing-room, and this room of yours, and that's all. Really now, where could we put them? The village elder's hut has been cleaned up for them: Michael Matveev says its quite clean now.'

'And we could have chosen a bridegroom for you from among them, Lizzie – a fine hussar!'

'I don't want an hussar; I'd rather have an uhlan. Weren't you in the uhlans, uncle? . . . I don't want to have anything to do with these hussars. They are all said to be desperate fellows.' And Lisa blushed a little but again laughed her musical laugh.

'Here comes Ustyushka running; we must ask her what she has seen,' she added.

Anna Fedorovna told her to call Ustyushka.

'It's not in you to keep to your work, you must needs run off to see the soldiers,' said Anna Fedorovna. 'Well, where have the officers put up?'

'In Eromkin's house, mistress. There are two of them, such handsome ones. One's a count, they say!'

'And what's his name?'

'Dazarov or Turbinov . . . I'm sorry – I've forgotten.'

'What a fool; can't so much as tell us anything. You might at least have found out the name.'

'Well, I'll run back.'

'Yes, I know you're first-rate at that sort of thing . . . No, let Daniel go. Tell him to go and ask whether the officers want anything, brother. One ought to show them some politeness after all. Say the mistress sent to inquire.'

The old people again sat down in the tea-room and Lisa went to the servants' room to put into a box the sugar that had been broken up. Ustyushka was there telling about the hussars.

'Darling miss, what a handsome man that count is!' she said. 'A regular cherubim with black eyebrows. There now, if you had a bridegroom like that you would be a couple of the right sort.'

The other maids smiled approvingly; the old nurse sighed as she sat knitting at a window and even whispered a prayer, drawing in her breath.

'So you liked the hussars very much?' said Lisa. 'And you're a good one at telling what you've seen. Go, please, and bring some of the cranberry juice, Ustyushka, to give the hussars something sour to drink.'

And Lisa, laughing, went out with the sugar basin in her hands.

'I should really like to have seen what that hussar is like,' she thought, 'brown or fair? And he would have been glad to make our acquaintance I should think . . . And if he goes away he'll never know that I was here and thought about him. And how many such have already passed me by? Who sees me here except uncle and Ustyushka? Whichever way I do my hair, whatever sleeves I put on, no one looks at me with pleasure,' she thought with a sigh as she looked at her plump white arm. 'I suppose he is tall, with large eyes, and certainly small black moustaches . . . Here am I, more than twenty-two, and no one has fallen in love with me except pock-marked Ivan Ipatich, and four years ago I was even prettier . . . And so my girlhood has passed without gladdening anyone. Oh, poor, poor country lass that I am!'

Her mother's voice, calling her to pour out tea, roused the country lass from this momentary meditation. She lifted her head with a start and went into the tea-room.

The best results are often obtained accidentally, and the more one tries the worse things turn out. In the country, people rarely try to educate their children and therefore unwittingly usually give them an excellent education. This was particularly so in Lisa's case.

Anna Fedorovna, with her limited intellect and careless temperament, gave Lisa no education – did not teach her music or that very useful French language – but having accidentally borne a healthy pretty child by her deceased husband she gave her little daughter over to a wet-nurse and a dry-nurse, fed her, dressed her in cotton prints and goat-skin shoes, sent her out to walk and gather mushrooms and wild berries, engaged a student from the seminary to teach her reading, writing, and arithmetic, and when sixteen years had passed she casually found in Lisa a friend, an ever-kind-hearted, ever-cheerful soul, and an active housekeeper. Anna Fedorovna, being kind-hearted, always had some children to bring up – either serf children or foundlings. Lisa began looking after them when she was ten years old: teaching them, dressing them, taking them to church, and checking them when they played too man pranks. Later on the decrepit kindly uncle, who had to be tended like a child, appeared on the scene. Then the servants and peasants came to the young lady with various requests and with their ailments, which latter she treated with elderberry, peppermint, and camphorated spirits. Then there was the household management which all fell on her shoulders of itself. Then an unsatisfied longing for love awoke and found its outlet only in Nature and religion. And Lisa accidentally grew into an active, good-natured, cheerful, self-reliant, pure, and deeply religious woman. It is true that she suffered a little from vanity when she saw neighbours standing by her in church wearing fashionable bonnets brought from K––, and sometimes she was vexed to tears by her old mother's whims and grumbling. She had dreams of love, too, in most absurd and sometimes crude forms, but these were dispersed by her useful activity which had grown into a necessity, and at the age of twenty-two there was not one spot or sting of remorse in the clear calm soul of the physically and morally beautifully developed maiden. Lisa was of medium height, plump rather than thin; her eyes were hazel, not large, and had slight shadows on the lower lids; and she had a long light-brown plait of hair. She walked with big steps and with a slight sway – a 'duck's waddle' as the saying is. Her face, when she was occupied and not agitated by anything in particular, seemed to say to everyone who looked into it: 'It is a joy to live in the world when one has someone to love and a clear conscience.' Even in moments of

vexation, perplexity, alarm, or sorrow, in spite of herself there
shone – through the tear in her eye, her frowning left eyebrow,
and her compressed lips – a kind straightforward spirit unspoilt by
the intellect; it shone in the dimples of her cheeks, in the corners
of her mouth, and in her beaming eyes accustomed to smile and to
rejoice in life.

10

The air was still hot though the sun was setting when the squadron
entered Morozovka. In front of them along the dusty village street
trotted a brindled cow separated from its herd, looking around and
now and then stopping and lowing, but never suspecting that all
she had to do was to turn aside. The peasants – old men, women,
and children – the servants from the manor-house, crowded on
both sides of the street and eagerly watched the hussars as the latter
rode through a thick cloud of dust, curbing their horses which
occasionally stamped and snorted. On the right of the squadron
were two officers who sat their fine black horses carelessly. One
was Count Turbin, the commander, the other a very young man
recently promoted from cadet, whose name was Polozov.

An hussar in a white linen jacket came out of the best of the huts,
raised his cap, and went up to the officers.

'Where are the quarters assigned us?'

'For your Excellency?' answered the quartermaster-sergeant,
with a start of his whole body. 'The village elder's hut has been
cleaned out. I wanted to get quarters at the manor-house, but they
say there is no room there. The proprietress is such a vixen.'

'All right!' said the count, dismounting and stretching his legs as
he reached the village elder's hut. 'And has my phaeton arrived?'

'It has deigned to arrive, your Excellency!' answered the quartermaster-sergeant, pointing with his cap to the leather body of a
carriage visible through the gateway and rushing forward to the
entrance of the hut, which was thronged with members of the
peasant family collected to look at the officer. He even pushed one
old woman over as he briskly opened the door of the freshly
cleaned hut and stepped aside to let the count pass.

The hut was fairly large and roomy but not very clean. The
German valet, dressed like a gentleman, stood inside sorting the

linen in a portmanteau after having set up an iron bedstead and
made the bed.

'Faugh, what filthy lodgings!' said the count with vexation.
'Couldn't you have found anything better at some gentleman's
house, Dyadenko?'

'If your Excellency desires it I will try at the manor-house,'
answered the quartermaster-sergeant, 'but it isn't up to much –
doesn't look much better than a hut.'

'Never mind now. Go away.'

And the count lay down on the bed and threw his arms behind
his head.

'Johann!' he called to his valet. 'You've made a lump in the
middle again! How is it you can't make a bed properly?'

Johann came up to put it right.

'No, never mind now. But where is my dressing-gown?' said the
count in a dissatisfied tone.

The valet handed him the dressing-gown. Before putting it on
the count examined the front.

'I thought so, that spot is not cleaned off. Could anyone be a
worse servant than you?' he added, pulling the dressing-gown out
of the valet's hands and putting it on. 'Tell me, do you do it on
purpose? . . . Is the tea ready?'

'I have not had time,' said Johann.

'Fool!'

After that the count took up the French novel placed ready for
him and read for some time in silence: Johann went out into the
passage to prepare the samovar. The count was obviously in a bad
temper, probably caused by fatigue, a dusty face, tight clothing,
and an empty stomach.

'Johann!' he cried again, 'bring me the account for those ten
rubles. What did you buy in the town?'

He looked over the account handed him, and made some
dissatisfied remarks about the dearness of the things purchased.

'Serve rum with my tea.'

'I didn't buy any rum,' said Johann.

'That's good! . . . How many times have I told you to have rum?'

'I hadn't enough money.'

'Then why didn't Polozov buy some? You should have got
some from his man.'

'Cornet Polozov? I don't know. He bought the tea and the sugar.'

'Idiot! . . . Get out! . . . You are the only man who knows how to make me lose my patience . . . You know that on a march I always have rum with my tea.'

'Here are two letters for you from the staff,' said the valet.

The count opened his letters and began reading them without rising. The cornet, having quartered the squadron, came in with a merry face.

'Well, how is it, Turbin? It seems very nice here. But I must confess I'm tired. It was hot.'

'Very nice! . . . A filthy stinking hut, and thanks to your lordship no rum; your blockhead didn't buy any, nor did this one. You might at least have mentioned it.'

And he continued to read his letter. When he had finished he rolled it into a ball and threw it on the floor.

In the passage the cornet was meanwhile saying to his orderly in a whisper: 'Why didn't you buy any rum? You had money enough, you know.'

'But why should we buy everything? As it is I pay for everything, while his German does nothing but smoke his pipe.'

It was evident that the count's second letter was not unpleasant, for he smiled as he read it.

'Who is it from?' asked Polozov, returning to the room and beginning to arrange a sleeping-place for himself on some boards by the oven.

'From Mina,' answered the count gaily, handing him the letter, 'Do you want to see it? What a delightful woman she is! . . . Really she's much better than our young ladies . . . Just see how much feeling and wit there is in that letter. Only one thing is bad – she's asking for money.'

'Yes, that's bad,' said the cornet.

'It's true I promised her some, but then this campaign came on, and besides. . . However if I remain in command of the squadron another three months I'll send her some. It's worth it, really; such a charming creature, eh?' said he, watching the expression on Polozov's face as he read the letter.

'Dreadfully ungrammatical, but very nice, and it seems as if she really loves you,' said the cornet.

'H'm . . . I should think so! It's only women of that kind who love sincerely when once they do love.'

'And who was the other letter from?' asked the cornet, handing back the one he had read.

'Oh, that . . . there's a man, a nasty beast who won from me at cards, and he's reminding me of it for the third time . . . I can't let him have it at present . . . A stupid letter!' said the count, evidently vexed at the recollection.

After this both officers were silent for a while. The cornet, who was evidently under the count's influence, glanced now and then at the handsome though clouded countenance of Turbin – who was looking fixedly through the window – and drank his tea in silence, not venturing to start a conversation.

'But d'you know, it may turn out capitally,' said the count, suddenly turning to Polozov with a shake of his head. 'Supposing we get promotions by seniority this year and take part in an action besides, I may get ahead of my own captains in the Guards.'

The conversation was still on the same topic and they were drinking their second tumblers of tea when old Daniel entered and delivered Anna Fedorovna's message.

'And I was also to inquire if you are not Count Fedor Ivanych Turbin's son?' added Daniel on his own account, having learnt the count's name and remembering the deceased count's sojourn in the town of K—. 'Our mistress, Anna Fedorovna, was very well acquainted with him.'

'He was my father. And tell your mistress I am very much obliged to her. We want nothing but say we told you to ask whether we could not have a cleaner room somewhere – in the manor-house or anywhere.'

'Now, why did you do that?' asked Polozov when Daniel had gone. 'What does it matter? Just for one night – what does it matter? And they will be inconveniencing themselves.'

'What an idea! I think we've had our share of smoky huts! . . . It's easy to see you're not a practical man. Why not seize the opportunity when we can, and live like human beings for at least one night? And on the contrary they will be very pleased to have us . . . The worst of it is, if this lady really knew my father . . . ' continued the count with a smile which displayed his glistening white teeth. 'I always have to feel ashamed of my departed papa.

There is always some scandalous story or other, or some debt he has left. That's why I hate meeting these acquaintances of my father's. However, that was the way in those days,' he added, growing serious.

'Did I ever tell you,' said Polozov, 'I once met an uhlan brigade-commander, Ilyin? He was very anxious to meet you. He is awfully fond of your father.'

'That Ilyin is an awful good-for-nothing, I believe. But the worst of it is that these good people, who assure me that they knew my father in order to make my acquaintance, while pretending to be very pleasant, relate such tales about my father as make me ashamed to listen. It is true – I don't deceive myself, but look at things dispassionately – that he had too ardent a nature and sometimes did things that were not nice. However, that was the way in those times. In our days he might have turned out a very successful man, for to do him justice he had extraordinary capacities.'

A quarter of an hour later the servant came back with a request from the proprietress that they would be so good as to spend the night at her house.

11

Having heard that the hussar officer was the son of Count Fedor Turbin, Anna Fedorovna was all in a flutter.

'Oh, dear me! The darling boy! . . . Daniel, run quickly and say your mistress asks them to her house!' she began, jumping up and hurrying with quick steps to the servants' room. 'Lizzie! Ustyushka! . . . Your room must be got ready, Lisa, you can move into your uncle's room. And you, brother, you won't mind sleeping in the drawing-room, will you? It's only for one night.'

'I don't mind, sister. I can sleep on the floor.'

'He must be handsome if he's like his father. Only to have a look at him, the darling . . . You must have a good look at him, Lisa! The father *was* handsome . . . Where are you taking that table to? Leave it here,' said Anna Fedorovna, bustling about. 'Bring two beds – take one from the foreman's – and get the crystal candle-stick, the one my brother gave me on my birthday – it's on the what-not – and put a stearine candle in it.'

At last everything was ready. In spite of her mother's interference Lisa arranged the room for the two officers her own way.
She took out clean bed-clothes scented with mignonette, made
the beds, had candles and a bottle of water placed on a small table
nearby, fumigated the servants' room with scented paper, and
moved her own little bed into her uncle's room. Anna Fedorovna
quieted down a little, settled in her own place, and even took up
the cards again, but instead of laying them out she leaned her
plump elbow on the table and grew thoughtful.

'Ah, time, time, how it flies!' she whispered to herself. 'Is it so
long ago? It is as if I could see him now. Ah, he was a madcap!. . .'
and tears came into her eyes. 'And now there's Lizzie . . . but still,
she's not what I was at her age – she's a nice girl but she's not like
that . . .'

'Lisa, you should put on your *mousseline-de-laine* dress for the
evening.'

'Why, mother, you are not going to ask them in to see us? Better
not,' said Lisa, unable to master her excitement at the thought of
meeting the officers. 'Better not, mamma!'

And really her desire to see them was less strong than her fear of
the agitating joy she imagined awaited her.

'Maybe they themselves will wish to make our acquaintance,
Lizzie!' said Anna Fedorovna, stroking her head and thinking,
'No, her hair is not what mine was at her age . . . Oh, Lizzie, how
I should like you to . . .' And she ready did very earnestly desire
something for her daughter. But she could not imagine
a marriage with the count, and she could not desire for her
daughter relations such as she had had with the father; but still she
did desire something very much. She may have longed to relive
in the soul of her daughter what she had experienced with him
who was dead.

The old cavalryman was also somewhat excited by the arrival of
the count. He locked himself into his room and emerged a quarter
of an hour later in a Hungarian jacket and pale-blue trousers, and
entered the room prepared for the visitors with the bashfully
pleased expression of a girl who puts on a ball-dress for the first
time in her life.

'I'll have a look at the hussars of today, sister! The late count was
indeed a true hussar. I'll see, I'll see!'

The officers had already reached the room assigned to them through the back entrance.

'There, you see! Isn't this better than that hut with the cockroaches?' said the count, lying down as he was, in his dusty boots, on the bed that had been prepared for him.

'Of course it's better; but still, to be indebted to the proprietress . . .'

'Oh, what nonsense! One must be practical in all things. They're awfully pleased, I'm sure . . . Eh, you there!' he cried. 'Ask for something to hang over this window, or it will be draughty in the night.'

At this moment the old man came in to make the officers' acquaintance. Of course, though he did it with a slight blush, he did not omit to say that he and the old count had been comrades, that he had enjoyed the count's favour, and he even added that he had more than once been under obligations to the deceased. What obligations he referred to, whether it was the count's omission to repay the hundred rubles he had borrowed, or his throwing him into a snow-heap, or swearing at him, the old man quite omitted to explain. The young count was very polite to the old cavalryman and thanked him for the night's lodging.

'You must excuse us if it is not luxurious, Count,' (he very nearly said 'your Excellency,' so unaccustomed had he become to conversing with important persons), 'my sister's house is so small. But we'll hang something up there directly and it will be all right,' added the old man, and on the plea of seeing about a curtain, but mainly because he was in a hurry to give an account of the officers, he bowed and left the room.

The pretty Ustyushka came in with her mistress's shawl to cover the window, and besides, the mistress had told her to ask if the gentlemen would not like some tea.

The pleasant surrounds seemed to have a good influence on the count's spirits. He smiled merrily, joked with Ustyushka in such a way that she even called him a scamp, asked whether her young lady was pretty, and in answer to her question whether they would have any tea he said she might bring them some tea, but the chief thing was that, their own supper not being ready yet, perhaps they might have some vodka and something to eat, and some sherry if there was any.

The uncle was in raptures over the young count's politeness and praised the new generation of officers to the skies, saying that the present men were incomparable superior to the former generation.

Anna Fedorovna did not agree – no one could be superior to Count Fedor Ivanych Turbin – and at last she grew seriously angry and drily remarked, 'The one who has last stroked you, brother, is always the best . . . Of course people are cleverer nowadays, but Count Fedor Ivanych danced the *écossaise* in such a way and was so amiable that everybody lost their heads about him, though he paid attention to no one but me. So you see, there were good people in the old days too.'

Here came the news of the demand for vodka, light refreshments, and sherry.

'There now, brother, you never do the right thing; you should have ordered supper,' began Anna Fedorovna. 'Lisa, see to it, dear!'

Lisa ran to the larder to get some pickled mushrooms and fresh butter, and the cook was ordered to make rissoles.

'But how about sherry? Have you any left, brother?'

'No, sister, I never had any.'

'How's that? Why, what is it you take with your tea?'

'That's rum, Anna Fedorovna.'

'Isn't it all the same? Give me some of that – it's all the same. But wouldn't it after all be best to ask them in here, brother? You know all about it – I don't think they would take offence.'

The cavalryman declared he would warrant that the count was too good-natured to refuse and that he would certainly fetch them. Anna Fedorovna went and put on a silk dress and a new cap for some reason, but Lisa was so busy that she had no time to change her pink gingham dress with the wide sleeves. Besides, she was terribly excited; she felt as if something wonderful was awaiting her and as if a low black cloud hung over her soul. It seemed to her that this handsome hussar count must be a perfectly new, incomprehensible, but beautiful being. His character, his habits, his speech must all be so unusual, so different from anything she had ever met. All he thinks or says must be wise and right; all he does must be honourable; his whole appearance must be beautiful. She never doubted that. Had he asked not merely for refreshments and sherry but for a bath of sage-brandy and perfume, she would not have been surprised and would not have blamed him but would have been firmly convinced that it was right and necessary.

The count at once agreed when the cavalryman informed them of his sister's wish. He brushed his hair, put on his uniform, and took his cigar-case.

'Come along,' he said to Polozov.

'Really it would be better not to go,' answered the cornet. '*Ils feront des frais pour nous recevoir.*'

'Nonsense, they will be only too happy! Besides, I have made some inquiries: there is a pretty daughter . . . Come along!' said the count, speaking in French.

'*Je vous en prie, messieurs!*' said the cavalryman, merely to make the officers feel that he also knew French and had understood what they had said.

12

Lisa, afraid to look at the officers, blushed and cast down her eyes and pretended to be busy filling the teapot when they entered the room. Anna Fedorovna on the contrary jumped up hurriedly, bowed, and not taking her eyes off the count, began talking to him – now saying how unusually like his father he was, now introducing her daughter to him, now offering him tea, jam, or home-made sweetmeats. No one paid any attention to the cornet because of his modest appearance, and he was very glad of it, for he was, as far as propriety allowed, gazing at Lisa and minutely examining her beauty which evidently took him by surprise. The uncle, listening to his sister's conversation with the count, awaited, with the words ready on his lips, an opportunity to narrate his cavalry reminiscences. During tea the count lit a cigar and Lisa found it difficult to prevent herself from coughing. He was very talkative and amiable, at first slipping his stories into the intervals of Anna Fedorovna's ever-flowing speech, but at last monopolizing the conversation. One thing struck his hearers as strange; in his stories he often used words not considered improper in the society he belonged to, but which here sounded rather too bold and somewhat frightened Anna Fedorovna and made Lisa blush to her ears, but the count did not notice it and remained calmly natural and amiable.

Lisa silently filled the tumblers, which she did not give into the visitors' hands but placed on the table near them, not having quite recovered from her excitement, and she listened eagerly to the count's remarks. His stories, which were not very deep, and the hesitation in his speech gradually calmed her. She did not hear from him the very clever things she had expected, nor did she see that elegance in everything which she had vaguely expected to find in him. At the third glass of tea, after her bashful eyes had once met his and he had not looked down but had continued to look at her too quietly and with a slight smile, she even felt rather inimically disposed towards him and soon found that not only was there nothing especial about him but that he was in no wise different from other people she had met, that there was no need to be afraid of him though his nails were long and clean, and there was not even any special beauty in him. Lisa suddenly relinquished her dream, not without some inward pain, and grew calmer, and only the gaze of the taciturn cornet which she felt fixed upon her, disquieted her.

'Perhaps it's not this one, but that one!' she thought.

13

After tea the old lady asked the visitors into the drawing-room and again sat down in her old place.

'But wouldn't you like to rest, Count?' she asked, and after receiving an answer in the negative continued, 'What can I do to entertain our dear guests? Do you play cards, Count? There now, brother, you should arrange something; arrange a set – '

'But you yourself play *préférence*,' answered the cavalryman. 'Why not all play? Will you play, Count? And you too?'

The officers expressed their readiness to do whatever their kind hosts desired.

Lisa brought her old pack of cards which she used for divining when her mother's swollen face would get well, whether her uncle would return the same day when he went to town, whether a neighbour would call today, and so on. These cards, though she had used them for a couple of months, were cleaner than those Anna Fedorovna used to tell fortunes.

'But perhaps you won't play for small stakes?' inquired the uncle. 'Anna Fedorovna and I play for half-kopeks . . . And even so she wins all our money.'

'Oh, any stakes you like – I shall be delighted,' replied the count.

'Well then, one-kopek "assignats" just for once, in honour of our dear visitors! Let them beat me, an old woman!' said Anna Fedorovna, settling down in her armchair and arranging her mantilla. 'And perhaps I'll win a ruble or so from them,' thought she, having developed a slight passion for cards in her old age.

'If you like, I'll teach you to play with "tables" and *misère*,' said the count. 'It is capital.'

Everyone liked the new Petersburg way. The uncle was even sure he knew it; it was just the same as 'boston' used to be, only he had forgotten it a bit. But Anna Fedorovna could not understand it at all and failed to understand it for so long that at last, with a smile and nod of approval, she felt herself obliged to assert that now she understood it and that all was quite clear to her. There was not a little laughter during the game when Anna Fedorovna, holding ace and king blank, declared *misère* and was left with six tricks. She even became confused and began to smile shyly and hurriedly explain that she had not got quite used to the new way. But they scored against her all the same, especially as the count, being used to playing a careful game for high stakes, was cautious, skilfully played through his opponents' hands, and refused to understand the shoves the cornet gave him under the table with his foot or the mistakes the latter made when they were partners.

Lisa brought more sweets, three kinds of jam, and some specially prepared apples that had been kept since last season and stood behind her mother's back watching the game and occasionally looking at the officers and especially at the count's white hands with their rosy well-kept nails which threw the cards and took up the tricks in so practised, assured, and elegant a manner.

Again Anna Fedorovna, rather irritably outbidding the others, declared seven tricks, made only four, and was fined accordingly, and having very clumsily noted down, on her brother's demand, the points she had lost, became quite confused and fluttered.

'Never mind, mamma, you'll win it back!' smilingly remarked Lisa, wishing to help her mother out of the ridiculous situation. 'Let uncle make a forfeit, and then he'll be caught.'

'If you would only help me, Lisa dear!' said Anna Fedorovna, with a frightened glance at her daughter. 'I don't know how this is . . .'

'But I don't know this way either,' Lisa answered, mentally reckoning up her mother's losses. 'You will lose a lot that way, mamma! There will be nothing left for Pimochka's new dress,' she added in jest.

'Yes, this way one may easily lose ten silver rubles,' said the cornet looking at Lisa and anxious to enter into conversation with her.

'Aren't we playing for assignats?' said Anna Fedorovna, looking round at them all.

'I don't know how we are playing, but I can't reckon in assignats,' said the count. 'What is it? I mean, what are assignats?'

'Why nowadays nobody counts in assignats any longer,' remarked the uncle, who had played very cautiously and had been winning.

The old lady ordered some sparkling home-made wine to be brought, drank two glasses, became very red, and seemed to resign herself to any fate. A lock of her grey hair escaped from under her cap and she did not even put it right. No doubt it seemed to her as if she had lost millions and it was all up with her. The cornet touched the count with his foot more and more often. The count scored down the old lady's losses. At last the game ended, and in spite of Anna Fedorovna's attempts to add to her score by pretending to make mistakes in adding it up, in spite of her horror at the amount of her losses, it turned out at last that she had lost 920 points. 'That's nine assignats?' she asked several times and did not comprehend the full extent of her loss until her brother told her, to her horror, that she had lost more than thirty-two assignats and that she must certainly pay.

The count did not even add up his winnings but rose immediately the game was over, went over to the window at which Lisa was arranging the *zakushka* and turning pickled mushrooms out of a jar onto a plate for supper, and there quite quietly and simply did what the cornet had all that evening so longed, but failed, to do – entered into conversation with her about the weather.

Meanwhile the cornet was in a very unpleasant position. In the absence of the count, and more especially of Lisa, who had been keeping her in good humour, Anna Fedorovna became frankly angry.

'Really, it's too bad that we should win from you like this,' said Polozov in order to say something. 'It is a real shame!'

'Well, of course, if you go and invent some kind of "tables" and "*misères*" and I don't know how to play them . . . Well then, how much does it come to in assignats?' she asked.

'Thirty-two rubles, thirty-two and a quarter,' repeated the cavalryman, who under the influence of his success was in a playful mood. 'Hand over the money, sister; pay up!'

'I'll pay it all, but you won't catch me again. No! . . . I shall not win this back as long as I live.'

And Anna Fedorovna went off to her room, hurriedly swaying from side to side, and came back bringing nine assignats. It was only on the old man's insistent demand that she eventually paid the whole amount.

Polozov was seized with fear lest Anna Fedorovna should scold him if he spoke to her. He silently and quietly left her and joined the count and Lisa who were talking at the open window.

On the table spread for supper stood two tallow candles. Now and then the soft fresh breath of the May night caused the flames to flicker. Outside the window, which opened onto the garden, it was also light but it was a quite different light. The moon, which was almost full and already losing its golden tinge, floated above the tops of the tall lindens and more and more lit up the thin white clouds which veiled it at intervals. Frogs were croaking loudly by the pond, the surface of which, silvered in one place by the moon, was visible through the avenue. Some little birds fluttered slightly or lightly hopped from bough to bough in a sweet-scented lilac-bush whose dewy branches occasionally swayed gently close to the window.

'What wonderful weather!' the count said as he approached Lisa and sat down on the low window-sill. 'I suppose you walk a good deal?'

'Yes,' said Lisa, not feeling the least shyness in speaking with the count. 'In the morning about seven o'clock I look after what has to be attended to on the estate and take my mother's ward, Pimochka, with me for a walk.'

'It is pleasant to live in the country!' said the count, putting his eye-glass to his eye and looking now at the garden, now at Lisa. 'And don't you ever go out at night, by moonlight?'

'No. But two years ago uncle and I used to walk every moon-light night. He was troubled with a strange complaint – insomnia. When there was a full moon he could not fall asleep. His little room – that one – looks straight out into the garden, the window is low but the moon shines straight into it.'

'That's strange: I thought that was your room,' said the count.

'No. I only sleep there tonight. You have my room.'

'Is it possible? Dear me, I shall never forgive myself for having disturbed you in such a way!' said the count, letting the monocle fall from his eye in proof of the sincerity of his feelings. 'If I had known that I was troubling you . . . '

'It's no trouble! On the contrary I am very glad: uncle's is such a charming room, so bright, and the window is so low. I shall sit there till I fall asleep, or else I shall climb out into the garden and walk about a bit before going to bed.'

'What a splendid girl!' thought the count, replacing his eyeglass and looking at her and trying to touch her foot with his own while pretending to seat himself more comfortably on the window-sill. 'And how cleverly she has let me know that I may see her in the garden at the window if I like!' Lisa even lost much of her charm in his eyes – the conquest seemed too easy.

'And how delightful it must be,' he said, looking thoughtfully at the dark avenue of trees, 'to spend a night like this in the garden with a beloved one.'

Lisa was embarrassed by these words and by the repeated, seemingly accidental touch of his foot. Anxious to hide her confusion she said without thinking, 'Yes, it is nice to walk in the moonlight.' She was beginning to feel rather uncomfortable. She had tied up the jar out of which she had taken the mushrooms and was going away from the window, when the cornet joined them and she felt a wish to see what kind of man he was.

'What a lovely night!' he said.

'Why, they talk of nothing but the weather,' thought Lisa.

'What a wonderful view!' continued the cornet. 'But I suppose you are tired of it,' he added, having a curious propensity to say rather unpleasant things to people he liked very much.

'Why do you think so? The same kind of food or the same dress one may get tired of, but not of a beautiful garden if one is fond of walking – especially when the moon is still higher.

From uncle's window the whole pond can be seen. I shall look at it tonight.'

'But I don't think you have any nightingales?' said the count, much dissatisfied that the cornet had come and prevented his ascertaining more definitely the terms of the rendezvous.

'No, but there always were until last year when some sportsman caught one, and this year one began to sing beautifully only last week but the police-officer came here and his carriage-bells frightened it away. Two years ago uncle and I used to sit in the covered alley and listen to them for two hours or more at a time.'

'What is this chatterbox telling you?' said her uncle, coming up to them. 'Won't you come and have something to eat?'

After supper, during which the count by praising the food and by his appetite has somewhat dispelled the hostess's ill humour, the officers said good-night and went into their room. The count shook hands with the uncle and to Anna Fedorovna's surprise shook her hand also without kissing it, and even shook Lisa's, looking straight into her eyes the while and slightly smiling his pleasant smile. This look again abashed the girl.

14

'I say, aren't you ashamed of yourself?' said Polozov when they were in their room. 'I purposely tried to lose and kept touching you under the table. Aren't you ashamed? The old lady was quite upset, you know.'

The count laughed very heartily.

'She was awfully funny, that old lady . . . How offended she was! . . . '

And he again began laughing so merrily that even Johann, who stood in front of him, cast down his eyes and turned away with a slight smile.

'And with the son of a friend of the family! Ha-ha-ha! . . . ' the count continued to laugh.

'No, really it was too bad. I was quite sorry for her,' said the cornet.

'What nonsense! How young you still are! Why, did you wish me to lose? Why should one lose? I used to lose before I knew how to play! Ten rubles may come in useful, my dear fellow. You must look at life practically or you'll always be left in the lurch.'

Polozov was silenced; besides, he wished to be quiet and to think about Lisa, who seemed to him an unusually pure and beautiful creature. He undressed and lay down in the soft clean bed prepared for him.

'What nonsense all this military honour and glory is!' he thought, looking at the window curtained by the shawl through which the white moonbeams stole in. 'It would be happiness to live in a quiet nook with a dear, wise, simple-hearted wife – yes, that is true and lasting happiness!'

But for some reason he did not communicate these reflections to his friend and did not even refer to the country lass, though he was convinced that the count too was thinking of her.

'Why don't you undress?' he asked the count who was walking up and down the room.

'I don't feel sleepy yet, somehow. You can put out the candle if you like. I shall lie down as I am.'

And he continued to pace up and down.

'Don't feel sleepy yet somehow,' repeated Polozov, who after this last evening felt more dissatisfied than ever with the count's influence over him and was inclined to rebel against it. 'I can imagine,' he thought, addressing himself mentally to Turbin, 'what is now passing through that well-brushed head of yours! I saw how you admired her. But you are not capable of understanding such a simple honest creature: you want a Mina and a colonel's epaulettes . . . I really must ask him how he liked her.'

And Polozov turned towards him – but changed his mind. He felt he would not be able to hold his own with the count, if the latter's opinion of Lisa were what he supposed it to be, and that he would even be unable to avoid agreeing with him, so accustomed was he to bow to the count's influence, which he felt more and more every day to be oppressive and unjust.

'Where are you going?' he asked, when the count put on his cap and went to the door.

'I'm going to see if things are all right in the stables.'

'Strange!' thought the cornet, but put out the candle and turned over on his other side, trying to drive away the absurdly jealous and hostile thoughts that crowded into his head concerning his former friend.

Anna Fedorovna meanwhile, having as usual kissed her brother, daughter, and ward and made the sign of the cross over each of them, had also retired to her room. It was long since the old lady had experienced so many strong impressions in one day and she could not even pray quietly: she could not rid herself of the sad and vivid memories of the deceased count and of the young dandy who had plundered her so unmercifully. However, she undressed as usual, drank half a tumbler of *kvas* that stood ready for her on a little table by her bed, and lay down. Her favourite cat crept softly into the room. Anna Fedorovna called her up and began to stroke her and listen to her purring but could not fall asleep.

'It's the cat that keeps me awake,' she thought and drove her away. The cat fell softly on the floor and gently moving her bushy tail leapt onto the stove. And now the maid, who always slept in Anna Fedorovna's room, came and spread the piece of felt that served her for a mattress, put out the candle, and lit the lamp before the icon. At last the maid began to snore, but still sleep would not come to soothe Anna Fedorovna's excited imagination. When she closed her eyes the hussar's face appeared to her, and she seemed to see it in the room in various guises when she opened her eyes and by the dim light of the lamp looked at the chest of drawers, the table, or a white dress that was hanging up. Now she felt very hot on the feather bed, now her watch ticked unbearably on the little table, and the maid snored unendurably through her nose. She woke her up and told her not to snore. Again thoughts of her daughter, of the old count and the young one, and of the *préférence*, became curiously mixed in her head. Now she saw herself waltzing with the old count, saw her own round white shoulders, felt someone's kisses on them, and then saw her daughter in the arms of the young count. Ustyushka again began to snore.

'No, people are not the same nowadays. The other one was ready to leap into the fire for me – and not without cause. But this one is sleeping like a fool, no fear, glad to have won – no love-making about him . . . How the other one said on his knees, "What do you wish me to do? I'll kill myself on the spot, or do anything you like!" And he would have killed himself had I told him to.'

'Suddenly she heard a patter of bare feet in the passage and Lisa, with a shawl thrown over, ran in pale and trembling and almost fell onto her mother's bed.

After saying good-night to her mother that evening Lisa had gone alone to the room her uncle generally slept in. She put on a white dressing-jacket and covered her long thick plait with a kerchief, extinguished the candle, opened the window, and sat down on a chair, drawing her feet up and fixing her pensive eyes on the pond now all glittering in the silvery light.

All her accustomed occupations and interests suddenly appeared to her in a new light: her capricious old mother, uncritical love for whom had become part of her soul; her decrepit but amiable old uncle; the domestic and village serfs who worshipped their young mistress; the milch cows and the calves, and all this Nature which had died and been renewed so many times and amid which she had grown up loving and beloved – all this that had given such light and pleasant tranquillity to her soul suddenly seemed unsatisfactory; it seemed dull and unnecessary. It was as if someone had said to her: 'Little fool, little fool, for twenty years you have been trifling, serving someone without knowing why, and without knowing what life and happiness are!' As she gazed into the depths of the moonlit, motionless garden she thought this more intensely, far more intensely, than ever before. And what caused these thoughts? Not any sudden love for the count as one might have supposed. On the contrary, she did not like him. She could have been interested in the cornet more easily, but he was plain, poor fellow, and silent. She kept involuntarily forgetting him and recalling the image of the count with anger and annoyance. 'No, that's not it,' she said to herself. Her ideal had been so beautiful. It was an ideal that could have been loved on such a night amid this nature without impairing its beauty – an ideal never abridged to fit it to some coarse reality.

Formerly, solitude and the absence of anyone who might have attracted her attention had caused the power of love, which Providence has given impartially to each of us, to rest intact and tranquil in her bosom, and now she had lived too long in the melancholy happiness of feeling within her the presence of this something, and of now and again opening the secret chalice of her heart to contemplate its riches, to be able to lavish its contents thoughtlessly on anyone. God grant she may enjoy to her grave this chary bliss! Who knows whether it be not the best and strongest, and whether it is not the only true and possible happiness?

'O Lord my God,' she thought, 'can it be that I have lost my youth and happiness in vain and that it will never be . . . never be? Can that be true?' And she looked into the depths of the sky lit up by the moon and covered by light fleecy clouds that, veiling the stars, crept nearer to the moon. 'If that highest white cloudlet touches the moon it will be a sign that it is true,' thought she. The mist-like smoky strip ran across the bottom half of the bright disk and little by little the light on the grass, on the tops of the limes, and on the pond, grew dimmer and the black shadows of the trees grew less distinct. As if to harmonize with the gloomy shadows that spread over the world outside, a light wind ran through the leaves and brought to the window the odour of dewy leaves, of moist earth, and of blooming lilacs.

'But it is not true,' she consoled herself. 'There now, if the nightingale sings tonight it will be a sign that what I'm thinking is all nonsense, and that I need not despair,' thought she. And she sat a long while in silence waiting for something, while again all became bright and full of life and again and again the cloudlets ran across the moon making everything dim. She was beginning to fall asleep as she sat by the window, when the quivering trills of a nightingale came ringing from below across the pond and awoke her. The country maiden opened her eyes. And once more her soul was renewed with fresh joy by its mysterious union with Nature which spread out so calmly and brightly before her. She leant on both arms. A sweet, languid sensation of sadness oppressed her heart, and tears of pure wide-spreading love, thirsting to be satisfied – good comforting tears – filled her eyes. She folded her arms on the window-sill and laid her head on them. Her favourite prayer rose to her mind and she fell asleep with her eyes still moist.

The touch of someone's hand aroused her. She awoke. But the touch was light and pleasant. The hand pressed hers more closely. Suddenly she became alive to reality, screamed, jumped up, and trying to persuade herself that she had not recognized the count who was standing under the window bathed in the moonlight, she ran out of the room . . . .

15

And it really was the count. When he heard the girl's cry and a husky sound from the watchman behind the fence, who had been roused by that cry, he rushed headlong across the wet dewy grass into the depths of the garden feeling like a detected thief. 'Fool that I am!' he repeated unconsciously, 'I frightened her. I ought to have aroused her gently by speaking to her. Awkward brute that I am!' He stopped and listened: the watchman came into the garden through the gateway, dragging his stick along the sandy path. It was necessary to hide and the count went down by the pond. The frogs made him start as they plumped from beneath his feet into the water. Though his boots were wet through, he squatted down and began to recall all that he had done: how he had climbed the fence, looked for her window, and at last espied a white shadow; how, listening to the faintest rustle, he had several times approached the window and gone back again; how at one moment he felt sure she was waiting, vexed at his tardiness, and the next, that it was impossible she should so readily agreed to a rendezvous; how at last, persuading himself that it was only the bashfulness of a country-bred girl that made her pretend to be asleep, he went up resolutely and distinctly saw how she sat but then for some reason ran away again and only after severely taunting himself for cowardice boldly drew near to her and touched her hand.

The watchman again made a husky sound and the gate creaked as he left the garden. The girl's window was slammed to and a shutter fastened from inside. This was very provoking. The count would have given a good deal for a chance to begin all over again; he would not have acted so stupidly now . . . 'And she is a wonderful girl – so fresh – quite charming! And I have let her slip through my fingers . . . Awkward fool that I am!' He did not want to sleep now and went at random, with the firm tread of one who has been crossed, along the covered lime-tree avenue.

And here the night brought to him all its peaceful gifts of soothing sadness and the need of love. The straight pale beams of the moon threw spots of light through the thick foliage of the limes onto the clay path, where a few blades of grass grew or a dead branch lay here and there. The light falling on one side of a bent bough made it seem as if covered with white moss. The silvered leaves whispered now and then. There were no lights in the house and all was silent; the voice of the nightingale alone seemed to fill the bright, still, limitless space. 'O God, what a night! What a wonderful night!' thought the count, inhaling the fragrant freshness of the garden. 'Yet I feel a kind of regret – as if I were discontented with myself and with others, discontented with life generally. A splendid, sweet girl! Perhaps she was really hurt . . . '

Here his dreams became mixed: he imagined himself in this garden with the country-bred girl in various extraordinary situations. Then the role of the girl was taken by his beloved Mina. 'Eh, what a fool I was! I ought simply to have caught her round the waist and kissed her.' And regretting that he had not done so, the count returned to his room.

The cornet was still awake. He at once turned in his bed and faced the count.

'Not asleep yet?' asked the count.

'No.'

'Shall I tell you what has happened?'

'Well?'

'No, I'd better not, or . . . all right, I'll tell you – draw in your legs.'

And the count, having mentally abandoned the intrigue that had miscarried, sat down on his comrade's bed with an animated smile.

'Would you believe it, that young lady gave me a rendezvous!'

'What are you saying?' cried Polozov, jumping out of bed.

'No, but listen.'

'But how? When? It's impossible!'

'Why, while you were adding up after we had played *préférence*, she told me she would be at the window in the night and that one could get in at the window. There, you see what it is to be practical! While you were calculating with the old woman, I arranged that little matter. Why, you heard her say in your presence that she would sit by the window tonight and look at the pond.'

'Yes, but she didn't mean anything of the kind.'

'Well, that's just what I can't make out: did she say it intentionally or not? Maybe she didn't really wish to agree so suddenly, but it looked very like it. It turned out horribly. I quite played the fool,' he added, smiling contemptuously at himself.

'What do you mean? Where have you been?'

'The count, omitting his manifold irresolute approaches, related everything as it had happened.

'I spoilt it myself: I ought to have been bolder. She screamed and ran from the window.'

'So she screamed and ran away,' said the cornet, smiling uneasily in answer to the count's smile, which for such a long time had had so strong an influence over him.

'Yes, but it's time to go to sleep.'

The cornet again turned his back to the door and lay silent for about ten minutes. Heaven knows what went on in his soul, but when he turned again, his face bore an expression of suffering and resolve.

'Count Turbin!' he said abruptly.

'Are you delirious?' quietly replied the count. 'What is it, Cornet Polozov?'

'Count Turbin, you are a scoundrel!' cried Polozov and again jumped out of bed.

16

The squadron left next day. The two officers did not see their hosts again and did not bid them farewell. Neither did they speak to one another. They intended to fight a duel at the first halting-place. But Captain Schulz, a good comrade and splendid horseman, beloved by everyone in the regiment and chosen by the count to act as his second, managed to settle the affair so well that not only did they not fight but no one in the regiment knew anything about the matter, and Turbin and Polozov, though no longer on the old friendly footing, still continued to speak in familiar terms to one another and to meet at dinners and card-parties.